The GLITTERING COURT

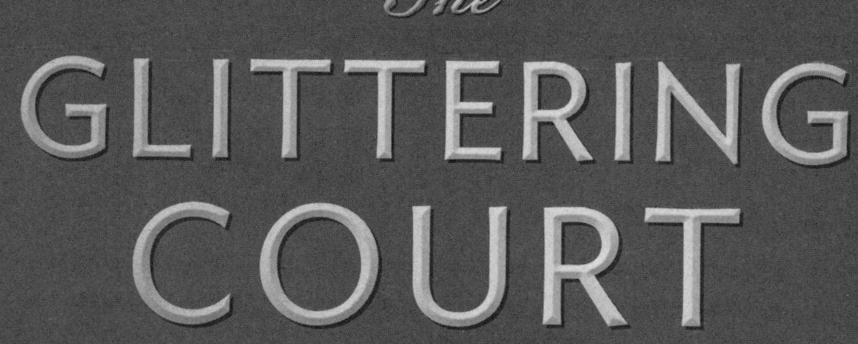

The Glittering Court

RICHELLE MEAD

RAZORBILL
An Imprint of Penguin Random House

An Imprint of Penguin Random House
Penguin.com

ISBN: 978-1-59514-842-1

Printed in the United States of America

1 3 5 7 9 10 8 6 4 2

Interior design by Lindsey Andrews

For Jay,
Looks like I unlocked the code.

CHAPTER 1

I'D NEVER PLANNED ON STEALING SOMEONE ELSE'S LIFE.

Really, at a glance, you wouldn't think there was anything wrong with my old life. I was young and healthy. I liked to think I was clever. I belonged to one of the noblest families in Osfrid, one that could trace its bloodline back to the country's founders. Sure, my title might have been more prestigious if my family's fortune hadn't evaporated, but that was easily fixed. All I had to do was marry well.

And that was where my problems started.

Most noblemen admired a descendant of Rupert, First Earl of Rothford, great hero of Osfrid. Centuries ago, he'd helped wrest this land from savages, thus forming the great nation we enjoyed today. But few noblemen admired my lack of resources, especially in these times. Other families were fighting their own financial crises, and a pretty face with an exalted title no longer held the appeal it once might have.

I needed a miracle, and I needed one fast.

"Darling, a miracle's happened."

I'd been staring at the ballroom's velvet-embossed wallpaper as dark thoughts swirled in my head. Blinking, I returned my attention to the noisy party and focused on my grandmother's approach. Though her face was lined and her hair pure white, people always remarked on what a handsome woman Lady Alice Witmore was. I agreed, though I couldn't help but notice she'd seemed to age more in the years since my parents had died. But just now, her face was alight in a way I hadn't seen in some time.

"How, Grandmama?"

"We have an offer. *An offer.* He's everything we've hoped for. Young. A substantial fortune. His family line's as prestigious as yours."

That last one caught me by surprise. The blessed Rupert's line was tough to match. "Are you sure?"

"Certainly. He's your . . . cousin."

It wasn't often that words failed me. For a moment, all I could think of was my cousin Peter. He was twice my age—and married. By the rules of descent, he would be the one to inherit the Rothford title if I died without children. Whenever he was in town, he'd stop by and ask how I was feeling.

"Which one?" I asked at last, relaxing slightly. The term "cousin" was sometimes used loosely, and if you looked far enough in the family trees, half the Osfridian nobility was related to the other half. She could be referring to any number of men.

"Lionel Belshire, Baron of Ashby."

I shook my head. He was no one I knew.

She linked my arm with hers and drew me toward the opposite side of the ballroom, winding our way through some of the city's most powerful people. They were swathed in silks and velvets, adorned with pearls and gems. Above us, crystal chandeliers covered the entire ceiling, like our hosts were trying to outdo the stars. Such was life among Osfro's nobility.

"His grandmother and I were both ladies in the Duchess of Samford's coterie, back in the old days. He's only a baron." Grandmama leaned her head toward me to speak more quietly. I noted the pearl-studded cap she wore, in good shape but unfashionable for at least two years. She spent our money on clothing me. "But his blood is still good. His line comes from one of Rupert's lesser sons, though there was some scandal that Rupert might not actually have been his father. His mother was noble, though, so either way, we're covered."

I was still trying to process that when we came to a halt in front of a floor-to-ceiling window that overlooked Harlington Green. A young man stood with a woman my grandmother's age, speaking in low tones. Upon our arrival, they both looked up with keen interest.

Grandmama released my hand. "My granddaughter, the Countess of Rothford. My darling, this is Baron Belshire and his grandmother, Lady Dorothy."

Lionel bent over and kissed my hand while his grandmother curtseyed. Her deference was a show. Sharp eyes raked over every part of me. If propriety had allowed it, I think she would have examined my teeth.

I turned to Lionel as he straightened. He was the one I had to size up. "Countess, it's a pleasure to meet you. It's a shame this hasn't happened sooner, seeing as we're family. Descendants of Earl Rupert and all that."

Out of the corner of my eye, I saw Grandmama arch a skeptical eyebrow.

I gave him a demure smile, not deferential enough to diminish my superior rank but enough to make him think his charm had flustered me. His charm, of course, was yet to be assessed. At a glance, it might be all he had going for him. His face was long and pointed, his skin sallow. I would have expected at least a flush, considering how the crush of bodies had heated the room. The sagging of his narrow shoulders gave the impression he was about to cave in upon himself. None of it mattered, though. Only the marriage logistics did. I'd never expected to marry for love.

"We're definitely overdue for a meeting," I agreed. "Really, we should all be having regular Rupert reunions, as a tribute to our progenitor. Get everyone together and have picnics on the green. We could do three-legged races, like the country folk do. I'm sure I could manage it with the skirts."

He stared at me unblinkingly and scratched his wrist. "Earl Rupert's descendants are spread out all over Osfrid. I don't think a gathering of that sort would be feasible. And it's not just unseemly for nobility to do those three-legged races; I don't allow the tenants on my estates to do such things either. The great god Uros gave us two legs, not three. To suggest otherwise is an abomination." He paused. "I don't really approve of potato-sack races either."

"You're right, of course," I said, keeping the smile fixed on my face. Beside me, Grandmama cleared her throat.

"The baron has been very successful with his barley production," she said with forced cheer. "Quite possibly the most successful in the country."

Lionel scratched his left ear. "My tenants have converted more than eighty percent of the land to barley fields. We recently bought a new estate, and those lands too now have a booming crop. Barley as far as the eye can see. Acres and acres. I even have my house servants, in both estates, eat it every morning. To boost morale."

"That's . . . a lot of barley," I said. I was starting to feel sorry for his tenants. "Well, I hope you let them splurge every once in a while. Oats. Rye, if you're feeling exotic."

That previous puzzled look returned to his face as he scratched his right ear. "Why would I do that? Barley is our livelihood. It's good for them to remember that. I hold myself to the same standard—a higher one, actually, as I make sure to include a portion of barley in *all* of my meals. It sets a good example."

"You're a man of the people," I said. I eyed the window beyond him, wondering if I could jump out of it.

An awkward silence fell, and Lady Dorothy tried to fill it. "Speaking of estates, I understand you just recently sold your *last* one." Here it was, a reminder of our financial situation. Grandmama was quick to defend our honor.

"We weren't using it." She lifted her chin. "I'm not so foolish as to waste money on an empty house and tenants who've grown lazy without supervision. Our town house here in the city is much more comfortable and keeps us close to society. We were invited to court three times this winter, you know."

"Winter, of course," said Lady Dorothy dismissively. "But surely summers in the city are dull. Especially with so much of the nobility at their own estates. When you marry Lionel, you'll live in his Northshire estate—where I live—and want for nothing. And you may plan as many social gatherings as you like. Under my close supervision, of course. It's such a lovely opportunity for you. I mean no offense—Countess, Lady Alice. You maintain yourselves so well that no one would guess your true situation. But I'm sure it'll be a relief to be settled into better circumstances."

"Better circumstances for me. A better title for him," I murmured.

As we spoke, Lionel first scratched his forehead and then his inner arm. That second bout went on for some time, and I tried not to stare. What was going on? Why was he itching so much? And why was it happening all over his whole body? I couldn't see any obvious rashes. Worse, the more I watched him, the more I suddenly wanted to scratch. I had to clasp my hands together to stop myself.

The excruciating conversation went on for several more minutes as our grandmothers made plans for the nuptials I'd only just learned about. Lionel continued to scratch. When we finally extracted ourselves, I waited all of thirty seconds before voicing my opinion to Grandmama.

"No," I said.

"Hush." She smiled at various guests we knew as we walked to the ballroom's exit and told one of our host's manservants to order our carriage around. I bit off my words until we were safely alone inside it.

"No," I repeated, sinking back into the carriage's plush seat. "Absolutely not."

"Don't be so dramatic."

"I'm not! I'm being sane. I can't believe you accepted that offer without consulting me."

"Well, it was certainly difficult choosing between that and your *many other offers*." She met my glare levelly. "Yes, dear, you're not the only one around here who can be pert. You are, however, the only one who can save us from eventual ruin."

"Now who's being dramatic? Lady Branson would take you with her into her daughter's household. You'd live very well there."

"And what happens to you while I'm living very well?"

"I don't know. I'll find someone else." I thought back to the flurry of guests I'd met at the party this evening. "What about that merchant who was there? Donald Crosby? I hear he's amassed a pretty big fortune."

"Ugh." Grandmama rubbed her temples. "Please stop talking about the nouveau riche. You know how it gives me a headache."

I scoffed. "What's wrong with him? His business is booming. And he laughed at all my jokes—which is more than can be said for Lionel."

"You know what's wrong with *Mister* Crosby. He should never have been at that party. I don't know what Lord Gilman was thinking." She paused as a particularly large pothole in the cobblestone street caused our carriage to lurch. "How do you think your exalted ancestor Rupert would feel about you mingling his line with such common blood?"

I groaned. It seemed as though, lately, we couldn't have a conversation without invoking Rupert's name. "I think someone who followed his lord across the channel to carve out an empire would place a pretty big emphasis on keeping one's self-respect. Not selling it out to a boring cousin and his tyrant grandmother. Did you count how many times she said 'under my close supervision' when we were talking about the future? I did. Five. Which is seven less times than Lionel scratched some body part."

Grandmama's expression grew weary. "Do you think you're the first girl who's had an arranged marriage? Do you think you're the first girl to resent it? Stories and songs are full of tales of woeful maidens trapped in such circumstances who escape to a glorious future. But those are stories. The reality is that most girls in your situation . . . well, endure. There's nothing else you can do. There's nowhere else you can go. It's the price we pay for this world we live in. For our rank."

"My parents would have never made me endure," I grumbled.

Her eyes hardened. "Your parents and their frivolous investments are the reason we're in this situation. We're out of money. Selling the

Bentley estate has kept us living as we always have. But that's going to change. And you won't like it when it does." When my obstinate glare continued, she added, "You'll have people making choices for you your entire life. Get used to it."

Our home was located in a different—but equally fashionable—district of the city from the party. Upon our arrival, servants swarmed to attend us. They helped us out of the carriage, took our wraps and shawls. I had my own flock of maidservants who accompanied me to my suite to remove my formal attire for me. I watched as they smoothed the red velvet overdress, with its trumpet sleeves and gold embroidery. They hung it up with countless other decadent frocks, and I found myself staring at the bureau after they'd left. So much of our family's fading wealth spent on clothes that were supposed to help me achieve the opportunity to change my life for the better.

My life was certainly about to change, but for the better? That I was skeptical of.

And so, I treated it as though it wasn't real. It was how I'd dealt with my parents' deaths as well. I'd refused to believe they were gone, even when faced with the tangible proof of their graves. It wasn't possible that someone you loved so much, someone who filled up so much of your heart, could no longer exist in the world. I tried convincing myself that they would walk through my door one day. And when I couldn't make myself believe that, I simply didn't think about it all.

That was how I dealt with Lionel. I put him out of my mind and went on with my life as though nothing at that party had ever happened.

When a letter came from Lady Dorothy one day, I finally had to acknowledge his existence again. She wanted to confirm a date for the wedding, which was to be expected. What wasn't expected was her directive to cut our household staff in half and get rid of the majority of our possessions. *You won't need them when you get to Northshire,* she wrote. *The staff and items you need will be provided, under my close supervision.*

"Oh, sweet Uros," I said when I'd finished reading.

"Don't take the god's name in vain," Grandmama snapped. Despite her sharp words, I could see the strain on her. Living under someone else's thumb wasn't going to be easy for her either. "Oh. And Lionel sent you a present."

The "present" was a container of a proprietary barley cereal blend he ate each morning, with a note saying it would give me a taste of what was to come. I wanted to believe he'd intended the pun, but I sincerely doubted it.

Grandmama began fretting about how to split up the household as I walked out of the room. And I kept walking. I walked out of the town house, out through the front courtyard. I walked right out through the gate that sheltered our property from the main thoroughfare, earning a puzzled look from the servant who was manning it.

"My lady? Is there something I can help you with?"

I waved him back when he started to rise. "No," I said. He glanced around, uncertain what to do. He'd never seen me leave our property alone. No one ever had. It wasn't done.

His confusion kept him where he was, and I soon found myself swallowed up in the foot traffic moving about the street. It wasn't the gentry, of course. Servants, merchants, couriers . . . all the people whose labor helped the city's rich survive. I fell in step with them, unsure of where I was going.

Some crazy part of me thought maybe I should go make an appeal to Donald Crosby. He'd seemed to like me well enough in our minutes-long conversation. Or maybe I could seek passage somewhere. Go off to the continent and charm some Belsian noble. Or maybe I could just lose myself in the crowd, one more anonymous face to blend into the city's masses.

"Can I help you, my lady? Did you get separated from your servants?"

Apparently not so anonymous.

I'd ended up on the edge of one of the city's many commercial districts. The speaker was an older man who carried parcels on his back that looked far too heavy for his slight frame.

"How do you know I'm a lady?" I blurted out.

He grinned, showing a few missing teeth. "Ain't too many out alone dressed like you."

I glanced around and saw he was right. The violet jacquard dress I wore was a casual one for me, but it made me stand out in the sea of otherwise drab attire. There were a few others of higher classes out shopping, but they were surrounded by dutiful servants ready to shield them from any unsavory elements.

"I'm fine," I said, pushing past him. But I didn't get very far before someone else stopped me: a ruddy-faced young boy, the kind who made his living delivering messages.

"Need me to escort you home, m'lady?" he asked. "Three coppers, and I'll get you out of all this."

"No, I . . ." I let my words drop as something occurred to me. "I don't have any money. Not on me." He started to leave, and I called, "Wait. Here." I pulled off my pearl bracelet and offered it to him. "Can you take me to the Church of Glorious Vaiel?"

His eyes widened at the sight of the pearls, but he hesitated. "That's too much, m'lady. The church is only over on Cunningham Street."

I pushed the bracelet into his hand. "I have no idea where that is. Take me."

It turned out to be only about three blocks away. I knew all the major areas of Osfro but little about how to travel between them. There'd never been any need to know.

There were no services today, but the main doors were propped slightly open, welcoming any souls in need of counsel. I walked past the elegant church, out to the graveyard. I moved through the common section, through the nicer section, and finally to the noble section. It had a wrought-iron gate surrounding it and was filled with monuments and mausoleums, rather than ordinary gravestones.

I might not know my way around Osfro streets, but I knew exactly where my family's mausoleum was in this graveyard. My guide waited near the iron gate as I walked over to the handsome stone building labeled WITMORE. It wasn't the biggest one on the property, but I thought it was one of the most beautiful. My father had loved art of all kinds, and we'd commissioned exquisite carvings of the six glorious angels on all the exterior walls.

I had no way to enter, not without prior arrangements with the church, and simply sat on the steps. I ran my fingers over the names carved amid those listed on the stone placard: LORD ROGER WITMORE, SIXTEENTH EARL OF ROTHFORD, AND LADY AMELIA ROTHFORD. Above them, my grandfather's name was listed alone: LORD AUGUSTUS WITMORE, FIFTEENTH EARL OF ROTHFORD. My grandmother's name would join his one day, and then the mausoleum would be full. "You'll have to find your own place," Grandmama had told me at my father's funeral.

My mother had died first, catching one of the many illnesses that ran rampant in the poorer parts of the city. My parents had been greatly interested in investing in charitable establishments among the less fortunate, and it had cost them their lives, my mother getting sick one summer, my father the next. Their charities fell apart. Some said my parents had been saintly. Most said they'd been foolish.

I stared up at the great stone door, which held a carving of the glorious angel Ariniel, the gatekeeper of Uros. The work was gorgeous, but I always thought Ariniel was the least interesting of the angels. All she did was open the way for others and facilitate their journeys. Was there some place she'd rather be? Something else she'd rather do? Was she content to exist so that others could achieve their goals while she stayed at a standstill? Grandmama had said I'd always have choices made for me. Was that way of both humans and angels? The scriptures had never addressed such questions. Most likely they were blasphemous.

"My lady!"

I turned from that serene face and saw a flutter of color at the gate. Three of my ladies were hurrying toward me. Far beyond them, near the church's entrance, I saw our carriage waiting. Immediately, I was swarmed.

"Oh, my lady, what were you thinking?" cried Vanessa. "Did that boy behave inappropriately?"

"You must be freezing!" Ada tossed a heavier cloak over my shoulders.

"Let me brush the dirt from your hem," said Thea.

"No, no," I said to that last one. "I'm fine. How did you find me?"

They all began talking over one another, but it basically came down to their noticing my disappearance and questioning the boy at our town house's gate and pretty much every person I'd passed in my outing. I'd apparently made an impression.

"Your grandmother doesn't know yet," said Vanessa, urging me forward. She was the cleverest of them. "Let's get back quickly."

Before I stepped away, I looked back at the angel, back at my parents' names. *"Bad things are always going to happen,"* my father had told me in his last year. *"There's no way to avoid that. Our control comes in how we face them. Do we let them crush us, making us despondent? Do we face them unflinchingly and endure the pain? Do we outsmart them?"* I'd asked him what it meant to outsmart a bad thing. *"You'll know when the time comes. And when it does, you need to act quickly."*

The maids couldn't stop fussing over me, even on the carriage ride home. "My lady, if you'd wanted to go, you should have just let us arrange a proper visit with a priest," Thea said.

"I wasn't thinking," I murmured. I wasn't about to elaborate on how the letter from Lady Dorothy had nearly given me a nervous breakdown. "I wanted the air. I decided I'd just walk over on my own."

They stared at me incredulously. "You can't do that," said Ada. "You can't do that on your own. You . . . you can't do anything on your own."

"Why not?" I snapped, feeling only a little bad when she flinched. "I'm a peeress of the realm. My family name commands respect everywhere. So why shouldn't I be free to move everywhere? To choose to do whatever I want?"

None of them spoke right away, and I wasn't surprised that it was Vanessa who finally did: "Because you're the Countess of Rothford. Someone with a name like that can't move among the nameless. And when it comes to who you are, my lady . . . well, that's something we never have a choice in."

CHAPTER 2

I REALIZED THEN THAT I WAS TAKING THE FIRST approach to this "bad thing" with Lionel: I was letting it crush me. And so, I decided then and there that I would choose the nobler, unflinching approach. I would endure the pain.

In the following weeks, I smiled and made my quips and acted as though our household wasn't being torn apart. While the servants worked and worried about their futures, I calmly went about tasks that were appropriate to young noblewomen, painting pictures and planning my wedding attire. When callers came to wish us well, I sat with them and feigned excitement. More than once, I heard the arrangement referred to as a "smart match." It reminded me of when I was six, when my mother and I had watched Princess Margrete's wedding procession go by.

The princess had sat in a carriage, waving and stiffly smiling as she held hands with a Lorandian duke she'd only met the week before.

"She looks a little green," I'd said.

"Nonsense. And if you're lucky," my mother had told me, "you'll make a smart match like that."

Would my mother have allowed this if she were still alive? Would this have turned out differently? Probably. A lot of things would've turned out differently if my parents were still alive.

"My lady?"

I looked up from the canvas I'd been painting, a field of purple and pink poppies copied from one of the great masters in the National

Gallery. A page stood in front of me. From the tone of his voice, I could tell this wasn't the first time he'd spoken to me.

"Yes?" I asked. The word came out a bit more harshly than I'd intended. I'd had an argument with Grandmama this morning about the dismissal of my favorite cook, and it still bothered me.

He bowed, relieved at finally being acknowledged. "There's a gentleman caller here. He's, um, making Ada cry."

I blinked, wondering if I'd misheard. "I'm sorry, what?"

Thea and Vanessa sat beside me, busy with sewing. They looked up from their work, equally perplexed.

The page shifted uncomfortably. "I don't really understand it myself, my lady. It's some sort of meeting arranged by Lady Branson. I think she was supposed to be here to supervise but was delayed by business. I settled them into the west drawing room, and when I returned to check on them, Ada was quite hysterical. I thought you would want to know."

"Yes, certainly."

And here I'd thought this would be a boring day.

The other ladies started to rise when I did, but I urged them to sit down. As I followed the page back into the house, I asked, "Do you have any idea what this so-called gentleman is here for?"

"Another position, I believe."

I felt a small pang of guilt. Staff cuts had begun, and Ada was one of the ladies being dismissed from my entourage. I'd been able to keep only one. Lady Dorothy had assured me the replacements who'd been selected under her close supervision were exemplary, but I was pretty sure their chief function would be to spy on me.

As I made my way to the drawing room, I pondered what could have caused this unexpected morning drama. Lady Branson was my grandmother's chief lady. If she'd arranged a position for Ada, I had to imagine it would be something respectable and not worthy of a breakdown.

"These weren't tears of joy?" I asked the page, just to clarify.

"No, my lady."

We entered the room, and sure enough, there was poor Ada, sitting on a sofa and sobbing into her hands. A man, his back to me, was bent over, trying awkwardly to comfort her by patting her shoulder. Immediately, my heart hardened as I wondered what kind of monster had brought this about.

"Lady Witmore, Countess of Rothford," announced the page.

That startled both Ada and her guest. She lifted her face from her hands, still sniffling, and managed to rise for a small curtsey. The man also straightened, turning to look at me. As he did, the images I'd been building of some old, twisted scoundrel vanished.

Well, maybe he was a scoundrel, but who was I to say? And the rest of him . . . my eyes burned at the sight of him. Deep auburn hair swept back in a short, fashionable tail revealed a face with clean lines and high cheekbones. His eyes were an intense blue-gray, contrasting with skin tanned from being outdoors. That wasn't fashionable among nobles, but I could've deduced he wasn't one of us from a mile away.

"Your ladyship," he said, giving a proper bow. "It is a pleasure to meet you."

I gestured the page away and sat down, a signal for the other two as well. "I'm not sure I can say the same, seeing as you've sent my lady-in-waiting into hysterics."

A chagrined expression crossed that handsome face. "Er, that wasn't my intent. I'm just as surprised as you. I'd been under the impression that Lady Branson had settled things with her."

"She did," exclaimed Ada. I could see new sobs bubbling up within her. "But now that it's here . . . I just . . . I just don't know if I want to go!"

He turned on a smile for her, one so confident and so practiced that I was certain he must use it regularly to get his way. "Well, a few nerves are understandable. But once you've seen how the other girls live at the Glittering Court—"

"Hold on," I interrupted. "What is the Glittering Court?" It sounded vaguely brothelish, but that seemed unlikely if Lady Branson had arranged it.

"I'd be happy to explain it, my lady. Assuming you don't find the logistics boring."

I looked him over. "Believe me, there's absolutely nothing about this situation I find boring."

He turned that gallant smile on me, no doubt hoping it would win me over as it did others. It kind of did. "The Glittering Court is an exciting opportunity for young women like Ada, an opportunity that will transform their lives and—"

"Hold on one more time," I said. "What's your name?"

He stood and bowed again. "Cedric Thorn, at your service." No title, but again, that didn't surprise me. The more I studied him, the more intrigued I was. He wore a brown coat of light wool that flared slightly at the knee, longer than current trends. A brown brocade vest under the coat caught the light. It was a respectable, subdued outfit, one a prosperous merchant might wear, but a bright amber pin in the hat he held told me he wasn't entirely without flair.

"My lady?" he asked.

I realized I'd been staring and offered a grand wave of my hand. "Please continue explaining this Gleaming Court of yours."

"Glittering, my lady. And as I was saying, it's an exciting opportunity for young women to move up in the world. Ada here is exactly the type of bright and promising girl we're looking for."

I raised an eyebrow at that. Ada was by far my most uninteresting maidservant. She was pretty, which, I'd learned, tended to be synonymous with "bright and promising" for most men.

He launched into what had to be a well-rehearsed speech. "The Glittering Court is a highly respected enterprise on both sides of the ocean. My father and my uncle founded it ten years ago after learning just how few women there are in Adoria."

Adoria? That's what this was about? I nearly leaned forward and then remembered myself. Still, it was hard not to be taken in. Adoria.

The country discovered across the Sunset Sea. Adoria. The very sound of it inspired adventure and excitement. It was a new world, a world far removed from the one in which I was required to marry my itching cousin—but also a world without galleries and theaters and luxuriously dressed nobility.

"There are plenty of Icori women there," I remarked, feeling the need to say something.

Cedric's smile broadened, warming his features. Were his eyelashes longer than mine? That certainly seemed unfair.

"Yes, but our colonists aren't looking for savage Icori wives in kilts and tartans. Well," he added, "most of our colonists aren't looking for savage wives. I suppose there's always someone who finds that appealing."

I nearly asked what he found appealing and then again reminded myself I was a lady of exalted rank.

"*Most* of our settlers are looking for gentle, cultured Osfridian wives—especially those men who've made their fortunes there. Plenty set sail for Adoria with nothing more than the clothes on their backs and now have found success as businessmen and plantation owners. They've become pillars in their communities, men of prestige." Cedric held up his hands grandly, a performer on his stage. "They want suitable wives to start families with. His Majesty wants it too. He's ordered the founding of several other colonies and the expansion of current ones—but it's very difficult when Osfridian men outnumber women three to one. When women do go, they're usually ordinary, working-class girls who are already married. That's not what the new nobility is looking for."

"New nobility?" I asked. I was getting sucked into his pitch. It was a new experience, having someone else turn the powers of persuasion on me.

"The new nobility. That's what we call them—these ordinary men who've found extraordinary greatness in the New World."

"It's very catchy. Did you come up with it?"

He looked surprised by the question. "No, my lady. My father did. He's a master of publicity and persuasion. Far more so than me."

"I find that incredible. Please—continue with your new nobility."

Cedric studied me for a beat, and there was something in his eyes. A calculation, or maybe a reassessment. "The new nobility. They don't need a title or right of birth to claim power and prestige. They've earned it through hard work and have become a nobility—of sorts—and now need suitably 'noble' wives. But since women of your rank aren't exactly lining up to sail over, the Glittering Court has taken it upon itself to create a cohort of young women willing to transform. We take lovely girls like Ada here, girls of common birth, girls with no family—or maybe too much family—and we train them up to greatness."

He'd smiled briefly when he made his comment about noblewomen lining up, like it was a joke between us. I felt a pang in my heart. Little did he know that just then, faced with a lifetime shackled to a sullen cousin and an overbearing grandmother-in-law, I would have given up my regal world and sailed to the colonies in an instant, savage conditions or no. Not that I could have ever made it to the docks without dozens of people trying to usher me back to my proper sphere of society.

Ada sniffled, reminding me she was still here. I'd known her for years, barely giving her a second thought. Now, for the first time ever, I felt jealous of her. She had a world—a new world—of potential and adventure opening up right before her.

"So. You're going to take Ada to Adoria," I said. It was difficult keeping my tone light, lest my envy show.

"Not right away," said Cedric. "First, we have to make sure she's trained up to Glittering Court standards. I'm sure she's received some education in your service—but nothing to match your own. She'll spend a year in one of my uncle's manor houses with other girls her age, learning all sorts of things to make up for that. She'll—"

"Wait," I interrupted. My grandmother would've been appalled at the completely haphazard way I was managing this conversation, but this whole situation was too strange for me to get caught up in formalities. "You're saying she'll have an education that'll match mine. In a year?"

"Not an exact match, no. But she'll be able to pass herself off among upper classes—maybe even the nobility—after that time."

Knowing Ada as I did, I was again skeptical, but urged him on. "Continue."

"We'll start by polishing up her basic education in reading and accounting, and then expand into other more genteel areas. How to run a household and manage servants. Music lessons. How to throw social engagements. What to talk about at social engagements. Art, history, philosophy. Foreign language, if there's time."

"That's very extensive," I said, casting a curious glance at Ada.

"That's why it takes a year," Cedric explained. "She'll live in one of my uncle's manors learning all these things and then sail over to Adoria with all the girls from the other manors. If she chooses to go."

At this, Ada finally came to life. Her head jerked up. "I don't have to go?"

"Well, no," said Cedric, a little surprised at the question. He produced a roll of paper from his coat—with a bit of a flourish, if I wasn't mistaken. "At the end of your year, your contract states you can either choose to go to Adoria to have a marriage made for you or you can leave the Glittering Court, at which point we'll find a suitable work arrangement to reimburse us for your education."

Ada looked immensely more cheerful, and I realized she probably thought said arrangement would involve a job similar to what she had now.

"I'm guessing he means a workhouse or a factory," I said.

Her face fell. "Oh. But it'd still be here. In Osfrid."

"Yes," said Cedric. "If you want to stay. But honestly? Who'd pick those kind of long work hours over a chance to be on the arm of a wealthy, doting husband who'll drape you in silks and jewels?"

"I don't get to choose him," she argued.

"That's not entirely true. When you arrive in Adoria, you and the other girls will have a three-month period in which you'll be presented to those eligible men who've shown interest in our jewels—that's what my uncle calls the Glittering Court girls." He turned his smile to its most dazzling, trying to reassure her. "You'll love it there. The colonial men go crazy when we bring new girls. It's a season of parties and other social engagements, and you'll get a whole new wardrobe for it all—Adorian fashions are somewhat different from ours. If more than one man makes an offer for you, then you can choose the one you want."

Once again, I found myself brimming with jealousy, but Ada still looked uncertain. No doubt she'd heard tales of danger and savagery about Adoria. And, in fairness, some weren't unfounded. When settlers from Osfrid and other countries had landed in Adoria, there'd been terrible bloodshed between them and the Icori clans living there. Many of the Icori had been driven away, but we still heard stories of other tragedies: diseases, storms, and wild animals, to name a few.

But what were those things compared to the riches and greatness that Adoria offered? And wasn't there danger everywhere? I wanted to shake some sense into her, to tell her she should take this opportunity and never look back. Surely there could be no greater adventure than this. But she'd never had a sense of adventure, never seen the promise of taking a chance on something she didn't know. That was part of the reason I hadn't picked her to come with me to Lionel's household.

After much deliberation, she turned to me. "What do you think I should do, my lady?"

The question caught me unprepared, and suddenly, all I could think of was my grandmother's words: *You'll have people making choices for you your entire life. Get used to it.*

I felt myself softening. "You have to make your own choices—especially since you'll be on your own once you leave my service." I looked over at Cedric, and for the first time, I saw uneasiness on those striking features. He was afraid Ada was going to opt out. Did the Glittering Court have quotas to meet? Was he on the hook to come back with someone?

"Mister Thorn has made it all sound very lovely," she replied. "But I kind of feel like some trinket being bought and sold."

"Women always feel that way," I said.

But in the end, Ada accepted Cedric's offer anyway because, as she saw it, she had nowhere else to go. Over her shoulder I scanned the contract, which was mostly a more formal explanation of what Cedric had told us. When she signed, I did a double take.

"That's your full name?" I asked. "Adelaide? Why don't you go by that?"

She shrugged. "Too many letters. It took me years to learn to spell it."

Cedric seemed to struggle to keep a straight face. I wondered if he was starting to question this choice and if Ada could really be made into part of his "new nobility."

Contract in hand, he stood up and bowed to me. To her, he said, "I have other contracts to deliver this afternoon and some errands to run at the university. You can take the day to pack your things, and our carriage will come to retrieve you this evening and take you to your manor. My father and I will join you along the way."

"Where is this manor?" I asked.

"I'm not sure which one she'll be assigned to," he admitted. "I'll know by tonight. My uncle maintains four for the Glittering Court, with ten girls each. One is in Medfordshire. Two are in Donley, another in Fairhope."

They were true country houses then, I noted, placing each location on a mental map. They were each at least half a day from where we were in Osfro.

He delivered a few more last-minute instructions before making motions to leave. I offered to walk him out, which was a bit unorthodox, and took him back toward the garden I'd been in earlier. "University. So you're a student then, Mister Thorn."

"Yes. You don't sound surprised by that."

"It's in your manner. And your coat. Only a student would set his own fashion standards."

He laughed. "I didn't. It's actually an Adorian fashion. I've got to look the part when I go with the girls."

"You get to go too?" Somehow, that made this entire thing even more agonizing. "You've been there before?"

"Not in years, but—"

He drew up short as we rounded a corner and heard more sniffling. Old Doris the cook was trudging toward the kitchen, trying not to cry as she walked.

"Don't take this the wrong way . . ." Cedric began. "But there are a lot of tears in your household."

I shot him a wry look. "Much is changing. Doris won't be going with us either. She's blind in one eye, and my cousin doesn't want her."

He turned to study me, and I averted my gaze, not wanting him to see how much this decision pained me. In her condition, Doris wasn't going to have an easy time finding work. It was another argument Grandmama had won. I was losing my edge.

"Is she good?" Cedric asked.

"Very."

"Excuse me," he called out to her.

Doris turned in surprise. "M'lord?" Neither of us bothered to correct her error.

"Is it true that your services are for hire? I can understand if someone else has already hired you on."

She blinked, her one good eye focusing on him. "No, m'lord."

"There's an opening over in one of the university's kitchens. Four silvers a month and room and board. If you're interested, it's yours. Although if the thought of cooking for so many is daunting—"

"M'lord," she interrupted, pulling herself up to her full but short height. "I have overseen seven-course dinners hosting a hundred nobles. I can handle swaggering boys."

Cedric's expression remained dignified. "Glad to hear it. Go to the university's north office tomorrow and tell them your name. They'll give you more information."

Old Doris's mouth dropped, and she looked to me for confirmation. I nodded encouragingly.

"Yes, yes, m'lord! I'll go right after breakfast's served. Thank you—thank you so much."

"Well, that's lucky," I told him, once we were alone again. I certainly wouldn't say so, but I thought it was incredibly kind of him to offer such a thing, let alone notice her. Most didn't. "Lucky that there was an open position."

"There isn't, actually," he said. "But I'll stop by and talk to the office today. By the time I'm done, they'll have an opening."

"Mister Thorn, something tells me you could sell salvation to a priest."

He smiled at the old adage. "What makes you think I haven't?"

We reached the garden and were nearing the exit when he halted again. An expression of disbelief crossed his face, and I turned toward what had caught his eye. My poppies painting.

"That's . . . Peter Cosingford's *Poppies*. I saw it in the National Gallery. Except . . . ?" He trailed off, face full of confusion as he took in the canvas and the pigments beside it.

"It's a copy. My attempt at a copy. I have others. It's just something I do for fun."

"You make copies of great works for fun?" Belatedly, he added, "My lady?"

"No, Mister Thorn. That's what *you* do."

The smile on his face was genuine, and I found I liked it better than the show ones. "Well, I'm pretty sure I could never copy *you*."

We'd reached the front gate, and his words made me come to a halt. It was less about their meaning than the way he'd said them. The tone. The warmth. I tried to think of a witty retort, but my normally quick mind had frozen up.

"And if you won't take offense at me speaking openly . . ." he added quickly.

"I'd be disappointed if you didn't."

"It's just . . . well, *I'm* a little disappointed I probably won't ever get a chance to see you again." Perhaps realizing that was *too* open, he gave a hasty bow. "Farewell, and best of luck to you, my lady."

One of the guards outside the gate unlocked it for him, and I watched him walk out the gate, admiring the way the velvet coat hugged his body.

"But you will be seeing me again," I murmured. "Just wait."

CHAPTER 3

THE PLAN HAD BEEN FORMING IN THE BACK OF MY MIND ever since Ada had tearfully signed her contract. I had a chance to outsmart the bad things looming over me. And, as my father had advised, I needed to act quickly. As more and more details became clearer, my excitement grew, and it was all I could do not to shout it to the heavens.

Mastering myself, I walked quickly—but sedately—out of the garden, back to the drawing room, where Ada sat morosely. I dodged two servants lugging my grandmother's chaise lounge and was glad Cedric hadn't seen that. It looked like we were being looted.

"Well, you must be excited," I said cheerfully to Ada. "Such an exciting opportunity ahead of you."

She rested her chin in her hands. "As you say, my lady."

I sat down beside her, feigning astonishment. "It's a great thing for you."

"I know, I know." She sighed. "It's just . . . it's just . . ." Her attempts at self-control failed utterly, and tears ran down her cheeks. I offered her a silk handkerchief. "I don't want to go to a strange land! I don't want to sail across the Sunset Sea! I don't want to get married!"

"Then don't go," I said. "Do something else when Grandmama and I leave. Get another job."

She shook her head. "I signed the contract. And what can I do? I'm not like you, my lady. I can't just walk away. I don't have the means, and no other noble families are hiring—at least not at this level. I've looked."

Walk away? Did she really think *I* could? Ada looked at my ancestry and wealth as if that was power, but really, a commoner had more freedom than me. Which was why, perhaps, I needed to become one.

"You're the Countess of Rothford. Someone with a name like that can't move among the nameless."

"What would you do then? If you had the means?"

"If I wasn't working here?" She paused to wipe her nose. "I'd go to my family in Hadaworth. I have cousins there. They have a nice dairy farm."

"Hadaworth's as far north as you can get," I reminded her. "That's not an easy journey either."

"There's no ocean!" she exclaimed. "It's still in Osfrid. And there are no savages there."

"You'd rather work on a dairy farm than marry an Adorian adventurer?" Admittedly, this played into my plans better than I'd expected. But it sounded so comical, I couldn't help but ask, "How did you even end up being referred to this Glittering Court?"

"Lady Branson's son John attends the university with him—Master Cedric. Lord John heard him talking about how he needed pretty girls for some task his father had set him. Lord John knew you were disbanding the household and asked his mother if there were any girls who needed a place to go. When she approached me . . . well, what could I do?"

I took her hand in an unusual show of informality between us. "You'll go to Hadaworth. That's what you'll do."

Ada gaped, and I led her up to my bedroom where other maids were sorting clothes. I sent them off to new tasks and then produced some topaz earrings from my jewelry box.

"Here," I said, handing them over to Ada. "Sell them. More than enough to buy passage with a reputable group traveling to Hadaworth." I'd expected her to have some greater lifelong dream, one I might not be able to afford. This was a bargain.

Her eyes widened. "My lady . . . I . . . I can't. I can't take these."

"You can," I insisted, my own heart racing. "I, uh, can't bear the thought of you being miserable. I want you to be with your family and find happiness. You deserve it." That wasn't entirely a lie . . . but my true motivations were hardly so altruistic.

She clutched the earrings in her hands, and hope started to bloom on her face. "I—no. I can't. That contract! That's binding. They'll find me and—"

"I'll take care of it—no need to worry. I'll get you out of it. I can do those kinds of things, you know. But to make sure it will all, um, work out, you need to leave now. Right away. It's just after midday. Most of the traveling merchants will be finishing business and heading north soon. And then you need to disavow all knowledge of the Glittering Court. Never, ever tell anyone they approached you."

Her eyes were huge. "I won't, my lady. I won't. Never a word. And I'll go now—as soon as I pack."

"No, don't. I mean, don't take too much. Pack lightly. You can't look like you're leaving for good. Act like you're just going off on an errand." I didn't want anyone noting her departure, possibly stopping her and asking her questions.

She nodded at the wisdom of my words. "You're right, my lady. Of course you are. Besides, with these, I can buy new clothes when I reach Hadaworth."

Upon my advice, she gathered only a few small things: a change of clothes, a family locket, and a pack of Deanzan cards. She flushed, seeing my raised eyebrow at that last one.

"It's just a lark, my lady. We read the cards for fun. People always have."

"Until the Alanzans made them a key part of their religion," I said. "The priests are burning them these days. Don't get yourself arrested as a heretic."

Her eyes widened. "I don't worship demons! Or trees!"

Everything else she left behind. The household was so busy getting ready for the move that no one paid us a second glance as we sneaked around about our tasks. I took her remaining possessions—which weren't much, only a few items of clothing—back to my room and hid them while I covertly saw her off. She startled me with a quick, highly inappropriate hug, tears shining in her eyes.

"Thank you, my lady. Thank you. You've saved me from a terrible fate."

And you may have done the same for me, I thought.

Upon my instructions, she walked casually out the front gate as though she were just going on a market errand. I don't think the sentry on duty even noticed her leaving. She was invisible, something I couldn't even comprehend . . . yet. As soon as she was gone, I returned to my painting in the garden, trying for all the world to look as though I were going about my usual attempts to pass the time while the rest of the household labored. Whenever I could work it into conversation with other servants, I mentioned casually that Ada had left for a new position and how wonderful it was that it had been arranged for her. Everyone knew someone had come asking about her before, but no one knew the details of that conversation. Many other servants had moved on already, so her departure was nothing new.

As evening wore on, word came that my grandmother and Lady Branson had been detained for dinner while out visiting a friend. That development couldn't have suited me better, though I did have a moment of pause when I realized I might never see Grandmama again. We'd exchanged harsh words that morning, but that didn't diminish my love for her . . . or hers for me. Everything she'd done in this mess with Lionel had been to benefit me, and there would be a huge fallout when it disintegrated.

Don't falter now, I told myself. I took deep breaths, forcing calm. *Grandmama can deal with whatever happens. And when the scandal dies down, she'll live with Lady Branson and her daughter. She'll be much happier there than under Lady Dorothy's close supervision.*

Even if we were apart, there was still the chance Grandmama might very well walk through my door, some far-off day. But oh, how she'd worry about me. I hoped that if—no, when—we met again, she'd understand why I'd had to do this. I couldn't marry into a life of luxury if it meant leaving my soul at the door.

After dinner, I complained of a headache and retired to my room. It was about the only reason I could have to be alone, and even that wasn't easy. As soon as I'd shooed my doting maids away, I changed out of the fine silk dress I'd worn for dinner and put on Ada's simpler linen one—which gave me some difficulty. I usually had maids helping me in and out of my clothes and wasn't accustomed to managing buttons without extra hands. Ada's dress was dark blue in color, with no ornamentation. The white chemise I put on under it was equally plain. I'd never truly noted until then how drab my ladies' clothing really was. Still, it would help conceal me, as did the gray hooded cloak I wore over it. I packed the rest of her clothing into a small satchel and then hurried down a narrow servants' staircase little used this time of night. After ascertaining no one was around, I slipped out a back door.

That put me in the courtyard by our stables, which were now darkened with twilight's shadows. Servants bustled about here, winding things down for the night, and no one noticed me as I huddled in the darkness. This was the most dangerous part of this endeavor, the part where it could all fall apart if anyone got a good look at me. I had to walk across the courtyard, toward the stable's back gates. The spring weather had cooled considerably, and I wasn't the only one with a hood. I just prayed no one would take a look at my face as I walked.

The stable boy guarding the back gate was busy whittling, his attention turned to anyone trying to get in, not out. If he noticed me, he saw only the back of one of the servant girls who came and went about the household's tasks. Once I was out of the enclosure, I hurried around the corner of our home, out toward the busy thoroughfare of our front street. Traffic on it had slowed since earlier in the day, but there were still horses and pedestrians out for the evening, their steps clattering on the cobblestone street. Most didn't give me a second glance. I was a lady's maid, not a lady.

An errant priest of Uros stood on a corner, preaching against the Alanzan heretics. He pointed accusingly at me, his finger right up in my face. "You wouldn't worship the sun and moon, would you, girl?"

There was a fanatic, feverish gleam in his eyes, and I was so astonished that I froze before him.

"You! Stay right there!"

I gasped as two city sentries came running toward me. I was barely across the street from my home! How had they known to come for me already?

But it wasn't me they were after. They seized the priest, one holding the thrashing man while the other bound his wrists. "How dare you lay hands on one of Uros's chosen!" bellowed the priest.

One of the sentries snorted. "You're no true follower of Uros. See how strong your faith is after a few nights in prison." He dragged the shrieking priest away while the other sentry turned to me. I quickly looked down, feigning shyness, so he wouldn't see my face.

"You all right, miss? Did he hurt you?"

"I'm fine. Thank you. Sir."

He shook his head in disgust. "I don't know what the world's coming to when heretics walk the street. You'd best get back to your master's house before it gets darker."

I bobbed my head and quickly walked away. The religious atmosphere was dangerous in Osfrid these days. These radical wandering priests might claim to worship the one god Uros, but their practices challenged the established church almost as much as the Alanzans and their fallen angels. The orthodox priests and officials were no longer as tolerant as they'd once been, and it took very little to make you suspect.

It was a relief when I reached the Glittering Court's carriage. It was two blocks away in the opposite direction, exactly as Cedric had told Ada it would be.

It was all black, sleek and shiny, with the Glittering Court's seal on the outside: a circle of golden chain with little jewels interspersed between the links. The carriage was of modest size, not nearly as grand as the one my grandmother or I rode in, but I supposed it would be extraordinary to a girl who knew no different. I walked around to the front where a driver sat waiting over four white horses. I called a greeting to him, loud enough to make my voice heard over the noise from the street but hopefully not enough to attract the attention of the great house on the other side of it.

"Hey," I called. "You're here to pick me up. My name is Adelaide."

I'd decided on that when I concocted this plan. I'd made Ada disappear and received her promise that she wouldn't mention any of this, but as far as the Glittering Court officials knew, they had the right girl. Calling myself Ada didn't seem right. What I was doing already felt like theft, but I certainly couldn't go by my own name anymore. So, I'd use the beautiful name Ada had been given at birth, the one she had trouble spelling. I felt like I deserved it, just as I deserved this opportunity that terrified her.

The driver gave a curt nod. "Yeah, well, hop in. We're meeting Master Jasper and Master Cedric along the way."

Master Cedric.

As much as I'd enjoyed looking at him, seeing him now could most certainly create a problem in this brilliant plan I'd created . . . but I'd have to deal with that later. For now, I had other issues.

"Hop in?" I asked, putting my hands on my hips. "Aren't you going to come down and open the door for me?"

The man gave an amused snort. "Listen to you, acting like a lady already. You aren't a 'jewel' yet, missy. Now get in—we've got two more stops to make, and one's by the Sirminican district. I don't want to be out *there* any later than I have to. Those Sirminicans will rob you blind if you're not watching 'em."

I fumbled with the coach's handle and finally figured out how to open it. Ungracefully, I half-stepped, half-tumbled into the carriage's interior, without the benefit of a stool or pillow offered by a servant. Inside, the carriage was dim, lit only by what light made its way in through the smoky windows. As my eyes adjusted, I could see that the cushioned seat I sat on was made of a burgundy velvet of middling quality.

Without bothering to make sure I was comfortable, the driver set the horses on their way, causing me to jerk forward. I gripped the walls for support, staring out the darkened glass as the lights of my family's home moved farther and farther away. I held my breath as I watched the retreating house, expecting a group of servants to come tearing out at any moment, swarming the carriage until it stopped and released me. No one came, though. The house went about its nighttime duties, soon vanishing into the night. Or maybe I was the one vanishing. Maybe I would be forgotten quickly, my face and voice gone from the minds of those I'd once known. The notion made me sadder than I'd expected, and I had to shift my focus back to the plan.

Presuming no one thought to check on my headache tonight, I'd have until morning before my absence was discovered, at which point I'd hopefully be long gone into the country. And that was assuming, of course, that Ada didn't get cold feet and come back—if she'd even left the city. If things were on track, she'd have already bought passage with some group of travelers heading north.

There were a lot of "if"s in this plan, a lot of things that could go wrong.

The rocking carriage made its way through the city, into parts I'd never seen before. I was terribly curious about it all, but as the evening deepened, I could see less and less by the glow of the gas lamps used to illuminate the streets. The carriage finally came to a halt, and I heard a muffled conversation. Moments later, the door opened, and a girl my age stood framed in the doorway, her fiery red hair shining even in the twilight. She shot me a calculating look and then, like me, climbed in without benefit of a stool. Only she managed it better. She shut the door, and the carriage continued on its jerky ride.

We sat there, sizing each other up in silence as we moved down the cobblestone streets. Light from outside lamps came and went, creating a flickering show of shadows inside. When that intermittent illumination came, I could see that her dress was even plainer than mine, threadbare in some places. At last, she spoke, her voice tinged slightly with a working-class accent: "How'd you get your hair like that? All those curls lying just so?"

It wasn't a question I'd expected. It also seemed blunt until I realized she thought we were of equal social rank. "It's naturally wavy," I said.

She nodded impatiently. "Yes, yes. I can tell, but the way those curls are all arranged so perfectly . . . I've tried that myself, like the highborn ladies do? I think I'd need half a dozen hands to do it."

I nearly said I *had* had half a dozen hands helping me and then bit off the words. I'd thought I was so clever changing into Ada's dress, but had gone off on this adventure with the same elaborately styled hair I'd had from this morning—which my maids had helped curl and pin in the latest fashion, cascading all around my shoulders. I gave my companion a tight smile back.

"Someone helped me," I said. I thought about Ada's backstory and tried to make it my own. "Since it's a, uh, special occasion. I worked as a lady's maid, you see, so I have friends who are really good at this kind of thing."

"A lady's maid? Well, that's bloody lucky. I wouldn't want to leave that post. Explains why you talk so well—you'll have a leg up on the rest of us." She sounded impressed . . . and also a little envious.

"It's not a competition," I said quickly.

There was another fleeting flash of light from outside, showing me a wry expression on her face. "The hell it isn't. How we do and how well we learn affects who they offer us to as wives. I'm going to be a banker's wife. Or a statesman's. Not some farmer's." She paused to reconsider. "Unless he's some dirty rich plantation owner, where I can order around the servants and the household. But an ordinary farmwife? Sweeping floors and making cheese? No, thanks. Not that any old farmer could afford one of us. My mother heard from one of her friends that the Glittering Court got a marriage price of four hundred gold dollars for one of their girls. Can you even imagine that sort of money?"

Vaguely, I recalled Cedric talking about suitors making "offers." The contract had further elaborated how the Glittering Court's agents made a commission off each girl's marriage price. Cedric might have spoken in lofty tones about his new nobility providing a service to the New World, but it was obvious this was a huge money-making venture for the Thorn family.

The other girl was regarding me strangely, waiting for a response.

"I'm sorry—you'll have to forgive me if I sound scattered. This was all kind of last-minute," I explained. "The family I worked for was dismissing most of their staff, and so when Ced—Master Cedric was looking for girls, someone referred me to him."

"Oh, you're one of his, huh? I heard about that too," my companion said. "He hasn't ever recruited before, you see. His father's one of the best procurers, and Master Cedric made a big deal about how he could be just as good, so his father let him pick a couple of girls. Caused a big family stir."

"You sure do know a lot," I said. She'd apparently received a more extensive pitch than Ada and me.

"I was delivering laundry to their house," she explained. "My mother washes clothes, and I helped her. But no more." She held up her hands and studied them, but I couldn't get a good look. "I'm not meant to be a laundress. I'm never washing anyone's damned clothes again."

Her ambition radiated off her. I wasn't sure if that sort of initiative would be useful to me or not, but when in doubt, I'd found friendliness was usually the best course of action.

"I'm Adelaide," I told her warmly. "It's so nice to meet you, Miss . . . ?"

She hesitated, as though deciding if I was worth the next piece of information. "Wright. Tamsin Wright."

The carriage began to slow, bringing us to our next stop. Both of us dropped the thread of our conversation as we waited to see who would enter next. When the door opened and revealed a girl standing outside, Tamsin's breath caught. At first, I thought the poor lighting was distorting the newcomer's appearance. Then, I realized the tawny hue of her skin was natural. It was almost like caramel. I recalled the driver saying we were going near the Sirminican quarter. It was one of the poorest districts in the capital, and I could just make out a few dirty, run-down buildings in the distance. I knew by reputation that it was overcrowded with refugees from Sirminica, which had been locked in civil war for the last few years. Once, it had been a great nation, and its monarchy had even intermarried with ours. Rebels had recently overthrown the royal family, and now the country was generally avoided as a chaotic war zone. This girl waiting by the coach's door, with her lovely skin and luxurious black hair, bore all the signs of being one of those refugees.

She was also stunningly, breathtakingly beautiful.

The driver had hopped down to admit her, giving her a wary look as she stepped forward. She carried herself with dignity and, after glancing between Tamsin and me, settled in on my side of the carriage. Her dress was even more worn than Tamsin's, but a shawl around her shoulders, stitched with intricate embroidery, was exceptional.

Recalling his slurs, I wondered if the driver had come down to ensure she didn't rob us blind. When he continued waiting by the open door, I realized more was happening. Soon, two male voices carried to my ears—one of which I recognized.

"—pretty enough, I suppose, but you have no idea how hard it's going to be to sell a Sirminican."

"That's not going to matter—not over there."

"You don't know 'over there' like I do," came the biting reply. "You just threw away your commission."

"That's not—"

The words were abruptly cut off when the two speakers reached the carriage's doorway. One of them, an older man in his forties, had only the faintest touch of silver in his brown hair. There was a dashing look about him, and he bore enough resemblance to Cedric Thorn to make me realize this must be his father, Jasper.

The other man joining us was, of course, Cedric Thorn himself.

My mouth went dry as our gazes locked. Even while being chastised by his father, Cedric had swaggered up to the carriage with that same self-assured ease I'd seen previously. Now, he came to an abrupt halt, so suddenly that he nearly tripped over his own feet. He stared at me like I was an apparition. His mouth opened to speak and then shut abruptly as though, perhaps, he didn't trust himself.

Jasper beamed when he saw Tamsin, oblivious to the silent drama occurring between Cedric and me. "So lovely to see you again, my dear. I trust your pickup was fine?"

Tamsin's earlier calculation and wariness vanished as she returned his smile. "Oh, everything's been lovely, Mister Thorn. The carriage is beautiful, and I've already made a new friend."

His eyes fell on me, and I had to drag myself away from Cedric's pinning gaze. I noticed that Jasper, at least, regarded me with approval. "And you must be our other lovely companion. Ada, right?" Jasper extended his hand to me, and after several awkward moments, I realized he expected to me to shake it. I did, hoping my unfamiliarity with the gesture didn't show. "You, I have no doubt, will have men beating down our door in Adoria."

I wet my lips, having difficulty finding my voice. "Th-thank you, sir. And you can call me Adelaide."

Somehow, that comment seemed to snap Cedric out of his daze. "Oh. Is that what you're calling yourself now?"

"It's an improvement," I said pointedly. "Don't you think?"

When Cedric didn't answer, Jasper nudged him. "Stop delaying. We need to get going."

Cedric studied me a beat more, and I felt as though we both stood on a precipice. He was the one who'd determine which way we tipped. "Yes," he said at last. "Let's go."

Jasper entered ahead of him, sitting beside Tamsin and taking up most of the seat on that side. Obligingly, the Sirminican girl scooted over on our side, creating extra space. Recognizing the cue, I moved as well. After a slight hesitation, Cedric sat down beside me. It still made for close quarters, and our arms and legs touched. My grandmother would have been scandalized. He barely moved, and I could feel that his body was as rigid as my own, both of us tense as we came to terms with this new situation.

Most of the subsequent conversation was carried by Jasper and Tamsin. I learned the Sirminican girl was called Mira, but she said as little as Cedric and I did. I commented once on the beauty of her shawl, and she drew it closer. "It was my mother's," she said softly, her words laced with a Sirminican accent. There was a sadness in her voice I understood, one that stirred up an ache in my chest that had never entirely gone away. Without knowing anything else about her, I instantly felt a connection and asked her no more.

When the carriage came to a full stop after about twenty minutes, Jasper looked up with satisfaction. "Finally. The gates. Once we're outside the city, we can get some real speed." We could hear agitated voices on the other side of the carriage door, and as the delay increased, Jasper's expression grew annoyed. "What's taking so long?" He opened the door and leaned out, calling to the driver.

The driver hurried to the door, two gate guards behind him. "Sorry, Mister Thorn. They're checking everyone leaving. Looking for some girl."

"Not some girl," corrected one of the guards harshly. "A young noblewoman. Seventeen years old. A countess."

I stopped breathing.

"Who are these girls?" demanded the other guard, peering inside.

Jasper relaxed. "Certainly not countesses. We're with the Glittering Court. These are common girls, bound for Adoria."

The guard was suspicious, studying each of us in turn. I wished again I'd thought to change my hair.

"What's this girl look like?" asked Jasper conversationally.

"Brown hair and blue eyes," said one of the guards, his gaze lingering fractionally longer on me. "Same age as this lot. Ran away earlier this evening. There's a reward."

I almost felt indignant, since I liked to think my hair was more of a *golden* brown. But it was a common enough description that it could apply to half the girls in the city. The vaguer, the better.

"Well, we've got a Sirminican, a laundress, and a housemaid," said Jasper. "If the reward's big enough and you want to pass one of them off as a countess, be my guest, but I assure you, we've seen where they come from. Hardly posh conditions . . . although, Cedric, weren't you in some noble's house today? Isn't that where you got Adelaide? Did you hear anything?"

The first guard's gaze locked onto Cedric. "Sir? Where were you?"

Cedric had been staring straight ahead this whole time, perhaps hoping a lack of eye contact would render him invisible.

"Sir?" prompted the guard.

The world seemed to move in slow motion, and all I could hear for several moments was the hammering of my own heart. I was reminded of that precipice again, only now I was losing my footing. All it would take was one word from Cedric, one word to get me hauled back to my grandmother and Lionel. I didn't doubt Cedric was clever enough to spin the situation to make himself sound innocent. And for all I knew, Cedric might think collecting a reward now was easier than earning a commission in Adoria.

Cedric took a deep breath, and as if putting on a mask, he became the swaggering young man from before. "I saw Lord John Branson," he said. He nodded toward me. "She was mending some fine lady's clothes at his house when I retrieved her, though. Does that count?"

"This is hardly a joking matter," snapped the guard. But I could tell he was already losing interest in us, ready to move on. There were probably a lot of travelers trying to leave before curfew, and they didn't want to be delayed by one unlikely carriage. A runaway noblewoman would be skulking out, not sitting with reputable businessmen.

"You can go," said the other guard. "Thank you for your time."

Cedric, still putting on a good face, smiled back. "Not a problem. I hope you find her."

The door closed, and the carriage started forward, finally moving at a steady pace now that we'd cleared the stops and starts of the city. I exhaled, all the tension melting out of me as I sank into the seat. I dared a brief glance at Cedric but couldn't read his expression or intentions. All I could hope was that maybe, finally, I'd be free.

CHAPTER 4

THE JOURNEY TOOK ALL NIGHT, AND I DRIFTED IN AND out of sleep. My body wanted rest, but my mind was too keyed up, fearful I'd hear horses and angry shouts behind us. But the night passed uneventfully, the rocking of the carriage lulling me into more of a calm daze than a true sleep. I came fully awake when I heard Jasper say, "Ah, here we are." The carriage's steady gait began to slow, and I lifted my head, startled and embarrassed to realize I'd been resting it on Cedric's shoulder. His cologne smelled like vetiver.

My companions' reactions were mixed. Tamsin's face was eager, ready to take on this new adventure and seize what she saw as her destiny. Mira was more apprehensive, wearing the expression of one who had seen much and knew better than to trust initial appearances.

Jasper helped each of us out of the carriage, and as I waited my turn, I had a momentary flash of panic at what I might find. I'd gone to a great deal of trouble last night, striving for a destination grounded more in my own fantasies than any fact. Cedric had wooed me with his pitch to Ada, but there was a very real chance I was about to walk into a situation far worse than a life of barley with Lionel. I could be walking into a life of sordidness and danger.

Jasper took my hand, and I got my first good look at Blue Spring Manor. To my immediate relief, it looked neither sordid nor dangerous on the outside. Blue Spring Manor was a country estate, set out among the moors with no village or other community in sight. No one searching for me would casually pass by. It wasn't quite as big as some of my family's former holdings, but it was still old and impressive. The morning sun rose just beyond its roof, illuminating Tamsin and Mira's awestruck faces.

A middle-aged woman dressed all in black met us at the door. "Well, here they are, the last of them. I was worried they weren't going to show."

"We had a few delays," Jasper explained, glancing at Mira. "And some surprises."

"I'm sure they'll settle in soon enough." The woman turned to us with a stern expression. "I'm Mistress Masterson. I run the house and will manage your day-to-day affairs. I'll also be in charge of teaching you etiquette—which I expect you to excel in. We've got one room left that'll hold the three of you nicely. You can put your things away and then join the other girls for breakfast. They've just sat down."

She asked the Thorns if they wanted breakfast as well, but I barely heard their response. I was too busy processing Mistress Masterson's comment about the three of us sharing a room. I'd never shared a room with anyone in my life. No—I'd never shared my *rooms* with anyone. No matter which residence my family had stayed in, I'd had a suite to myself. At most, I'd had a maid sleeping outside the door or in an antechamber to answer my summons.

Cedric gave me a sharp look, and I wondered if perhaps my astonishment showed on my face. I quickly schooled my expression to neutrality and followed Mistress Masterson inside. She led us up a winding staircase that I had to admit was elegant. Bright paintings lined the house's walls—some portraits of Thorn family members, and others hung simply for their beauty. I recognized a few of the artists and nearly slowed to study them in more detail before remembering I needed to keep up.

The room Mistress Masterson took us to was decently appointed, with lacy curtains framing a window that looked down on the manor's grounds. The room also held three claw-foot beds with matching dressers—but didn't seem nearly big enough for any of that, let alone three occupants. Tamsin and Mira's wide eyes suggested otherwise.

"It's so bloody big," exclaimed Tamsin.

"Language, please." Mistress Masterson's prim face softened a little as she looked us over. "You'll soon get used to it, and if you're lucky and study hard, you'll likely have a room this size all to yourself when you marry in the New World."

Mira ran her fingertips lightly along the flowered wallpaper. "I've never seen anything like this."

Mistress Masterson swelled with pride. "Nearly all of our rooms are wallpapered—we try to maintain high standards, just as good as the capital's. Now, then. Let me take you down to the other girls. You can get acquainted with them while I speak with Master Jasper and his son."

We left our meager belongings in the room and followed her back down the staircase. The rest of the manor's corridors bore the same décor, with old portraits and elegant vases scattered about. We entered the dining room, also beautifully done, sporting striped wallpaper and deep green rugs. The table was covered with a scallop-edged linen cloth and set with china and silver. Tamsin had attempted an unimpressed expression when we walked into the room but faltered at the sight of it.

I immediately focused my attention on the table's occupants, consisting of seven girls who fell silent at our arrival. They looked to be the same age as us and were all very attractive. The Glittering Court might claim to find girls who could learn to behave like nobler classes, but it was clear our appearances were a big part of the criteria that got us here.

"Ladies," said Mistress Masterson, "this is Tamsin, Adelaide, and Mirabel. They will be joining our home." To us, she added, "Everyone else has just arrived within the last week. Now that you're all here, we'll formalize the schedule and of course work on overhauling everyone's wardrobes. You'll dress better than you ever have in your lives and learn to style yourselves as befits the upper classes." She paused and looked me over. "Though your hair is already quite nice, Adelaide."

She urged us to sit down and then left to speak with Jasper and Cedric. Silence continued as everyone sized each other up or continued eating. I was surprisingly hungry and wondered when a servant would enter. After a few minutes, I realized no one was coming and that we had to do our own serving. I reached out to a nearby teapot and had the novel experience of pouring for myself.

Breakfast was a selection of fruit and delicate pastries. Tamsin's calculation and Mira's apprehension couldn't hold out against an array like that, and they reached eagerly for the serving plate. I wondered if they'd ever eaten such things in their lives. Both were thin. Maybe they'd never eaten much of anything.

I purposely selected a fig-and-almond tart, something that required a little effort. It was traditionally eaten by being first cut into small, equally sized pieces, and I used the delay as an excuse to study my companions. The first thing I noticed was a uniformity in their clothing. Sure, the dresses varied in color and fabric choices, but my guess was that they'd all gone through the outfitting process Mistress Masterson had spoken about. The dresses were pretty and flirty, as opposed to the more serviceable one I'd inherited from Ada. The fabric quality in mine was at least as good, however, if not better. Mira and Tamsin's attire didn't even warrant comparison to the rest of us, though I had to assume most of the girls had arrived in a similar state.

The others also appeared to have had a few rudimentary etiquette lessons already, which they were trying to implement with varying degrees of success. They might be dressed and styled decently, but these were the daughters of laborers and tradesmen. A couple of girls managed the ten-piece silverware setting reasonably well. Others made no effort whatsoever and ate largely with their hands. Most fell in the middle, visibly struggling to figure out which utensil to use, no doubt trying to recall whatever Mistress Masterson had taught them in their brief time here. Tamsin, I suddenly noticed, was eating a fig-and-almond tart too. Unlike other girls who were simply lifting and biting it, Tamsin cut hers perfectly, with exactly the right tools. Then I realized her eyes were locked on my plate, imitating everything I did.

"What are you?" one girl asked boldly. "Myrikosi? Vinizian? Surely not . . . Sirminican."

There was no question about whom she was speaking to, and all eyes swiveled to Mira. She took several moments to look up. She'd been nicely cutting her lemon roll but was using the wrong fork and knife. No one else knew any better, and I certainly wasn't going to point it out. "I was born in the City of Holy Light, yes."

Santa Luz. The grandest, oldest city in Sirminica. I'd learned about it in my governess's history lessons, how it had been settled by the ancient Ruvans centuries ago. Philosophers and kings had lived and ruled there, and its monuments were legendary. At least, they had been until revolution ravaged the country.

A girl at the opposite end of the table regarded Mira with undisguised derision. "There's no way you can get rid of that accent in a year." She glanced around knowingly at some of the others. "I'm sure they need servants in the New World. You won't need to talk much if you're busy scrubbing floors."

This brought a few snickers from some, uncomfortable looks from others. "Clara," warned one girl uneasily. I carefully set down my fork and knife, crossing them in a perfect X, as a lady did when pausing in her meal. Fixing a level gaze on the girl—Clara—sitting at the end of the table, I asked, "Who did your makeup today?"

Startled by my question, she turned from smirking at her neighbor to study me curiously. "I did."

I nodded in satisfaction. "Obviously."

Clara frowned. "Obviously?"

"Well, I knew it couldn't have been Mistress Masterson."

A girl beside me hesitantly offered: "We haven't been here long. Cosmetics haven't been part of the curricu—curricu—"

"Curriculum," I said, helping her with the unfamiliar word. I glanced back at Clara before returning to my tart. "Obviously it hasn't."

"Why do you keep saying that?" she demanded.

I drew out the tension by eating another piece before answering. "Because Mistress Masterson would have never directed you to use cosmetics like *that*. Red lips aren't in style in Osfro anymore. All the highborn ladies are wearing coral and dusky pink. And you've applied the rouge in the wrong spot—it goes higher, up on your cheekbones." That's what I'd heard, at least. I'd certainly never applied my own cosmetics. "Where you've got it right now makes you look like you have mumps. You've got a steady hand on the kohl, but everyone knows you have to smudge it to get the proper look. Otherwise, your eyes look beady. And everything—*everything*—you've applied is far too dark. A light touch goes a long way. The way you're wearing it now makes you look . . . how shall I put it . . . well, like a lady of questionable morals."

Two spots of color appeared in the girl's cheek, making her badly applied rouge look even worse. "Like *what*?"

"Like a prostitute. That's another word for 'whore,' in case you're not familiar with it," I explained, using as formal a tone as my former governess would use while teaching Ruvan grammar. "That's someone who sells her body for—"

"I know what it means!" the girl exclaimed, turning even redder.

"But," I added, "if it's any consolation, you look like a very high-class one. Like one who would work in one of the more expensive brothels. Where the girls dance and sing. Not like the ones who work down by the wharves. Those poor things don't have access to true cosmetics at all, so they have to make do with whatever they can scrape together. Be grateful you haven't hit that low." I paused. "Oh. And, by the way, you're using the wrong fork."

The girl stared at me openmouthed, and I braced myself for a backlash. It'd be no more than I deserved, but she'd certainly deserved my belittling. I didn't know Mira well, but something about her resonated with me—a mix of sorrow shielded by pride. Clara had the air of someone who preyed on others frequently. I knew that type of girl. They apparently existed in both upper and lower classes, so I felt no remorse for what I'd done.

Until her eyes—and those of everyone else at the table—lifted to something beyond me. A cold feeling welled up in the pit of my stomach, and I slowly turned around, unsurprised to see Mistress Masterson and the Thorns standing in the entryway to the dining room. I wasn't sure how much they'd heard, but their shocked expressions told me they'd heard enough.

No one acknowledged it, however, as Cedric and Jasper joined us at the table. Really, no one acknowledged much of anything as the meal progressed. I wanted to shrink into my seat but remembered a lady must always sit straight. The tension had been thick before, but now I could feel it pressing upon my shoulders. I regretted finishing the tart because then I had nothing to occupy myself or fix my gaze upon. I poured another cup of tea, stirring it endlessly until the Thorns rose to leave and Mistress Masterson formally dismissed us to our rooms.

I was one of the first to hurry out, hoping if I escaped Mistress Masterson's eye, she'd eventually forget about the scene she'd witnessed. Surely she had better things to worry about. The other girls turned toward the spiral staircase, but just as I was about to, a flash of color caught my eye at the opposite end of the foyer. Everyone was preoccupied going their own way and paid little attention when I turned from the stairs. At the far end of the great hall was the entrance to the drawing room, and beside it hung a painting of surpassing beauty.

I recognized the artist as I drew nearer. Florencio. The National Gallery in Osfro also held one of his paintings, and I'd studied it many times. He was a Sirminican renowned for painting landscapes in his own country, and I was surprised to find one of his works in this country manor. Closer scrutiny made me think it was one of the artist's earlier works. Certain techniques weren't quite as refined as the gallery portrait. It was still exquisite, but those imprecise details might explain how the painting had ended up here.

I admired it a little longer, trying to puzzle out some of his methods, and then turned around to go back to the staircase. To my astonishment, I saw Jasper and Cedric headed my way down the corridor. Neither had noticed me yet. They were too engrossed in their own conversation. I quickly stepped around a corner, cringing back into a small nook to the side of the drawing room's entrance that was out of sight of the main hall.

". . . knew it was too good to be true," Jasper was saying. "You had two chances. Two chances, and you blew them both."

"You don't think you're being a little extreme?" asked Cedric. His tone was light, laconic even, but I could sense the tension underneath it.

"Did you hear the mouth on that girl?" Jasper exclaimed. "Atrocious."

"Not really. She was quite polite about it all. No improper language." Cedric hesitated. "And her grammar and diction are quite excellent."

"It's not the language so much as the attitude. She's bold and impertinent. The men in Adoria don't want shrews for wives. They want mild, compliant young woman."

"Not too mild if they're going to survive in Adoria," Cedric said. "And she was defending Mira. I thought it was noble." Well, that answered one question. They'd heard the whole exchange after all.

Jasper sighed. "Oh, yes. Defending the Sirminican—that justifies it all. *That* one's going to have to get used to being put down. Clara's not going to be the only one to do it."

"I don't think Mira's the type who will ever 'get used to' being put down," said Cedric. I thought about the dark glitter of her eyes and was inclined to agree with him.

"Be that as it may, you've thrown away both commissions. You'll be lucky to get anything for them in Adoria—unless you can get Adelaide to close her mouth long enough for us to marry her off. She's pretty enough to snare some fool. The Sirminican is too," Jasper added, almost grudgingly. "There's nothing wrong with your eyes, I'll give you that. It's the rest of you I don't know about. Letting you procure this year was a bad idea. You should've stayed here with your classes. Maybe a few more years would have taught you some sense."

"What's done is done," said Cedric.

"I suppose so. Well, I have to finish up some paperwork, and then I'll meet you at the carriage. We need to check on Swan Ridge."

I heard the sounds of Jasper's footsteps departing and waited for Cedric to do the same. Instead, he moved forward, coming into my view as he looked at the same painting I'd admired before. I froze where I was, praying he wouldn't look off to his side. After several moments, he sighed and turned to follow his father. And as he did, he caught sight of me in his periphery. Before I could draw another breath, he darted into my little alcove, trapping me between him and the wall.

"You! What in Ozhiel's name have you done?" he hissed, pitching his voice low. "What are you doing here?"

"Um, getting ready to be part of the new nobility."

"I'm serious! Where's Ada?" he demanded.

"Long gone," I said, with a shrug. "Guess you're stuck with me. Besides, I thought you wanted to see me again?"

"When I said that, I meant that I wanted—" He stopped that thought, looking only briefly flustered as countless unvoiced possibilities lingered tantalizingly in the air between us. His composure was back in moments. "My lady, this isn't a game. You have no business here! I was supposed to get Ada."

"And I'm telling you, she's long gone. I gave her some money and sent her on her way. She'll be happily milking cows in no time." My words were bold—impertinent, as Jasper would no doubt say—but inside, I was panicked. Cedric had covered for me in Osfro, but this wasn't over yet. "I helped you by coming here. Ada would've probably bolted on her own. Wouldn't you have gotten in trouble for showing up short a girl?"

"Do you know how much trouble I'll get in for smuggling away a countess? They'll imprison me! Presuming your husband-to-be doesn't just kill me himself." Seeing my surprise, he said, "Yes, I know about your engagement, my lady. I read the society papers."

"Then you should know you're in no real danger from Lionel. He's not the violent type—unless you're an itch."

"Do you think my future's a joke? Is all of this a joke to you?"

I met his gaze, looking unblinkingly into those gray-blue eyes. "Actually, this is anything but a joke. This is my future too. My chance to be free and make my own choices."

He shook his head. "You don't realize what you've done—what you may have cost me. I have so much depending on this, more than you can know."

"I haven't cost you anything. Help me with this—don't betray me, and I'll owe you a favor." I caught hold of his sleeve. "Haven't you ever known something in your heart, known you needed to do something or be somewhere? That's how this is for me. I *need* to do this. Help me, and I swear, I'll make it up to you some day."

A fleeting smile played over his lips. "The Countess of Rothford could have done a lot more for me than a simple girl bound for Adoria."

"You'd be surprised. The Countess of Rothford couldn't do much for herself, let alone anyone else." I looked up at him through my lashes. "And don't assume I'm simple."

He made no response and instead studied me for a long time. We were in very close quarters, which gave that scrutiny a disconcertingly intimate feel. "This will be harder than you think," he said at last.

"I doubt it," I said, putting my hands on my hips. "All those things you're teaching the other girls? I already know them. I could teach classes in this place."

"Yes. That's exactly the problem. You know too much. Your manners, your diction—even your hair."

"I wish everyone would stop talking about my hair," I muttered.

"You stand out, my lady. This is a world you don't understand—where you can't wield the privilege you've known. Where your title won't get you access or even let you be taken seriously in some places. And there are plenty of things the other girls know that you don't. Can you start a fire in the hearth? Can you even dress yourself?"

"I put this on myself," I told him. "I mean, the buttons took a little figuring out, but I eventually did it."

He looked like he was on the verge of rolling his eyes. "My lady, you have no idea what—"

"Adelaide," I corrected. "If we're going to pull this off, you must call me that. No more titles."

"Well, then, *Adelaide*, let me give you some advice. Don't be too good at anything—you don't want to attract extra attention. Think twice before you correct someone, even if it's Clara." His tone as he said her name made me think he hadn't actually minded my putting her in her place. "And above all, watch the other girls. Watch their mannerisms. Listen to the way they talk. Every little detail. One slip, and both our lives will be ruined. You'll give yourself away in ways you don't even realize."

At those words, I had a sudden flash of how I'd already messed up in the last twenty-four hours. The carriage door. The tart. The cosmetics lecture. And yes, the hair.

You'll give yourself away in ways you don't even realize.

"I won't," I said fiercely. "I'll do this—you'll see. I'll do all the right things. I'll get a dozen Adorian offers and land you the biggest commission of them all."

"No—don't stand out." He paused, and a hint of that earlier flirty smile resurfaced. "Well, as much as you can help it."

"You said you've got a lot depending on this. What is there? More than the commission?"

He grew sober again. "Nothing for you to worry about. Just get to Adoria without being discovered, and we both might survive this." He glanced around. "We need to go. We're going to be missed."

I thought about the harsh way Jasper had spoken to him, the way he'd dismissed Cedric's efforts. A wise part of me knew better than to comment on that. Instead I asked, "Any other words of wisdom before you leave?"

He turned back, looking me over in that way that felt oddly personal. But it didn't unsettle me as much this time. Neither did our proximity. "Yes," he said. He reached forward and wound one of my curls around his fingers, inadvertently brushing my cheek in the process. "Do something about this hair. Mess it up. Tie it back. Anything to make you a little more disheveled and less like you're being presented at court."

I lifted my chin. "First, this isn't a court style—which you'd know, if you'd spent any time with the *old* nobility. And second, I can mess up as many etiquette lessons as you like . . . but disheveled? I don't know if I can do that."

The smile returned, warmer and wider than before. "Somehow, I'm not surprised." He sketched me a bow, almost a caricature of the one he'd given at our first meeting. "Until next time, my—Adelaide."

He turned and, after a quick check around the corner, walked back down the great hall. I waited an appropriate amount of time and did the same. I'd hoped to catch a glimpse of him, but he was already out of sight. It was just as well. Putting him from my mind, I climbed the staircase up to my new life in the Glittering Court.

CHAPTER 5

I RETURNED TO MY ROOM, NOT ENTIRELY SURE WHAT TO expect. I was still shaking from the encounter with Cedric, how close I'd been to everything falling apart around me. Taking a deep breath, I threw my shoulders back and pushed the door open.

Calm and silence met me. My two roommates were each sitting on their respective beds. Mira's knees were drawn up to her, creating a makeshift desk as she read a battered book. Tamsin sat cross-legged, furiously writing what looked like a letter. Seeing me, she quickly folded the paper up. I didn't know if it was coincidence or not, but the beds they'd chosen were opposite each other in the room.

"I hope you don't mind the bed by the window," Mira said. "Tamsin was worried it'd be bad for her complexion."

Tamsin lightly touched her cheek. "You have no idea what sunlight can do to freckles. But that doesn't matter right now. What happened downstairs? They didn't kick you out, did they?"

I sat down on the edge of the bed between theirs, the one that agitated freckles. "Not yet." I nearly said that Mistress Masterson hadn't chastised me at all but then thought better of it, lest I have to explain what I'd really been doing. "Just a, uh, stern talking-to."

"Well, you're lucky," said Tamsin. "But this kind of changes everything. I'm not sure what to do about you now."

It took me a moment to follow. "Are you chastising me too?"

"No. I mean, yes. I don't know. But I'm not sure if being associated with two troublemakers is going to help me around here."

Mira looked startled. "What did I do?"

"Nothing yet." Tamsin *almost* seemed chagrined. "But you saw how it was down there after just five minutes. People like Clara aren't going to let up on you."

"So you want to be associated with someone like Clara?" I asked.

"Hell no. But I've got to plan my strategy here. I can't fail." There was the slightest tremor in her voice at that last part—vulnerability, more than arrogance. Mira caught it too.

"You won't fail," she said kindly. "Just keep up with everything. Cedric said as long as we score in a passing range, we're guaranteed to go to Adoria." Her use of his first name, with no honorific, wasn't lost on me.

"I have to do more than just pass." Tamsin glanced down at the folded paper in her hands and then looked up with renewed determination. Her other fist clenched beside her. "I have to be the best. The best in our manor. The best in all the other manors. And I have to do whatever it takes to make the best marriage in Adoria—the wealthiest man I can find, one who'll do anything for me. If that means being cutthroat here? So be it."

"Who needs cutthroat when you've got me? If you want to be on top, then I'm your best bet. I already know half of all this from being in a grand lady's house. Stick with me, and you're guaranteed to succeed. Stick with both of us," I added, with a glance at Mira.

I still knew nothing about her, but that sense of connection remained. I didn't know much about Tamsin either, aside from her willingness to become "cutthroat"—which didn't exactly come as a surprise after our brief acquaintance. But Cedric's words were weighing on me, about how important it was that I not screw up and give myself away. I was more likely to pull that off if I had backup.

Were these two the best backup I might have chosen? Unclear. But as my roommates for the next year, they were the best candidates.

"You're probably not the only one thinking this place is cutthroat," I continued. My persuasive skills hadn't exactly been top-notch recently, but after winning Cedric to my side, I was starting to feel confident again. "So you know the others are going to be ruthless—especially if you are the best."

"There's no 'if,'" said Tamsin.

"Right. Well, then, someone like Clara's going to target you for sure. And you know she'll surround herself in cronies too. She'll have eyes and ears everywhere—you'd better have them too. Who knows if she'll stoop to sabotage? And you might think I'm a troublemaker, but I'm also a troublemaker who knows the difference between *sec*, *demi-sec*, and *doux* wine."

"Demi-what?" asked Tamsin.

I crossed my arms over my chest, triumphant. "Exactly."

"So you've got the insider information. I'm obviously the leader." Tamsin's eyes fell on Mira. "What do *you* have to offer?"

When Mira simply met her gaze unblinkingly, I supplied, "Well, she apparently survived a war zone. I somehow doubt this is going to be harder."

Tamsin looked as though she was trying to decide about that. Before the conversation could continue, a knock sounded at the door. Mistress Masterson entered with clothing slung over one arm. "Here are some day dresses for you to wear today. We can make adjustments later. Put them on, wash your faces, and be downstairs in fifteen minutes." Her eyes fell on me. "And Adelaide, I expect there will be no more outbursts from you of such a . . . candid nature. The Thorns employ me to make you into exemplary young ladies. I don't need that undermined within your first hour."

"Yes, of course." She looked at me expectantly, and I added, "Ma'am." When that still didn't lift her gaze, I tried "Uh, I'm sorry?" I had rarely had to apologize in my position and wasn't entirely sure of the process.

Looking exasperated, Mistress Masterson draped the dresses and chemises over a chair. "Please just think before you speak next time."

That I understood. It was advice my grandmother had been giving me for years.

When Mistress Masterson was gone, Tamsin pounced on the dresses and began examining each one. Mira, however, studied me. "I thought you said she already scolded you?"

I put on a wry smile. "I guess she wanted to make sure I got the message. Or embarrass me in front of you."

A groan from Tamsin drew our attention elsewhere. "Damn it. This is too long."

She was holding a cream-colored dress, scattered with green flowers, up to her. I got up and sifted through the rest of the clothes. "Wear this one. It's shorter."

Tamsin gave the russet calico a dismissive look. "That's not my color. I'd think any sort of proper lady's maid would know orange doesn't go with red hair."

"I know that wearing a dress that doesn't fit you will look a lot worse. Sloppy, even."

Tamsin wavered a moment and then snatched the dress from me, tossing back the green in return. It was too long for me too, and I handed it to Mira, the tallest of us. That left me with a gray-striped dress of lightweight wool. As the others began to undress, I backed up, suddenly feeling self-conscious. It was silly, I supposed, considering I'd had people dressing me my entire life. But that had been utilitarian. It was my servants' job. Changing clothes now, with others around, was a reminder of the new lack of privacy I had. The room suddenly felt small, like it was closing in around me.

I turned my back to them and began working through all those buttons that had given me such trouble before. It was slightly easier than initially fastening them up, but the loops they went through were sewn under the edge of the fabric, requiring some dexterity. And good grief, why did there have to be so many of them? When I finally made it to the bottom of the dress, I glanced behind me and saw Tamsin and Mira staring in astonishment. Both were already in their new chemises and dresses.

"Our best bet, huh?" asked Tamsin.

"It's harder than it looks," I retorted. "A new style. One I'm not used to." I turned away from them again and at least managed to wriggle out of it in a timelier manner than the unbuttoning. Ada's chemise was of better quality than this new one, but I removed it too and put on the whole ensemble.

"Are these dresses torn?" asked Mira, studying one of her sleeves.

It was clear neither girl had ever worn a chemise as anything other than a basic undergarment. In fact, I was pretty sure Mira hadn't had one on at all. These new dresses were the same style of many I'd worn before—albeit mine had been more expensive materials—where the chemise was meant to be displayed as part of the dress. I knew how it was supposed to look but wasn't entirely sure of how to implement it. I did my best to explain it, and after a fair amount of tugging and straightening, we all finally managed to look fashionable. The delicate white fabric of my chemise was pulled and puffed out through slashes in the overdress's arms, creating a color contrast. Lace from the chemise's neckline peeped out around my bodice.

All of our extra maneuvering had taken time, and we were the last ones to arrive downstairs. We weren't exactly late, but Mistress Masterson's sharp eyes told us we shouldn't have cut it so close. Then, taking in our appearance, her expression turned approving. "You three have styled those chemises very nicely. I've been trying to teach the others all week, but they just keep bunching up the fabric."

I gave Mistress Masterson my sweetest smile. "Thank you, ma'am. We're happy to help the other girls if they keep having trouble. I see Clara's is *really* bunched up in the back. I can help her out after today's lessons." Clara shot me a murderous look, and I noticed much of her makeup had been scrubbed.

"That's very kind of you," said Mistress Masterson. "And such a refreshing attitude. Most girls come here being so . . . cutthroat. Mira, is there something wrong?"

Mira had a hand to her mouth, trying to cover her laugh. "No, ma'am. Just a cough."

Mistress Masterson gave her a wary glance and then beckoned for us all to follow her to the conservatory. Mira and Tamsin fell into step with me, one on either side.

"That was excessive," said Tamsin. But she too was smiling—and this time, there was no show or calculation.

I smiled back. "Best. Bet."

And so my life as a commoner began, the days flying by faster than I expected.

Cedric didn't need to worry about my hair giving me away. I'd never styled it on my own in my life, and after its first washing at Blue Spring, there was no way I could have ever replicated what I'd come in with that first day. No one demanded that level of detail on a regular basis, and mostly we were expected to pull our hair back neatly into buns or braids. I wasn't very good at that either. Disheveled became part of my daily life.

And Cedric was right about the other things. Although we were being trained to fit into the upper classes, freeing the girls from many of the labors they'd grown up with, there were still a lot of skills taken for granted that I couldn't perform. I did what he'd advised, watching the other girls avidly and imitating them as best as I could. I succeeded with varying degrees of luck.

"Don't mix it!" Tamsin exclaimed. She darted across the kitchen, jerking a spoon from my hand.

It was a month into our stay at Blue Spring, and we'd fallen into a regular routine of classes and activities. I pointed at the open cookbook on the counter. "It says to break the butter into the flour."

"That's not the same as mixing. This thing'll be as dense as some tosser's skull."

I shrugged, not understanding, and she nudged me aside to take over. Culinary skills weren't something I'd expected to learn here. The hope was that most of us would have servants or at least a house cook to prepare meals in Adoria. But the mistress of a large household was still expected to oversee what was being cooked, and that meant instructing us in the preparation of finer food. The dishes we made here were beyond what most of the girls had ever dined on, but a lot of the basic principles were still familiar to my housemates. Me? I'd never cooked a thing, nor had I had to supervise anything. I'd had servants to supervise my other servants.

I watched as Tamsin deftly chopped up the butter and put it into the flour in pieces. "Let me try," I offered.

"No, you'll just mess it up. We all still remember what happened when you 'blanched' the asparagus."

"Look, 'bleached' and 'blanched' sound very similar," I said through gritted teeth.

Tamsin shook her head. "I just don't want to screw up our first cooking test, especially after Clara's group got such good marks yesterday. Go measure the currants. Mira, can you warm the cream instead?"

Mira slid the bowl of currants over, exchanging an amused glance with me. My roommates and I had also fallen into comfortable roles, not to mention a growing closeness. Despite Tamsin's initial proclamations, I ended up being looked to as the unofficial leader—though we still usually let her dictate our actions. It was easier than going against her. We all wanted to succeed here, but her undisguised ambition and razor-sharp focus kept Mira and me working at a pace we might otherwise have missed. It was useful having her on my side, but her scrutiny made me nervous sometimes. She rarely missed anything.

"How did you ever survive in your lady's home?" she asked, regarding her butter and flour with satisfaction. It wasn't the first time I'd been asked that question. Along with being the unofficial leader, I suspected I also served as regular entertainment for them, thanks to both my wit and my mishaps.

I shrugged. "I never had to cook. There were others to do that." That wasn't a lie. Ada might have had to cook growing up in her mother's household, but she'd never had to in mine. "I sewed and mended. Dressed my lady. Styled her hair."

Both Mira and Tamsin raised an eyebrow at that. They'd seen my hair efforts.

I successfully deflected from that when I saw Tamsin take out a ceramic platter for plating our pastry. "No, use glass," I told her.

"Why the hell—I mean, why would we do that?" Tamsin had made a lot of progress in her word choice this last month but still often slipped.

"It's how they're serving it now. On glass, decorated with sugar and extra currants."

I might struggle with commonplace activities, but I knew these small, luxurious details—things our instructors often hadn't gotten around to yet in our education. It was like the chemises. I saw Tamsin's eyes narrow, immediately filing this away. It was why she often looked past my other inadequacies—both real and contrived. These small things gave us an edge, and it was proven later when the cooking instructor came by to survey our work.

"This is lovely," she said, studying the artful swirls of sugar on the glass platter that I'd made. "None of the other girls have focused much on aesthetics, but they're just as important as the quality of the food. Visual appeal is part of taste appeal, you know."

We didn't see what she wrote down on her paper, but her pleased look spoke volumes. Tamsin could barely contain her smugness.

"There'll be no living with her now," Mira told me when we walked to our dance lesson afterward. She nodded to where Tamsin was animatedly telling another girl about our excellent marks. "She's doing that for spite. She knows it'll get back to Clara."

"You're saying Clara doesn't deserve a little spite?" Clara had continued to make life difficult for Mira, though she'd backed off a bit when she realized taking on Mira meant also taking on Tamsin and me.

"I'm just saying that we don't need to further petty rivalries when there's already so much evil in the world we need to stop."

She might not have Tamsin's frenetic energy, but Mira was an ally—and a friend—I'd long come to appreciate. There was a calmness and strength to her that soothed me and even neurotic Tamsin. Mira was the rock we could both lean on. She gave the impression that the politics and drama in the house were of no concern to her after witnessing the ravages of war and subsequent hardships of the Sirminican ghetto in Osfrid. Her comment about the world's evils was a rare allusion to her past, but I didn't push her when she didn't elaborate.

Instead, I linked my arm through hers as we entered the ballroom. "You should have been a nun with that kind of diplomatic attitude. Hide away in some cloister and meditate."

"You can't fight evil with meditation," she replied. I wouldn't have been surprised if she was quoting from one of her most prized possessions: an old book of heroic tales, smuggled out of Sirminica.

A dance mistress rotated among the different manors each week, and here was an area in which I had to consciously dumb down my abilities. I'd had formal dance lessons since childhood. The other girls had never had any, and most still struggled after only a month. It was one of those areas Cedric had warned I'd stand out in, so I was overly cautious about not attracting Miss Hayworth's attention—to the point where I almost seemed hopelessly inept.

"Adelaide," she said wearily. "Are you dancing the gentleman's part?"

We were in the middle of a complicated line progression, in which it was common for us to alternate standing in for the opposite gender. "Yes, ma'am," I said. "I thought we were supposed to take turns doing that?"

She threw up her hands. "Yes, but it's your turn to dance the lady's part—the part you'll be doing in Adoria. You're trampling all over poor Sylvia's feet."

"Oh. That explains it." I gave her a sunny smile, and she moved on. Cedric might be able to sell salvation to a priest, but I could make my instructors find me endearing despite my frustrating progress.

We did a few more rounds and then paused for one of Miss

Hayworth's infamous pop quizzes. I promptly snapped to attention. These were not anything to slack on, as those who performed badly were often put on clean-up duty.

"Caroline, how many passes in a Lorandian two-step loop?"

Caroline—Clara's chief sidekick—hesitated. "Three?"

"Correct."

Miss Hayworth turned to the next girl, going down the line. When my turn came, I answered promptly and perfectly, earning a puzzled look from Miss Hayworth—seeing as the question had been about the dance I just botched. She walked past me.

"Mira, at what round is the twirl performed on the allegro circuit?"

I saw Mira's face go blank. She had a natural instinct for the movements and did well in the actual steps—but these quizzes stumped her. Mira always worked so much harder than the rest of us, having to catch up on things many of us already knew as Osfridians—particularly with the language. She spent so much time working on her speech that technical dance facts just weren't a priority.

Miss Hayworth's back was to me, and I caught Mira's eye with a small gesture, holding up four fingers.

"The fourth, Miss Hayworth." Although her accent was still noticeable, Mira's dedication to improving her Osfridian was already apparent.

"Correct."

Miss Hayworth moved on, and Mira gave me a nod of thanks. I nodded back, happy to have helped. The lesson closed with us drilling repetitive steps on a new dance. Naturally, I pretended to fumble through it.

"I saw what you did," Clara hissed, sidling up beside me while Miss Hayworth's attention was elsewhere. "You gave her the answer. You do it all the time. As soon as I get proof, I'm going to bust you and that Sirminican slut."

"Don't call her that," I snapped.

Triumph flared in Clara's face. I'd become pretty good at ignoring her jabs, and it had been a while since she'd gotten a rise out of me. Someone as nasty as her lived for that kind of thing.

"Why not?" she asked. "It's true, you know. I'm not just making it up."

"Of course you are," I said. "Mira's one of the most decent girls here—which you'd know if you weren't such a bigot."

Clara shook her head. "How do you think she got here? How in the world do you think a Sirminican refugee managed to snag a spot in an establishment like this—one whose whole point is to train elite *Osfridian* girls?"

"Cedric Thorn saw potential in her."

Clara smirked. "Oh, he's seen a lot more of her than that."

I didn't have to fake my next stumble. "You're such a liar. I should report you for slander."

"Am I? Did you see the way he dotes on her when he visits? The way he defied his father to get her and risk his commission? They made a deal. She went to bed with him in exchange for a spot here. I've heard other people talking about it."

"Who?" I asked. "Your toady friends?"

"Say whatever you want, but there's no getting around the truth. Your Sirminican friend is a dirty, shameless—"

I did what I did next without a second thought. Clara had moved close to me in order to keep her voice down, and I used that proximity to snake my foot out and strike her in the ankle. The results were spectacular, throwing both of us off-balance. Mishaps weren't uncommon for me, but she was one of the better dancers. I was thrown off by my move, falling backward and striking a bureau rather painfully. It was worth it to see Clara go sprawling on the floor, causing the whole class to come to a standstill.

"Girls!" exclaimed Miss Hayworth. "What is the meaning of this?"

I straightened up, smoothing my dress from where it had snagged on the bureau's elaborate handles. "I'm sorry, Miss Hayworth. It was my fault—my clumsiness."

She looked understandably exasperated. "How can you understand the principles so well and not execute them? And oh, look—you've torn your dress. We'll both get in trouble with Mistress Masterson for that."

I looked down and woefully saw that she was right. These dresses might not be the silks and velvets I'd once worn, but they were a substantial investment by the Glittering Court. Respect for them had been drilled into us. Clara's embarrassment might have come at a greater cost than I'd expected.

"Well," said Miss Hayworth, leaning close, "it looks like it should be an easy enough fix, thankfully. You may go early to take care of it."

I stared up at her in confusion. "Take care of it?"

"Yes, yes. It's a quick mend. Go now, and you probably won't be late for Mister Bricker's lesson."

I didn't move right away as I let the impact of her words sink into me. "A quick mend," I repeated.

Annoyance filled her features. "Yes, now go!"

Spurred by her command, I hurried out of the classroom, taking only small satisfaction from Clara's outrage. When I was alone in the great hall, I surveyed my skirt's tear and felt despair sink in. For anyone else, this probably was an easy mend—unless you'd never mended anything. I'd occasionally done fancy, very fine needlework, and if she'd wanted me to embroider flowers on the dress, I could've managed that. I had no idea how to mend something like this, but dutifully borrowed one of the manor's sewing kits and went to my room.

There, I found a housemaid cleaning. I retreated, not wanting her to see my ineptitude, and instead chose to work in the conservatory. It was unoccupied; the music teacher wouldn't be here for two days. I unlaced my overdress and settled down on a small sofa. I wriggled out of the voluminous garment and spread the fabric over my knees. It was a light, rose-colored wool, suitable for our late spring weather. It was thicker than the fine silks I'd embroidered, so I randomly chose a larger needle and set to work.

My maids had always threaded my embroidery needles for me,

so that alone took time. And once I started sewing, I knew it was hopeless. I didn't know how to seamlessly mend the tear. My stitches were uneven and badly spaced, creating obvious puckers in the fabric. I paused and stared at it morosely. My regular excuse about being a lady's maid wouldn't get me out of this. Maybe I could make up a story about how my abysmal sewing skills had gotten me dismissed.

The sound of the conservatory door opening broke my rumination. I feared someone had come to check on me, but to my astonishment, it was Cedric who entered. Remembering I was in my chemise, I promptly exclaimed, "Get out!"

Startled, he jumped back and nearly obeyed me. Then, curiosity must have won him over. "Wait. Adelaide? What are you doing? Are you . . . are you . . ."

"Half-naked?" I draped the overdress over me. "Yes. Yes, I am."

He shut the door, looking more curious than scandalized. "Actually, I was going to ask . . . are you sewing? Like with a needle and everything?"

I sighed, irritation overcoming my embarrassment. I wondered what he was even doing here. He'd stopped by the manor only once since my initial arrival. "Can you please go before this situation gets any worse?"

He moved closer, daring a hesitant look at the dress I was clutching to me. The torn part of the skirt hung near my knee, and he knelt down to get a better look. "You *are* sewing. Or well, something sort of like sewing."

The dry remark was enough for me to ignore his being so close to my leg. I snatched the torn skirt away from him. "Like you could do any better."

He straightened up and sat on the couch beside me. "I could, actually. Let me see it."

I hesitated, unsure of giving up my coverage—or revealing my ineptitude—and then finally handed the dress over. The chemise I'd worn under it was deep blue but still thinner than modesty allowed.

I crossed my arms over my chest, angling myself away as best I could while still managing to look over and observe him.

"This is a quilting needle," he said, pulling out my stitches. "You're lucky you didn't tear holes in this." He replaced the needle with a smaller one and threaded it in a fraction of the time it had taken me. He then folded over the torn fabric and began sewing with neat, even stitches.

"Where did you learn to do that?" I asked reluctantly.

"There are no doting maids at the university. We've got to learn to make our own repairs."

"Why aren't you there today?"

He paused and glanced up, carefully keeping his eyes trained above my neck. "No classes. Father sent me out to get status reports from here and Dunford Manor."

"Well, I'm sure you'll have a lot to say about my progress."

His response was a smile as he returned to his work. His hair was casually unbound today, framing his face in soft auburn waves. "I'm afraid to ask how this happened."

"Defending Mira's honor once again." As I spoke, I realized with a pang what the accusation had been—and his role in it. I had to avert my eyes briefly before turning back to him. "Clara was being typically mean."

This caused another pause as he looked up with a frown. "Are they still harassing her?"

"Less than they used to, but it's still going on. She handles it well, though."

"I'm sure she does," he said. "She's got a strong spirit. Not easily broken."

A strange feeling settled in the pit of my stomach as he returned to his work. There'd been no missing the regard in his voice. A warmth, even. My stomach sank further when he added, "I hope you'll keep helping her. I'll worry a lot less if I know she's got a strong defender. Only a fool would cross you—I certainly wouldn't."

I couldn't take in the compliment. A terrible thought had seized hold of me.

Had Clara been right?

Had Mira gotten here by sleeping with Cedric?

He certainly treated her with more than the indifference one might have toward an acquisition. He admired her and was concerned for her. And Clara was right that bringing her here had been a risk for him. I didn't want to believe such things about quiet, resilient Mira, who had such pride and strength in her every action.

And I definitely didn't want to believe it of Cedric.

Studying his profile now, the fine cheekbones and gently curved lips, I felt the unease spread from my stomach, tightening my chest. In my mind's eye, I had a sudden flash of those lips on my friend, of those deft fingers running through her luxurious hair. I swallowed, trying to push down the inexplicable dismay I felt.

He looked up again, his expression softening as he took in my face. "Hey, it's going to be all right. This is almost done. No one will know."

I must have been wearing my emotions, and he'd misunderstood. I lowered my gaze, murmuring a stiff thanks, as opposed to one of the usual biting remarks we so often traded.

"There we are," he said a few minutes later, holding up the over-dress. "As good as new."

Looking at it, I saw that he was correct. The stitches were barely visible unless you were right next to it. It would hopefully be enough to evade Mistress Masterson's notice. I took the dress, turning away from him as I pulled it over my head. I was surprised that in so short a time, it had picked up the fleeting scent of the vetiver he wore.

It took me a few minutes to get the ensemble back together, fastening all the tiny pearl buttons on the bodice and smoothing the petticoat to lie flat. Then, of course, came the tedious process of arranging the contrasting chemise so it peeked out properly. When I finally turned around, Cedric was regarding me with amusement.

"Were you watching me get dressed?" I exclaimed.

"Don't worry, I didn't see a thing," he said. "Except how much progress you've made in putting on your own clothes. I guess this finishing school is really paying off."

"Someone should send *you* to a finishing school," I retorted as we moved toward the door. "You have no sense of decency."

"Says the girl who let me come in."

"I told you to leave! You were the one who ignored me and marched right in anyway, despite the state I was in."

That easy, confident grin returned. "Don't worry, it's easily forgotten."

"Well," I said huffily, "it shouldn't be *that* easily forgotten."

"Would you like it better if I say I'll eventually forget it but not without a great deal of struggle and torment?"

"Yes."

"Done."

We parted, and I made my way toward the drawing room, where Mister Bricker gave us lessons about both history and current affairs. The door was ajar, and I lingered outside, reluctant to enter. I didn't want to be called out for being late. I also didn't really want to listen to his lecture. He was explaining the Alanzan heresy and its growing concern to the Osfridian church. All good, Uros-fearing people knew that six glorious angels had served the god since the beginning of creation and that six wayward angels had fallen and become demons. The Alanzans worshipped all twelve angels, dark and light alike, putting them on nearly the same level as the great god in bloodthirsty, sordid rituals.

I knew much of this, as it was a hot topic in noble drawing rooms—one to be marveled at and then dismissed as something "other people" did. I started to push the door open but stopped when I caught sight of Mira, listening avidly, her eyes focused on Mister Bricker. Alanzans were a big faction in Sirminica.

But instead of pondering if she'd encountered them, I found myself admiring her beautiful profile. It was impossible not to. Her quiet, fearless manner made her mysterious and alluring in a way few could match. Certainly not me. Were those striking eyes holding a dark secret? Had she been Cedric's mistress?

That ugly feeling started to rise up within me again, and I banished it as I pushed open the door and stepped inside. I took my seat, hoping the scent of vetiver would soon fade from my dress.

CHAPTER 6

I SAW LITTLE OF CEDRIC IN THE MONTHS THAT FOLLOWED. With so many other things to keep me busy, it was easy to push him off to a place in the back of my mind. I filed other things there—like the memories of my parents, and how worried my grandmother must be—and made a point of visiting that mental place as little as possible. It was only on occasional late nights, when I'd lie restless in bed, that I'd allow myself a peek at those dark corners of my mind.

My tenure at the Glittering Court soon became the happiest time of my life to date, excepting when my parents were alive. Despite the regimented schedule, the endless drills and classes, I felt a freedom I'd never known. I moved around the manor with a lightness in my chest, heady with the feeling that I could do anything and had the world at my fingertips. Certainly, I was scrutinized, but nowhere near the levels of Osfro.

That wasn't to say I didn't still face some challenges.

"Hey, are you ready to— What have you done?"

I looked up as Tamsin and Mira entered the kitchen. Even though we'd now spent nearly eight months learning the ways of upper-class ladies, Mistress Masterson wanted us—or some of us—to remember our humble roots. That meant occasional household chores, such as the dishes I was currently washing.

They hurried over to my side, peering at the copper kettle I was attempting to wash. "Is that bleach? That *is* bleach! I can smell it."

Without waiting for a response, Tamsin grabbed the kettle and dumped its contents into a tub of wastewater. "What were you thinking?"

"Something got burned in it, and scrubbing wasn't working. I saw you use bleach to get out that stain from your dress the other day, so I thought—"

"Stop," said Tamsin. "I don't want to hear any more. I can't hear any more."

Mira picked up a cloth and rubbed the inside of the pot. "It came out, and the bleach wasn't in long enough to cause damage."

I felt triumphant. "So it did work."

"Soaking in water, followed by a lemon scrub, would have done the same with a lot less risk." Tamsin took one of my hands and held it up. One side was red from the bleach. "Deepest hell. Go rinse them off. You've got the best hands of all of us. Don't ruin that."

Tamsin's own hands showed the signs of having scrubbed laundry since childhood, and it vexed her to no end. She was constantly applying moisturizers in an effort to undo—or at least minimize—the damage.

Mira took my apron and hung it up while Tamsin gave me a quick inspection. "No other harm done. The dress is intact, and I daresay that's the nicest chignon I've ever seen you do. Did someone help you?"

I patted my hair, affronted at her suspicious tone. "We share the same room. Do you think someone sneaked in and helped me?"

"It wasn't me," said Mira, seeing Tamsin's gaze fall on her. "Adelaide's come quite a long way. I saw her fold a blanket the other day, and there were almost no creases in it."

I pushed the kitchen door open, and the other two followed me. "Oh, stop, both of you. It's our off day. It wouldn't matter if I did have sloppy hair."

Tamsin narrowed her eyes in thought. "No, something's going on. Mistress Masterson wouldn't have ordered us to the ballroom otherwise. This is usually the day she has it cleaned."

My slowness on the dishes had made us the last to arrive, but we weren't late yet. Even if we were, I didn't think Mistress Masterson would have noticed. She was busy directing one of the house servants to set up large tables on the far side of the room. In the middle of the ballroom itself, we were met with the astonishing sight of blankets spread across the floor and our housemates sitting on them.

"What's going on?" I asked Rosamunde.

She glanced up at us from her blue-flowered quilt. "No idea. Mistress Masterson just told us to sit down and wait."

Puzzled, my friends and I made it across the room to an unoccupied blanket, an enormous fuzzy one with red and yellow stripes. Around us, the other girls' conversation buzzed as they too wondered what was happening. Tamsin groaned. "Damn it. I knew I should have worn my church dress."

"You think we're having a service in here?" I asked.

"No. But I think this is a test. A pop quiz. Maybe how to entertain and throw a get-together on short notice." Tamsin pointed to the entrance. "Look. Here comes food."

Three men in plain workmen's clothes entered, hauling large platters that Mistress Masterson directed to the tables. As she uncovered them, I could tell even from this distance that they contained finger sandwiches and fruit. The workmen left and returned with a second load of food, as well as plates and linen napkins. I'd thought Tamsin was paranoid, but there was no doubt we had much more food than our coterie needed. After the tables were filled, the workmen left and didn't return. Mistress Masterson stood by the doorway, an expectant look on her face.

"Damn it," Tamsin repeated. She took a deep breath. Her eyes grew as steely as those of a general preparing for battle. "Okay. No problem. We can do this. We can do this better than the others because none of them have realized what's happening. We've got an edge. Think back to our lessons on greeting strangers at a party. All the acceptable topics. Weather. Upcoming holidays. Animals are all right too. No religion. No politics, unless it's in support of the king and his latest policy.

Always look dignified—who knows what kind of posh guests the old lady's dug up? Keep your posture good and—"

That crafty countenance dissolved into disbelief, and Tamsin let out a very undignified shriek. In a flash, she was on her feet, sprinting across the room. And she wasn't the only girl. Others were on the move as well, and the buzz turned into an outright cacophony of chaos and excitement. Turning my gaze back to the entryway, I saw strangers entering, strangers who could hardly be called posh. My housemates lost themselves in the crowd, swept away in a flood of hugs and tears.

"Their families," said Mira softly. She and I were the only two still sitting down. A smile spread over her face as we watched Tamsin throw herself against the chest of a big, burly man with a red beard. A thinner woman stood smiling beside him, and three red-haired children hovered nearby. Two, a girl and a boy, looked to be in their mid-teens. The third was a young girl only a few years old. Tamsin swept her into her arms as though she weighed nothing and then tried to simultaneously draw the other two into a hug, resulting in laughs and confusion. There was no guile on Tamsin's face. No cunningness or sizing up the situation. The tight control she always maintained was gone, her emotions pure and raw. There was a lightness about her that made me realize that, until that moment, I'd never truly comprehended just how much weight she carried.

"Do you have anyone coming?" I asked Mira.

She shook her head. "No. No other family came with me from Sirminica. But I do wonder what my parents would think of all this if they could see it. They'd be shocked."

I couldn't help a laugh, even though I didn't feel very cheerful. "Mine too. Mine too."

But surprisingly, it wasn't the thought of my parents that made my heart ache just then. It was Grandmama. She'd taken care of me these last few years, working so hard to salvage our situation. I still stood by my decision to leave, but as the initial excitement had faded, I'd had more time to consider the consequences of what I'd done—and feel guilty. Cedric had covertly slipped me a clipping from the society papers mentioning Lionel's marriage to some minor noble, only a few weeks after my disappearance. Cedric had scrawled on it: *Such a hasty marriage. Probably the only way the poor man could console himself after such a great loss.* That had closed the door on that chapter, but still left a lot of other questions unanswered.

I spoke without thinking. "I wish I could see my grandmother."

Mira regarded me with mild surprise. "You've never mentioned her before—I don't believe it. They're here!" She slowly got to her feet, her eyes widening as she stared across the room to a wizened Sirminican couple. "Pablo and Fernanda. They came with me on the journey from home. Excuse me."

She walked away without looking back, and although I was glad to see her hug the little old man and woman, the ache in my heart only intensified. Most of the other girls were too overwhelmed with their own loved ones to notice much else, but a few cast curious glances my way. I'd worried about standing out in other ways, but never this one. Even those without blood relatives at least had friends visiting. I was the only one alone. The only one without any family. The only one without a past.

Or maybe not.

"Adelaide's over there, behind Sylvia's family," I heard Mistress Masterson say. "Sitting on the striped blanket."

A woman stepped around a crowd of people, beaming when she saw me. "There's my Adelaide!"

I stared. I'd never seen her before in my life. She looked to be twice my age and had a voluptuous figure that was enhanced—more than it should be—by a faded red dress that was one size too small. Generous kohl lined her eyes, and a straw hat with fake flowers sat atop brassy hair.

"Well?" she asked, standing over me with hands on her hips. "Aren't you going to give your aunt Sally a hug?"

Beyond her, I saw Mistress Masterson watching curiously. Not wanting to draw extra scrutiny, I stood up and embraced the strange woman and was flooded with the cloying scent of tea roses. "Just play along," she whispered in my ear.

We stepped apart, and I forced a smile that I hoped hid how bewildered I was. Mistress Masterson nodded approvingly and then moved on.

"Aunt Sally" relaxed but still kept her voice low as she spoke to me. "My name is Rhonda Gables, great star of some of the biggest theatrical productions in Osfro. You've probably heard of me."

I shook my head.

"Well, a girl of your station probably doesn't make it out to the theater very much, so that's understandable." My family owned box seats and had seen every major show in the capital, and I felt certain that if Rhonda had been in any of them, I'd remember.

"What are you doing here?" I asked.

She peered around conspiratorially. "I'm here to play your aunt. I was hired by—well, I never got his name, but he paid in silver. Nice-looking young man. Brown hair. Good cheekbones. Why, if I was twenty years younger, I'd have liked to—"

"Yes," I interrupted. "I think I know the young man in question. Do you know why you're here?"

"Just that I was supposed to come out here to Uros-knows-where in the moors with the rest of this lot. Carriages picked us up in the city and told us we'd be fed, and who am I to turn down a free meal? There's the man that organized it." She pointed across the room as Jasper entered. "Do you know if they're serving wine here?"

Jasper clapped his hands for attention, and the din died down as we stepped closer to hear him. He was in full showman mode.

"First, let me welcome you here today to Blue Spring Manor. You are our guests, and we are all at your service. Second, I want to thank you for the sacrifice I know you must have made in the last eight months by lending us your daughters." He paused to make eye contact with random people, nodding and smiling. "But it has been our privilege and our honor to have them, to help them develop the potential you surely knew they had all along. Today you'll get a glimpse into the world they've entered—a world that will be dwarfed by the riches and splendor they'll get when they marry in Adoria."

That last bit hit home. Nearly all of the visitors were in awe of the ballroom, with its crystal chandelier and gilded wallpaper. The idea that more wealth than this might be waiting was simply incomprehensible.

"Normally, we invite friends and family later in the spring, so that we can picnic in warmer conditions." Jasper smiled conspiratorially, nodding toward a large window covered in ice crystals. "But, as you can see, that's not possible today. So, we'll have an indoor picnic. Fill your plates and cups, find a spot, and learn just how much your daughters' futures truly glitter."

I tried not to roll my eyes. It was hard for me to take his fine words seriously, recalling how harshly he'd spoken to Cedric in private, but everyone else was quite charmed. Families clustered together and made their way over to the buffet. Rhonda had noticed there was rum punch and had already shot over to that section of tables. I hurried after her, delayed by loved ones strolling and taking their time to catch up. As I waited for Caroline's grandmother to teeter past, I overheard Jasper speaking to Mistress Masterson.

"It's always such a delicate balance, this meet and greet," he said to her quietly. "You never know if some of them might get homesick and bolt. But once the Adoria trip is official, I find the risk of running is actually greater then. If they've been bolstered up by their dazzled loved ones beforehand, they're more likely to want to do them proud."

I frowned at that as I caught up with Rhonda. If I hadn't known sailings to Adoria were always done in spring and summer, I'd have thought his tone suggested something more immediate.

Rhonda downed a cup of punch and went for another. I pulled her away as Clara's mother watched disapprovingly. "Now, now, Aunt Sally. Not until you've had some lunch. Remember what happened at last year's Midwinter party."

Fortunately, Rhonda was just as happy to load up on food, and we carried plates of cucumber sandwiches, cold chicken, and sliced pears back to the striped blanket. Mira sat on its edge with Pablo, speaking rapidly in Sirminican. Tamsin, radiant with joy, was too excited to eat. Her family shared that happiness but could hardly turn down such a meal. The teenage siblings—twins, I learned—were named Jonathan and Olivia and snuggled up on each side of Tamsin, eating and talking at the same time. The littlest girl was introduced to me as Merry and sat on Tamsin's lap, happily munching on a pear. All of them had the same red hair.

"Look at your hands," exclaimed Tamsin's mother. "You'll never be able to do a load of clothes again."

Tamsin beamed. The hands she considered inferior beside mine were smooth and delicate compared to her mother's, which were hard and rough from a lifetime of scalding water and scrubbing.

"I don't intend to," Tamsin replied. "And once I'm married to the richest man in Adoria, you won't have to either."

Her father let out a bellowing laugh, one that made everyone else at our blanket smile too. "My dreamer. Just get yourself over there first."

"She's not wrong," Jasper said, sidling up to us. I'd noticed him making the rounds to other families too. He crouched down. "Tamsin's known around here for her ambition—for her determination to accept no less than perfection. I was just talking to our music teacher the other day, and she couldn't stop raving about Tamsin's remarkable progress on the piano."

Her mother turned to her in astonishment. "You can play the piano?"

It was perhaps the most tangible amazing thing Jasper could have picked. In the circles Tamsin had come from, they never even saw pianos. Playing one was like speaking a foreign language.

She flushed with pleasure. "I'm still learning—but I can do some basics. If my husband has a piano, I can keep practicing."

Jasper winked at her. "And if he doesn't, I'm sure you can talk him into one."

He turned to me, and I wondered what trivia he'd pull out. I sincerely doubted he'd spoken to our music instructor. I was guessing he'd gotten a crash course on each of our strong areas this morning from Mistress Masterson. In his previous visits, Jasper had simply done cursory checks of us and then talked business with her. The most personal comment I'd ever heard him give a girl was to tell Caroline to reduce the number of breakfast pastries she ate each morning.

"Adelaide here carries herself with such poise and elegance, it's like she's done this her whole life," he said. I wasn't surprised he'd gone with something external. I was purposely hit or miss with my studies. "And with her beauty, we know we'll have men beating down our door over there."

Rhonda nodded as she drank from another cup of rum punch, which I had no idea how she'd managed to get a hold of. "That's how it's always been with our lovely girl. Ever since she was a little one. Boys lining up in the streets. Boys at our door. Boys in our house. If Adelaide was around, you could be sure there was a boy with her."

Uncomfortable silence fell, and I attempted a light laugh that sounded more like I was choking. Jasper mercifully turned toward Mira. Tamsin leaned over Merry and whispered to me, "I can see why you've never mentioned her."

"And Mira . . ." Jasper was still smiling, but it was hard to gauge his true feelings. "Well, Mira continues to surprise us all. I'm sure she will in Adoria too."

"You are Mister Thorn's father?" asked Pablo. "Mister Cedric Thorn? I thought he might be here."

Mira might get a hard time about her accent, but it was nothing compared to his. It took me several moments to parse his words, and I could see Jasper doing the same.

"He's back in Osfro, finishing up his finals." Jasper frowned. "How do you know my son?"

Pablo hesitated. "I met him when he came to get Mirabel. He seems like a good man."

I expected some cutting remark from Jasper, but he never broke character. “He is. And I’m sure you never would have let Mira go with anyone less. If you’ll excuse me now, I must speak with the others.”

He straightened up and moved on to the next group. I recalled his words to Mistress Masterson, about this all being a show to ensure we would go to Adoria with our family’s blessings. I couldn’t shake the feeling that there was something underhanded going on.

Fernanda scoffed when he was gone. “We cannot *let* Mirabel do or not do anything. She makes her own way.”

I turned back to them and tried to shake off my worries. “You knew each other back in Sirminica?”

“While the factions were fighting each other, most ordinary people just wanted to stay out of the way. And when that wasn’t possible, people began to flee,” explained Mira. She gestured to Pablo and Fernanda. “We fell in with the same group of refugees trying to make it to the border. The roads weren’t safe—they still probably aren’t. Sometimes there was safety in numbers. Sometimes. Even in a group, a lone girl wasn’t always safe. I tried to protect others. I tried.”

Mira’s expression darkened, and Fernanda squeezed her hand. “Mira did protect others. War brings out the monsters among humanity, and there’s only so much anyone can do to—” Her eyes fell on the red-haired children, who were hanging on every word. “Well. As I said, Mira did plenty of protecting.”

Rhonda set her empty cup down. “You know, I have no problem with Sirminicans. I say, Osfrid is open to all. Anyone who wants to come and find a new life here is welcome to it. I have great respect for all peoples. And some of my dearest friends are Sirminican, you know. There’s a gentlemen who runs a crepe shop over by the Overland fountain. He’s my friend—more than a friend, if you catch my meaning. He makes some of the best crepes in the city. And he makes me—”

“I know the shop you’re talking about,” said Tamsin’s mother. “And he’s not Sirminican. He’s from Lorandy.”

“He most certainly isn’t. I couldn’t understand a word he said. And his name ends in an *o*, just like the rest of you." Rhonda accompanied that last part with a nod to Mira and her friends.

"His name's Jean Devereaux," Tamsin's mother insisted. "I've washed his laundry. He speaks Lorandian."

"And crepes are from Lorandy," I added.

Rhonda shot me an affronted look. "You doubt me now, too? So much for blood being thicker than water. Well, it doesn't matter. Sirminican, Lorandian. They all sound alike, and really, the two of us didn't do much speaking anyway, if you know what I mean."

I felt guilty when the family picnic ended a couple of hours later, mainly because I was so happy about it. The rest of my housemates were not, and Tamsin in particular took it hard. Everyone was making their goodbyes in the front hall as the carriages prepared to take the visitors back to the city. I saw Tamsin hand a huge bundle of paper to her mother, and I realized it was the culmination of those letters she was always writing. I'd noted she did it daily, but seeing the full sum of them was astonishing.

It was her expression that threw me, though. Where it had been so full of open joy earlier, she now looked devastated. I had never seen such emotions on her face. Such vulnerability. She gave her parents fierce hugs goodbye, and when she went to lift Merry, Tamsin looked as though she might start crying. I had to avert my eyes. It felt wrong to stare during that kind of moment.

Rhonda stood beside me. I'd lost track of how many cups of punch she'd consumed. "Well," she said, putting an arm over my shoulders, "I hope you'll spare some time to come visit your old aunt Sally the next time you're in the capital. I know you'll be a grand lady and all by then, but don't you forget where you came from, girl. You hear me?"

Several people near us heard her. The more she drank, the more she had trouble regulating her volume. I couldn't decide if Cedric had done me a favor in hiring her or not.

A carriage driver called for the first group of passengers, which included Tamsin's family. She watched them walk out, grief-stricken. As soon as they were gone, she turned on her heels and fled from the foyer. There was so much commotion and buzz from the other guests still waiting for their rides that no one but me noticed her departure. Even Mira was distracted, speaking with one of the workers. Snaking my way through the bystanders, I hurried off to find Tamsin, ignoring Rhonda's shouts that I'd better not forget to come visit her.

I found Tamsin in our room, crying on her bed. Her head shot up when I entered, and she furiously wiped at her eyes. "What are you doing here? Shouldn't you be telling your aunt goodbye?"

I sat down beside Tamsin. "She'll do just fine without me. I came because I was worried about you."

She sniffed and wiped her eyes again. "I'm fine."

"It's okay to be homesick," I said gently. "You don't have to be ashamed about missing them."

"I'm not ashamed . . . but I can't let them—the others—see me like this. I can't show weakness."

"Loving your family isn't weakness."

"No . . . but around here? I have to be strong. All the time. Always moving forward." That familiar determined look gleamed in her eyes again. "I can't let anything stop me from getting what I want. What I need." I didn't say anything. I just put my hand over hers, and after a moment, she squeezed it. "I know everyone thinks I'm cold and unfeeling. That I'm mean to people."

"You've never treated me that way."

She glanced up. "Well, of course not. How else am I going to learn that damned Belsian waltz if you don't practice with me? I have to keep you on my good side. But seriously . . ." She pulled away and clasped her hands in front of her. "You have to understand that I'm not doing all this because I'm just inherently a bitch. There's a reason I have to do this—keep pushing to be the best and get the best in

Adoria. If you only knew what I had—what I had on the line—" Her voice started to crack.

"Then tell me," I pleaded. "Tell me, and maybe I can help you."

"No." Tamsin brushed away a few more rebellious tears. "If you knew, you'd never look at me the same."

"You're my friend. Nothing's going to change how I feel about you."

Yet, as I spoke, I wondered if I'd be so quick to believe those words if someone wanted to pry my secrets out of me. I was pretty sure neither Tamsin nor Mira would act the same if they knew they were sharing a room with one of the mighty Rupert's descendants.

"I can't," she said. "I can't risk it."

"Okay. You don't have to tell me anything you don't want to. But I'm always here. You know I am."

Her smile was weary but sincere. "I know."

The door opened, and Mira rushed in. "There you are. Everyone's—Are you okay?"

Tamsin got to her feet. "Fine, fine. What's going on?"

Mira glanced at me for confirmation, and I gave her a small nod. She studied Tamsin a few more moments in concern before continuing.

"Everyone's gone—the families. Jasper's calling for all of us to assemble back in the ballroom."

The last of Tamsin's emotional outburst vanished. She gave herself a cursory check in the mirror and then followed Mira. "I knew it. I knew something was happening."

We hurried back downstairs and found everyone in the ballroom. Tamsin was by no means the only one suffering from her loved ones' departure, and I had to wonder if Jasper's plan would really have the outcome he'd hoped for.

Mistress Masterson brought us to attention as Jasper stepped forward to speak. "I hope you all enjoyed your day. It was a true delight for me to meet the wonderful people who helped raise you. But their visit isn't the only surprise you're getting today."

He waited, building up the tension in the room. Although his disposition was sunny and reassuring, Mistress Masterson's strained expression told me all wasn't well. My sense of foreboding returned.

"I hope you're all excited about Adoria, because we're going there—two months earlier than planned."

CHAPTER 7

NO ONE SPOKE. EVERYONE WAS TOO STUNNED. IT WAS Jasper's next proclamation that really elicited a reaction.

"As a result, you will also be taking your exams early. They'll start in one week."

Beside me, Tamsin gasped and put a hand to her chest. Other girls, wide-eyed, turned to each other in alarm and began whispering. "Hush," warned Mistress Masterson. "Mister Thorn isn't finished speaking."

"I know this change in plans is unexpected," Jasper continued. "But really, it's a reflection of your outstanding progress that we feel confident in bringing you to Adoria early. In just a couple of months, you'll be in a whole new world—adored and coveted like the jewels you are. I know my brother will be overcome when he sees this year's class."

Charles Thorn, the Glittering Court's chief financial backer, alternated procurement with Jasper each year. He was in Adoria now and would sail back to Osfrid in the spring to recruit the next batch of girls while Jasper oversaw our progress in Adoria.

"I have no doubt you'll all perform excellently in your exams," Jasper continued. "I'd love to stay but must check in on the other manors as well. Cedric, however, will be coming soon to supervise during your exams and offer moral support."

I cleared my throat and stepped forward. "Isn't it dangerous?"

Jasper frowned. "Cedric offering moral support?"

"No. Making the crossing in late winter. Isn't that still storm season?"

"I like to think of it more as early spring. And I'd hardly make the journey myself if I thought we'd be in danger. Surely, Adelaide, you haven't gained some sort of nautical knowledge I don't know about, have you? Surpassing mine and that of the ship's captains who agreed to take us?"

It was a ridiculous question to answer, so I didn't. Of course I didn't have any seafaring expertise, but I had read the countless books on Adoria's history that were part of the curriculum here. And there'd been plenty of tales about early settlers learning the hard way that winter crossings weren't advised.

We were dismissed to our rooms, and Tamsin, as I expected, had a lot to say. She flounced down on her bed, uncaring of wrinkling her lawn dress.

"Can you believe this? They've moved up our exams! To *next week*."

Mira also looked uneasy, and I remembered to appear appropriately concerned. We could've taken them today, and it would have made no difference to me.

"That's not a lot of time to study," Mira said.

"I *know*!" wailed Tamsin. "But on our way out, I heard Mistress Masterson say that at this point, we either know it or we don't."

"She's right," I said, earning astonished looks from both of them. "Come on, you don't think we can all get passing grades in every subject? None of us are going to get cut." A girl would have to fail in multiple subjects to get removed from the Glittering Court's trip to Adoria, and anyone doing that badly would have long since been asked to leave.

"I don't want to just get a passing grade," said Tamsin. "I want the best grades. I want to be the diamond."

"The what?" Mira and I asked in unison. I'd heard her talk about excelling many times, but I'd never heard mention of any diamond.

Tamsin leaned forward, her brown eyes alight. "It's this year's theme. When they present us in Adoria, they always have some sort of theme. They tailor our wardrobes around it and assign each of us roles roughly equivalent to our scores. Last year it was flowers, and the top girl was an orchid. The next was a rose. Then a lily. I think the year before that, it was birds. This year, it's jewels."

"And the top girl is a diamond," I guessed.

"Yes. The top three girls across all manors get invited to the most parties in Adoria and get special introductions to the most eligible men. I mean, technically we're all exceptional, but Jasper and Charles build up a lot of mystique around those three. It creates demand—and increases the marriage fees. And that increases the surety money that we get to keep for ourselves."

Again, it was of little concern to me. I'd make sure I placed in the middle of the scores, just as I always did. Tamsin unquestionably did the best in Blue Spring, and I couldn't believe there was any girl in the other manors who was more motivated.

As the exams loomed nearer, the next week became a flurry of activity. Our regular lessons were cancelled, so that we could each devote our time to studying in those areas that needed the most work. The instructors who rotated through all four manors stopped by more frequently, offering tutoring to those who requested it. The manor was in nonstop motion.

As for me, I had to contrive areas of study to make myself look busy. Tamsin became withdrawn, isolating herself with books, and I was surprised at how much I missed her frenetic energy. Mira didn't even really need me to drill her in language anymore. She slipped into her accent during casual conversation, but when prompted, her Osfridian was nearly indistinguishable from a native's. In fact, it was better than that of some of the other girls, who'd come in with atrocious lower-class dialects. Sometimes Mira even practiced the accents of other languages for fun.

I needed to look like I was doing something, so I spent my time rereading a book on what Mistress Masterson delicately referred to as

"Female Studies." Along with the particulars of pregnancy and childbirth, it also included information on what led to those. "A pleasing wife is pleasing in the bedroom. Your warmth and affection will ensure a happy husband," Mistress Masterson had said in our lessons, often in what was perhaps the least warm voice imaginable. It was pretty much the only area of study that hadn't been part of my previous life. Most of the girls had been mortified when we'd had those lectures, but I couldn't help but regard it with a guilty fascination.

"Isn't that the third time you've read that?" Mira teased on the day before exams. She was on her bed with language books while Tamsin, on a rare break, was writing another letter.

Flushing, I closed the book. "I just think it's more puzzling than almost everything else, that's all."

Mira glanced back at her papers. "I don't know. I think it'll just work itself out when the time comes."

"I suppose," I said, wondering not for the first time if it was an area she already had firsthand experience with. Her cool countenance betrayed nothing.

"There's nothing to know," Tamsin said, not even bothering to look up from her letter. "Except that we need to wait until our wedding nights and then let our husbands teach us what they want."

Mira set her book aside and leaned back against the headboard. "I don't like that. The idea that it's all up to them. That they're in control. Shouldn't we have the right to figure out what we want too?"

This drew Tamsin's attention at last. "And how would you do that? I knew a girl back home who gave her virtue to a man who promised to marry her. And you know what? He didn't. He was promised to another and told her it had all been a misunderstanding. It ruined her. So *don't* get another crazy idea."

"Another?" I asked.

"She was going on the other day about how she was going to pay her own marriage price," said Tamsin.

"I didn't say I was going to for sure," Mira corrected. "Just that it was possible. The contracts don't state we have to get married—just that our fees have to be paid. If you got the money, you could buy yourself out and be free."

"You want to go to one of the workhouses?" I exclaimed. I remembered that first day with Ada, when Cedric had explained how girls unwilling to fulfill their contracts would be sent off to other, less desirable employment.

"No, no." Mira sighed. "But I mean if you could find some other way to raise the money while you were meeting suitors in Adoria, you could just pay it off on your own terms. That's all."

"How would you raise that kind of money?" asked Tamsin. "The minimum price for any of us is one hundred gold. Sometimes higher."

"I'm just saying it's possible, that's all."

I smiled and returned to my scandalous book. Mira sometimes gave the impression that she could easily take or leave the Glittering Court. It wasn't surprising she'd come up with such an idea—though Tamsin was right: It would be difficult to implement.

When the first exam day came, we were all called down to a meeting in the great hall. Our entrance was much different than the initial shuffling of our early days. We descended the grand staircase one by one, moving at a sedate, graceful pace that allowed us to be admired by those gathered below. As I made my way, I spotted Cedric standing with our instructors, making me more self-conscious than I would have normally been.

Still, I completed the journey perfectly and lined up with the other girls, standing in an elegant pose long drilled into us. Mistress Masterson inspected us, and when she'd moved past, I glanced over and saw Cedric watching me. He met my eyes briefly and then shifted his gaze to Mira.

Mistress Masterson issued some instructions about how the day would proceed and then turned to Cedric. "Any inspiring words?"

He smiled his showy smile. "Nothing to say except 'good luck'—not that I think any of you'll need it. I've seen you over the last eight months. You're all exceptional." Unlike his father, Cedric was telling the truth about keeping tabs on our progress. He'd always chatted with each girl on his visits, genuinely wanting to learn more.

As we dispersed for the exams, he caught my sleeve. "How was your visit with Aunt Sally?"

I rolled my eyes. "Honestly, was that the best you could dredge up? I think I would have been better off alone and pathetic."

"Not true. You're too likeable for anyone to believe you don't have at least one friend who'd show up to support you. And I didn't have much notice to find someone. I only heard about the schedule change at the last minute."

"Why *did* it change?"

"Along with you girls, Father transports all sorts of goods for trade to the colonies. If he can get there ahead of the other spring ships, he can turn a better profit. When he finally got a couple of ships willing to make the early crossing, he jumped on it," Cedric explained. "And so, I had to find an actress for you."

"Not just any actress. A great star of some of the biggest theatrical productions in Osfro. Or so I hear."

Cedric raised an eyebrow at that. "Trust me, I did *not* find her starring in a big theatrical production. But it was better that people noticed your crazy relative than wondered how you had no one in the world."

"I suppose that's true." Grudgingly, I added, "Thank you."

"I'm always at your service. But you'd better go before you're late. I hope you do well."

"I won't. I'll do just good enough."

And I held to that as the exams began. All the information we'd been drilled in over the last eight months was suddenly condensed into three days. Some of the exams were written. Some, like dance, had to be conducted in a more hands-on way. It was exhausting, even for me, particularly as I had to pick and choose which areas to succeed in and which to do poorly in. It was definitely a balancing act, but I was certain I'd place comfortably in the middle. I'd make good on my promise to Cedric to attract no unnecessary attention.

"Adelaide, dear," Miss Hayworth said, halfway into my dance exam. "What are you doing?"

"The waltz?" I offered.

She shook her head, making a few notes in her papers. "I don't understand. You executed this perfectly last week and completely botched the new rigaudon. Today, it's reversed."

I tried to keep my face blank. "Nerves will do that to you, ma'am."

"Continue," she said, waving us on and wearing the exasperated look I often brought out in her.

Nearby, I saw Clara smirk at my critique. In her time here, she'd come to excel in this area, so much so that Miss Hayworth had suggested she lead the opening dances in Adoria. She needed these scores to offset the abysmal ones she had in academic areas, and really, I didn't care what she thought anyway.

Tamsin's thoughts, however, were something I deeply cared about. Farther across the room, I saw her watching me with a puzzled look. She soon slipped back into the rhythm of the dance, but I could've kicked myself for my error. Alternately excelling and failing was easy enough to do around here. Keeping track of which areas I was allegedly deficient in was more difficult. This wasn't the first time I'd mixed something up—and this wasn't the first time Tamsin had noticed.

Written tests followed dance, something that made me much more comfortable. No one but the instructors knew if I mixed something up. But another slip followed on the second day, during our music exam. While we weren't expected to be experts on any one instrument, we were supposed to have a passing knowledge of each one. Rather than quiz us on all of them for our final, our instructor simply selected three and based our score on that. I hadn't anticipated that. The first two, the flute and harp, were ones I'd always purposely performed poorly on. I assumed the last instrument she'd produce would be a harpsichord or lute—which I always showed my true proficiency on. Instead, she chose the violin. It wasn't played much by women in Adoria, so I'd always regarded it as a safe choice to botch here. Now,

I realized, to pull a decent music score, I needed to excel in something. And so, to the amazement of her and my peers, I produced a perfectly executed melody on the violin.

"Well, look at that," Mistress Bosworth said, beaming. "You've been practicing."

"You have *not* been practicing," whispered Tamsin later, once the exam was over and we were on break to go to dinner. "Where did you learn to do that?"

I shrugged. "From her."

"The last time she brought out the violin, you couldn't even hold the bow straight!"

"Tamsin, I don't know. Sometimes I get anxious and mess things up. What's it matter? You've been doing great."

As hoped, that distracted her. "I have," she said proudly. "I answered all of those religious and political essays for Mister Bricker perfectly. *And* I know I got almost everything on the Adorian culture and society test right too. That's one of the most important, you know."

I smiled, genuinely happy for her. "You'll get your diamond rank in no time."

"*If* I can beat out the girls in the other manors. I know I'm the best here." She said it as a fact, not even bragging. "But who knows about the other three houses?"

I wasn't worried for her, particularly as the rest of the exam days went by. That zeal and intense resolve I'd seen since the first day were fully turned on, and she threw herself into each exam. When she returned to our room each night, she'd fight her exhaustion and study more.

After the tests ended on the third and final day, we were all worn out, even those who hadn't studied as much as Tamsin had. Everyone was weary and drawn, and I gratefully went to bed as soon as we were excused from dinner. Neither my roommates nor I said much of anything, choosing instead to drop into sleep with a sigh of relief.

The next morning was a different matter. Rested and free of exams, we were hit by the truth: We had done it. We'd completed what we set out to do when we'd joined the Glittering Court. We didn't have our results yet, but the triumph of our accomplishment was heady. Mistress Masterson gave us the whole day off, with plans for our first big celebration that night in honor of Vaiel's Day, greatest of the winter holidays. We'd all been assigned specific tasks to ready for the party, and none of us minded applying our hard-won abilities.

"I love Vaiel's Day," Tamsin said as we put on our day dresses. "The food. The smells. The decorations. Seems a shame we're doing it all so last-minute."

She was right. Usually, winter festivities started weeks ahead of the angel of wisdom's holy day, allowing the cheerful atmosphere to last most of the month. "Well, if Jasper hadn't moved up our timeline, our celebrations wouldn't have gotten shoved aside for his profit," I reminded her.

"At least we get some sort of celebration. You know those poor heretics of Uros—the barefoot priests? They don't celebrate at all. Say it's idolatry. But maybe nothing at all is better than what the Alanzans do. Who'd want to be out there worshipping trees in this weather?"

"*Among* the trees," corrected Mira. "Vaiel's Day is Midwinter for them—the longest night of the year. The Alanzans pray outside to Deanziel for insight and then will give thanks tomorrow to Alanziel for a return of the sun and the days getting longer."

I regarded her with some surprise. It wasn't often she pulled out a fact I didn't know, but then, she'd also probably met real Alanzans. Like so many areas, her religious beliefs were something I never inquired about. She attended orthodox services to Uros with us, which was really all that mattered.

"Doesn't matter what they worship. It's all pagan superstition." Satisfied with her appearance, Tamsin turned toward the door. "Well, time to get to work. I can't wait until we have other people to do this for us."

Most of the girls—like Tamsin—had been assigned to cooking the formidable feast that Mistress Masterson had planned. A few were in charge of games and music, and I was on decorating duty, along with Clara, of all people. She and I managed the task by splitting the rooms and staying out of each other's way.

When it came time to decorate the drawing room, I was surprised to find Cedric and Mira talking inside. He'd made himself scarce during our exam days.

"You're respectable today. Back to being a proper Adorian," I said. He'd been dressed that way at our first meeting but often slipped into Osfridian styles for informal occasions. His overcoat, made of a heavy blue fabric edged in gold, hung nearly to his knees, as opposed to the shorter ones more common here. His boots were also higher than those of continental fashion trends. He didn't just look proper. He looked dazzling—not that I'd ever tell him. "It's like you've been to finishing school."

"Well, some people might have trouble dressing themselves, but I never have," he said. "We'll be on our way in another month, so I figured I should look the part. My father and I need to be nearly—though not quite—as grand as the rest of you if we're going to show we're legitimate brokers. It's all about image, or so my uncle says."

In the months that had passed, I'd given little thought to Clara's malicious accusations about Cedric and Mira. Now, having walked in on the two of them talking, my curiosity was piqued. "Are you distracting Mira from her tasks?" I asked, keeping my tone light.

Mira exchanged a knowing smile with him. "Cedric is explaining a game called hexbones to me. Mistress Masterson put me in charge of entertainment, but I don't know many Osfridian games."

"Hexbones?" I asked incredulously. "That's just a dice game stableboys and messengers play." I bit off any other words as Cedric shot me a sharp look.

"It's a game played by *many people*," he amended. "Most girls here grew up with it. The elite classes don't play it, true, and it's smart of you to be thinking ahead like that. But I'm sure for one night we can all relax a little."

"Yes, of course," I said. It'd been a while since I'd slipped like that. "But where are you going to get the dice? You think Mistress Masterson has a spare set?"

"Oh, I think Nancy Masterson might be more of a rebel than we think." Although he still smiled, Cedric had an unusual air about him tonight. I couldn't quite put my finger on it, but he seemed almost melancholy—certainly not a mood I generally associated with him.

"Did you call for me?"

Mistress Masterson stuck her head in the doorway, having just been passing by at that moment.

"Ah, no," said Cedric. Mira and I tried not to laugh. "Adelaide was just discussing her plans for the room and was hoping you'd approve."

Mistress Masterson looked at me expectantly, and I tried not to glare at Cedric for shifting the focus to me. Quickly, I mustered a plan. "Uh, candles in all the windows and those gilt-edged blue runners for the tables. And if I move that sofa over there, it'll open up that corner for conversation. It'd be nice to get some of that spiced incense too."

Mistress Masterson nodded in approval. "Sounds like you've got it well in hand, dear."

"And holly," I suddenly said, looking at the mantel. "We should've gotten holly to make boughs. We always used to do that for winter parties in the capital."

"That would've been nice," Mistress Masterson agreed. "I didn't even think about it with everything going on. Too late to get any now—the sun's almost down." She nodded toward a darkened window and, seeing my disappointed face, added, "Don't worry. Clara had the foresight to go get fresh ivy and make some garlands. That's almost as good."

That only made things worse, knowing that Clara had one-upped me. Mistress Masterson left, and Mira gazed at the window for long moments before turning to Cedric. "Weren't there some things you needed to take care of?"

"Yes . . . I should do that soon."

When he made no motions to leave, Mira added, "You'll have plenty of time before the party. Everyone's very busy right now."

"Yes . . . yes." His smile returned, but I could see a tightness behind it, reinforcing that odd sense I'd gotten from him. "I'll take care of that now."

He started to walk out of the room and then paused by me. "Here." I smiled as he pressed a set of dice into my hand.

"Of course. Of course you have a set."

"It's my spare, actually. We play all the time at school."

"Are you any good?" I asked. "Never mind. I already know you are. It's a game that involves reading people and manipulating them."

"Exactly," he said. "You'd be a natural."

Despite that jest, he still seemed tense. "He's acting very strangely," I told Mira when he was gone.

"Is he? I don't know him well enough to know."

"Don't you?" I asked pointedly.

Her face was completely innocent as she shook her head. "I'm sure everything's fine. Do you want me to help you move the sofa before I leave?"

She and I lugged it across the room, both of us surprised at its weight. "I'm starting to agree with Tamsin," I said. "It'll be nice to have flocks of servants to do this for us."

Mira grinned back. "We'll see. I don't know if I did well enough to get a husband with *one* servant, let alone flocks."

"Not like Tamsin," I said.

"Not like Tamsin." She laughed. Her face grew serious. "But I hope I did well enough to get . . . I don't know. A choice. Or at least someone I can respect."

"Still want to buy out your contract?"

She helped straighten the sofa. "I think Tamsin was right about that. I'd need some sort of job on the side—and I'm guessing that's not allowed."

"Um, yeah. Jasper would probably frown on that kind of thing. But it won't matter. I know you'll have your pick of amazing men. And if you're worried about your scores, you can always retake the tests."

"Right. They were *so* fun the last time." She stepped back and joined me to survey our work with the sofa. "Do you need anything else before I go?"

"Not unless you can make some holly materialize," I said wistfully. "It just doesn't feel like winter without it."

"I wouldn't know, since we don't have it in Sirminica, but I think this room will be fine."

After she left, her remark made me feel worse—as though I owed her holly for a true Osfridian experience. When I finished with the drawing room, Mistress Masterson released me from my duties early to go get ready for the party. Neither Tamsin nor Mira had returned yet. I put on my best dress, a full-skirted gown of sky-blue brocade scattered with pink flowers. A pink chemise was worn under it, peeping through the slashed sleeves and around the boned bodice. As I laced it up, I thought ahead to what it would be like when we switched to Adorian fashions. The skirts were slimmer and more maneuverable, the bodices less structured.

I wandered downstairs, looking for ways to help. No one needed me, and Cedric was gone. I'd kind of wanted to brag to him about having laced up the dress in under a minute. So, I busied myself by going over my decorative handiwork but found no flaws in it—except the absence of holly. A check of the clock told me I had an hour until dinner, and I made an impulsive decision.

I traded my delicate party shoes for sturdy boots and donned a wool cloak. Even so, I wasn't prepared for the blast of cold that hit me when I went outside through one of the back doors. I questioned my decision for a moment, watching as my breath made frosty clouds, and then plunged forward.

I knew what Mistress Masterson would have said about me traipsing alone through the woods at this time of day. My grandmother would have said the same thing. But I'd been all over Blue Spring's property in my time here, taking walks and picnics with the other girls. No dangerous animals roamed the grounds, and we were too far out of the way to have any vagabonds coming by. The only person I was likely to see was the kindly old groundskeeper.

It was the shortest day of the year, and sunset had come early. The light was almost gone from the western horizon, and the rest of the sky already glittered with stars. A rising moon and my own memory of the way to the holly trees made navigation easy. The cold was my biggest obstacle, and I regretted not bringing gloves. A thin coat of snow crunched softly as I passed over it.

I found the holly trees where I remembered, on the farthest edge of the property. Here, the grounds gave way to what was left of the wilder, original forest. Those who'd built Blue Spring long ago had cleared the trees around the house, replacing them with vast manicured lawns and ornate specimen plantings. It was a common practice among fashionable estates, and these sorts of wild woods were becoming scarce.

I'd had enough sense to bring a knife, and set to cutting off branches of holly. I wouldn't be able to fashion them into a true wreath, but I'd have enough to make some nice arrangements for the mantels that would certainly outdo Clara's ivy. I'd just about finished when I noticed something in my periphery.

At first, I thought my eyes were playing tricks on me. I could see fairly well out here. The moon reflected off the snow, and stars spilled across the sky. Squinting at what had caught my eye, I wondered if I was seeing just another reflection. But no—this wasn't the pale, silvery light of moon and snow. This was warmer. The golden light of a flame.

It was coming from even farther into the old woods, in a copse of hazel and oak. I crept forward to investigate. Most likely it was the groundskeeper. If not, and it was some trespasser, I could easily sneak away without being seen, and report it. Again, I knew Mistress Masterson and my grandmother would have a lot to say about this reasoning, but I didn't care.

Clutching my holly boughs and knife, I crept forward, keeping to the shadows and concealment of the trees. As I drew closer, I saw that there were actually twelve lights: tiny lanterns in the snow, arranged in a diamond formation in a clearing canopied by the skeletal branches of ancient trees. Standing in the middle of the diamond, facing the most venerable of oaks, was a man in a billowing greatcoat that glowed scarlet in the lantern light. He knelt down, facing the diamond's eastern point, and bowed to it, murmuring something I couldn't make out. Then he knelt to the south and repeated the ritual.

Terror filled the pit of my stomach as I realized what was happening. I'd dismissed Tamsin's joking comments about Alanzans and Midwinter, but here, before my very eyes, was one of those heretics conducting some arcane ritual in the night. I might not know as much about them as Mira, but I'd learned enough from whispered conversations in Osfro to know that the diamond made of twelve points was sacred to the Alanzans. It represented the twelve angels, six light and six dark.

A heretic is using our lands! I needed to get back and report it. Quietly, I started to retreat, just as he turned toward the northern point—facing me. It illuminated his face, revealing features I knew. Features I'd seen less than an hour ago. Features I'd spent far too much time contemplating.

Cedric.

CHAPTER 8

IN MY SHOCK, THE HOLLY SLIPPED FROM MY ARMS. I attempted to recover it—covertly—but it was too late. I'd already made too much noise and alerted him to my presence. He shot to his feet, and I considered running but knew I wouldn't get far in these skirts. In a moment, he was before me, staring down in disbelief.

"Adelaide? What are you doing out here?"

"Me? What are you— Never mind. I know what you're doing!" I backed up, swinging my small knife. "Stay away from me!"

"Put that down before you hurt someone." There was a hard set to his face, not angry . . . just resigned. "It's not what you think."

The words were so ludicrous, it drew me up short in my retreat. "Oh? Are you saying you're not in the middle of a heretical Midwinter ritual?"

He sighed. "No. I'm saying the Alanzans aren't whatever bloodthirsty creatures you've been told we are."

The use of "we" wasn't lost on me. "But . . . but you're saying you're one of them?"

He took a long time in answering. A chill wind blew, ruffling my hair and freezing my skin. "Yes."

The world seemed to sway around me. Cedric Thorn had just admitted to being a heretic.

He reached toward me. "I mean it. Will you please put that down?"

"Don't touch me!" I said, brandishing the knife higher. Behind him, the lanterns glowed with a sinister light, and I suddenly wondered if he was going to attempt some Alanzan curse on me. I'd heard plenty about them but never expected to be the victim of one. But then, I'd never really been in this situation before with someone I thought I knew. I wondered if anyone in the house would hear me if I screamed.

"Do *not* scream," said Cedric, anticipating me. "I swear, there's nothing to be afraid of. Everything's the same. I'm the same."

I shook my head and felt the knife tremble in my hand. "That's not true. You believe in communing with demons—"

"I believe the six wayward angels are every bit as holy as the six glorious ones. They aren't demons. And I believe divinity is all around us in the natural world, free to anyone," he said calmly. "Not something only accessible through the priests in their churches."

It sounded less sinister when he put it like that, but I'd had too many warnings drilled into me.

"Adelaide, you know me. I covered for you when you ran away. I got your old cook a job. Do you really think I'm some servant of darkness?"

"No," I said, lowering the knife at last. "But . . . but . . . you're confused. You need to stop this. Stop . . . um, being a heretic."

"It's not something I can just stop being. It's part of me."

"They could kill you if you're caught!"

"I know. Believe me, I'm well aware of that. And it's something I've long come to terms with." I shivered as another icy wind passed over us. He looked me over, his face turning incredulous. "Come on, let's talk somewhere warmer before you get hypothermia."

"Like the drawing room?" I asked. "I'm sure your dangerous and illegal beliefs will make compelling conversation back at the party! We're not going anywhere until I understand what's going on. I'm fine. I put on a cloak."

"Then why are you turning blue?"

"You can't see that well out here!"

"I can see that cloak is just meant to cover you going from a carriage to a party. Not prancing around on the longest night of the year.

If you won't go inside, then go over there at least." Off to the side of the clearing was a small lean-to, open on two sides, used to store tools and wood. I squeezed inside it and found it blocked some of the wind. Cedric joined me, and I started to cringe as he approached, still frightened by the memory of him in the firelit diamond, living out the tales of horror I'd heard.

To my surprise, he unbuttoned his scarlet greatcoat and pulled me toward him, enveloping me in the folds of the heavy fabric. The warmth it offered dampened my fear. I smelled the familiar cologne I liked so much and could make out nearly every detail of his face in the moonlight now that we were closer. Out of necessity, I moved closer to the warmth he offered and realized what he'd said was true. It was just him, the same Cedric I'd known for nearly a year. And that made the situation even more terrifying.

"They could kill you," I repeated, the full weight of that hitting me.

The Osfridian ecclesiastical courts sometimes offered soft sentences to women or foreigners caught practicing the Alanzan faith. Imprisonment. Fines. But an Osfridian citizen—a man? That could—and often did—result in execution. The priests were getting zealous about keeping Osfrid pure. And the king was uneasy about a religion that advocated every member having a voice instead of one all-powerful leader.

"And that's why you need to go to Adoria," I suddenly realized, speaking my thoughts aloud. "It's why you fought for all of this with your father and put your classes on hold, isn't it? So you can practice safely in Cape Triumph." Although the Osfridian colonies still fell under the crown's law, a number of them had charters allowing for certain exceptions and liberties. Religion was one that came up a lot. Shipping heretics across the sea was easier than trying to stamp them out in the motherland, so long as it resulted in taxes and trade goods being sent back.

"It's not legal in Cape Triumph," he said. "No colonies sanction Alanzan worship. Not yet."

I tilted my head, having to do some complicated maneuvering to look him in the eye while still staying in the protection of his greatcoat. I understood now why these coats were so popular in the rugged conditions of Adoria.

"Is there going to be one?" I asked.

"Well, not strictly Alanzan. But there's a charter being drawn up for a colony called Westhaven that would allow freedom of religion to all who lived there. Us. The errant priests. And the Heirs of Uros—those who haven't already gone north, at least."

"So you can go there and be safe," I said, surprised to feel relief on his part.

"It's in the very early stages." Some of that earlier melancholy underscored his words. "The boundaries and laws are still being established. It's not open to all settlers yet—only those who buy a stake in the company's initial charter. It's a great opportunity to be one of the early investors—lots of potential for leadership and immediate safety if you can get that membership. But it's not cheap."

"And that's why you procured, isn't it?" I asked. "It wasn't enough to simply get passage to Adoria on family business. You needed money of your own."

"Yes. But I'm going to come up short."

I winced. "Because you recruited a Sirminican and an imposter who are going to get you mediocre commissions."

"You're only an imposter when it comes to sewing and 'bleaching' vegetables."

I smacked his chest, too annoyed to wonder how he'd heard about the asparagus incident. "This is serious! You need to get out of Osfrid. You need to get to this safe place . . . if there is such a thing for someone like you."

I couldn't say for sure, but it seemed as though he flinched at *someone like you*. "It's not just about safety. It's about freedom. Freedom to be who I am without putting on a show for everyone else." He gestured back at the diamond. "Without having to sneak around."

His words echoed my own, spoken months ago when I'd begged him to keep my cover. I understood his longing for freedom, even if I didn't understand the motivation behind it. I'd fought hard to get on a path that would let me seize control of my life, and it had been with his help.

"Well, you don't have that freedom yet. So why worship right on the Glittering Court's grounds?"

"I didn't expect anyone to be out here," he said pointedly. "If it had been up to me, I wouldn't have come to the manor at all today—I'd be off worshipping with others instead of doing a solitary ritual. You're celebrating the end of exams, but for me, this is one of the holiest nights of the year. I had to come offer praise before your party started."

It was hard for me to reconcile the brash Cedric I thought I knew with this one who was so seriously discussing spiritual matters—matters that sounded nonsensical to someone raised in the orthodox worship of the one god Uros, worship that took place inside solid churches with orderly services. When I looked away and didn't respond, Cedric remarked softly, "It's funny—I knew when this came out, others would look at me differently. Reject me. I braced myself for it. But somehow, I didn't expect it'd bother me so much that you think less of me . . ."

I glanced back up at him, taken in by the tone of his voice. What I saw in his face confused me, especially when he drew the greatcoat more tightly around us. I swallowed and moved to a somewhat safer topic. "Is there some other way to get the money and get a stake in the colony? Can't you ask your father or uncle?"

"You know my father," Cedric scoffed. "He has no idea I'm part of this. He'd probably turn me in himself. I discovered the Alanzans when I started at the university a couple of years ago, and finally, something just made sense for me in the world. It felt so right, but I knew better than to breathe a word of it to anyone, even my own kin. My uncle wouldn't help either—he just follows my father's lead. As for other funds . . . I could find some kind of work over there, but it would take a while to make the money needed for the colony, especially if I don't finish my degree here. I'd probably end up as a laborer, going when the colony opened to all settlers—but that won't happen right away. Anyone outside the initial charter members settling in the colony probably wouldn't get citizenship until next year."

"Well, you can't stay here to finish your degree," I said firmly. "Surely there must be other ways of quickly making money."

He chuckled. "If they existed, would your family have been struggling? I mean, yes, there are plenty of get-rich-quick schemes in the New World—and some of them work. But really, the Glittering Court's one of the best. Moving any kind of luxury goods—even young women—can have big returns over there. They don't have access to the kinds of things we do here."

"What kind of luxury goods?" I asked, trying to ignore my increased shivering.

"Spices, jewelry, china, glass." He paused to think. "My father makes a fortune on the side selling fabric. He brings it over with the girls, and it more than covers what gets spent on your wardrobes—which he then resells for more profit once you're all married. One-of-a-kind things are valuable too. Antique furniture. Art."

That pulled me in. "Art? What kind of art?"

"Any kind. There are no galleries over there, no great masters. And few people here go to the trouble of shipping their rare paintings or sculptures over the ocean to sell there. Too complicated. Too risky. But—if they did, there's a huge profit to be made. Damn it—I can hear your teeth. We need to go."

He started to lead me in the direction I'd come, but I pushed obstinately back, keeping us where we stood. "Then . . . if you could sell a painting, that'd go a long way in helping earn your fee."

He shook his head. "If I could sell the right kind of painting to the right buyer, I could more than cover my stake in Westhaven."

"Then you need to get a painting."

"Valuable ones aren't exactly lying around. I mean, they are in my uncle's manors, but I won't steal from my own family."

"You don't have to steal one if you can make your own," I said excitedly.

"I can't make any—"

"Not you. *Me.* Don't you remember that day in Osfro? The poppy painting?"

He fell silent. His eyes were dark in the dim lighting, surveying me thoughtfully. "I thought that was some kind of game."

"It wasn't. Well, I mean it was . . . it's hard to explain. But I can do it. I can replicate all sort of famous paintings. Or if you don't want an exact duplicate, I can imitate an artist's style and claim we found some lost work. That Florencio hanging by the drawing room? I could do that easily, given enough time."

"You want to sell a counterfeit painting in Adoria?" he asked in disbelief.

"Do you think they'd honestly know the difference?" I challenged.

"If we were caught—"

"Add it to the list of the other things we could get in trouble for."

"It's becoming kind of a long list." But that initial worry was giving way to a warmth and enthusiasm I knew. The Cedric I knew—the schemer and salesman. He looked down at me for long moments as the wind whistled around us. "Do you know what you're getting into by doing this?"

"No more than what you did when you protected me that night at the Osfro city gates. I told you I'd owe you a favor."

I could feel the decision settle around him. "Okay then. We'll do this. But first—we need to get inside."

We left the meager safety of the lean-to, both of us shivering. He doused the lanterns while I picked up my holly. Watching him, I felt that previous unease begin to stir within me as all the warnings from dour priests played through my mind. Then Cedric returned to me, his face alight and eager with a plan before us, and those warnings faded to background noise. He draped the greatcoat around me as best he could as we walked back toward the manor, huddled together.

"How in the world," he remarked, already planning ahead, "are we going to even find a way for you to secretly paint this masterpiece?"

"You'll have to figure out those logistics," I said. "And I'll concentrate on finding a husband so you can get that mediocre commission."

"Right. Wouldn't want to distract you from that. I'll figure something out."

The lights of the manor glowed before us in the night, and despite my earlier confidence, I couldn't help a bit of uncertainty. Not about the painting. I was still confident I could do that. But the logistics *would* be difficult. Getting the materials, let alone a place for me to do it, wouldn't be easy. Between that and the potential problems of even selling it in Adoria, Cedric's chances of getting the money he needed were not certain by any means.

Just before we reached the back door, he stopped and met my eyes. "I meant what I said about the stories you've heard not being true. Alanzans are ordinary people. Normal people with vocations and morals. We just have a different view on how the world works."

"Cedric, I don't think less of you. I've always felt . . ." I couldn't finish and had a feeling I should have never begun. I turned away, but he caught my arm and pulled me toward him.

"Adelaide . . ." Words escaped him as well, and he released his hold on me. "Okay. Let's go."

We made it inside, earning surprised looks from Mistress Masterson, our other instructors, and the rest of the girls who'd been assembling for dinner. I knew my face was flushed and my hair windswept, but Cedric was quick to cover for me, like always. "Adelaide couldn't rest unless she got her holly, so I offered to go out with her." His smile was as easy as ever, in no way indicating he practiced a controversial religion that could get him executed.

Mistress Masterson tsked at me. "I admire your dedication, dear, but these aren't fit conditions to be out in. Thank you for looking after her, Master Cedric."

But who was going to look after him? The question plagued me throughout the rest of the evening. I went through the motions of dinner, games, and conversation, but always, my eyes strayed to Cedric. He too was being sociable, but I could see he didn't go out of his way to engage others. Now that I understood what was happening, I could easily spot the worry weighing on him. Again, I wondered if my forged painting—if we could pull it off—would even be enough to save him.

"Where's your head tonight?" Tamsin strolled over to me from across the drawing room. She wore a blue dress that looked striking with her reddish hair, though she was still quick to tell us green was her best color.

"I'm worried about my exams," I lied.

"Are you?" she asked in surprise. "You always seem to go through classes and studying as though it didn't make any difference to you."

"I guess the reality of it is catching up with me now."

She studied my face closely. "I suppose so. Well, go sneak an extra glass of wine when Mistress Masterson's not looking. Or, if you're really worried, retake them after you get your score."

"Retake them?" I'd suggested it to Mira but had never even considered it for myself.

"Sure," Tamsin said. "I'm going to. I mean, I think I did pretty good, but why not make sure? I can't leave anything up to chance."

Her words hit me like a slap in the face. I stared at her for several long moments and then turned my gaze back to the crowded drawing room. Cedric stood near the fire, talking to a wildly gesticulating Mister Bricker, whom I suspected had had multiple glasses of wine. As though sensing me, Cedric glanced up and gave me a small smile before returning to the conversation.

"Adelaide? Are you okay?" Tamsin asked.

I glanced back at her. "Yeah . . . yeah. It's just, something hit me I hadn't thought of before."

"What?" she asked.

"It's not important." I mustered a cheerful expression. "Tell me how you think everyone here will rank."

It was a topic she was more than happy to expound on, seeing as she'd spent a lot of time analyzing our housemates. As she launched into an explanation, I nodded and smiled appropriately, all the while making plans for what I had to do next.

Cedric needed money to get to Westhaven and stay alive. Could my forged painting do it? Yes—if everything fell into place. And if everything didn't fall into place? Then he needed a backup plan. I'd pondered this all evening, feeling useless. I had no power to give him money. But I realized now that I did have that power. Could I guarantee he'd be able to pay the entire fee for his stake in Westhaven? No, but I *could* guarantee he'd have a good start.

And the only way to do that was to make sure he did not, in fact, get a mediocre commission for me.

CHAPTER 9

CEDRIC LEFT THE MORNING AFTER MIDWINTER, AND the exam results were in a few days later. They arrived with Jasper and Miss Garrison, one of the Glittering Court's dressmakers. She immediately wanted to start designing our themed wardrobes. Mistress Masterson strode in sedately to the library, where we all waited anxiously in neat, orderly rows. She propped up the framed list on the mantel and then stepped back. There was a moment of hesitation, and then we broke rank to crowd forward and look.

The list showed the scores for all girls across the four manors. I immediately found my name, exactly in the middle, as I'd once hoped. It was a fine score, and scores only helped in the Glittering Court's promotion in Adoria. A prosperous man entranced by a girl's looks might not care how she ranked in the exams—but those with the highest scores would have more opportunities to meet said gentlemen.

Mira, standing beside me, let out a small exclamation of delight. I found her name several above mine, in a very respectable seventh across all manors—and one spot higher than Clara. "Can you believe it?" Mira asked. "Maybe I won't have to clean floors after all." Around us, the room was buzzing with other girls' chatter.

I hugged her. "Of course I can believe it. You've been so worried about the accent, but you've worked so hard in all the other—"

The wail of a familiar voice drew me up short. I immediately spied Tamsin standing on the opposite side of the group, her eyes wide. She turned to Mistress Masterson incredulously. "How am I ranked third?

The girls above me have the same score as me!" A quick study of the list showed two girls from other manors in the first and second spots.

"Yes," Mistress Masterson agreed. "You all tied—it was very impressive. Really, what it came down to is aesthetics." She nodded toward Miss Garrison. "Winnifred, the first girl, would look so lovely in the diamond coloring. Ruby's the next most precious stone, and that obviously wouldn't suit you with your hair. So third, as a sapphire, seemed like—"

"Sapphire?" interrupted Tamsin. "*Sapphire*? Everyone knows green is my best color. Isn't an emerald rarer than a sapphire?"

"My green fabric hasn't arrived yet," said Miss Garrison. "Isn't likely to show until about a week before you sail."

Mistress Masterson nodded. "And the categories are flexible—it's more of a gemstone *range* we're going for. We thought it best just to go forward with sapphire so that she could start on your wardrobe. Otherwise, she'd be working at the last minute."

Tamsin fixed the seamstress with a sharp eye. "Well, maybe she could just sew a little damned faster."

"Tamsin!" snapped Mistress Masterson, shifting back to the stern instructor we knew. "You are out of line. You will take sapphire and be grateful that you're among the top three. *And* you will watch your language."

I could tell Tamsin was still upset, but she took a deep breath and visibly calmed before speaking again. "Yes, Mistress Masterson. I apologize. But I can retake the exams I did poorly on, right?"

"Yes, of course. Every girl can. Though, I'll be honest, with a ninety-nine percent rating, there's isn't much else to achieve."

"Perfection," replied Tamsin.

Most of the girls were content with their scores. Even the lowest ranked would still be dazzlingly displayed in Adoria, and enduring exams again wasn't so appealing.

Miss Garrison and her assistants set about measuring everyone and holding fabric swatches to them as other gemstone themes were decided. I approached Mistress Masterson and asked if I could retake the exams.

"Certainly," she said, looking surprised. As mediocre as I'd always been, this initiative had to be unexpected. She rifled through some papers and produced one that broke down my scores, detailing each area. "Which would you like to retake?"

I barely glanced at the sheet. "All of them."

"All?" she repeated. "That almost never happens."

I shrugged by way of answer.

She pointed to a couple of scores. "You performed very well in these areas. I doubt there's any need."

"I'd still like to do it."

She hesitated and gave a curt nod. "It'll take a bit of scheduling for you to meet with all the instructors, but it's every girl's right. Between you and me, in all the time I've done this, most girls who retake an exam only go up a few points. Miss Garrison and I currently have you placed as an amethyst, and her purple fabrics are gorgeous. It's unlikely your score would shift enough to warrant a new theme, and would you really want one?"

"I want to retake them," I reiterated.

"Very well. But in the meantime, we'll still have you fitted so Miss Garrison can start on the amethyst wardrobe."

She was right about the fabrics. Of all the ones Miss Garrison had brought, the amethyst ones were among the most beautiful. She held up swathes of lavender silk and purple velvet, clucking in approval each time.

But an amethyst girl wouldn't give Cedric the commission he needed.

"You've got the coloring to pull off anything," she remarked. "For some of the other girls, the originally planned palettes aren't going to work."

Mira was one such case. They'd decided her theme would be topaz, but after having her try some of the fabrics, it was clear the yellow-brown fabrics just didn't suit her. "Deep reds are the way to go,"

Miss Garrison told Mistress Masterson. The dressmaker's gaze fell on Clara. "We could switch them—give Mira garnet."

Jasper, observing the conversation, nodded in agreement. "It's a little more of a common stone, so it might be fitting."

I didn't have a chance to be affronted by the insult to my friend because Clara's scowl told me how much the change upset her. That made up for a lot. Afterward, I heard her mutter to Caroline, "I *hate* yellow. It always makes me look sickly."

Tamsin was one of the last to complete her fittings, largely because she kept pointing out how unacceptable the blue fabric was. When she finally finished and walked up to our room with us, she muttered, "I can't wait until the retakes put me at the top. Then they'll see what a bad choice they made. I'd look just as good in white as green."

I stumbled on the stairs and had to catch the railing for support. In my plan to retake the exams, I somehow hadn't considered Tamsin. If I managed to vault myself to the top of the list, where would that put her? Her words rang in my ears: *You don't know what I have on the line.*

No, I didn't. But I knew what Cedric had on the line. His life. No matter how dire, could Tamsin really have anything comparable to that? And *was* it really dire? Her feelings had seemed genuine the day of the family visit, but I'd seen a lot of theatrics from her in our time together. Was her fixation to be the best just a matter of pride? A yearning for riches?

I had to choose between them. My best friend or . . . who? The man who'd helped save me? No matter where Tamsin placed, she'd have a prosperous future in Adoria. My placement could affect Cedric's life. There was only one choice I could make.

Content with her scores and theme, Mira was able to relax in the days that followed, spending a lot of time engrossed in her beloved tome of adventures. Tamsin and I, however, endured the stress of retaking our exams as our various instructors scheduled time throughout the week among all the manors. Like Mistress Masterson, Tamsin was baffled that I'd retake all of them.

"Why would you do that?" she asked on our way to the dance exam. "You think things will change? And why would you want them to? Your clothes look great on you. Not like *some* of us."

I had to look away, still feeling guilty in spite of my resolve. "I just need to see what I can do."

Miss Hayworth met with us and Caroline, the only other girl retaking the dance exam, in the ballroom. "Same format as before. We'll go through every single dance and see if you've improved."

Tamsin had marginally improved in the step that continually gave her trouble. For some reason, the beats tripped her up. Caroline hadn't improved at all. In fact, she did worse, but luckily, Mistress Masterson would only count the highest of her two scores.

And me? Well, I was something else altogether.

It was hard to say who among the three of them was the most astonished. I executed every dance perfectly on both technical and artistic levels, and it was a relief to finally let my true self show through. I'd spent most of the last year hiding what I could do with the façade I'd created. Now, all the years of instruction and formal parties came back to me, and I actually enjoyed myself.

The other exams had similar results. As before, the written ones allowed me to conceal my answers from my housemates. But in the public tests, all my "new" skills were on display for my peers. Since no other girl was retaking every single exam, no one else really got a full sense of how well I did in each subject.

That all changed when the results came in the following week.

There was no posted list this time, simply a meeting called by Mistress Masterson in the drawing room. We lined up in our rows. Jasper Thorn was with her again, and both of them wore expressions that weren't grave so much as . . . perplexed. Just as she was about to speak, Cedric came hurrying in. I'd neither seen nor heard from him in the last couple of weeks, leaving me to wonder what his plans were for our painting project.

I saw him murmur what looked like an apology as he took his place beside his father. Jasper said nothing, maintaining that pleasant cover he always had in public with his son.

Mistress Masterson nodded a greeting to him and then turned to address us. "I know some of you have been waiting for your retake results, so you'll be pleased they're in. Most of you showed improvement—for which I'm particularly proud. But there was nothing significant enough to warrant a change in rank or theme." She paused. "With one exception."

Beside me, Tamsin straightened up, lifting her chin proudly. I could feel her trembling with excitement as she awaited the news that she'd trumped the two girls who'd beat her on the list.

"Adelaide," said Mistress Masterson, her gaze falling heavily on me. "The improvement you showed is . . . remarkable, to put it mildly. I've never, ever seen a girl make such a leap in scores. And . . . I've never seen a girl get a perfect overall score." She let those words sink in, and I felt the eyes of everyone in the room upon me. Tamsin's were widest of all. "We rarely have theme changes based on retakes, though of course it happens. And in this case, it's absolutely warranted."

Jasper stepped forward, taking the lead from her. He was as ostensibly cheerful as ever, but somehow, I didn't think he was overly thrilled about the turn of events. "Adelaide, my dear, you've replaced Winnifred from Dunford Manor as our diamond. Everyone else who scored above your last result will move down a notch. All girls will still keep their gemstone themes, with a few exceptions."

"As Master Thorn said, you'll have diamond," Mistress Masterson explained. "You and Winnifred are of similar size, and Miss Garrison should have little difficulty fitting you into her clothes. Since her score was so high, it'd hardly seem fair to assign her a semiprecious stone like the amethyst. We think she'll show best as a sapphire, and we've done a couple of other last-minute switches—which means, Tamsin, you can be an emerald after all. Miss Garrison expects the green fabric to arrive next week, and she and her assistants will work around the clock to make sure you're properly outfitted."

Tamsin still looked dumbstruck, like Mistress Masterson was speaking a different language. "But . . . if the ranks shifted, then that means . . . I'm fourth."

"Yes."

It was a rare moment of Tamsin being stunned into silence, and I felt a lump in my throat. Jasper, seeing her dismay, gave her a stiff smile. "You'll dazzle them as an emerald. Even if you aren't invited to *all* the elite parties, I know you'll be in high demand. I'm proud of you. I'm proud of all my girls—though it looks like my son managed to find the top jewel this season." Jasper didn't sound particularly proud of that. The top three had previously been all his acquisitions.

With the sudden dramatic turn of events, I'd nearly forgotten Cedric was here. I looked at him now and saw that he was quite possibly the most shocked person in the room. He couldn't even fake a smile.

Jasper gave a few more encouraging words for the whole group, telling us how excited he was to take us to Adoria next week. He had significant trade to do and had chartered two ships for the journey. We'd be traveling with the girls from Guthshire Manor. Swan Ridge and Dunford would be in the other ship.

When we were dismissed, a flurry of excitement broke out, and I was immediately swarmed by girls wanting to know how I'd achieved such a feat. It was a relief when Mistress Masterson pulled me away to discuss a few logistics.

"It really is remarkable," she told me in the privacy of the study. "Master Jasper wondered if there might be some deceit involved, but I told him if you'd found a way to cheat in playing the harp or dancing the Lorandian two-step, then that itself deserved some sort of reward. Remarkable."

I swallowed. "I guess I just learned more than I realized. A lot of lessons from when I was a lady's maid came back to me."

"Well, we'll all work hard to get these initial bumps fixed. I think it should come together fairly easily. The diamond attire is all white and silver, which will look nice on you as well. You'll have to set aside some extra time for Miss Garrison to alter the clothes for you this week."

"It's no problem," I said, still stunned at just how well my plan had worked. "Let me know what you need from me."

Cedric appeared in the doorway, his earlier shock now covered by a jovial grin. "Mistress Masterson, do you mind if I borrow Adelaide when you're done? I know this change must be a little daunting, and I just wanted to give her some encouragement."

Mistress Masterson beamed. "Yes, of course. We're all set."

Winter still held its grip, but the sun had come out enough to make the day pleasant. Cedric suggested we go for a walk to enjoy the weather, but I suspected he just wanted to ensure we weren't overheard. I felt small relief that he led us to a grove of hawthorn, rather than the old forest where he'd held the Midwinter ritual.

"What," he demanded, "have you done? Are you completely out of your mind?"

"I've *saved* you, that's what I've done!" I'd expected surprise but was a little taken aback by his vehemence.

He raked a hand through his hair, messing up where it had been neatly tied in the back. "You weren't supposed to attract attention. I told you that on the first day! Didn't you hear Mistress Masterson? No one does this. No one makes a score change that vast. No one gets a perfect score! *No one.*"

"I—"

"Do you think everyone's just going to marvel about this?" he continued, pacing around. "Do you think they'll all just chuckle and shake their heads? Someone's going to ask questions! Someone's going to wonder how a lady's maid from a countess's house performed so perfectly after months of average behavior! Someone's going to make the connection that maybe that maid isn't actually a maid!"

I strode up to him, hands on my hips. "So what if they do? Better I'm caught as a runaway noble than you outed as a heretic! Besides, in a couple of weeks, we'll be on our way to Adoria. None of this will matter."

"Don't be so sure," he said darkly. "These kinds of things can follow you anywhere."

"What's the worst that can happen? They haul me back to Grandmama? I'd rather that than you on the Osfro gallows!"

"You don't think they'd hang me for kidnapping a peeress of the realm?" he asked, leaning toward me.

"No. I'd make sure you were innocent of any involvement. I'd take the full blame—but it's not going to happen. Even if someone follows us to Adoria, I'll be married before they can lay claim to me. And that," I added proudly, "is the whole point of this. These scores are just the beginning. Wait until I'm there. I'll dazzle them all. There'll be a bidding war. I'll have men eating out of my hand."

"I don't doubt it," he grumbled.

"Don't make fun of me," I returned. "Because of what I've done, you'll get the biggest commission of the season. You can even have some of my surety money. Maybe it won't cover your whole stake in Westhaven, but it'll certainly make things easier if the painting scheme falls through."

He looked me over and declared, "Nothing involving you has ever been easy."

I balled my fists at my sides. "The words you're looking for are 'Thank you, Adelaide, for going to all this trouble to help me out.' "

"The risk is too great." He shook his head. "You shouldn't be doing this."

And as I spoke, I realized he wasn't talking about the risk to himself. He wasn't really concerned about being implicated in my disappearance. It was exposing me as a fraud and taking me away that he wanted to prevent.

"Why shouldn't I?" I said. "After what you did for me. You saved me, Cedric. I was drowning back there in Osfro. Of course I should do this. I'll do more, if that's what it takes to keep you alive in spite of yourself."

He'd been regarding me very intently as I spoke, as though he couldn't quite believe my words. At that last bit, his face broke into a smile, finally easing the tension. "In spite of myself?"

"Well, you're the one who chose to complicate your life with heresy."

"You don't choose it. It chooses you."

"If you say so," I said. I kept my tone light and dismissive, but inside, I was relieved to no longer be fighting with him. "How did it choose you anyway? Don't take this the wrong way . . . but you don't really seem like the type who'd think too much about godly affairs."

He beckoned me toward the house, and I fell in step with him. "A lot of things bothered me about the world, ever since childhood. My parents are married, but they might as well not be. They've almost always lived apart, and we were all supposed to pretend that was normal. Emotional reactions weren't allowed about that or, well, anything. It was all duty and keeping up appearances, just like the traditional churches teach. Then I learned how the six wayward angels aren't evil—they just govern emotion and instinct, something the rigid priests of Uros fear. I learned it was okay to embrace that emotional side of me—to accept my true nature. That it was okay to let my passions run wild."

The idea of Cedric and passions running wild was enough to make me momentarily lose track of his ardent explanation.

"And the rest of the Alanzan worship just made sense too," he continued. "Spirituality without boundaries. All voices heard. Reverence for the natural world. We don't need to attend lavish services paid for with prayer fees and massive tithes . . . while beggars and others starve outside the cathedrals. It's not fair for one group to have so much wealth and another so little."

"I've seen your wardrobe choices. You're no ascetic. And here you are, ironically, doing business with men who are massively wealthy in the New World."

"But there's a difference between building wealth through honest business and building it by taking it from those who look to you for hope and spiritual guidance. Don't you see, Adelaide, the orthodox priests are preaching good will toward all men but actually hoarding—"

"No." I held up my hand. "Stop now. I can see where you're going with this. I'll keep your secrets, but do not try to convert me to your pagan ways."

He laughed. "Wouldn't dream of it. But it's nice to know you draw the line somewhere."

The house grew closer and closer, and the momentary lightness faded. "I really am sorry if I made things more complicated," I said softly.

"This was already complicated. Just be careful . . . no one's safe until you've got some wealthy Adorian's ring on your finger."

"It'll be weighted with a diamond," I told him, earning a return of the smile.

Inside, I was relieved to see that most of the other girls had gone on to their rooms or other tasks, freeing me from a deluge of questions. Or so I thought.

When I got to my room, I found Tamsin and Mira. It was clear they'd been waiting for my return. Tamsin leapt to her feet.

"What have you done?" she cried, echoing Cedric.

"I'm, uh, not sure what you mean."

"The hell you don't!" It was a lapse into her former dialect that would've scandalized Mistress Masterson. "Has this all been some kind of joke? Coast along and then swoop in at the end to crush everyone else?"

I remembered Cedric's accusations when I first came here—that I'd treated impersonating Ada as a joke too. Was that how my actions would always be perceived by people? Would I never be taken seriously?

"How did you do that?" continued Tamsin. "How did you score perfectly on everything?"

"I learned a lot of it when I worked in my lady's house. I was around nobility all the time, and I guess I picked up their ways. You know that."

Tamsin wasn't buying it. "Oh yeah? Where were those ways in the last nine months? You've botched things continuously—but not always the same things! You run hot and cold, perfect at some things and then failing at the most basic ones. What kind of game are you playing?"

"It's no game," I said. "My nerves just got the best of me. Things finally came together during the retakes."

"Impossible," she stated. "I don't understand how or why you've been doing this, but I know something's going on. And if you think you can just ruin my life and—"

"Oh, come on," I interrupted, switching from defense to offense. "Your life is far from ruined."

Fury filled her features. "That's not true. I had it. I was in the top three, and then *you* came along and pulled that out from under me. You knew how it important it was to me but still went ahead and destroyed everything I've worked for."

I threw up my hands. "Tamsin, enough! I've gone along with your theatrics for nine months, but this is going too far. Exactly what in your life has been destroyed? You can converse about current politics, eat a seven-course meal, and play the piano! Maybe you'll miss out on a few parties, but you're still going to marry some rich, prestigious man in the New World. You've come a long way from being a laundress's daughter, and if you were my friend, you'd be happy at how far I've come too."

"That's the thing," she said. "I can't tell how far you've come. I've lived with you all these months but don't know anything about you. The only thing I'm sure of is that you've been lying to us all, and this 'triumph' of yours just proves it!"

There was a jumble of emotions in my chest. Anger. Sadness. Frustration. I hated the lies and subterfuge. I wanted to tell Tamsin and Mira about everything. My title. Lionel. Ada. Cedric. Westhaven.

Those secrets burned within me, wanting—no, needing—to get out. But I couldn't let them. The consequences were too great, and so I had to bury them back within me and let that terrible animosity hang in the air.

"Tamsin," said Mira, speaking up at last. "That's not fair. What's wrong with her wanting to do well? It's what we all want. And she told you, nerves always got the best of her—"

"That's the biggest lie of all. She's been fearless from the first day, facing down Clara and traipsing out in the night for holly. The jokes, the carefree air . . . it's all been a cover." She pointed an accusing finger at me. "Nerves aren't your problem. I refuse to be sucked into your web of lies, and I will never have anything to do with you again."

That drew even diplomatic Mira to her feet. "Isn't that a little extreme? You're being irrational."

"*And* you're acting like a child," I added. The stress of today's events was catching up with me. Between the shocking announcement, Cedric, and now this, I was having a hard time remaining calm.

Tamsin turned on Mira, ignoring me. "I'm refusing to let her manipulate me like she has everyone else. And if you know what's good for you, you'll do the same."

"Tamsin," pleaded Mira. "Please stop and talk this out."

"No." Tamsin moved toward the door and paused to fix me with a stony glare. "I'm never speaking to you again."

My control snapped. "Should be easy enough—seeing as we'll be hanging out in different social circles in Adoria."

She took it like a physical blow but held good to her threat. She didn't say a word to me, and the only response I got was the slamming of the door as my first real friend stormed away from me.

CHAPTER 10

I HONESTLY DIDN'T BELIEVE HER. AFTER MONTHS OF wild emotions and dramatics, I figured Tamsin would calm down and make amends. But she never did.

The next couple of weeks were a whirlwind of activity. Fittings continued at an accelerated pace as the seamstresses worked around the clock to finish up everyone's wardrobes. It was a daunting task for our house alone, and I knew it had to be just as busy in the three other manors. Tamsin's green fabric arrived, and I caught sight of her at one of her fittings. She looked stunning in it, and I told her so, but she acted as though I hadn't spoken.

My clothes were equally beautiful. I'd loved the purple attire, but this new set transcended even that. Some of the dresses, particularly the daytime ones, were of purest white, made of delicate fabrics that rivaled those I'd worn in my former life. The evening and ball gowns were radiant confections of velvet and satin, done in gleaming white and glittering silver, embellished with jewels and metallic lace.

The Adorian styles took a little getting used to. Although the long skirts were full and layered with petticoats like ours, there was no extra bustle to pad the hips. I didn't mind that so much; it made them infinitely more maneuverable. Adorian sleeves were close fitting to the elbow, with a spill of lace or other embellishment at the cuffs, rather than a chemise revealed through slashing up the arms. It was the bodices, however, that gave me the most pause. They were significantly lower cut than Osfridian fashion, with a scoop neckline that could reveal a lot with a particularly ambitious corset.

"It's how they do it there," Miss Garrison said when I'd remarked upon it. "It's a New World, so they claim—a bolder world. They're trying not to be held back by our 'stuffy' ways here." Her tone suggested she didn't entirely approve, even if creating such things was part of her job. "Well, at least it's done where you're going in Cape Triumph. Up in the northern colonies? Where those crazy Heirs of Uros live? I hear that's a whole other story."

I nodded politely, more concerned with my cleavage than a conservative group of Uros devotees. Honestly, with the threat hanging over Cedric for his Alanzan faith, I kind of felt that my life would be a lot simpler avoiding religion of any kind.

If not for the fight with Tamsin, all this preparation would've been an enjoyable time. "She'll come around," Mira told me one day. "I know she will." Mira had still been playing diplomat, talking insistently with both of us in the hopes of mending the rift.

"Will she?" I asked. "Has she given any sign she will?"

Mira made a face. "No. But it can't last—not even for her. Maybe once we're there, and she's got her choice of suitors, she'll let go of things."

"Maybe," I agreed. My unexpected advancement was still a subject of much speculation in the house, though no one came anywhere near to guessing the truth. I knew Mira was among those who wondered, but she was friend enough not to push me on it. It seemed she carried her own secrets and could respect those of others.

The final blow in the feud with Tamsin came on the day we set sail. We'd traveled to the port city of Culver, in western Osfrid, where Jasper's two commissioned ships waited. It was a cold, blustery day, and as we huddled near the docks, I overheard some of the sailors muttering about a winter crossing. Mistress Masterson had also mentioned it to Jasper, and he'd shrugged it off, saying we were close enough to spring to be free of storms. If he got the jump on other traders coming over in the spring, he could get a higher profit for the rest of the goods he was transporting.

Mistress Masterson and the other manor mistresses had come with us, though not all would be going to Adoria. "You'll be in the capable hands of Mistress Culpepper when you arrive," Mistress Masterson told us. The cold sea wind whipped around us, and I pulled my cloak tighter. "She runs things on the Adorian side and will look after you."

Despite her confident words, I could see concern in Mistress Masterson's features. She'd taught us with a prim—and often strict—countenance, but the gentleness in her features now showed her underlying affection.

"Listen to what you're told there and remember what you've learned here," advised the Swan Ridge mistress.

"And don't talk to the sailors," said another mistress. "Keep to yourselves, and always go in groups if you leave your quarters."

She didn't have to tell us that. The sailors loading our belongings and Jasper's cargo were a burly, rough-looking lot. I avoided eye contact as they moved past us with their loads. My understanding was that they'd been very strongly warned against socializing with us, but one could never be too careful. Jasper's eye was on them now as he directed which ships would carry which goods. Between us and his trade, he was certain to make a good profit from this trip, and I thought it a shame he couldn't use that money to help his son. But from what I'd observed, Cedric was right to guess his father wouldn't endorse alternative religious beliefs.

Cedric himself showed up near boarding time, running typically late. By then, the goods were on board, and it was our turn. Jasper read our names from a list, indicating which ship we'd take. Our manor was traveling on the *Good Hope*, so it was a shock when I heard Tamsin's name read for the *Gray Gull*.

Even Mira was surprised. Like me, I don't think she'd actually thought Tamsin would take our fight to this extreme. "Tamsin . . ." she said in disbelief, watching as our friend walked past us.

But Tamsin didn't look back, and her only pause was to hand Mistress Masterson a stack of letters and say, "Thank you for taking care of these." Then she continued on. My heart sank as she boarded the other ship. I'd chosen Cedric's interests over hers, and sometimes, particularly when I had those middle-of-the-night wakings, I'd question if I'd made the right choice.

"She'll come around," reiterated Mira as we walked up the dock. She didn't sound as confident as usual. "She has to. This journey will give her a lot of time to think."

Our cabin on the *Good Hope* was small, as to be expected, with six narrow bunk beds. Mira and I were rooming with three other Blue Spring girls, as well as one named Martha from Swan Ridge Manor. She was the one Tamsin had managed a trade with. Our rooms were near those of the other Glittering Court girls, as well as that of Miss Bradley, the mistress from Dunford Manor. She met with us in the small common room we'd be using for our meals, reiterating much of what we'd heard on the docks about where we could go and what we could do. The options were limited, and two months in such cramped quarters seemed like a very long time.

When we finally set sail, we all went above deck to observe. My heart hammered as I watched the lines brought in and sailors at work. I'd done many things as the Countess of Rothford, but never a journey of this magnitude. I'd been on a ship to Lorandy once as a child but remembered little of it. That trip took only a day across the narrow channel that separated Osfrid from its continental neighbor. Beside us, the *Gray Gull* was also casting off, and I could make out Tamsin's bright hair among the girls gathered there.

"Did you come from Sirminica by ship?" I asked Mira, suddenly realizing I'd never asked her before. Her eyes were on Osfrid's retreating shore, and I wondered if she regretted leaving the country she'd taken refuge in.

"Some of it. It's expensive to do the whole journey by ship, and most of us fleeing the war couldn't afford it. The group I was with traveled overland and then took a ship from Belsia." She smiled, struck by a memory. "If you think our cabin's small, you should've seen that Belsian ship. No one even had a bed—we were in the cargo hold. Fortunately, that trip was only a few days."

I squeezed her arm, realizing I'd never fully comprehended how much she'd gone through. "It must have been awful."

She shrugged. "It was what it was. It's the past."

"And you're moving on to better things now," Cedric said, strolling up beside us. His hands were in the pockets of the scarlet greatcoat, reminding me of that night I'd found him in the Alanzan ritual. In this clothing, he looked like a proper merchant or scholar, but the wind wreaking havoc on his hair gave him an untamed edge, reminding me of when he'd spoken of letting his passions run wild. I shivered.

"I hope so," said Mira. "What kind of room do you have?"

"I suppose you're staying in a luxury stateroom," I teased.

"That would be my father. I'm in a cabin like yours, bunking with other passengers." He nodded toward a group of men on the other side of the deck, their clothing and manners displaying a wide variety of backgrounds.

"Who are they?" I asked, curious as to who else was going to the New World. One man, with black hair whipping in the wind, was studying me. If he'd shaved and put on unwrinkled clothes this morning, he might have been dashing. When he saw I'd noticed him, he gave a polite nod and looked away.

"Mostly merchants. A few adventurers. The ones I'm rooming with are nice enough—terribly curious about you girls, as one might imagine."

"Any potential suitors?" I asked. "Should I be putting on the charm?"

"I didn't know it ever went away." Cedric studied the men a few moments and shook his head. "Well, I don't think they're that successful yet. None of them could afford any of you."

A few girls standing nearby overheard his words and turned

speculative gazes to the cluster of men. Maybe this group wasn't wildly successful, but some of them looked like they were doing well enough with their lives. I could guess my peers' thoughts. For most of them, coming from impoverished backgrounds, any of these gentlemen would be a great step up in the world. What was in store if the men in Adoria surpassed this?

After the thrill of our departure wore off, most of the girls retired to their rooms. Not long into our journey, some returned above deck once seasickness set in. I felt a little queasy now and then but soon overcame it. Mira never went through it at all.

Miss Bradley preferred we stay down below but didn't discourage our strolls, so long as we did them in groups. Her biggest concern seemed to be that we apply daily moisturizers to our faces, lest the salt water roughen our skin before we got to Adoria. Mira was particularly restless and hated being cooped up. I accompanied her as often as I could, though I knew she sneaked up on her own sometimes.

"What do you think Tamsin's doing?" I asked one day. Mira and I stood at the rail, watching the *Gray Gull*. It was never out of our sight, and I squinted, hoping to catch sight of red hair.

"Making plans," said Mira. "Sizing up the other girls and figuring out how to best them."

I smiled at the thought, knowing she was right. "Her rivals are there, aren't they? The girls who tied her?"

Mira nodded. "Maybe this was all a ruse so that she could spy on the competition."

"I wish it was." There was always an ache in my chest when I studied the other ship. It was amazing how much I missed Tamsin's calculating ways, and the rift between us seemed to overshadow any pleasure I might have taken from this journey.

Mira, brave as ever, walked right up to the railing and peered down at the water. It made me shiver. I had a constant fear of her being pulled over the edge. Averting my eyes from her, I studied the far reaches of the bluish-gray sea. Not unlike Cedric's eyes, I supposed.

"So beautiful," I murmured.

"Your first voyage?"

I turned and saw the man who'd been watching me that first day, the one who either needed to shave or just grow a proper beard. In fact, the more I studied him, the more I just wanted to . . . well, neaten him up. His rumpled clothing was respectable enough but, as Cedric had pointed out, hardly in the class of someone who could afford us.

"I'm sorry," he said, smiling. "We're not supposed to talk without a formal introduction, right?"

"Well, these aren't very formal settings," I said as Mira came to stand beside me again. "I'm Adelaide Bailey, and this is Mira Viana."

"Grant Elliott," he replied. "I'd take my hat off if I had one, but I learned long ago that it's not even worth wearing one out in this wind."

"You've been to Adoria before?" Mira asked.

"Last year. I have a stake in a store that outfits people for exploration and wilderness survival. My partner ran it over the winter, and now I'm coming back."

Mira's eyes lit up. "Have you done much exploring yourself, Mister Elliott?"

"Here and there," he replied, turning from her and focusing back on me. "Nothing you'd find interesting. Now, help me understand how your organization works. You're ranked by gemstone, right? And you're the top one?"

"The diamond," I affirmed. "And Mira's a garnet."

"So, that means you'll get to go to all sorts of—"

"There you are." Cedric strolled up to us, smiling when he saw Grant. "Looks like the three of you have already met. Mister Elliott is one of the men who shares a cabin with me. Adelaide, I need to borrow you for a moment." He nodded toward another group of our girls a short distance away. "Mira, will you be able to go back down below with them when they leave? I think they're going soon."

"Of course," said Mira. "And perhaps Mister Elliott could tell me more about his business."

Grant shook his head. "I'd love to, but I just remembered something I have to follow up on."

He walked away, and Mira wandered over to the other girls. Cedric beckoned me to follow him, and I expected us to simply find some private part of the deck to talk. Instead, he went below, leading me through the ship's narrow inner passages until we reached a cargo hold piled high with crates.

"What in the world are we doing here?" I asked as he shut the door behind us.

He waved me forward past several rows of crates and then gestured grandly. "Your art studio, madam."

I peered into a narrow space shielded by a large stack of boxes and found a canvas and some paints.

"I smuggled them aboard and waited until I could find a place seldom visited," he explained, clearly proud of his cunning.

I knelt down to look at the paints, spreading my skirts around me. I examined the pots one by one. "Oils."

"Does that make a difference?" he asked.

"It affects what I can do. I can't do a Florencio. His medium's different."

Cedric's earlier pride faltered. "I didn't know. Will you be able to do *something*?"

"Sure." I ran through a mental list of various artists' works I'd seen, including the types of pigments and canvases used. I had a pretty good memory for detail. The question would be choosing which style was within my skill set. "Thodoros," I said at last. "A Myrikosi painter. I can do one of his. A lot of their trade goes through Sirminica, and with all the chaos there right now, a rogue painting being smuggled out wouldn't be that extraordinary."

"Can you do it in a little less than two months?"

I hesitated. "I suppose—especially if I can get a couple of hours each day."

"I'll make sure of it," he said adamantly. "We'll make this happen."

When he simply stood there and watched me expectantly, I exclaimed, "What, right now?"

"Why not? We're short on time."

"I can't just jump into a major work. Especially with you staring at me the whole time."

He backed up—but not by much. "Well, I can't leave you. I need to be around in case someone comes in."

"Well, if they do, it's not going to save us from being caught in art forgery," I snapped.

"It'll save you from some wandering sailor. Now. Is there anything else you need?"

"More space. More time. A ship that isn't constantly swaying. And maybe something to eat that isn't dried out and preserved. I'd kill for a honey cake." Seeing his exasperated look, I said, "Hey, you try just jumping into reproducing one of the greatest artists out there. I want to help you, but I need to think this through."

After pondering Thodoros's works for the better part of an hour, I finally set to sketching charcoal on the canvas and began planning out the scene. Thodoros was famous for a series of four paintings called *The Lady of the Fountain.* Each also had a number. They were all different angles and poses of a young woman standing by a fountain and had been created at different times. Occasionally, another person would be included—a man, a child. Passing off a fifth, just-discovered one would hopefully be viable.

My marks were tentative at first. The bizarre, cramped setting didn't help any. Neither did the constant rocking of the ship. I finally decided a back view of the woman would be easiest, and I had to remember the exact position of the fountain and number of trees around it. As time passed, I grew more confident and was happy to get lost in the work. It took my mind away from the deception I was enmeshed in and that constant ache over Tamsin.

I forgot Cedric was there and jumped when he spoke. "Adelaide, we've got to go."

"Do we?" I nodded toward the canvas. "I'm not done with the sketch."

"We've already been gone longer than we should have. It's nearly dinnertime, and I'm hoping Miss Bradley hasn't been looking for you."

I reluctantly surrendered the charcoal and watched as Cedric neatly concealed everything away. "Be careful," I warned. "Don't tear that canvas."

"Maybe it'll just add to the authenticity of being smuggled out through dangerous conditions."

"Maybe," I said, stretching my cramped muscles. "But a painting that makes it out intact will fetch a better price for poor, penniless heathens. A buyer won't question the miracle to have something neat and tidy hanging in his home."

"Well, this poor, penniless heathen is grateful."

We left the cargo room but stopped again in the narrow corridor just before we reached the Glittering Court's set of rooms. He lowered his voice. "Where *did* you learn to do that anyway? The painting? Lots of people know how to paint. Not many can do that kind of imitation."

Another weighty question. "My father," I said after several long moments. "It was a game we played. To test my memory."

He quickly noticed the change in me. "I'm sorry. I didn't mean to bring up something upsetting. But he must have been remarkable to have that kind of faith in you. From what I've seen, most noblemen just care about their daughters behaving politely and marrying well."

"He was interested in those things too. But I don't think what I'm about to do is exactly the marriage he had in mind. Do you know about Rupert, First Earl of Rothford?"

"Of course. All Osfridians know about him." Cedric gave me a meaningful look. "And I know who his direct descendants are."

"Throughout my entire life, I've had the importance of that drilled into me. What a responsibility that title is." I leaned against the rough wooden wall, thinking of Grandmama. "Sometimes I wonder if I'm tarnishing that heritage. I don't know."

Cedric's expression softened. "Well, I know two things. For you to be countess, he's one of the rare progenitors to let his title be passed to his female descendants. Most don't do that, which means he wasn't someone who believed in abiding by archaic rules. You should be proud of that."

"You don't need to pitch me on my own ancestor. What's the other thing you allegedly know?"

"There's no 'allegedly' about it. Rupert left a comfortable life back on the continent, sailing west to a savage land he knew little about. He didn't do it because it was the safe choice or because it was the easy choice. He did it because it was the *right* choice, because he knew in his bones that staying in the old land was draining him and he had to move on to greater things. He didn't tarnish his heritage. He was brave and bold." Cedric looked at me meaningfully. "Sound like anyone we both know?"

"Are you talking about yourself?"

I started to turn away before he could see my smile, but he caught my hand and pulled me back. When I looked at him, I felt my mirth vanish. There was something disconcertingly serious in his face. The hall suddenly seemed very small, the space between us even smaller.

"Never underestimate your own worth," he told me. "I certainly never have."

I wanted him to smile again or make a joke, and when he didn't, I broke away. "I have to go. I'll see you later." I hurried off to my room, afraid of what I'd see if I looked back.

CHAPTER 11

Cedric was nervous in those first days. He'd expected me to put brush to canvas and start instantly creating people and scenery. Those things would come, but first, I had to do the groundwork. I sketched and laid base colors, and slowly, bit by bit, the work began to come to life. Each time I finished a session, I always felt as though I hadn't had enough time. The minutes flew by, and I'd have a pang of worry that I wasn't going to be able to finish before the end of our journey.

Outside of my makeshift art studio, however, my painting time was noticeably long.

"There you are," exclaimed Miss Bradley one evening. I hadn't been able to leave the storage room until some paint had properly set, making me late for dinner in our common room. All the other girls were seated, their eyes locked on me as I stood in the doorway. On a long trip like this, anyone getting in trouble was high entertainment.

"I'm sorry, ma'am." I clasped my hands in front of me and tried to look contrite. "I was taking a walk on the deck, and when I started to come back, there was a group of sailors in my way in the stairwell—doing some sort of repair. I didn't want to have to pass so close to them, so I waited—discreetly—until they were done. I thought that was the proper thing to do."

Miss Bradley tsked. "The proper thing to do would have not been to go above deck alone." At least I wasn't alone in this crime. A few other girls with cabin fever had been chastised repeatedly too.

"I'm sorry," I said again. "I just needed some air. I get nauseous down here sometimes."

She surveyed me a moment longer and then nodded for me to take a seat. "Very well, but don't let it happen again. And that goes for *all* of you."

Everyone nodded meekly, knowing full well this would probably happen again. I breathed a sigh of relief and settled next to Mira. Since this business with Cedric had started, I hadn't been able to spend much time with her. At first, she'd commented on it and tried to include me in excursions, but she'd eventually given up. Now, when I wasn't painting, I'd sometimes find her alone in our room rereading her Sirminican swashbuckling stories. Other times, I couldn't find Mira around at all.

"Another decadent meal," she said, handing me a basket of hardtack.

I picked up one of the stiff biscuits with a scowl and then added some pickled cabbage from a serving platter. Our lessons in fine dining and etiquette weren't of much use at the moment as we subsisted on this simple ship's fare. The food in and of itself didn't bother me so much as eating the same thing each day did.

I'd lifted the hardtack to my mouth when Clara suddenly said, "Isn't it raining up above? Why aren't you wet, Adelaide?"

I froze as all eyes once again swiveled toward me. "I . . . kept under cover," I said at last. "I knew Miss Bradley wouldn't want us to ruin our clothes—or even our hair. Maybe we aren't in Adoria yet, but we should still maintain certain standards." Sure of my footing now, I smiled sweetly at Clara. "I can understand why you might not think of those things on a trip like this. But as our cohort's diamond, I find it's something I must constantly keep in mind."

"Excellent point," said Miss Bradley. "Just because we're in rough conditions, it doesn't mean we should be any less diligent about our manners and appearances. You are going to have to be in best form the instant we reach Adoria. As soon as word of our ship's arrival spreads, there'll be prospective suitors down at the docks to watch you come ashore and size up this year's group."

Those words took all of us aback for a moment. It wasn't anything that had ever come up before. I suppose I shouldn't have been surprised, however. Everything we'd done had been scrutinized at Blue Spring Manor, with the understanding that we'd continue to be scrutinized in the New World. Why not from the first moment we stepped on shore?

"Sized up like livestock." Mira pitched her voice low, but Miss Bradley heard her.

"There are young ladies begging in the streets of Osfrid who'd love to have the opportunity to be dressed up and 'sized up,'" she said sharply. "I'm sure if you'd like to join them, arrangements can be made for you to return with the Thorns to Osfrid at the end of the summer." While most of our household now accepted Mira, Miss Bradley obviously hadn't come to terms with having a Sirminican in our cohort.

"Of course not, ma'am," said Mira. "Forgive me." Her tone was as apologetic as mine had been, and like me, she wasn't sincere.

"I think if Mira had her way, she wouldn't get married," I told Cedric on our way to the cargo room one day. Long weeks had passed, and amazingly, this ocean journey was nearing its end. "Sometimes I just feel like she's here because she has nothing better to do."

He put his hand on my back to guide me around a pile of netting taking up part of the hall. Since this enterprise had begun, we'd grown remarkably casual around each other. "Compared to Sirminica, this *is* probably better," he said.

"I suppose. But I wish she was more on board with what's in store. Whatever the means, this journey ends in us marrying in Adoria. She'd be happier if she was excited about that, just like the rest of us."

As we neared the cargo room, we saw the captain and one of his men hurrying through. We stepped to the side, letting them pass. As they did, I heard the sailor say, "It's no problem, Cap'n. I can handle it."

"I'm sure you can," came the gruff response. "But I don't like the looks of it. It came up too fast. I'll steer us the next hour and then hand off."

Once they were clear of us, Cedric came to a halt. "Did you hear that?" he asked.

"Which part exactly?"

"The part about the captain taking the wheel."

"So?"

Cedric's face was alight with excitement. "So, it means he won't be in his stateroom for a while. How would you like to add another crime to our growing list of offenses?"

I eyed him warily. "What are you talking about?"

"Come on." He linked his arm through mine and turned us in a different direction from the cargo room. We soon entered the part of the ship used mostly by the crew. It made me uneasy, but Cedric walked with self-assurance. It seemed to make the crew members assume we were supposed to be there, and most of them were hustling about and preoccupied anyway.

We reached an ornate door that marked the captain's chambers. After a furtive glance around, Cedric pushed it open and hurried me inside. "I'm surprised it's unlocked," I said.

"He usually only locks it when he sleeps. During the day, most crew wouldn't have the nerve to come in."

"And we do?" Even so, I couldn't help being fascinated by what I saw. The captain's room was a combination office and bedroom and was more than twice the size of my room at Blue Spring Manor. An ornate desk immediately drew the eye to the center of the room, as did the window behind it. I couldn't even believe there *was* a window in here. Gray sky and a deeper gray sea showed through it. Brocade cloth hung around a bed on the room's far side, and other rich furnishings warmed the space as well: candelabras, leather-bound books, and more. It was incredible to believe such a room existed when the rest of us were crammed into such humble quarters.

Another wave sent us rolling, and Cedric put a hand on the desk to steady himself. "I know you once said I could sell salvation to a priest . . . but there are some things even I can't get a captain to barter for. So . . . we'll just, ah, take them."

"We steal now?" I asked.

"He won't miss it. You'll understand soon." Cedric walked up to a wall covered in shelves, directing his gaze to a closed cupboard up by the ceiling. He glanced around, expression turning puzzled. "We want to get in there . . . but the ladder's gone. There was a small one in here the last time Father and I ate with him."

I walked over to the desk's chair, but it was bolted down. Perhaps I should've viewed that as a sign we needed to get out, but I was too intrigued. I had to know what would actually reduce him to stealing. Seeing no other options, I returned to Cedric's side.

"Okay, then. Lift me up."

"Hold on, what?"

"I can climb on those bookshelves—use them for footholds. I'll just need you to get me started. Unless you've changed your mind?"

"Eh, no . . ." The shocking suggestion seemed to give even him pause. "But can you climb in a dress?"

"Wouldn't be the first time," I said, thinking of childhood days when I used to get scolded for climbing trees on our country estate. "I could take it off, but then you'd have to deal with the shock of seeing me half-naked again."

"I'm still recovering from the first time," he said wryly. He stood by the shelves. "Okay, let's go. No risk, no gain."

He put his hands around my waist and helped hoist me high until I could place my feet on one shelf and grip a higher one with my hands. I was pretty sure he got a face full of skirts and petticoats in the maneuver, but in a few moments, he was able to let go as I maintained my hold and slowly scaled upward.

"I'll catch you if you fall," he said helpfully.

"I won't fall. You've got me confused with some helpless girl who balks at dishonest behavior."

"My mistake."

Despite my bold words, I nearly lost my grip when the ship rocked sharply again. We'd had relatively calm waters so far, and today's troubled conditions had already made normal movement around the ship difficult—let alone when attempting to climb shelving in a dress.

I reached the upper cupboard and opened it, marveling at what I saw. Food. But not the dried, flavorless kind we consumed daily. A variety of jarred delicacies were displayed before me: dried currants, nuts, caramel brittle, lemon cookies . . . Along with them, mysterious boxes and bags contained other hidden delights.

"Do you see a small green tin?" Cedric asked. "That's what we want."

After several moments of searching, I found it. I tossed the tin down to him and began my descent. It was a little easier this time, both because I was surer of my footholds and less scared of injury the nearer I got to the floor. When I was almost there, Cedric took hold of my waist again and swung me down the rest of the way.

"Easy," I declared.

He started to let go, but another wave threw us both off. He held me tighter, shifting his weight so that we stayed upright. Some of the items in the room slid around with the sudden movement, but most were bolted down. Only when things calmed did he release me.

"Well?" I asked. "Was it worth it?"

He opened the tin. "You tell me."

"Honey cakes! How?"

"The captain has a sweet tooth, and after you said you'd kill for some, I figured I'd better take action for everyone's safety. Want one?"

"No, I want them all," I said. "But let's go back to the cargo room before we're caught here."

We checked the hall before making a break for it, but again, most crew barely noticed us. They moved swiftly and deftly over the rolling floor while Cedric and I had to occasionally stop and hold the walls. When we finally completed the journey to our room, we hurried back to my art corner to divvy up our spoils.

"You said you wanted them all," Cedric teased when I held the tin out to him.

"You can have some as a commission of sorts. Even though I really did all the work."

I plucked one out and popped it into my mouth, closing my eyes as that sweetness flooded me. "I ate these all the time back home," I said after I'd swallowed it. "Never thought much of it. But after all that hardtack . . . I swear, this is now pretty much the best thing I've eaten in my entire life."

We quickly went through the tin, and Cedric urged me to take the last one. "I should give this one to Mira," I demurred. "She's the only friend I've got left."

Cedric looked up. "Oh?"

"Well, I'm sure that's what Tamsin would say."

"And the rest of us are just partners in crime."

"The rest are just—oh." I felt foolish. "Sorry. I wasn't thinking. I mean, yes. Of course you're my friend. I think."

His smile was hard to read as he stretched his limbs before leaning against the wall beside me. "I don't think that makes me feel any better."

"No, you are. I've just never thought of men as friends before. In my life they've always been . . . a means to an end."

"Still not making me feel any better."

"Conquests?"

"A slight improvement. Maybe being your conquest wouldn't be so bad."

"After I got you to help me that first day? I figured you already were." I looked over at him and saw a bit of honey near his lips. Without thinking, I leaned over and gently dabbed at it with my fingers.

As soon as I brushed his lips with my fingertips I felt my pulse quicken and a flush of heat sweep over me. Unable to resist, I traced the edges of his lips, suddenly wondering if they would taste just as sweet as the honey.

Cedric took hold of my hand and laced his fingers with mine. The heat in his gaze made me heady, its intensity burning right through me. He didn't let go, and I felt as though the world around us was slowing down. I finally managed to ask, "What about me? Am I your friend?"

He closed his eyes briefly, wrestling with some great dilemma, and then exhaled. "You are—"

Before he could finish answering, the door to the cargo hold suddenly opened. Both of us jumped. A sailor appeared in the doorway, an older man with a shaved head and a slanted scar across his cheek. I was also pretty sure he was missing two fingers on his left hand. He seemed equally astonished to see us, and Cedric immediately straightened up, angling himself between me and the door. He put one arm protectively around me and rested his other hand on the pocket of his coat. The painting at least wasn't in view of the door.

"What are you doing here?" the sailor demanded. Before either of us could answer, a smirk suddenly crossed the man's face. "Oh. I see how it is. Getting a little alone time, eh? I guess Thorn's blushing beauties aren't so innocent after all."

It took me a moment to understand, and then I realized how it must look. Cedric's proximity and arm around me made it look as though, at the very least, we'd been cuddling. Understanding the implications, I did, indeed, blush.

"We're not—"

"She's having second thoughts about marrying in Adoria," said Cedric, interrupting my outrage. "She wants to turn around and go back to Osfrid. If my father finds out, *I'll* be the one who gets in trouble."

I slipped into the act and crossed my arms over my chest. Nerves would be a lot easier to explain to Jasper than a slur on my virtue. "I told you! There's nothing you can say to change my mind."

Cedric sighed dramatically. "Why won't you just listen to reason?"

The sailor's eyes shifted between the two of us, and I didn't like the way he looked at me. I also didn't think he believed us.

Cedric removed his hand from his pocket and reached for the opposite one, producing a small bag. He withdrew three silver coins from it and held them out to the sailor. "I'm sure you understand the need for discretion until I can talk her out of this. No need for anyone else to know."

The sailor didn't hesitate to snatch up the coins. I'd been right about the fingers. "Yes, sir. I certainly do. I'm as discreet as they come. You can trust Old Lefty, that you can. I won't tell anyone about your, uh, doubts."

He bobbed his head deferentially and then picked up a small crate before retreating. He gave us one last leer and then exited, closing the door behind him.

I groaned and sank back against the wall. "Great, just great. I knew it was only a matter of time before this all fell apart."

"It did nothing of the sort," Cedric replied. "He didn't see the painting, and he's not going to talk anyway."

"Really? You think so? I'm sorry, but I can't feel that confident about trusting our fate to someone called Old Lefty." I paused. "And why is he called that if that's the hand missing the fingers? Why not take a positive spin and go with 'Old Righty'?"

"He's not going to talk," Cedric reiterated. "The silver will ensure that—and future silver, seeing as I'm sure he'll approach me later wanting a bonus to further his 'discretion.' "

I raised an eyebrow. "I wasn't aware you had all that much silver to just throw around."

"I don't . . . but some expenses are necessary. And if all of this works out, it won't matter."

"Let's hope so." My gaze fell on the pocket of his coat. "What's there? Why'd you reach for it?"

Cedric hesitated and then produced a gleaming dagger. The hilt was silver, engraved with an intricate tree pattern. "A ritual blade. The angel Ozhiel's blade. That's the Tree of Life that connects all living things in this world to the next."

I was too surprised to even make a joke about him worshipping trees after all. "You were . . . going to attack him with that?"

"If that's what it took. I didn't know his intentions." Cedric grew thoughtful a few moments and then held out the dagger to me. "Here."

"It's beautiful, but I don't really want some pagan knife."

"Forget the religious implications. Keep it in case you find yourself in a situation where you need it."

"That night I got the holly, you told me to drop my knife before I hurt someone."

"Well, I was worried you'd hurt *me*. But anyone else? They're fair game."

"I don't really know how to use this," I said, taking the weapon in spite of myself.

"You'll figure it out—you've always been good at defending yourself. But here's a tip to get you started: If someone attacks you, just point the blade away from you and start hacking."

"I see. I didn't know you had a second job as a weapons master."

The strongest wave we'd hit so far tumbled us into each other. A few items nearby shifted violently, and I nearly stabbed Cedric. "Probably not a good idea to have that out with all these waves," he said.

I tucked the blade away, knowing I'd have to conceal it carefully among my belongings lest I be caught with an Alanzan artifact. I glanced around us as the ship swayed. "Is it just a few waves? We got into this because the captain went to take the wheel, remember?"

I could see Cedric considering this, that maybe we should've paid more attention to why the stateroom we'd raided had been abandoned in the first place. "I'm sure it's—" Another jolt sent us reeling, and a crate fell, smashing beside us. "I think we should go," he said.

I followed him out of the cargo room as wave after powerful wave rocked us. With no formalities or care for who saw, he hurried me quickly down the corridor, taking me to the Glittering Court's common room. Just before we entered, I pulled him back.

"Cedric . . . you never told me. What am I to you?"

"You are . . ." He started to lift a hand to my face and then dropped it. "Out of my reach."

I closed my eyes for a heartbeat as I let those words burn through me. My world swayed, and not because of the storm outside. I turned away, scared to meet his eyes, and entered the room. There, a pale-faced Miss Bradley paced, surrounded in the rest of our girls.

"Thank Uros you're here," she said, upon seeing us. "I just heard from Master Jasper—we're in some kind of storm. The captain said it came out of nowhere. We're ordered to stay below."

"I need to go back out," Cedric said.

I'd been about to sit and shot back up. "What? It's dangerous! Now isn't the time to do something stupid."

"Adelaide," scolded Miss Bradley, obviously not aware of the informality between Cedric and me.

"No more stupid than usual," he replied and disappeared out the door.

I looked around the room, assessing my cohorts. Some stood alone, fighting their fear in their own stoic way. Others huddled in groups, crying and wailing. I did a quick head count and noticed we were one short.

"Mira! Where's Mira?"

Miss Bradley shook her head, clearly distracted by her own panic. "I don't know. We'll just have to hope she took refuge in some other room."

A sickening feeling—intensified by the almost constant rolling and rocking of the ship—welled up within me. Mira wasn't in some other room, I was certain of it. She'd probably been on one of her illicit above-deck excursions. She was resourceful—but would she be able to get below in time?

I strode to the door, my gait unsteady. "I have to find her. I have to make sure she's safe." I struggled to make my voice heard above the creaking of the ship and wind wailing outside, both of which seemed to be increasing by the minute.

"Adelaide!" exclaimed Miss Bradley. "You will most certainly not!" She took a step toward me, but a wave threw her off-balance. I moved out the door, not looking back.

Getting through the corridor was a terrifying ordeal. The lurching of the ship kept slamming me into the walls, and my progress was slow. My whole world was disordered, and I became more aware than ever that I was in a great expanse of water in a small enclosure of wood. I'd never, ever felt such fear—not even when sneaking out of Osfro. Then, I'd risked the punishment of man. This was the wrath of nature.

I finally reached one of the hatches that allowed access above. I climbed upward and was entirely unprepared for the mighty wind that slammed into me. It pushed me back, sharp and cold with stinging sleet. The sky above us was a sickly greenish-gray, and everything around me was in motion. Sailors ran, following the barked orders of the captain and first mate, grabbing lines and securing loose items. I was soaked in an instant, pushed into a post by another blast of wind. A wave that seemed to reach up to the sky rolled into us, nearly turning the ship on its side. My grip on the pole held me steady, but I saw many sure-footed sailors tossed about, screaming and desperately seeking to hold on to something—anything.

Between the haze of the blowing sleet and the stinging of my eyes, I could barely see. But then, across the deck, I caught sight of a familiar form. Mira sat on the deck, pinned by a large, broken beam that had fallen across her. She was dangerously close to the ship's edge, giving me a sudden sense of déjà vu to all the times I'd worried about her standing by it. Without hesitation, I hurried to her—as much as I could hurry in such conditions. Most sailors didn't even notice me in their frantic scrambling, but I got a second glance when I passed Old Lefty.

"What are you doing, girl?" he shouted. "Get below!"

I pointed to Mira. "Get help! You have to get it off her."

"*You* get it off her," he snapped back. "We've got to keep this ship from sinking."

He left, and I moved swiftly to Mira's side. Fine. If it was up to me to move it, I would do it. I knelt and tried to pull the beam away from her but couldn't budge it. "It's too heavy," she yelled to me. "Leave me, and get back below."

"Never," I shot back, tugging and pulling more. Splinters dug into my fingers, and my muscles burned. I managed to shift it slightly, but I was nowhere near setting her free. If it was so immobile, I supposed that meant Mira wasn't going to fly off the ship anytime soon, but I'd feel better if she were below with everyone else. Steeling myself, I strained again, swearing I'd get it off her no matter the cost to myself. Nearing tears, I was startled when another set of hands suddenly joined me. It was Grant Elliott. I hadn't seen him throughout most of the voyage. He'd made a couple more attempts to talk to me during our first week aboard, and after that, he'd all but disappeared.

"Pull with me," he barked, in a tone much different than the genteel one he'd used on me. He glowered when the beam remained obstinate. "Damn it, are you even trying, girl?"

"Of course I am!" I yelled back.

"You both need to go—" attempted Mira.

"Be quiet," Grant snapped to her. To me, he said, "We'll do it on the count of three. Put all the strength you've got into it, and then dig up some you didn't even know you had. One—two—three!"

We pulled, and I did what he'd ordered, digging deep into my reserves. I felt like my own arms were going to get ripped off, but Grant and I finally lifted the beam just enough for Mira to slide out her leg and free herself. He helped her unsteadily to her feet. "Can you walk?"

She gave a shaky nod, but as she moved forward, it was obvious her ankle was slowing her down. Grant and I each took one of her arms and helped her, making our coordination that much more difficult in the treacherous conditions. Winds wailed around us, mingling with the sailors' cries. More than one yelled at us to get below, but most rushed past, uncaring if we fell overboard.

We finally made it across the rolling deck to one of the entrances below. As we were about to enter, Mira pointed and cried, "Adelaide."

I followed where she indicated. It took a moment to see what she was pointing to, since nearly everything was a blur from the storm. But then, far out on the dark waters, in the haze of the tempest, I could make out what her sharp eyes had seen. The *Gray Gull.* It was a little farther out than it usually was from us, and from this distance, it appeared to be tossed about on the waves like a child's toy, rocking precariously back and forth. Sometimes it tipped so far right or left that I was certain there was no way it could right itself.

Tamsin. Tamsin was aboard it.

Did we look the same to them? Were we flailing that much? I had no time to give it much thought. "Stop gaping! Go!" Grant ordered us. "Hurry!"

We made it below, but all we gained was a reprieve from the sleet and wind; the ship still pitched frightfully. Grant saw us back to the Glittering Court's common room and turned around. "Where are you going?" Mira asked.

He barely glanced back. "To see if any other fools need help."

Mira watched him dash away, her eyes smoldering with anger. "Men get to do everything."

"You want to go back out there?"

"I'd rather do something useful than sit around and worry about my dress being wet."

Miss Bradley caught sight of us in the doorway. "Girls! Get in here! Thank Uros you're safe."

A number of the girls were praying to the god. A few others had gotten sick, but that was a small thing, compared to everything else going on. Mira and I found a corner and sat down, wrapping our arms around each other.

"Are you sure you're okay?" I asked.

She nodded, touching her ankle. "It's sore, but nothing's broken. A sprain, at most. I was lucky. The beam just fell in a way to trap me but didn't crush it."

I held her closer, trying to hold back my tears. "You saw that ship. Tamsin's over there."

"She'll be okay," Mira said fiercely. "She's a survivor. She won't let a storm stop her from landing a rich husband."

But neither of us could find any humor in the thought. And really, I supposed we should worry just as much about ourselves as the roiling seas continued to toss us around. We clung to each other like that for hours, each of us holding our breath when we hit one of those tremendous waves that seemed certain to capsize us. It must have been the middle of the night by then, but there was no way any of us could sleep.

A lull came at one point, making me think we'd escaped, but it was short-lived before the storm swept us up again, plunging us into another excruciating vigil. When the heaving subsided again, returning us to a calmer pace, I didn't trust it. I braced myself for another return of the tempest, but it didn't come. Mira lifted her head from my shoulder and raised her gaze to mine, each of us thinking the same thing: Was it possible this was over?

Our answer came a little while later when Cedric arrived in our room. He too was pale, obviously shaken by what we'd just endured. He scanned the room, taking note of Mira and me in particular, and then turned to Miss Bradley.

"My father talked to the captain, and we're out of it. Amazingly, no one was lost, and there was no damage to the ship. It's unclear how the cargo fared, but we'll figure that out later." Around me, girls gave small cries of relief. "It's still night, and as soon as the clouds clear, the captain can assess our position. In the meantime, get what rest you can."

He left, and many of the girls took him up on the suggestion. Mira and I couldn't sleep. We stayed together, adrenaline pushing us past exhaustion. The seas remained calm, and I did manage kind of a hazy trance near the end. Mira, who must have been keeping track of the time in her head, looked over at Miss Bradley. Our chaperone hadn't slept either.

"It must be morning, ma'am," Mira said. "Can we go above to see what's happened?"

Miss Bradley hesitated. I knew her better judgment counseled we stay below, but her own curiosity won out. "All right," she said. "If we go together. They may send us back below."

She led us and the girls who were awake through the corridor and then up to the deck. Gray morning light greeted us, and we found we weren't the only ones whose curiosity had been piqued. Many of our fellow passengers, including Jasper and Cedric, stood gazing around. Signs of damage and disarray were everywhere, but the ship sailed on strong and true. Sailors scurried around to make repairs and keep us moving.

"Look," said Grant, coming up beside us. He pointed to the west.

Mira and I turned, jaws dropping, when we saw a dark, greenish line on the far horizon.

"I could've sworn that storm blew us to the ninth hell—but if so, it apparently blew us back," he said. "That's Cape Triumph."

"Adoria," I whispered. Slowly, a burst of joy flowered within me, penetrating the numbed state I'd been in since the storm. I turned toward Mira and saw my excitement mirrored in her. "Adoria!"

Somehow, by the grace of Uros, we'd survived the storm and reached the New World. I glanced around eagerly, expecting to see all of my companions gleeful and dancing. A few girls shared our excitement, but almost everyone else was subdued. Grim even. That included Cedric and his father.

I caught Cedric's eye and was startled by the haunted look I saw there. "What's wrong?" I asked.

He nodded toward a sailor who was holding a broken piece of wood. I stepped closer, trying to identify it. It looked like part of a woman's face. I stiffened, knowing where I'd seen it before. The *Gray Gull*'s figurehead.

"Fished it out of the water," he said.

"No," I said. "No. It can't be."

And that's when I noticed our sister ship was nowhere in sight. Every day of the trip, it had been in orbit. Sometimes ahead, sometimes behind, but always—always—close by.

But not any longer.

The first mate, standing nearby, gave a sad nod. "The *Gray Gull* has been lost."

CHAPTER 12

DOCKING IN ADORIA WAS A BLUR. I STOOD ON THE DECK with the other girls, watching as the shore loomed closer and closer. Vaguely, I noted I'd never seen so many trees in my life. Though Cape Triumph was one of the oldest Osfridian cities in the New World, it was clear that the wilderness still wasn't tamed. And the trees were *huge*, like sentinels guarding this strange shore. Mira stood beside me, our hands tightly clenched. Her face, as I'm sure mine did, wore a haunted look.

I should've felt excitement. My heart should've hammered with anticipation. After all, this was what I'd been waiting for—the culmination of all my planning, starting with the day I'd sent Ada away. But I could take no joy in this moment. There was a leadenness inside of me, a coldness I was certain would never go away.

"Raise our banner," ordered Jasper.

His brisk command penetrated my haze, and I slowly turned my head. He'd been as stunned as the rest of us upon discovering the wreckage of the *Gray Gull*. Soon, he'd shifted to anger, berating the other ship's captain and crew for the great material and human loss he'd just suffered. That had ended when our captain curtly remarked that if anyone was to blame, it was Jasper himself for insisting upon a late-winter crossing, putting us at risk for storms like the one from last night.

And so, Jasper had soon shifted back to his indifferent, business-like mode, almost as though the storm had never happened. The crew raised the Glittering Court's banner, positioning it just under the great Osfridian flag. Jasper surveyed it with satisfaction and then turned to Miss Bradley.

"Once that's spotted, the word'll spread like wildfire." He jerked his head toward where the other girls and I huddled together. "We'll reach shore in a few hours. Make sure they're ready."

Miss Bradley's face was ashen in the gray morning light. "Ready, sir?"

"Half of our potential buyers will be down there, waiting to see what we've brought. I need this group dolled up to their finest, showing off everything they've learned last year. What happened to the *Gray Gull* changes nothing."

"Yes. Of course, sir," she replied, her face paling further. "Girls, you heard him. Let's go belowdecks and get you changed. You're a bedraggled lot."

The others started to move, used to following instructions, but I stood rooted to where I was. I stared incredulously at Jasper, grasping not for courage but for the right words to express my outrage. "*Changes nothing?* How can you say that? It changes everything! A ship full of people just died. Half our girls. My best friend. Don't you care? Do you really expect us to just prance off this ship and start flirting and smiling?"

Jasper regarded me unblinkingly. "I expect you to do what you came here to do—to make a match that's beneficial to you and me. The *Gray Gull* is a great loss. I'm perfectly aware of that, and my business will take a huge hit because of it. The rest of you are still able to carry out our purpose here. You'll put on the clothes I've bought you and walk off this ship looking as though you're happy to be here."

I took a step toward him, undaunted by neither his size nor status. "Well, I won't, and I'm not! I get that I'm here to play a part—that I'm here to be a doll you can display for the highest bidders. But nothing in my contract says I have to shut down my feelings—that I can ignore that tragedy. Maybe you should have added heartlessness to our curriculum, since you seem to be such an expert."

"Adelaide," said Miss Bradley, aghast. "How dare you speak to Mister Thorn that way?"

"You are certainly entitled to your opinion," Jasper told me coolly. "And Uros knows you've never hesitated to express it. But you signed a contract taking on this purpose—and this purpose is about to begin. If you'd rather opt out and return to a workhouse in Osfrid, that can be arranged."

"Maybe I will."

I turned my back on him and stormed away, ignoring Miss Bradley's protests. I paid little heed to where I was going, pushing past startled crew and passengers. I reached one of the entrances to the ship's interior and moved through the labyrinthine passages until I found myself back in the cargo room with the painting. I hadn't realized this was where I was headed, but I wasn't entirely surprised this was where my heart led. On this voyage, it was really the only space that had been my own.

I sank to the floor against the wall, burying my face in my hands as great sobs racked my body. Tears of anger mingled with sadness as I raged at the world. I hated the fickle winter weather that had brought us to this point. I hated Jasper for making us go on as though everything was normal. And I hated myself.

I hated myself most of all because if not for me, Tamsin would have never been on that ship.

I didn't notice Cedric coming in until he was right beside me. "Adelaide." When I didn't respond or look up, he repeated: "Adelaide."

My sobs diminished, but I was still sniffling as I finally lifted my head.

"The others are looking for you," he said, his face grave. "Miss Bradley's beside herself. She thinks some sailor carried you off."

"Then tell her I'm fine. That I needed to be alone."

"But you aren't fine."

That previous anger surged up in me, and I shot to my feet. "Why? Because I can't go through with this charade? Because I want to mourn, like a feeling human being?"

He rose to stand before me. "Everyone wants to mourn. No one's dismissing what happened."

"Your father is," I pointed out.

A pained expression passed over Cedric's face. "He's not . . . entirely unfeeling. But he's dominated by his business sense. And his business sense is telling him we need to make the same grand entrance that the Glittering Court always makes. Once we reach the house, I heard him telling Miss Bradley, we'll take a little more downtime than usual before the ball season kicks off."

"And then we go on like nothing's ever happened," I stated. "Dancing. Smiling. Dressing up."

"Adelaide, what do you expect? Yes, my father's callous, but he's right that we're here for a reason. We can't just call it off because of what happened to the *Gray Gull*."

I slumped against the wall and closed my eyes. "Tamsin was on that ship."

"I know."

"Do you know why?" I asked, focusing back on him. "Because of me. Because of what I did. Because of that stunt I pulled with the exams."

"Adelaide—"

"I don't regret helping you," I continued. "I owed you. But I should have told her. I should have told her about my past and trusted that, as my friend, she would keep my secrets. But I was too proud—too stubborn and caught up in my own importance. And now she's dead. Because of me."

He gently put his arms around me and tried to draw me to him. A fleeting memory of our moment with the honey cakes stirred within me, and I pushed back from him. I couldn't deal with that, not right now.

"You can't think like that," he said. "It's not your fault."

"Really? Then whose fault is it? Whose fault is it she was on that ship?"

"Hers. She made that decision, and she was just as stubborn as you. We're all in charge of our own lives—and we have to live with the consequences of the choices we make."

Those tears threatened to return, and I blinked, refusing to let them have power over me. "Just like I have since I traded places with Ada. And now you're saying I need to keep on with what I started. That I need to go catch my wealthy husband."

"I'm saying . . ." He paused, brow momentarily furrowed. "I'm saying I don't want you to go to a workhouse."

"Me either," I admitted. Here was that precipice, and the choice was solely on me: Grit my teeth and push on to Adoria, or skulk back to Osfrid. "Fine. I'll go play the game and get ready."

I started to turn toward the door, and he blocked my way. "Adelaide . . . I'm sorry. I really am."

"I know," I said. "I am too. But it can't change anything."

Back in the Glittering Court's wing, I found girls rushing between their own rooms and the common room, everyone too busy with hair and clothing to stop and speak to me. Few made eye contact, though I noted several giving me sidelong glances when they thought I didn't see.

In my room, I found Mira buttoning up her overdress. It was made of a rich, scarlet satin embroidered with golden flowers. Silk petticoats in that same gold flashed underneath the dress. She looked exotic and mysterious. Seeing me, she instantly stopped buttoning and swept me into her arms. I leaned into her and had to fight the tears back again.

"You have no problem doing this?" I asked. With her independent streak, I'd almost expected her to rebel too.

"Of course I do," she said matter-of-factly. As I studied her more closely and took in the emotion in her eyes and lines of her face, I realized that her calm tone masked a swelling of rage and sorrow. She was just better at keeping it locked down than I was. "But getting shipped back to Osfrid isn't going to accomplish anything. I need to go forward, get to the next stage. And you do too."

I pulled back and nodded. "I know. And I mean . . . I really do understand what I signed on for. I *want* to do it. But Tamsin . . ." I started to choke up, unable to go on. Mira squeezed my hand.

"I know," she said. "I feel the same way. But it's not your fault."

Cedric had said the same thing. I couldn't believe either of them.

But I followed Mira's lead, trying to go forward and on to the next stage. I put on a gown of gray velvet, worn over a chemise and petticoats of purest white. Bows of glittering silver decorated the sleeves and bodice, and a shawl of white lace covered my shoulders. The shawl would do little against the damp, cold weather, but Jasper had been adamant we not go out covered in heavy cloaks.

We pulled our hair up into elaborate buns and chignons, and my wavy hair allowed fine tendrils to frame my face. On board the ship, fires were limited, so those who didn't have naturally curly hair couldn't heat up the curling wands we usually used. Miss Bradley assured us that even if we weren't done up to our regular level of precise detail, we were still by far and away more than what usually came ashore in Denham Colony.

By the time we'd finished and come up to the deck, the *Good Hope* had nearly reached the docks. Sailors and the other passengers stopped and stared. My grief still weighed heavily on me, but I kept my expression cool as I assessed the approaching shore. Triumph Bay was a huge expanse of water, enclosed by land that "hooked" around it. Cape Triumph was located on the inside of the top of the hook. A great deal of our education had focused on the strategic location of this large port city, in an area protected by the worst of sea storms, creating safe waters for docking ships. The rest of Denham was accessible overland or by sailing along the coast. Opposite the city, on the far side of the bay, lay uncolonized lands whose rocky shore made docking more difficult.

I again studied the large and towering trees, many still standing despite years of colonists clearing them for lumber and farmland. This close, I could see some of the city's buildings now. I couldn't help but feel fascinated, despite my desire to remain indifferent. There was an entirely *other* feel, compared to Osfro. There, in Osfrid's capital city, everything was old. Stone castles and churches that had been around for centuries marked the skyline, surrounded by well-established wooden houses and shops that were sometimes fortified with stone or brick. Of course new construction and renovation took place all the time, but Osfro's overall feel was one of solidity and prestigious antiquity.

Cape Triumph was . . . new. Hardly any buildings had that venerable feel. Most were made of wood, with the planks' light color showing their young age. Much was still under construction as Cape Triumph grew in size and importance. None of the buildings, even some of the older ones, were very tall. There were no castles here as a memory of ages past. The largest structure I could see was a fort far off on a hill, and it too was mostly made of fresh timbers. That lack of stone, that lack of wear . . . it made everything feel so young. With such newness and instability, it seemed as though this town was fighting fiercely for its survival.

A crowd had gathered at the wharves, by far and away made up of men. These docks too had that same young feel, though some aspects were the same as in Osfrid's ports. Water lapped against the wooden posts, darkened by the gray sky overhead. The smell of fish and refuse washing up to shore filled the air.

The sailors tied up our ship, and much went into securing it before we were allowed to disembark. By then, the crowd had further increased. I could see men dressed in finery, who might very well be legitimate suitors, lined up with those in common clothes who'd simply come to see the show. All wore heavy cloaks and coats against the weather, and I regarded them with envy as a bitter wind cut through me.

A group of burly men with guns strode up to the dock, and Jasper walked down to meet them. I gathered by what little of the conversation I could hear that these were men hired by Jasper to see us around safely. While I was used to being escorted in Osfro, seeing that squad of rough-and-tumble men drove home what a different world we were in. I'd dreamed of the excitement and adventure of Adoria, but this was still a dangerous and untamed place.

When we were given permission to leave, Miss Bradley lined us up and put me at the head of the line. "You're the diamond," she explained. "You must be the lead."

I stared, speechless. I didn't fear the attention, exactly, but after everything I'd been through, this seemed like too much. Before I could protest, Mira asked, "Why are you putting me third?"

Miss Bradley fixed her with a look both hard and sad. "Because you *are* third now. Everyone else above you was on the *Gray Gull*."

The world swayed around me, as thoughts of Tamsin and that ship bobbing like a toy filled my mind.

"Adelaide," said Miss Bradley. "You need to go. Now."

I shook my head, rooted to the spot, and then I felt Cedric's steady presence beside me. "Follow me," he said. "We're just going straight to my father, that's all. Keep your eyes ahead."

He walked down the dock, and after a few deep breaths, I worked up the resolve to follow. My legs felt unsteady at first, accustomed to weeks in a rocking ship. Solid ground had become a foreign thing. I kept my eyes focused on Cedric's back as I put one foot in front of the other and tried to block out the gawkers around me. Even though I knew there was a whole line of other girls following me, I felt alone and vulnerable. Jasper, on the far side of the crowd, might as well have been miles away. His men had cleared a space where the dock ended, glaring threateningly at anyone who dared take a step closer.

But that didn't stop the whistles or catcalls. "Hey, girlie, hike up that skirt, and show us what a real jewel looks like!" and "Did they bring that Sirminican for the rest of us? When do I get my turn?" were only a few of the taunts. An angry flush swept over me, offering a small warmth against the cold. My rage was directed not just at the uncouth men but also at Jasper. Surely there were better ways of acquiring husbands for us than parading us around like the livestock Mira had remarked upon. All that training and culture, the alleged improvement of our minds, meant nothing when we were put on display in this wild land and judged by our looks alone.

And yet, was it any different than when I'd been shown off in the grand ballrooms of Osfro? Would this always be a woman's lot?

I had half an urge to tear the expensive clothing and dishevel the carefully styled hair. Instead, I held my head high and followed the scarlet of Cedric's coat. I wished I hadn't packed his dagger away in my trunk—not because I intended to use it, but simply because feeling the cold blade against my skin seemed comforting. *I'm better than these people,* I told myself. *Not because of my bloodline—but because of my character.*

At last, after what probably only lasted a few minutes, I made it to Jasper. He stood with more of his men and some carriages, which were thankfully enclosed. Jasper nodded in approval. "Excellent, excellent," he said, beckoning us to the coaches. "I can already see the potential buyers. I suppose having half the set might drive up the prices."

I came to a halt, my jaw dropping. Mira pushed me on, into the coach. "How can you ignore that?" I exclaimed to her as we took our seats. Surely even her tight control had its limits.

"I'm not ignoring it," she said, rubbing her ankle. Fury simmered in her eyes. "But I pick my battles. Nothing can change what happened. Nothing's going to change his nature. But we can control our futures—that's what we must focus on."

I leaned back against the seat, wrapping my arms around myself. Now that the tension of that terrible procession was gone, the cold was hitting me again. I strived to be as calm as Mira, but it was hard. I wanted to go back outside and scream at Jasper, letting out all the tumultuous emotions trapped within me.

But it wouldn't bring back Tamsin or the *Gray Gull.*

So I sat in seeming complacency, letting my feelings boil within me. Two other girls joined us, and the carriage started off. I'd noted the lack of cobblestone streets here, even in a busy part of the city. The storm we'd faced had brought rain here, and I could feel the carriage struggle through the irregular, muddy roads. Once, our driver had to stop and get one of our escorts to help release a stuck wheel.

By the time we reached our lodging, it was late afternoon. Our temporary home in Adoria was a house called Wisteria Hollow. It seemed small and plain after the venerable Blue Spring, but I was told that by Adorian standards, it was a grand residence. It boasted a rare three floors and had real glass windows, which were also uncommon in Adoria. The land had mostly been cleared around it, but a few apple trees grew prettily near the front door, as well as the wisteria that gave the place its name. The wisteria vines were brown, and the buds on the apple trees were barely discernible, unlike the fuller ones back in Osfrid. Adoria's more severe climate brought a slightly later spring.

Warmth hit us inside the house, and we were finally offered blankets and cloaks to shake off the cold. A middle-aged woman with tightly bound dark hair and a pointed chin waited in the foyer, along with a well-dressed older man in spectacles. He embraced Jasper and Cedric, and I realized this must be Charles Thorn. He beamed at all of us until Jasper murmured something in his ear. Charles paled, and I realized he was learning about the *Gray Gull*.

"This is a tragedy beyond words," he said.

Jasper nodded but then shared his earlier revelation. "Indeed. It will increase the demand for this group."

Cedric shot his father a withering look and then turned to Charles. "Uncle, we told the girls they could have some time before beginning their social season."

"Yes, yes, certainly," said Charles, nodding his head. "My poor jewels—of course you must recover. But then you will have such fun once the season begins! Your promenade was only a taste of the delights to come."

Mira and I exchanged glances at that. Charles had seemed totally sincere. He might be more kindhearted than his brother, but he was also obviously more naïve about the glamorous lives we lived. I could understand why Jasper was the dominant force in this business.

"This is Mistress Culpepper," said Miss Bradley, nodding to the woman with the pointed chin. This felt vaguely like my arrival at Blue Spring.

Mistress Culpepper looked us over with a critical eye. "No doubt many of you think the New World is a looser place, where you will be allowed to run wild. But not while I am in charge of this house. You will follow all rules I set and adhere to their every detail. There will be no inappropriate or uncouth behavior under my roof."

I stared. Had she never seen the procession by the docks? Did she really think *we* were the ones who might be uncouth?

The Thorns and a few of the hired men had lodging in a downstairs wing. Our rooms were on the upper floors. We would've normally been placed three or four to a room, but with our numbers reduced, we were being roomed in twos. I was grateful I'd have privacy with Mira, but it only served as another slap in the face about Tamsin's fate.

"Change and rest," Charles told us cheerily. "We'll have supper soon and then help you prepare for the social season to come. Then, my jewels, the *real* fun will begin."

Chapter 13

I don't know if it was Jasper's intent or not, but our mourning period ended up being a good business move.

Our disappearance after that initial procession drove our prospective suitors into a frenzy. They'd seen us once and wanted to see more. Jasper, realizing the advantage this presented, became enigmatic about when our ball season would begin. Our mystique increased, and messengers constantly came on behalf of their masters, looking for more information. And soon, the masters themselves began to arrive.

I was one of the most despondent over the *Gray Gull*'s loss, but even I couldn't keep my curiosity at bay. The Thorns had a private office downstairs but would meet prospective clients in a luxury sitting room with a high ceiling that was open on one side to a walkway above. Here, we could crouch in the shadows behind a slatted railing and covertly observe the goings-on below. With no other contact with the outside world, aside from outlandish stories about pirates and Icori that our guards carried to us, this became grand entertainment for us. I welcomed the distractions, though they could never keep Tamsin far from my thoughts.

Some of the suitors came with general inquiries, and the Thorns slipped into their best sales modes to suggest possible matches to these suitors. Cedric was excellent at this, and not even Jasper could fault him. I was reminded of the Cedric from our first meeting, rather than the troubled religious dissident I'd come to know.

"Well, Mister Collins, a magistrate like you needs to be especially mindful of the kind of wife he chooses," Cedric said to an inquiring gentleman one day. Several of us were crowded above, trying to get a good view. A magistrate was of particular interest to us.

"I've put it off," the man admitted. He seemed to be older than us, mid-thirties if I had to guess. Cedric was handling the meeting alone, as was common. "I had been in talks with Harold Stone about his daughter, but then you arrived."

"I know of Mister Stone," Cedric said. "Good man, from what I hear. Successful farm, right? And I'm guessing his daughter is a pleasant, respectable girl, raised and educated at home with good values."

"Yes . . ." Mister Collins spoke warily, uncertain of where Cedric was leading.

"But is a pleasant farmer's daughter really going to help get you where you need to go?"

"What . . . what do you mean?" asked Mister Collins.

Cedric gestured grandly. "Look at you. You're a man in your prime, your career still rising. Is magistrate the most you want to achieve? There are almost certainly higher posts in the government that you'd be in the running for—in Denham and in some of the other fledgling colonies where they need capable men the most. A man hoping to rise needs to stand out. He needs every advantage he can get—including his choice of wife."

Mister Collins fell silent for several moments. "And you have someone in mind who would be suitable for this?"

Cedric's back was to me, but I could picture his winning smile. "I have several." He picked up a stack of papers and rifled through them. "Why, there's Sylvia, a petite brunette who charms everyone she knows. Received very high marks in social planning—exactly who you'd want to arrange dinners and parties to impress your friends. And then we've got Rosamunde. Golden blonde hair. Excellent knowledge of history and political affairs. She can hold her own in any conversation with the elite classes—in a genteel, ladylike way, of course."

Sylvia and Rosamunde, sitting near me, leaned forward eagerly.

"I do like blondes," said Mister Collins grudgingly. "Is she pretty?"

"Mister Collins, I assure you, they're *all* pretty. Beautiful. Stunning. Men are still reeling from the day they arrived in Cape Triumph."

"I wasn't there . . . but I've heard the stories." Mister Collins took a deep breath. "How much would someone like this Rosamunde cost?"

"Well," said Cedric, again going through the papers. I knew it was for show. He had all of our dossiers memorized and tended to make recommendations based on which girls simply hadn't been pitched to prospective clients, in an effort to give us all exposure. I had yet to be suggested. "Her *starting* price would be two hundred gold dollars."

"Two hundred!" exclaimed Mister Collins. "She'd cost two hundred gold?"

"Her *starting* price would, due to her rank. That number can easily go up if enough gentlemen bid and want to catch her attention. Between you and me . . ." Cedric leaned toward the other man conspiratorially. "Well, there's been *a lot* of interest this week. Like you, many gentleman are partial to blondes."

I'd only heard Cedric pitch Rosamunde as one of many other choices, but the idea that she was in demand was alluring to Mister Collins.

"That's a lot of money," he said uncertainly.

"That's an investment," corrected Cedric. I couldn't help but smile. He was so charming, so self-assured. He probably could have sold Mister Collins on buying ten wives. "Tell me, when the governor hosts a formal dinner and has a new position to fill, what will his wife—a baron's daughter, I hear—report back after conversing with Mister Stone's daughter? And should one of His Majesty's royal ambassadors visit, scrutinizing how well the New World is keeping pace with the old one, what will he say when he meets a farmer's daughter? Will she be able to discuss arts and music? Be well informed on the intricacies of Denham politics? You yourself are of middle-class upbringing, I understand. You've certainly surpassed that, but I imagine a young woman skilled in aristocratic ways could be *very* useful to you as you navigate political waters."

Cedric's body language reminded me of some predatory animal, braced and ready for his prey to show a sign of weakness so that he could move in for the attack. Mister Collins fell silent once more. At last, he said, "May I see her?"

"Of course—at our opening ball, with everyone else. I'll make sure you're on our invitation list when we announce it."

And that was how he left most of the men hanging, tantalizing them with the idea of a girl who was *perfect* for them but in demand by so many others. These gentlemen left consumed by the idea, soon imagining far more about us than Cedric could ever describe.

We'd been there about a week and a half when Cedric finally found a chance to pull me aside for a private conversation. "The painting and supplies are in the large cellar. Do you think you can find a chance to sneak in and finish?" The painting had been nearly complete when the storm hit, needing only a few last touches.

"If I can escape Mistress Culpepper. She watches everything we do—much more than Mistress Masterson ever did."

He nodded. "I'll find a way to get her out one afternoon. Tell her we need some emergency cloth or supplies for some girl or another. It's not entirely hard to believe—the opening ball is at the end of this week."

"Is it?" I asked. I'd known this lull couldn't last forever but was still startled.

"The announcement's being made tomorrow. This place'll be chaos as Mistress Culpepper gets you all ready. It should be easy enough for you to slip away. There'll be last-minute wardrobe problems and more men coming by to make another attempt at a private meeting before everyone gets a shot at you all."

I gave him a sidelong look. "Why don't you ever pitch me?"

"What?"

"I've watched most of your meetings. You rotate through all the girls, making sure each one gets highlighted to some suitor or another. But never me."

"I'm sure I have," he said lightly. "You probably just missed those particular meetings."

I found that unlikely. I'd watched almost all, and when I didn't, there was always some girl more than willing to rehash every single detail of the conversation. Before I could protest, Mistress Culpepper came hurrying into the dining room.

"Mister Thorn, there's a gentleman here to speak with you." It was the first time I'd seen her look unsettled.

Cedric raised an eyebrow. "I didn't think we had any appointments this afternoon."

"We don't, but sir, it's—it's the governor's son. Warren Doyle."

That caught even Cedric off guard. "Well, then. I guess you'd better show him to the sitting room." She hurried off, and he glanced at me. "And I suppose you'd better scurry off to your spy post."

I flashed him a grin and left the room. As I went upstairs, I caught sight of Jasper nearly running into the house. Apparently, word of the governor's son's visit had reached him. He might normally have no problem letting Cedric handle meetings alone, but this was clearly one Jasper wanted to be at.

All the girls gathered on the walkway above, even Mira, who tended to skip these covert viewings. We craned our necks, hoping to get a glimpse of the suitor who had caused both Cedric and Jasper to take notice.

"Not bad," murmured Clara. I had to agree. Warren Doyle was only a few years older than us—something of a relief, since many gray-haired gentlemen had graced our door. Even from this height, I could see a face with strong, handsome features and jet-black hair pulled back into the short fashionable tail popular on both sides of the Sunset Sea.

"Mister Doyle," said Jasper, taking the newcomer's hand. "It is an honor."

"Call me Warren, please. We might as well drop formalities since I plan on being quite straightforward here. It's how I am—and, well, I hope you'll forgive me. I'm no good with small talk."

Jasper exchanged the briefest of looks with his son and then returned his smile to Warren. "Of course. Please—sit down."

Warren did, clasping his hands in his lap. A daytime visit would have allowed more casual attire, but he was dressed formally in a russet coat and a vest of gold brocade. He could have attended our ball right now.

"I'm here about one of your girls. The top one—the one who led your procession, in the gray dress."

I tensed.

"Do you mean Adelaide?" asked Cedric uncertainly.

"Is that her name?" asked Warren, brightening. "She *is* the best one, right? Isn't that how your ranking works? She had brown hair—well, a golden brown. Very lovely."

Mira grinned beside me. "He got your hair right. That should make you happy."

"'Best' is a subjective term," said Jasper delicately. "All of our girls are—"

Warren smiled kindly. "You don't need to use your usual tactics on me. You don't need to try to sell them all to me. I'm already sold. I want her. I *need* her. You see, I've been given governorship of the new colony of Hadisen."

Jasper beamed, but I knew how he must be calculating. "Congratulations. That's an incredible accomplishment for a man of your age, if you don't mind me saying so."

"Thank you," said Warren, nodding eagerly. "I'm very, very fortunate. And that's why it's imperative I have an exemplary wife. She will be the first lady of the colony. Even in its rough stages, all will look to her as an example. And once we're truly established, she'll be the one in charge of all social affairs in my household. I need someone who excels in all areas—someone intelligent, cultured, and worthy of admiration. I assume, as your top girl—"

"Our diamond," corrected Jasper. "We call her our diamond."

"Your diamond then. I assume she must have surpassed all the others in every test. If I am to succeed in this venture, I must have an incomparable lady."

I could feel the eyes of my companions upon me, trying to gauge my reaction. Mostly, I was stunned. After never hearing my name come up, I was shocked at this turn of events. There could be no greater position than a governor's wife. And it hadn't escaped my notice that it had been my inner qualities and aptitude that caught his attention as much as my looks. Most of the men who'd come through here had made beauty a top priority.

"She is certainly incomparable," said Jasper. He managed to keep the sarcasm out of his voice. "And I'll tell you a secret—our opening ball is coming soon, so you only have to wait a few days to meet her."

"I don't really need to meet her," said Warren. "I'm sure she's exceptional. And I'd like to seal a marriage contract now."

"That's not . . . how it works," said Cedric stiffly. "The girls meet all potential suitors in our social season. Then they choose."

Warren was undaunted. "I don't want to risk losing her to someone who might woo her with a lot of flash and no substance. I'll put out a price to make it worth your while for removing her early—one I might not be willing to match if I have to wait. One thousand gold if you do the deal right now."

Some of the girls near me gasped. There'd never been a sum like that offered in the Glittering Court's history. It was double my starting fee.

Even Jasper couldn't believe it. "That is a very generous sum, Mister Doyle. Warren."

"I know what I'm asking is unorthodox," explained Warren, almost sheepishly. "And that's why I'm willing to compensate for altering your policy."

"Understandable," said Jasper, practically licking his lips. "And very considerate."

"Our policy," declared Cedric, shooting his father a warning glance, "is that she gets to see her options and choose. We can't just sell her behind her back."

"I wouldn't dream of it," said Warren. He seemed a little taken aback by Cedric's tone. "I can meet her today and then seal our deal."

"It would be a breach of our normal policy," said Jasper. "But I'm sure, given the circumstance, there'd be no harm in her at least meeting him now and—"

"She gets to see her options and choose," repeated Cedric. "It's in her contract. No preemptive deals."

I could tell Jasper was having a very difficult time maintaining his genial façade. He turned to Warren. "Forgive me; it's clear this is a matter we must discuss at more length. Let us do so, and we'll be in touch once we've made some decisions."

Warren looked hesitant about leaving with things up in the air but finally gave a conciliatory nod. "Very well then. I look forward to your reply—and an early meeting *before* the ball. Thank you again for indulging me in my unorthodox approach."

As soon as the Thorns had walked him out, Jasper pulled Cedric into their private office and shut the door. The rest of us retreated to our wing, where I was immediately accosted with questions and comments. I had no answers to give, and the chatter soon began to make my head ache. It was a relief when I was able to shut myself in my room with Mira. She gave me a sly smile.

"Well," she said. "That was certainly an exciting turn to the day."

I stretched out on my bed, still reeling. "That's an understatement."

"What will you do?" she asked.

"I don't think I can do anything. The Thorns will decide."

She sat down beside me. "If you went downstairs right now and said you'd take the deal, there'd be no protest. Not even from Cedric."

I straightened up. "Do you think I should?"

"It's not what I think that matters. But I know you've had your sights set high. And this is about as high as you can get."

"It would certainly speak well for my future. I mean, that *is* what we're here for." Although we didn't have to take the highest bidder's offer, a man putting down a lot of money generally suggested he had the means to provide generously for his wife. It gave the Thorns a higher commission and also increased the bride's surety money. "Although . . . it was kind of presumptuous, coming in here like that, wanting to buy 'the best' right now."

Mira laughed. "It certainly was—though even he seemed to recognize that. There was a brazen and bumbling charm to it. At least he wasn't one of the ones asking if he could buy 'the Sirminican' at a discount."

I squeezed her hand. That was an offer we'd heard many times. "It was nice that he seemed more concerned with my character than my looks."

"He already saw you. He doesn't have to worry about your looks."

"But you wouldn't take the deal. You still want to pay off your own contract."

She shrugged. "I told you, it's not about what I think. But no, I'd do as Cedric said and see the rest of my options. You can still choose him later."

"Tamsin would've taken the deal," I said sadly.

"Tamsin would've called for a priest and offered to marry him on the spot," Mira said.

My heart sank. "Tamsin should have been the one getting the offer. She should have been the diamond."

Word reached me later that Cedric had won out against his father: I wouldn't be meeting Warren until the ball. I suspected Jasper had caved in the hopes that, seeing me with other men, Warren might end up offering more. In the coming days, as the household was whipped into the frenzy Cedric had predicted, I found I had mixed feelings about what had happened with Warren. I respected what Cedric had fought for. On the other hand, I worried I might have cost Cedric the commission he needed. Really, what else was there to look for? Marrying Warren would put me in the closest position I could get to my former lifestyle here in the colonies. Hadisen was in no danger from the Icori. It was simply unsettled land needing a society to thrive in it and work its gold mines.

Somehow, amidst the pre-ball tumult, I found a chance to finish the painting when Mistress Culpepper was away. A small window in the cellar offered remarkably good light, and stepping back one day, I was astonished that I really had captured Thodoros's style. It was my greatest work. An inexperienced buyer certainly wouldn't know any different. An art expert probably wouldn't.

The cellar door creaked open, and I turned with a start, relaxing when I saw Cedric come down the stairs. He stopped next to me and stared.

"That's it," he said.

"That's it," I confirmed.

"Amazing. I thought the poppies were incredible the day we met, but this . . . this is something else altogether." He continued studying it, transfixed. "I'll smuggle this out of here tonight, over to my agent. He'll evaluate it and let me know what he thinks it'll get, but something tells me it'll be high. Enough to cover my Westhaven stake."

"You know what else would've helped with your stake?" I asked archly. "A twenty percent commission on one thousand gold."

Cedric turned from the painting and met my eyes. "Really? You came all this way and prepared for a season of galas only to skip them and marry the first man who wants you? Without even meeting him?"

"I would've met him eventually," I argued. "And I never said that's what I want. I'm just surprised you've taken such a stand. I thought securing an offer like that was top priority."

"Securing your self-respect is top priority. I didn't bring you into the Glittering Court so that you could be packed off to the first man who demands you."

"Hey," I retorted. "I brought myself into the Glittering Court."

"You're confirming my point. You're too strong, too opinionated, to just let yourself go with the first offer. You deserve more. You deserve to have them lined up in front of you. Maybe you'll want him after all, and that's completely fine—even if it results in a lower fee. Or maybe you'll like some other man. Maybe a few other men. Maybe there'll be a bidding war. Maybe someone will beat his offer."

"Maybe . . . but I find that last one unlikely. And I bet your father thinks it's unlikely too."

Cedric's sighed. "He does. The substantial sum aside, he thought it best we get you signed and engaged before you open your mouth and ruin your chances—his words, not mine."

"What?" I said, not even bothering to hide my indignation. "We'll see about that. There are going to be plenty of men who like a woman who speaks her mind."

"I agree. I certainly like your mouth." Cedric suddenly seemed to reconsider his words. "Er, that's not what I— Look. I just want you to have all your options. You deserve that."

"And I want you to stay alive."

"Me too." He turned back to the painting and sighed. "And between this, your charms, and a little luck, we might just pull it all off."

CHAPTER 14

THE DAYS TO THE OPENING BALL SOMEHOW MANAGED to fly by . . . and yet feel endlessly long.

I still grieved for Tamsin, but the pre-ball frenzy allowed me to keep those dark feelings at bay. This was what everything in the Glittering Court had been building up to. It wasn't unheard-of for girls to make marriage deals on that first night. Others would go through the season assessing and accruing offers.

"I just want to get out of this house," Mira said when the day finally came. "We're here in the biggest, most cosmopolitan city of the New World but haven't seen any of it!"

I thought of the ramshackle houses and muddy roads we'd passed on our first day. "I think 'cosmopolitan' might be an exaggeration."

"We only saw the harbor. The city's center is entirely different. Lively and busy and full of wonders."

"How do you know that?" I asked.

She shrugged. "Word of mouth."

I paced in front of the large mirror in our bedroom, a luxury in Adoria. We'd been outfitted for hours and were now waiting for the call to get in the coaches. Mistress Culpepper had wanted no last-minute wardrobe surprises.

Mira and I stood in stark contrast to each other. I wore silk of brilliant white, just like a bride. Silver lace peeped around the low neckline and spilled from the elbow-length sleeves. Tiny crystals—echoing diamonds—decorated the bodice in a filigree pattern and then spilled across the overdress's skirts like stars. Actual diamonds hung from my neck and ears, coming from a shared collection of jewelry used each year. Elaborate, often colored, wigs were fashionable in Adoria, but both Miss Bradley and Mistress Culpepper had been adamant I not wear any.

"Keeping with your theme would put you in white or gray," Mistress Culpepper had explained. "We don't want that. We need to show you as young and vibrant."

"It'll make you look more Osfridian for this first event, which isn't a bad thing," added Miss Bradley. "We want to be part of this society, obviously, but it's important you represent the Old World too—which is, of course, the pinnacle of fashion and culture."

So part of my hair was pulled up in the Adorian way, with the rest of it cascading in long curls in the Osfridian way. Strands of crystals had been woven into my hair, and everywhere I turned, I sparkled.

Mira's dress, also of silk, was a deep bloodred with a lower neckline than mine. The skirt opened in the front, revealing a ruffled black petticoat, a highly unusual color choice that had made Mistress Culpepper raise an eyebrow. The seamstresses in Osfrid had insisted it would look striking with the rest of the outfit—and they were right. Multifaceted beads of sparkling jet trimmed her neckline and sleeves, rather than the usual lace. Her hair, worn down, was adorned with a matching black crystal band from which hung strands of deep red hair that mingled seamlessly with her natural black. With Mira's rank unexpectedly moved up, the Glittering Court's heads were trying to pass her off as a ruby, rather than a garnet, now.

Mira came to stand with me in the mirror and smoothed the red locks with a frown. "Do you think these are real? Am I wearing some other woman's hair?"

"Does it matter when you look so stunning?" I asked.

Mira's expression told me it *did* matter, but she didn't pursue the topic. "Good luck," she said. "Not that you'll need it. You've already got an offer."

"You'll have plenty too," I assured her, my mind wandering to Warren. I'd been so uncertain that first day, wondering if I should have taken the deal. Now, I'd had more time to think, and I was glad Cedric had intervened. I wanted my options, even if it meant I might have sacrificed an unheard-of payment.

A call outside the door told us it was time to go. We squeezed each other's hands—no hugs, as that might wrinkle the dresses—and hurried to join the others. They too were a bright, sparkling array of jewels, some with natural hair like me and others with colored wigs. Clara wore a sunflower-yellow one that I thought looked kind of awful. Mistress Culpepper and Miss Bradley gave us one more inspection.

"Remember," said Miss Bradley. "Keep powdering—don't let your makeup run or turn greasy."

"And," added Mistress Culpepper sharply, "behave pristinely the entire night. I do not expect to see any of you frequenting the wine or punch."

Extra servants, guards, and carriages had been hired for this trip. We were put two to a coach in order to leave enough room for our dresses. Temporary maids came along in another carriage, ready to help any of us who need primping at the ball. Still another carriage was loaded with extra dresses, wigs, and jewelry, should an emergency occur. I didn't see the Thorns but knew they would be coming in their own carriage.

It being early evening, we could still see out the windows, and both Mira and I studied our surroundings eagerly. We passed other houses, none so big as ours, and I was again struck by the newness and jumbled layout. In Osfrid, even in a rural area like this with lots of land, each home's plot would be precisely laid out with clear boundaries, often with small stone walls to separate them. Everything would be claimed. Here, it was as though people had built at random and didn't seem to care about ownership. And of course, there were trees. Always trees.

They thinned out a little as we reached the heart of Cape Triumph, and here, I found Mira was right. Cobblestones covered the narrow roads, and the buildings were higher, with a greater sense of permanence. Shops of all kinds lined the streets, as well as places of entertainment—some looking more reputable than others. With evening approaching, brightly colored lanterns lit up the doorways. Groups of people moved through the street, displaying a diverse variety of backgrounds as they came home from work or sought evening entertainment. Most were dressed humbly or showed signs of the middle class. But obviously affluent citizens walked right among them with no indication there was anything unusual. And rich or poor, many seemed to make their own fashion choices, defying both Adorian and Osfridian customs. The populace was exotic and lively and impossible to look away from. In keeping with Adorian demographics, the majority of those I saw were men.

"I would love to get out and explore this," said Mira.

"I don't think Mistress Culpepper would approve." The streets didn't look unsafe, exactly, but it was certainly no place any of us would be allowed to go alone—especially after some of the behavior I'd observed at the docks. I pointed toward a man standing on a corner, wearing a deep green uniform. "Hey, a soldier. That's the first I've seen. I'd think there'd be more."

Mira followed my gaze. "They're around. But not as many as there used to be, now that most outside threats are gone."

"Then who keeps order inside? The militia?" I asked. Cape Triumph had no official city guard as Osfro did. The military was usually charged with primary law enforcement in the colonies, with the rest delegated to volunteer and locally organized groups.

"Them. Other agents of the crown. Pirates."

"Aren't pirates, by definition, breaking the law?"

"Not always. Haven't you heard how some of them walk the streets and help people in danger?" Mira's face was alight, caught up in the heroic drama she loved.

"No. When did *you* hear that?"

"I talk to the guards sometimes. It's more interesting than listening to all the visiting suitors."

"Oh. You mean the visiting suitors who'll play an influential role in your future?"

"Those are the ones," she answered with a grin.

Our destination was a vast hall on the opposite side of downtown. It was large, wooden, and plain, nothing at all like the grand ballrooms of Osfrid that were housed in ancient estates and castles. But this was apparently the largest place for a social function, and as we took in the crowds and guests gathered out front, I hoped it would be big enough to hold everyone. Our carriages traveled to a back door so that we could enter in private.

We gathered in an antechamber inside and were subjected to another inspection as Mistress Culpepper made sure our dresses and hairstyles had survived the journey. I spotted the Thorns huddled together, joined by a tall woman I'd never seen before. At first, I thought she was Sirminican, with her black hair and dusky complexion. But there was something about her that was different, the set of her high cheekbones and a general sense of . . . otherness. Her outfit, though made of nice fabric, resembled a riding dress with split skirts. It seemed out of place here, as did her hair, lying in one long braid down her back. That wasn't fashionable anywhere.

I turned back and started to say something to Mira about it when I discovered that Cedric had come up beside us. His hands were in the pockets of a long, fitted knee-length coat of a steel-blue damask that enhanced his gray eyes. I'd never seen him in that color and was struck by the effect. It set off the auburn of his hair and could have easily passed him off as Osfridian nobility. Except that I'd never met any noble who made me suddenly feel so flushed and warm.

I realized then that Cedric was staring at me too and that maybe, just maybe, I wasn't the only one feeling flushed. "You clean up well," I said.

"So . . . do you."

"Like you've ever seen me *not* clean up well."

"Well, I've seen you when you're . . ." He stopped, realizing Mira was here. ". . . when you're in less elaborate outfits. Like that, uh, one time."

"Of course you'd bring that up." I took a bold step toward him and twirled to show off the decadence of the dress. "But this *is* a serious improvement. It's like a dream. Not so much that *other* outfit."

"Well . . ." He looked me over in a way that made my blush deepen. "I guess it depends on the type of dream."

Mira cleared her throat and asked, "Is everything okay with your family? I thought I saw you and your father arguing earlier."

That seemed to pull him back to the present, and he finally looked away from me. "Just more of our usual dysfunction. We were 'discussing' who'd do Adelaide's introductions. He wanted to, but I argued it should be me, as you're my . . . acquisition." It was a term he'd always used freely in the past, but he stumbled over it tonight.

"And?" I prompted.

"I won."

I grinned. "When don't you?"

A rueful look crossed his face. "Well, it's on the condition that you meet Warren Doyle first. So long as I arrange that, my father's fine with everything else."

After we made our grand procession in the room, interested suitors would approach Glittering Court representatives to arrange dances and conversations with us. It was to prevent us from being mobbed.

"Are you making mine too?" asked Mira.

Cedric shook his head and gestured to the tall woman. "Aiana is."

Mira studied the woman curiously. "Who is she?"

"She's Balanquan," he said. "Does various jobs for us."

Mira and I exchanged astonished looks. The Balanquan people, like the Icori, had been in Adoria when Osfridians and others from across the Sunset Sea had arrived. There had been no wars or territorial disputes with the Balanquans as there had with the Icori. This was partially due to their northern lands being less hospitable and partially because they made a more formidable enemy than the less advanced Icori. Their culture was supposed to be sophisticated and rich—albeit very foreign from ours.

"What is she doing here?" asked Mira. The Balanquans had attempted some arbitration for the Icori and Osfridians but mostly stayed away from us.

"Uncle Charles contracts her," Cedric explained. "Usually, her job is following up with girls after they've married. If she sees anything amiss or any bad treatment, she . . . deals with it."

Before we could ask for more details, Mistress Culpepper called us into formation to make our grand entrance. Just as before, I would lead. My hands began to shake with nervousness, and I fiercely fought for control. I'd been announced and entered alone in countless parties back in Osfrid. I was no stranger to crowds or displays, unlike many of the other girls. They might have completed their training, they might look the part of nobility, but what we were about to do was beyond what many of them had ever experienced. Some were pale, others trembling.

Mistress Culpepper told me to go. I wished I could see Mira and get one last look of encouragement, but she was in line behind me and out of sight. Then, I caught sight of Cedric standing near the door. He met my eyes and nodded. I stepped forward.

"Adelaide Bailey, diamond," someone announced.

The hall might have been simple in nature, but the Thorns had gone to a lot of expense and labor to convince the guests otherwise. Flowers and candles, linen and crystal . . . if not for the rough wooden walls and exposed beams above, this could have passed for an affair back home. A walkway had been cleared through the room for us to proceed to a raised dais on the opposite side. Guests lined the aisle, orderly and quiet, with none of the coarseness from the docks. These were the elite of Adoria, well-dressed, with wineglasses in hand as they studied us politely. Women were mingled in the crowd: mothers hoping to help their sons, or society ladies who were simply curious.

I walked smoothly, serenely. I was the best of the Glittering Court. I was the new nobility *and* the old nobility, the descendant of Osfrid's founders. Soon, I would take my place with Adoria's founders. This was what all my struggles and manipulation had been for. As diamond, I would meet the city's most elite. I would attend the most exclusive functions. And I would pull in the highest price—and commission—ever seen by any of the Thorns' jewels.

I reached the dais, where one of Jasper's hired men helped me ascend the steps in my elaborate dress. I took my place at the center of a long table, which held glasses of water. Mistress Culpepper wouldn't allow us to eat here, so we'd had to do it beforehand. Although the next girl was making her entrance, I saw many eyes still on me, and I met them as confidently as Osfrid's queen might have.

Mira drew a lot of attention when she entered. In my opinion, she was the most beautiful of the group. Jasper might have grumbled, but I had no doubts that many men would be glad to have her as a wife, Sirminican or not. Thinking of her spirited nature, I thought the trouble might come in her consenting to be a wife. It made me smile, just as I met Warren Doyle's eyes in the crowd. He smiled back, thinking I'd done it for him.

When we were all seated, the high-society decorum degenerated a little. Cedric, Jasper, Charles, and Aiana were immediately solicited for introductions, with suitors and their representatives lining up to get a chance at us.

Mira, seated on my left, remarked, "It's going to be a long night."

Despite what seemed like initial disorder, things soon progressed. Cedric came for me and took my arm, escorting me across the floor. "Ready to meet your greatest admirer?" he asked.

"I thought you were my greatest admirer."

"I'm just a humble man. Not an absurdly rich and doting future statesman."

I studied Warren Doyle as we approached. His face was alight, and he shifted excitedly from foot to foot. His coat was cut like Cedric's, fitted and buttoned to the neck in a bronze shade. He looked like he was trying to remain calm and serious, but his face broke into a grin as we grew closer.

"If it makes you feel better," I said softly, "I like your coat better."

"Well, don't tell the poor guy. I think he'd burst into tears if he knew you thought less of him."

I managed to stop myself from laughing, but a grin still crept out—which Warren again thought was for him.

"Mister Warren Doyle," said Cedric with no trace of his prior teasing. "May I present Miss Adelaide Bailey."

I gave the delicate curtsey driven into us at Blue Spring, and Warren took my hand, still smiling broadly as he shook it. "I know I should be more decorous, but I can't help it . . . I'm just too excited. You probably think I'm uncivilized."

I smiled back, amused at his nervous eagerness. "Not at all, Mister Doyle."

Cedric gave a small bow and a wink to me that Warren didn't see. "I'll leave you two to talk, and then I'll come back for your next introduction."

He left, just as the string quartet began to play. Warren held out his hand and swept me into a dance. "You must call me Warren," he said. "I like to be straightforward."

"That's what I hear. You may call me Adelaide."

"I know our time tonight is brief. And I know you'll have a dozen men trying to turn your head with all sorts of charm and pleasantry." He paused. "I'm not always so good at that—at idle small talk, simply for appearance's sake. I know some ladies like that, but as I said—"

"You're straightforward," I finished.

"Exactly. If I know what I want, I pursue it. And I'll be honest, I want you. While we were waiting for your ship to arrive, I knew without a doubt I would come asking for the star of your cohort. Seeing you at the dock only confirmed my decision. And seeing you now . . ." He shook his head. "Well, I'll tell you simply. I didn't look at any of the other girls out there tonight. You truly are a diamond. And I can't imagine any other wife but you."

Even knowing what I did about him, I was bit overwhelmed. "Wow . . . you come on very . . ."

". . . straightforward?"

I laughed. "Yes, but I think 'strong' was what I had in mind. Or maybe 'intense.' You're very kind—very flattering. But I don't know that I deserve this when we hardly know each other."

He looked abashed and missed a step, but I was quick enough to recover for both of us. "I know, I know. And I'm sorry. I sound like a desperate fool, but I'm—you know what I'm facing, right? Governorship of Hadisen? At only twenty-three?"

"I've heard that as well. A great honor."

"And a terrifying one," he admitted. He glanced around uneasily. "I haven't told anyone that, certainly not my father, who helped secure the post. I'm glad—I really am. But it's not going to be easy, and I don't just mean the labor of setting up the colony—which is certainly formidable. I want Hadisen to be a strong place. A good place of upstanding and prosperous citizens. Not everyone will let me do that. People are always watching you in politics—always wanting you to fail. Even when they pretend to be your friends."

I didn't speak and simply gave him a nod of encouragement. But he'd touched upon an old memory, the way the nobility in Osfrid also put on pleasant faces only to attack when advantageous. Even across the sea, some things didn't change, and I found myself growing sympathetic to Warren Doyle.

"I have colleagues and advisors I think I can trust, but one can never be sure," he continued. "And that's why I need a smart, competent wife. My true ally. The one person I know I can trust, to give me good counsel while helping me keep up appearances with fashion and culture and all the other things the elite like to pick apart."

"I don't think you need much help with fashion and culture." No matter what I'd said to Cedric, Warren was dressed exceptionally.

"I'm surrounded by powerful family here—and a mother who keeps up with trends. There? I'll have nothing. Except you. And believe me when I'd say you'd have all you could dream of. Luxury at your fingertips. Complete control of the household."

"Again—flattering," I said. "But you don't know anything about me, aside from my rank. There's more to marriage than that. How do you know we're . . . compatible?"

His answer was swift. "Because you haven't instantly said yes. You're a thinking woman, a woman who can assess things. And that, Adelaide, is exactly what I'm looking for—what I most admire."

Cedric appeared at our side the instant the music ended. "Adelaide, it's time for your next introduction."

Warren caught hold of my hand as I stepped away. "Please—consider my offer. I know I must sound desperate and am certainly doing this all wrong—"

"Please, Mister Doyle," said Cedric. He seemed a little surprised but mostly amused at what he no doubt considered more of Warren's dizzy infatuation. "It's time for her to go."

Warren didn't release me, even when I tried to remove my hand. "You'll hear all sorts of offers tonight. All sorts of pretty words. You're beautiful beyond compare, but ask yourself, how many want you for your wisdom? To be a partner?"

Cedric's smile was gone. "Mister Doyle, your time is up—"

Warren was undaunted. "And how many will match the lifestyle I can give you? The queen of a colony?"

"That's enough," exclaimed Cedric, losing the civility. "You are not above the rules here, no matter your rank or resources, Mister Doyle. We've set down specific guidelines, and if you can't follow them, our guards will have to remove you." Cedric forcibly pulled me away, causing Warren to stumble and look understandably astonished.

"Did you just hear yourself?" I exclaimed, once Cedric had led me away. "I did. And so did several people nearby. You'd better hope your father doesn't find out what you just said."

"I don't care about him." Cedric's dark expression showed he no longer found Warren Doyle amusing. "That's twice now Doyle's been out of line."

"One last impassioned plea wasn't exactly out of line," I countered. "You could have been a little more diplomatic before turning to threats."

My next dance was with a major in Denham's army whose career was on the rise. He'd just been put in charge of leading soldiers out to Osfrid's southernmost colonies to investigate Icori border raids. He waxed on about my beauty, making all sorts of poetic analogies, like how my eyes were the color of bluebells in the spring. After him came another magistrate, one who ranked higher than Mister Collins. He was followed by a bishop of Uros—a man who seemed far more concerned with worldly than spiritual affairs.

On they went, running together. I was eventually given a break and sat on the dais with Mira, trying to cool myself with a crystal-covered fan.

"It's exhausting," I said.

"Tell me about it," she said, covertly rubbing her sore feet under the table.

"I take it more than a few men were fine with marrying a Sirminican?" I knew the answer; she'd been as busy as me.

"That remains to be seen," she said with a sly smile. "It's hard to know anything about them now. Mostly all they do is go on about my beauty and use pretty words."

I glanced at her in surprise. "That's almost exactly what Warren said."

"Really?"

I nodded. "That all these men would try to flatter me—but that he was the only one who'd make on offer to me based on my qualities and his need to have a partner whose counsel he could trust."

Her eyebrows rose. "I didn't hear anything remotely like that from my lot tonight. I still think that initial offer was presumptuous, but . . ."

"But?"

"Maybe you shouldn't dismiss him so quickly."

"Why, Mirabel Viana, I never thought you'd say such a thing."

She scoffed. "Well, that was before I'd heard my hair likened to the night sky."

"Was it the major?"

"Yes," she said, and we both fell into laughter.

We said little after that, enjoying our brief rest. We watched the crowd, the other girls dancing and flirting with their admirers. Most had overcome their initial shyness and were soaking up the attention. Clara in particular seemed to be loving it. She was dancing with the major, and I wondered what compliments he had for her. Apparently, he was trying to increase his odds by talking to all of us.

Mira suddenly stood up, a look of surprise on her face. "What is it?" I asked.

"I . . . it's nothing. But I need . . . I need to check something. I'll be right back."

She hurried down the dais without a glance. I looked around, trying to spot what had caught her notice, but all I saw was a sea of faces.

Soon, I was swept back up into the great game. When the party finally dispersed, nearly five hours had passed. The excitement and adrenaline had faded, and I only wanted my bed. My feet ached. As soon as I was back in the antechamber, I slumped against the wall, closing my eyes in relief.

Someone's arm linked through mine. "Easy there, my lady. Don't pass out yet."

I opened my eyes. "I told you not to call me that."

"I don't think anyone would think I was being literal tonight. Can you walk?"

"Of course." I straightened up, and Cedric slipped his arm farther around my back, letting me lean into him. Other girls were helping each other as well, all of us worn out as we made our way to the carriages.

"It'll be a lot easier after this," he said. "Smaller parties. Private homes. One-on-one visits at the house. This was just to get their attention."

"I hope it worked."

"For you it did. I had to turn away droves of them. There just wasn't time."

"Well, I hope you picked only the ones who—" I came to a halt near the carriage he was leading me to and glanced around. "Where's Mira?"

Cedric looked as well. It was nearly the middle of the night, and the scene behind the hall was one of chaos, filled with horses and coaches and Jasper's hired men. The girls glittered a little less now, and there was no need for the earlier meticulous order. Mostly we wanted to get in a carriage and go home.

"She's here somewhere," Cedric said. "Probably already inside one of these. Come on."

He started to help me into one of the coaches when a voice behind us said, "Adelaide?"

We both turned to see Warren Doyle approaching. I stepped back down. "How did you get through?" exclaimed Cedric. "Those guards are supposed to keep everyone out."

"Mister Thorn, I'm the governor's son. They don't keep me out of any place." Warren studied Cedric a few moments and then turned his enamored smile on me. "Adelaide, I know more invitations will flood your door now, so I wanted to issue mine in person. My hope is I'll get to call on you soon. But my mother is also hosting a dinner in a few nights, and we would love for you to join us. Along with a couple of other girls, of course."

"That's very kind," I said. "I'm sure—"

"We'll check her schedule and get back to you," Cedric interrupted. "As you said, we'll no doubt receive other invitations. And there are rules to be followed."

Warren looked Cedric over. "You're very big on rules, Mister Thorn. I admire your integrity."

"We'll be in touch," Cedric said pointedly.

"Thank you for the invitation," I said, offering Warren a smile in the hopes of relieving the tension. He smiled back, bowed, and then melted into the crowd.

I glared at Cedric. "It's like you don't even *want* a big commission."

He thought about it a moment. "I do. But maybe not from him."

"Why not?"

"I just don't think I like him."

"You don't even know him!"

"I know he's arrogant and full of himself."

"Sounds like someone else I know."

"Adelaide." He leaned toward me, dangerously and improperly close. "You saw how he was. How arrogant he acted."

"To *you*. Because you were provoking him. I'm not saying that I want to run off with him here and now, but we certainly can't cross him off yet. That's my decision to make—not yours." I glanced around and pitched my voice low. "We're supposed to be working together on this! I can't do my job here if you offend every suitor who comes my way."

"Your job?"

"Yes," I said. "I can read men. I know their romantic intentions better than you ever will."

Cedric's voice was snide. "Right. I'm sure you learned all about men's 'romantic intentions' after years of desperately throwing yourself at them in stuffy ballrooms. How exactly did that work out for you, my lady?"

A flush filled my cheeks. "I wouldn't expect you to understand the ways of the upper class. Between your common blood and pagan—"

"Is there room here?"

Sylvia strolled up to us with a weary smile. It was obvious she hadn't heard our conversation, or she might have been more uneasy. Cedric instantly put a charming expression back on and lent her a hand. "Of course."

When she was inside, he helped me up. As I was about to step in, he stopped me, holding my hand with his other arm around me. He leaned close to me so no one else would hear. That closeness threw me off, making me briefly forget everything but his eyes and lips.

"Adelaide, I'm not trying to—"

"What?" I demanded, my agitation returning. "What is it, exactly, that you're trying to do?"

We were suspended like that for a moment, and then his face hardened. "Nothing. Like you said, I've only got common blood. I'm not trying to do anything."

He lifted me inside and shut the door, telling the driver to go.

Chapter 15

My emotions were a storm within me when we got back to the house. I was fuming at Cedric, of course—and I had every right to, after the way he'd behaved. At the same time, I inexplicably felt like crying. Even in the tensest moments of our early times together, we'd never truly fought like that. Having left with that anger between us made my chest ache. As hurt and furious as I was, I couldn't stand the thought of us at odds. It was confusing, and my own heart was a mess.

My rumination slammed to a halt when I found my bedroom empty. I'd assumed Mira had been ahead of me since she hadn't been outside when I was talking to Cedric and Warren. *Nothing to worry about,* I thought. *She must have been in one of the later carriages.*

But as I prepared for sleep and the night wore on, there was still no sign of her. Everyone else was back, blearily making their way to bed. It left me with a dilemma. Should I tell Mistress Culpepper? What if something had happened to Mira? On the other hand, I knew Mira's ways. It was entirely possible she'd sneaked off to explore the city after all. Reporting her absence would get her in trouble. Cedric would have been a neutral party to go to, but after our fight, I wasn't willing to do that. Mira was tough, I told myself. She'd be okay.

And sure enough, when I woke up, she was in her bed.

"I was worried about you," I told her. I didn't ask her outright what had happened, but the expectant tone in my voice left no question that I was eager for more information.

"I'm sorry," she said, pausing to stretch and yawn. "I didn't mean to scare you. Thank you for not telling anyone."

When she still didn't offer any explanation, I asked, "Were you out exploring the city?"

She hesitated. "Yes. Foolish, I know."

"Something could have happened to you! Promise me you won't do it again. It's not safe for a woman alone."

"The world never is," she muttered.

I waited for more, but it didn't come. "You didn't promise."

"Because I can't."

"Mira—"

"Adelaide," she interrupted. "You have to trust that I wouldn't do anything—dangerous or otherwise—without a good reason. But . . . well, we all have our secrets. I know you do too, and I respect that."

I nodded, knowing that pushing her would make me a hypocrite when I held so much back. "Just tell me this," I said at last. "You weren't out with the Alanzans, were you?" I couldn't think of anything else covert she'd be doing and wasn't sure I could handle two heretics in my life.

She laughed in surprise. "No. Why would you think that?"

"Because, well, you're from Sirminica. And you always know so much about them."

"I do," she said, sobering a little. "I was raised among them, I'm sympathetic to them, but no, I'm not one of them. Their ways are just kind of etched in my mind. When I see a clear full moon, I think how it'd be perfect for one of their weddings. And I always know their holidays. Like, tomorrow is the Star Advent, not that I'll celebrate it."

"Star Advent," I repeated, unfamiliar with the term. "Is that some ritual full of sordid acts?"

"You're thinking of the Spring Rites—and they aren't actually so sordid. Plenty of Alanzans have strong morals. The Star Advent is a more solemn holiday."

I nodded, unsure how to feel about her actions. I was glad she wasn't in danger of being arrested for heretical religion . . . but if it wasn't that, then what other danger might she be entangled in?

I received no answers, and a whirlwind day soon ensued. There was no rest for us after last night's gala. The afternoon was packed with appointments from prospective suitors who wanted to speak to us in private. The house was put to full use as Mistress Culpepper arranged rooms for these meetings and assigned chaperones to each one. I had four meetings throughout the day, one with a gentleman I'd met last night and three who were new. Miss Bradley chaperoned two, and Aiana did the other two. She said little to me, only giving a smile of greeting.

So many men walked in and out of the house that day, but Cedric wasn't one of them.

It ate at me in a way I hadn't expected. Since leaving Osfrid, I'd seen him on a daily basis. His presence was a fixed part of my life now. A quip here, a knowing smile there. Without him, Wisteria Hollow seemed like an entirely different place. I felt like a different person. A very unhappy one.

He showed up that evening to play chaperone at a party being hosted for the top three girls: me, Mira, and Heloise. Heloise was the Swan Ridge girl who'd inherited the second spot. Like Mira, she'd originally had a slightly less precious stone, so they'd done a hasty upgrade from peridot to emerald, which allowed her to keep her green wardrobe. It was a painful reminder of Tamsin.

I tried striking up a conversation with him along the way, but he said no more than was absolutely necessary. He barely made eye contact. When we arrived at the home of one of Cape Triumph's most prosperous merchants, he melted into the background, letting us claim the attention at the party while he simply supervised.

The house was impressive by Adorian standards, a large estate with many servants. This was among the top positions a Glittering Court girl might marry into, and I tried to imagine myself as mistress of such a place. There were few in Denham that could match it, except perhaps the governor's home. Our merchant host was a pleasant, fairly attractive man who doted on all of us, but nothing special about him struck me. I smiled and made small talk but did little else to distinguish myself. If I were being mercenary and simply comparing men based on their resources, Warren still won handily—at least once he was established in Hadisen.

When we left, our host told us he'd be in touch, but it was obvious Heloise was his favorite. She beamed on the ride home, and I was happy for her.

"You three are going to the governor's house tomorrow night," Cedric told us. "For a private dinner. I won't be able to escort you, but I believe my father will."

Whatever Cedric might think of the governor and his son, he kept his face and manner perfectly businesslike. That ache in my chest intensified.

The rest of the girls were home from their engagements when we returned to the house. They were all still up, abuzz with the latest news from town—which was much more substantial than in previous days. Lorandian soldiers had been spotted near the northern borders of the Osfridian colonies. A man, drunk on too much wine, claimed he'd been rescued from thieves by two pirate vigilantes. To the west, Icori had been sighted on Osfridian lands, stirring up fears that they might march on us. Some even claimed the Icori were harassing the northern colonies. Back here, a merchant ship carrying sugar and spices had disappeared, meaning prices would rise. A pagan colony called Westhaven had received permission from the crown for settlement.

So much of the news was overly sensational that I had a hard time believing it was true. There was little fact to back it up. The only item I felt certain of was the news about Westhaven. I knew it was religiously tolerant, not exactly pagan, but for most people, those things were one and the same.

I went to bed, not interested in gossip. Mira stayed a little longer but soon followed me up. Yet, when I woke once in the middle of the night, I could see by the moonlight that her bed was empty. When morning came, she was back.

"Do you want to discuss what happened last night?" she asked as we got ready for the day.

"Are you talking about when you weren't in your bed again?"

She shook her head. "I'm talking about you and Cedric refusing to make eye contact."

"Oh." I turned back to the mirror and pretended to be fixated on pinning back a curl. "We had a fight, that's all."

"That can't be all, not if it's bringing you both down so much. If you were mad at someone like Jasper or Charles, I'd say not to worry about it. It's business. You don't ever have to see them again. But with Cedric . . . I can tell it's different. There's a bond there, something I can't quite put my finger on."

"I owe him," I said softly. "And that's forced me to make some hard choices." *Like choosing him over Tamsin,* I thought.

"Do you want to talk about them?"

"Yes. But I can't." She started to interrupt, and I held up a hand so I could continue. "I know, I know. I can tell you anything. But that doesn't mean I *should*. Not yet, at least. Some things have to stay secret, like why you go out at night. I keep hoping it's some romance with a dashing and wealthy man, but I doubt it. What I know is that you wouldn't do it without good reason and that you wouldn't keep it secret without good reason. That's how it is with this. There are lots of things I wish I could tell you—"

Mira caught me in a hug. "You don't have to tell me anything. I trust whatever you're doing. But . . ." She pulled back and looked me in the eye. "You need to fix things with Cedric. You're not yourself."

Her words stayed with me, but I never had a chance to fix anything. Cedric was gone again that day, and the schedule much like the previous one, packed with appointments. Heloise received a marriage offer from the wealthy merchant, which she readily accepted, making her the first of us to seal a contract.

Without her, Clara was bumped up to the top three and accompanied us to the governor's dinner. Jasper chaperoned us, as Cedric had mentioned, and told us that his son was out with friends. I wondered at that, since as far as I knew, Cedric didn't have any friends in town. It seemed more likely that Jasper simply wanted the honor of bringing us to such an important event.

"Welcome to our home," said Mistress Doyle, greeting us personally at the door. Warren's mother was a striking woman, with no gray in her black hair and a walk full of confidence. I remembered Cedric saying she'd been a baron's daughter, and the marks of nobility still remained. The governor joined her, and he too was a handsome man, showing a strong resemblance to Warren. His whole nature was gregarious but charismatic, which seemed appropriate for a politician. He soon wandered off, more interested in talking business with other men of the colony than investigating prospective daughters-in-law.

Warren greeted us as well, but it was me he honed in on. Clara and, to my surprise, Mira both made attempts to charm him. Equally astonishing was, well, how good Mira seemed to have become at it. I couldn't believe any man would be immune to that lovely, knowing smile of hers, but Warren was. As soon as it was polite to do so, he took my hand and led me through the party.

"I'm so glad you're here," he said. "I'm excited to show you my family's home and let you meet some of Denham's finest citizens."

Many of the guests I'd already met at the gala and last night's dinner, and I realized that although this get-together was for Warren's benefit, other bachelor friends of the governor were scouting us out too.

The house was even finer than the merchant's. I came to realize that no place in Adoria would have that old, regal feel of the elite in Osfrid. Affluence was displayed in a newer, more modern way, and once I got used to that, I could appreciate the magnificence of the Doyle estate.

"Of course we wouldn't have anything like this right away," Warren told me as we entered a conservatory holding a large harp and a few other instruments—great luxuries in the New World. "But I'd make sure we aren't in some shack either. Eventually, we could achieve this level. That's what my father did."

"Has he been governor for long?" I asked, studying a painting. It was by Morel, a famed Lorandian artist, and Warren had acquired it while studying in that country for a year. I wondered if Cedric's agent had considered the Doyles as potential buyers for my painting.

"Fifteen years." It was obviously a matter of pride for Warren. "Lord Howard Davis was the governor originally appointed by the king. My father was lieutenant governor, and together, they helped establish Denham and drive out the Icori. When my father took over, he continued that legacy—making this a safe and prosperous place."

"He's done an excellent job," I admitted. "Everyone knows Denham's the most successful colony. Money and trade flow back and forth between it and Osfrid."

Warren made a slight face. "Well, Osfrid seems to get more of the money, but—"

"Warren, dear?"

Mistress Doyle entered the room, gliding beautifully in a cream-colored satin dress. "You've monopolized this poor girl from the moment she entered, and there are two others to entertain. Let me take a turn and give her a break from your declarations of love."

Both Warren and I blushed at that, but he didn't deny it. He kissed my hand and obeyed his mother with obvious reluctance. She shook her head and gave me an indulgent smile as she linked arms with me.

"I apologize if he comes on strong," she said.

"Not at all, Mistress Doyle," I replied, even though it was exactly what I'd told him the night of the gala. "He's very charming."

"You must call me Viola. And thank you. He is charming, not that you'd know it from the scattered way he's conducted this courtship!" We strolled back out to the main party in the drawing room, but she kept us far enough away to speak in private. "But you must understand that he's been very anxious to wed. We had our sights set on one of the Glittering Court's girls, but it was unclear if your ship would arrive in time."

"When does he go to Hadisen?"

"In a little over a month."

"That's not a lot of time to contract a marriage."

Viola gave me a knowing look. "Isn't it? I hear one of you has already accepted an offer." She smiled when I didn't answer. "I understand your hesitation. It's wise on your part. Marriage is binding—you want to ensure you're making the right decision."

"Exactly," I said. A servant came by with champagne, but I shook my head. It was obvious both Warren and his mother had an agenda, and I didn't want to get tipsy and accidentally agree to something. "And I'm very flattered by your son's attentions. I just want to make sure this is good for him too—it seems like he would've arranged the marriage without ever meeting me."

She gave a small laugh. "No, he's not that far gone. If you'd seemed incompatible at your first meeting, he'd have resisted. And if I'd found anything amiss upon meeting you—I haven't, by the way—I'd have made my objections clear."

"Thank you."

"But let's be straightforward," she continued. That apparently was a shared trait in the Doyle family. "Marriages are rarely made for love—though certainly, love can follow. Why, I'd barely laid eyes on Thaddeus before we wed. And I could scarcely believe my parents would arrange such a thing—me, a noblewoman, married to a barrister bound for the New World. But, you see, he was a rich barrister. And my family was out of money."

"Ah," I said neutrally. "That must have been very difficult." I remembered suggesting a union with the nouveau riche to Grandmama on the day I'd met Lionel, ages ago. If she'd been more open to it, both of our lives would be very, very different now. "It was," she admitted. "But I've done my best to bring what I could of that noble lifestyle here. Just because many here in the colonies have humble roots, just because our towns are still rough-and-tumble . . . well, it doesn't mean we can't aspire to the great legacy of our mother country. That sort of transformation is really what your Glittering Court is about, isn't it?"

"I suppose so. Ced—Mister Cedric Thorn and his father call us the 'new nobility.'"

"Quaint." Her eyes fell upon Warren, who was chatting with Mira. She looked far more animated than I'd seen her around any other suitors, but Warren appeared distracted and kept glancing at us. Viola turned back to me. "I'm proud of what I've established here, and even though my husband is a good man, well . . . I can't forget the great dignity of those ancient bloodlines of Osfrid. I'm glad I was able to pass on some of my exalted heritage to my son, even if my old title means little here. And I'd like to see my grandchildren carry on a similar legacy. That, of course, is where you come in, my dear."

She looked at me expectantly, but I was thrown into complete confusion. "I beg your pardon?"

"My grandchildren, like my son, will become leaders in this land. Many—my husband included—will tell you hard work and character earn that position. And that is part of it. But blood is critical. And when you and Warren wed, I can rest easy that *two* noble bloodlines will be passed down to my descendants."

A strange, chilled feeling began to spread through me. "I . . . I don't know what you mean, Mistress Doyle."

"I told you—you must call me Viola. No need for titles among us, not even a countess's."

The room threatened to close in on me, and I thought I might faint. Sternly, I steadied myself, taking a deep breath as I worked to reveal nothing on my face. I hadn't come this far to let it all fall apart.

"I'm sorry—you must forgive me. I'm just not following this conversation."

"You're very good," she said. "You give nothing away. No doubt you've had to become good in this past year in order to achieve what you have. I might have doubted myself, had I not so vividly remembered seeing young Lady Witmore, Countess of Rothford, at a party five years ago. Your parents had just passed, and Lady Alice Witmore was already perfectly aware her family's fortunes were fading and that she'd have to secure a good marriage for you. You were too young at the time, but she was already at work. I recall thinking you were so lovely and that she'd have no difficulty in arranging things." Viola paused meaningfully. "But when I saw you on the docks at your arrival, I realized I must have been wrong. You look very much like you did five years ago—more mature, of course. Very much a woman. Maybe even more beautiful."

"Mistress Doyle," I said stiffly, refusing to use her first name. "You have made some sort of error."

She beckoned a servant to replace her champagne glass. "Or, is it possible you had a good match but didn't want the man? I can certainly understand *that*." Her eyes lingered briefly on the governor. "Whatever has led you here, I am glad. It was very adventurous of you, very risky, but as you can see, everything happens for a reason."

I stared off at the room, buzzing with guests I barely took note of. I hadn't expected this. I had nothing prepared. At last, conceding, I asked, "Does Warren know?"

"Of course. It's why he's so eager. Like me, he'd long dreamed of a worthy match. We'd assumed the Glittering Court, with its cheap imitations, was the best we could manage. I've met those girls in the past, you know. They do an admirable job, but their common roots often show. When I made inquiries about you that first week—and of course I did, after I recognized you—I learned how exemplary you were. Perfect in every exam they gave you, as though you'd been born to this."

I dragged my gaze from the room and met her squarely in the eye. "Mistress Doyle, what is it you want from me?"

"You already know. I want you to marry my son. I want you both to be happy and have a long, prosperous life together governing Hadisen." She paused again in that dramatic way of hers. "Even you can't find fault with this. You obviously came here in search of an advantageous marriage. Can you honestly tell me there's a better one available? One with such a future and a man who's smitten with you—he is, you know, regardless of your title. And securing a marriage early would certainly benefit you. As an unwed woman—still legally bound to your grandmother—you could very well be taken back to Osfrid by some enterprising bounty hunter. Marriage binds you to your husband. It frees you."

"Are you threatening me?" I asked.

"Lady Witmore," she said softly, "I'm simply laying out the facts for you."

Dinner was called, and I numbly took my place at the table. Viola, thankfully, was at the other end, but Warren sat right next to me, as happy as ever to see me. He chatted on about the great dreams he had for his colony and how he hoped to implement them. I nodded along, smiling appropriately as my own thoughts spun wildly.

After all the control I thought I'd seized in my life, I suddenly felt adrift—as helpless as the bobbing *Gray Gull* tossed on the storm. I felt alone and trapped, desperate for an ally. But Mira was seated far away, and Cedric . . . well, who knew where he was?

Back in Osfrid, at Blue Spring, discovery of my title would have been disastrous, almost certainly sending me back to Grandmama. Once I'd set foot in the New World, my security had increased exponentially. Even if I was recognized—and I'd never believed I would be—there was a whole ocean between me and Osfrid. For anyone to send word back and take action would be difficult and time-consuming, especially if I'd be engaged in the next few months.

Unless Viola was right. If someone forcefully tried to take me back now, hoping to gain a reward, I'd have no recourse. I'd be trapped on a ship for two months and promptly carted off to Osfro. Marriage made me independent—or, well, bound to someone else. Bound to someone I chose. At least, I thought I'd be able to choose.

Studying Warren now, I wondered if he was a bad choice. Before speaking to Viola, I hadn't thought so. She was right that instantly falling in love with anyone was far-fetched. The smart thing to do was secure my future with someone wealthy and reasonably nice. Warren was both.

But I didn't like being threatened. And I really didn't know just how much damage that threat might cause.

". . . and it helps that I've had so much guidance and experience under Father's rule," Warren was telling me. "I took part in some of the battles against the Icori savages. And even though they're gone, there's still work to be done in cleaning up Denham. Not just villains and highwaymen. There's the pirates, of course. And there are heretics skulking around, you know. In fact . . ." He glanced at the clock. "We're dealing with some very soon."

I blinked, trying to clear my head and refocus on him. "What do you mean?"

"Today's one of their dark holidays—the Alanzans, I mean. The demon worshippers. We've learned of where they're meeting, and we plan on arresting them."

He had me hanging on his every word now. "When?"

"We'll leave in two hours or so, maybe less, depending on how long it takes us to group and plan our course. I'm afraid that means I'll have to break from the party early," he said apologetically. "But I feel it's important I lead the charge—in light of both my current and future positions."

Tomorrow is the Star Advent, Mira had told me yesterday morning.

Cedric can't be here. He's out with friends tonight, Jasper had said on the way here.

And I knew. I knew Cedric wasn't out with friends, not exactly. He was out with other Alanzans, off celebrating this Star Advent in some grove or another. A grove that would very likely be raided by armed men. Desperately, I tried to keep my wits about me.

"This . . . this is so fascinating," I told him. "But you must forgive me—I'm getting the most terrible headache. It's hard to pay attention."

Warren instantly turned solicitous. “Is there anything I can do?”

“No, no, thank you. I think the best thing is for me to go home and rest.” I forced a smile. “I guess we’ll both be leaving early.”

I found Jasper and told him my story. He wasn’t happy about my leaving, but Warren’s impending departure softened the disappointment. Jasper arranged for one of his men to escort me home in the carriage and then return to wait for the other girls. Clara was deep in conversation with a banker, and Jasper had no interest in pulling her and Mira home early for my convenience.

I thanked the Doyles for their hospitality, and Warren again regarded me with concern. Viola looked as though she knew exactly why I had a “headache,” but she offered nothing but polite smiles.

On my way out, I pulled Mira aside. “Are you okay?” she asked. “Do you want me to come home with you?”

I shook my head. “No, but I do need your help. Answer two questions for me.”

She looked me over curiously. “Yes?”

“Do you know where the Alanzans will meet tonight? For their Star Advent?”

Mira stayed silent for several moments. “What’s your other question?”

“I need to know how you get in and out of the house undetected.”

“Those are big questions,” she said.

“And I wouldn’t be asking them without a good reason,” I returned, echoing what she’d said about her nightly escapes.

At last, she sighed. “You can’t tell anyone.”

“You know I won’t.”

“Of course not,” she said, giving me a weary smile. “I shouldn’t have suggested it.”

She told me what I wanted to know, and I thanked her with a hug. Jasper’s driver called for me, and I hurried off with him into the night—off to save Cedric.

CHAPTER 16

MOST OF THE GIRLS WERE STILL OUT WHEN I RETURNED to the house. Upon hearing my headache story, Mistress Culpepper immediately sniffed my face to make sure I hadn't been overindulging in any spirits. When she was finally satisfied with my excuse, she sent me off to my room.

As I shut my bedroom door, I experienced a weird feeling of déjà vu, recalling how I'd used another fake headache back in Osfro to win myself some privacy. It felt like a lifetime ago. I immediately stripped out of my elaborate lace party gown and began searching for the most practical thing I owned. There wasn't a lot. Most of our wardrobe was geared toward maintaining our grandiose image. Even our casual attire was embellished and rich. I finally found one of the day dresses I'd worn on board the ship, a simple one of pale pink lawn, scattered with white flowers. A light cloak and sensible shoes were the only other things I'd need in our warming spring weather. To make my escape, however, I put a large woolen night robe over it all.

Creeping down the hall, I peered in each direction before making a sharp right turn at the hall's end. There, just as Mira had said, was a door that led to a small staircase and a landing used for storage by the household staff. One flight below led to a hall behind the kitchen. One flight above provided access to the attic. I ascended quickly and came up under one of the roof's gables. In front of me was a window with a sliding panel that overlooked the house's back grounds.

I left the robe on the floor. That had been Mira's suggestion. "Wear the robe over your clothes going in and out. Then if you're spotted in the hall, it just looks like you got out of bed. A lot easier to explain that than why you're walking around in regular clothes in the middle of the night."

Outside the attic window was a trellis that more wisteria had climbed. Staring down, I reminded myself of how I'd successfully climbed the captain's shelves on a rocking ship. Of course, the distance hadn't been nearly so high, and I'd had Cedric to catch me.

Cedric. He was the reason I had to do this.

I swung out of the window and grabbed hold of the wooden slats. Mira had assured me the structure could hold my weight, and as I painstakingly inched my way down three floors, I saw she was right. The trellis stayed steady. I exhaled in relief when my foot touched the ground and allowed myself only a moment's rest before I headed across the property. As I did, I couldn't help but give a rueful head shake. If there was a secret way out of the house, of course Mira would be the one to find it.

A bright quarter moon and stars shone in the clear sky above as I moved at a steady jog. Warren's words rang in my head about how he was leaving soon to assemble his men. I had to hope there'd been some delay while they organized themselves in town, but they'd most certainly make that up if they traveled on horseback. Mira had been adamant about where the Alanzans in Cape Triumph would meet tonight. I only needed to follow her directions.

It didn't take long to reach a wooded area she'd described to the north. Whereas Blue Spring had acres and acres of manicured grounds, Wisteria Hollow's were almost immediately reclaimed by the wilderness. Little had been cleared, and there was no obvious path. Only the position of the moon let me know I was still going in the right direction. It was rough terrain, and I stumbled on fallen logs and branches, my skirt snagging on brush and other obstacles. It was a good thing these ship dresses were almost never worn anymore, because I'd have a lot of explaining to do if it was scrutinized.

I reached a highway of packed earth that was supposed to lead to a fork. Although uneven in places, the road made for much easier traveling, and I picked up my pace. But as more and more time passed and no fork appeared, I began to wonder if I'd misheard the directions. And where were Warren and his men? How much time had passed? Surely it was getting close to the two-hour mark. For all I knew, I'd show up just as Warren's men swooped down on Cedric. Or maybe they'd already arrived.

No, I told myself sternly. *That's not an option. I haven't gone to all this trouble to save him from persecution just to see him caught right in the open.*

The fork appeared at last, and I left the road as directed. I found a steep slope with a valley below and, eventually, an oak grove. At first, I wasn't sure how I'd locate the Alanzans. As I approached, I could soon discern the glow of tiny lanterns, just like the ones Cedric had used at Midwinter. I picked up my pace, moving at a jog across the open area of the valley, feeling conspicuous in the moonlight.

But no one called out to me, and when I reached the oaks, I could see the dark shapes of the Alanzans in a circle around the lanterns' diamond configuration. They seemed to be saying some sort of prayer in old Ruvan. I'd learned the language from an old governess. Most of the words seemed to be about stars and light and reconciliation, but the setting gave it a sinister edge. That old fear came back to me, bringing up all the stories I'd heard from priests and gossips. It was nearly enough to make me turn around and leave them to their fate.

But I knew Cedric stood among them somewhere, even if I couldn't pick him out in the silhouettes. I hoped there might be a natural break in their invocation, but it just kept going on. With time ticking, there could be no graceful way to get their attention.

"Hey!" I yelled. "You need to get out of here! The governor's men are coming!"

The chanting abruptly died away, and all those dark figures turned toward me. My heart stopped. This had been a terrible idea. Maybe they didn't use dark curses, but there were certain ugly physical ways of harming someone, especially an intruder to a sacred ceremony.

"Who is that?" demanded a deep male voice. "Somebody get hold of her before she reports us!"

"I'm trying to help you!" I shouted.

Two people surged toward me, and I started to scramble backward when a familiar voice in the circle exclaimed, "Adelaide? What are you doing here?"

The men reaching for me stopped and glanced back uncertainly. "Do you know her?" one asked.

"Yes." Cedric broke from the circle, his features becoming clearer as he approached. "What is this? You shouldn't be out here."

I clutched hold of his sleeve. "You have to get out of here. They're assembling—the governor's men. They know you're here and plan to attack."

"Impossible," said the first man, the one with the deep voice. As he came forward, I could make out long robes around him. They were almost like those an orthodox priest might wear, but these were dark on one side and light on the other. "No one knows we're here—this is private land, granted to me while the owner is away. And how could some girl possibly know what the governor's doing?"

Cedric stared down at me for long moments. "She would know," he said grimly. "We need to go."

"But the ceremony isn't over," one woman protested.

"It doesn't matter," said Cedric. "It's more important for us to—"

"Look!" someone cried.

There, on the far side of the valley, on the opposite slope, I could see men on horses charging down. A few carried torches. I couldn't be certain from this far away, but it looked as though all were armed.

"Scatter!" Cedric cried. "Different directions. Stick to the woods, where the horses can't follow."

Everyone instantly obeyed, and I wondered if they continually drilled for this sort of threat. Cedric grabbed my arm, and we ran toward the side of the valley I'd come from. For a while, all I could hear was the pounding of our feet and ragged breathing. Then, behind us, I heard shouts and, once, the sound of a pistol.

Cedric slowed to a stop and looked back. "What are you doing?" I demanded. "We have to get out of here!"

Another pistol shot sounded, and so help me, he started to move back toward the grove. I hurried forward, pushing myself in front of him.

"Cedric, don't!"

"They need me," he said. "I'm not going to run. I have to help them!"

"Help them by staying alive! Unless you've got more weapons than I can see, you'll only get yourself killed. And me."

That last part seemed to stir him. After another moment's hesitation, he turned and continued on our previous trajectory.

After what felt like an eternity, we finally reached the tree line and burst into the woods, barely slowing our pace. Branches whipped at me, further tearing the dress, and we both tripped on more than one occasion. I had no idea where we were when Cedric finally brought us to a halt. We stood there, both of us panting, as he looked around, scrutinizing every tree.

"We lost them," he said. "They didn't come in this direction. They either got delayed going after someone else or headed for more accessible areas."

"Are you sure?"

He studied the area once more, but all we heard were the ordinary sounds of a forest at night. "Positive. No horse could come through this, and we had too much of a head start on foot—because we let the others be caught instead." He made no attempt to hide the frustration within him.

I sagged in relief, unwilling to admit how terrified I'd been of being found with a group of heretics by the governor's men.

"How did you know where we were?" Cedric asked.

"Mira told me. She told me how to sneak out too. She's very resourceful."

He snorted. "She's not the only one, apparently. Do you realize what kind of danger you put yourself in? Sneaking out of the house? Going through the woods alone?"

"No more dangerous than religious dissidents who insist on holding services out in the open when their faith is punishable by death," I retorted. "Why do you keep doing that? Why don't you find some sacred, windowless basement to worship in? It's like you're trying to get caught."

Cedric sank to his knees. There was less light out here, but I could see him put a hand to his face. "The Star Advent *has* to be outside. I should've suggested another place. This one's privately owned, like Douglas said, but they've used it before—and that's dangerous. I should've been more prepared—helped them more."

I put a hand on his shoulder, moved by the anguish in his voice. "You helped them. They may have all gotten away. You gave them some warning before the riders came."

He stood back up. "Adelaide, why did you come out here?"

"Why do you think?" I asked. "Warren was bragging about how he was going to go round up some Alanzans tonight, and I knew my favorite heretic would be out with them."

"Adelaide . . ."

Although I wasn't able to truly meet his eyes in the darkness, I felt compelled to glance away from the intensity I could feel. There was no way I could tell him the truth, that Warren's words had filled me with dread, that my chest had tightened with the thought of something happening to Cedric—imprisonment, or worse. The bureaucracy of the Glittering Court, Viola's machinations . . . none of it had mattered if something happened to Cedric.

"And I didn't want to see your father steal your commission if you got yourself killed in some weird star-worshipping ceremony."

His amusement returned. "You don't know what Star Advent is?"

"How would I? I'm a devout worshipper of Uros."

"I'm pretty sure I saw you sleeping, the last I was in church with all of you."

I turned away and began walking in a random direction. "I'm going home to bed."

He took my arm and began leading me a different way. "Come on. You're in enough trouble, so let's make a detour."

"Is that a good idea?" I asked uneasily. "With them after us?"

"They aren't after us anymore—not you and me, at least. And we'll practically be on Wisteria Hollow's property anyway. I need to show you what Star Advent is. Don't worry," he added, guessing my thoughts. "There are no dark ceremonies, no heathens lying together under the moon."

"'Lying together under the moon'? I suppose that's a delicate way of referring to something sordid."

"It's not always so sordid. Sometimes it's part of the Alanzan wedding service," he explained. "Perfectly respectable."

I thought about what Mira had said, that Alanzan morals were the same as ours—but I didn't want him to know I'd asked about such things. "How so?"

"There's a line in the ceremony: 'I will take your hand and lie with you in the groves, under the light of the moon.'"

"Well, that's pretty," I said reluctantly. "But I take it *sometimes* lying together under the moon is as sordid as it sounds?"

He considered for several moments. "Yes. Yes, sometimes it is."

After cutting through more wooded areas for a while, we entered a field. It was desolate and overgrown with weeds, probably abandoned in one of the wars with the Icori.

"This should be open enough," Cedric said, though I noticed he stopped near the tree line so we weren't entirely exposed.

He spread his cloak out on the ground and lay down on one side, gesturing for me to do the same. Puzzled, I gingerly crouched down and then stretched out beside him. There wasn't a lot of room. He pointed.

"Look up. Away from the moon."

I did. At first, I saw nothing but the stars set across the darkness of the sky. It reminded me of Blue Spring, with so many more stars visible than around the lights of Osfro. I was about to ask him what I was looking for when I saw a streak of light in the sky. I gasped, and another soon followed.

"A shooting star," I said, delighted as I saw another. "Is that why you're out here? How did you know?" I'd seen one as a child, completely by chance.

"It happens every year around this time. I never know the exact dates, but the astronomers figure it out. We say they're the tears of the six wayward angels, weeping for their estrangement from the great god Uros."

Another star streaked above us. "You worship Uros?"

"Of course. He's the sky father. We acknowledge that—just as the orthodox do. And we pray during Star Advent that Uros and *all* the angels, glorious and wayward, will be reconciled. It's a time for us too to put away grudges and find peace."

I watched the stars. "I'd like to find peace with you. I'm sorry for what I said after the gala."

He sighed. "No, I'm sorry. You were right—Warren Doyle is a good match. His . . . approach rubbed me the wrong way, but that doesn't mean there's anything amiss."

"Eh . . . well, that might not exactly be true."

I told Cedric about the revelations at the party. Aghast, he propped himself up on one elbow and stared down at me. His body seemed to be only a heartbeat away from mine.

"What? Why are you only just mentioning this?"

"Well," I said drily, "I was kind of busy saving you and your heretic friends."

"Adelaide, this is . . . I don't know. This is bad."

"Yes . . . or is it?" I asked. "I mean, I didn't like her manner, but I was already considering Warren. I don't know."

"Before, it was your choice. Now, it's becoming blackmail."

"If I married him, she'd have no motivation to sell me out."

"But she'd always hold that over you. Someone who's threatening to do it now will never let that go. And if she does tell now . . ."

"Then some enterprising scoundrel in hope of a bounty carries me back to Osfrid. Unless I get the security of marriage—with Warren or someone else."

"I'll marry you myself before I let you do that." There was a hardness to his voice, no joking.

I still managed a laugh, but there was a catch in it. Maybe it was because of the earlier excitement. Maybe it was because we were lying out alone under the stars. Maybe it was simply the boldness of what he'd said—and what it would mean.

"Last I checked, you aren't in a position to 'let' me do anything." He was so close to me, his body leaning into mine. I could see the lines of his face, the shape of his lips. And of course, I could smell that damned vetiver. "Besides, what use could an art-forging, renegade noble possibly be to some tree-worshipping—"

I can't say the kiss was entirely unexpected. And I can't say I hadn't wanted it.

There was a hesitancy to it at first, as though he worried I might protest. He should've known better. I parted my lips and heard a small sound of surprise catch in his throat. And then all nervousness between us vanished. I'd say I yielded to him, except I was every bit as aggressive as he was. I wrapped my arms around his neck to pull him closer, crushing his lips to mine. It was the great release of months and months of pent-up . . . attraction? Lust? A deeper feeling? Whatever it was, I let it sweep me away.

I'd shared a few polite kisses in ballroom corners that seemed to belong to some other world. There was nothing polite here. It was hungry and consuming, almost an attempt by each of us to possess the other. I felt my whole body respond when he shifted his over mine. One of his hands cupped my face, and the other rested on my hip.

After years of virtue lectures, I'd always wondered how silly girls could give theirs up. Now, I understood.

When he brought his mouth down to my neck, trailing kisses to my collarbone, I thought I would melt. We clung to each other in the night, struggling to get closer and closer. Though all our clothes remained on, at one point I ended up on top of him, uncaring that it hiked my skirt up to my knee. He tangled his fingers in my hair as we kissed, freeing it from the carefully placed pins.

Then, at last, I paused for breath, managing to sit up—albeit in a very brazen way that still straddled his hips. He ran his fingers along the side of my face, tracing my cheekbone before sliding back to the unruly waves of my hair.

"Disheveled," I said, smoothing his own hair back. "Just like you always wanted."

"I . . . have wanted a lot more than that," he admitted, voice husky. But he dropped his hand with a sigh. "But your future husband won't thank me for this."

"'Future' being the important word. I don't have a husband yet. And until I do, I can make my own choice." I considered that for a few moments. "Actually, I intend to make my own choices even after I have a husband."

"I'm sure you do, but I'm also pretty sure my father would have some very, uh, strong opinions about this. We're your caretakers—your guardians. We're supposed to protect you and support you until you can move on to some extravagant marriage offer."

Words I'd heard so many times. "And get you an equally extravagant commission."

He sat up, gently shifting me off him. "I don't care about that."

I thought about our original plan. I thought about the riders in the night and the gunshots. Cedric needed to get out of here.

"I care about it," I said softly. "Have you had any luck with the painting?"

"Not exactly. No one really doubts its authenticity. But Walter—

my agent—is having trouble finding anyone with enough money."

I stood up and brushed off my skirt, more out of habit than anything else. "Then I guess it's up to me to secure your stake."

"Don't do anything you don't want," he warned, joining me and shaking out the cloak.

My heart still beat rapidly. *I want you,* I thought. *I want you to kiss me again and lay me back down in that field.*

But although my body was heated, my mind was cool. Maybe I was free to do what I wanted right now, but he was right that there would be terrible, terrible consequences if there was any whisper of what had just happened between us. We slowly continued our walk back to the house, both of us lost in thought. I hardened myself. Marriage wasn't about love and wanting. It was about business, and I needed to get back to that business. One slip could be forgiven, but not a second one—no matter what my heart wanted to tell me. And right now, it had a lot to say.

Cedric was apparently thinking along the same lines when Wisteria Hollow came into sight. We stopped on the far edge of the property, and he looked back down at me. "What do you want to do about Warren?"

"I don't know. I mean, I don't want to marry into that situation, but—"

"Then don't," he said firmly. "That's all I had to hear."

I eyed him warily. "What are you going to do?"

"Protect you from him. Keep him out of your schedule and put other suitors in. Maybe there'll be someone else you like."

I supposed he was right, but as we stood there, I doubted it. Because suddenly, I was pretty sure why every gentleman I'd met in the last week had seemed so lackluster. I was comparing everyone to Cedric—and there was no comparison.

"Your father isn't going to like your excluding Warren," I warned. "He'll fight you on it."

"Probably. But remember, it's always your choice. You can choose someone else—someone not holding a secret over you—even if he doesn't have as much money to give."

When we reached the house, Cedric told me he'd be going around to the front door and that no one would think anything of him coming in late after allegedly being out on the town with friends.

"Really?" I asked, unable to hide my bitterness. "How nice, to have no limitations on your movements. Meanwhile, every move we girls make is scrutinized."

"Hey, our job is to protect your virtue . . ."

Faint light from the house illuminated his features, and I saw his smile fade as he reflected that he had not, perhaps, done such a good job at that tonight.

"Well," I said. "At least your intentions were good."

"That depends on which intentions you're talking about." He shoved his hands in his coat pockets and looked up at the sky, his gaze resting on the moon. "Do you know why the six wayward angels fell?"

"I know what the priests say. It's probably not what you'll say."

"Alanziel and Deanziel were the first two to rebel. They fell in love, but that wasn't allowed, not for angels. They were supposed to be above human passions, but their love was so great, they were willing to defy the laws of gods and men. Uros banished them, and the other four wayward angels soon followed. They refused to close themselves off to emotion. They wanted to embrace the feelings within them and guide mortals to do the same."

I held my breath as he spoke, not sure what I was waiting for.

Cedric pointed at the moon. "Uros didn't just ban Alanziel and Deanziel from the divine realms for succumbing to their passions. They were banned from each other too. She is the sun, and he is the moon. And they're never together. Sometimes, at the right time of day, they can catch a glimpse of each other across the sky. Nothing more."

I exhaled. "What about during an eclipse?"

He took so long to answer that I thought he hadn't heard me. Then: "Those don't really happen every day."

"Seems like it'd only need to happen once."

He turned from the moon, and although his face was shadowed, I was pretty sure I could see him smiling. The tension between us faded—for now, at least. "Are we still talking about Alanziel and Deanziel?" he asked.

"How should I know? You're the heretic, not me."

"Right. You're just the daring escape artist who saves heretics like me. Now, tell me how you plan on getting back into the house." When I showed him the trellis I'd be climbing up, he was astonished. "That?"

I straightened up proudly. "Sure, why not? I told you a long time ago I can do stuff like this. And Mira does it all the time."

He winced. "I don't even want to know. And I guess I shouldn't be surprised. You're fearless. She's fearless. There's no going against either of you."

With a jolt, I remembered the old rumors. He'd acted very self-assured back there under the stars, with hands and lips that knew exactly what they were doing. It seemed naïve to think that, between his goings-on at the university and with the Alanzans, he wouldn't have some experience with women. But the idea that I might have been preceded by my best friend was particularly troubling.

I nearly asked him then and there. Instead, we bid each other an awkward good night, pointedly keeping distance between us. He watched me scale the trellis until I was safely in the attic before going on his own way. I reclaimed the robe and made it back to my room without detection.

Mira sat up in bed when I entered. Apparently I wasn't the only one who had trouble sleeping when friends were out doing foolish things.

"Did you get what you needed?" was all she asked.

It was a difficult question to answer, one that could have a lot of different meanings tonight.

"I don't know that I ever will," I replied.

CHAPTER 17

CEDRIC HELD TO HIS WORD ABOUT KEEPING ME AWAY from Warren. He didn't appear on the schedule for the next few days. I encountered him once on an outing into town with the other girls, but it was too brief and too public for him to go off on one of his impassioned pleas. He made no secret of how excited he was to see me, and I responded as politely as I could, even as he bragged about how they'd arrested three Alanzans the night of the Star Advent—something that caused me pain because I knew it caused Cedric pain. On the bright side, there was no sign of his mother or any indication she was acting upon her threat.

I should have been pleased with this development. I should have used this time to think about my next move and how best to navigate these uncertain waters Viola Doyle had cast me into.

But mostly, I just thought about Cedric.

If I was being honest with myself, Cedric had been on my mind since the moment we met. I'd just worked to keep my feelings pushed off to the side of my mind. But now that I'd unlocked my heart and admitted to those feelings . . . well, now there was no keeping him out of my head. I found myself constantly replaying every moment from that night under the stars. The exact moment our lips had met. The way his fingers had loosened my hair. The boldness of his hand moving up to the side of my thigh—but never any farther.

Sometimes, at the right time of day, they can catch a glimpse of each other across the sky. Nothing more.

I couldn't sleep. I could hardly eat. I moved around in a glorious haze, high on the thrill of what had happened between us, even though that high was dampened by the knowledge it wouldn't—that it couldn't—happen again.

At least he never told me it was a mistake. I always remembered that cautionary tale Tamsin had told us, about the girl she knew in Osfro who'd given up a lot more than kisses to a man who'd promised her everything, only to later tell her it had been a "misunderstanding."

But Cedric never spoke of regrets or any other humiliating excuses. In some ways, that made it worse. It meant that he didn't think it was a mistake. And I didn't either. Neither of us could deny, however, that it complicated things.

So, really, we found it best to speak as little as possible to each other—not because of any animosity but because we simply didn't trust ourselves. One day, however, communication was unavoidable. Several of us were about to go to a party, and he pulled me aside while the others were distracted. We stood several inches apart, and I counted every single one of them.

"I've found someone for you," he told me, casting a quick look back at the doorway. "A good man—I could tell when I spoke to him. And then I verified it with some sources who know his servants. You can always tell a lot about someone by their servants." Cedric hesitated. "And he's very . . . candid. Amusing. I thought . . . well, I thought you'd like that too."

Awkwardness joined the electric attraction between us. It was more than a little weird to have the man I so desperately wanted finding a suitable husband for me.

"Thank you for that," I said, not sure what else to say.

"He's out of town right now, but I've arranged for you to meet at the end of the week. There's just one problem . . ."

I couldn't help but smile. "Cedric, there are a *lot* of problems."

"Don't I know it. But he's . . . well, he's a lawyer. Still getting established. His house in town is small. Nice—but small. And he has only two servants."

"I see." A lawyer, while a respectable position here in the colonies, would not provide the luxury that, say, a plantation owner or shipping magnate would. Certainly not what a governor might offer. Two servants meant I'd most likely be helping with some of the household tasks.

"You'd always be provided for," said Cedric quickly. "You'd be comfortable—still part of some social events. Not the top-tier ones . . . but some. And I've heard he's good. He'll most likely advance, maybe even move into a government position over time. It would be an outstanding match for many of the girls here."

"But not necessarily the diamond."

"No," he agreed. "And he was uncertain you'd even want him—or that he could afford you. He could just afford your minimum bride price if he borrows, but there's no promise of surety money. I convinced him you'd be worth it."

I felt an ache in my chest. "Of course you did. You can sell salvation to a priest."

He winced. "Adelaide, I know it's not what you'd want—"

"No," I interrupted. "It's perfect. I'd rather live humbly with a man I can respect—maybe even like—than be pampered by someone who holds a sword over my head."

"You will like him—" The words caught in Cedric's throat.

I nearly reached for him but drew back before something happened I might not be able to control. I clenched my hand into a fist at my side. From the other room, I heard someone calling my name. Cedric and I stood together for a heartbeat, saying a million silent things, and then turned to join the others.

Mistress Culpepper clucked in disapproval when she saw me. "Adelaide, where is your jewelry? You've been forgetful all week—highly inappropriate for a girl of your rank."

"Sorry, Mistress Culpepper." My memory was so filled with details of a forbidden night, I supposed it had little room for much more.

Mistress Culpepper snatched the diamond necklace from a servant's hand and held it out to Cedric. "Mister Thorn, can you put this on her? I swear if we make it there in time, it will be nothing short of a miracle! Now stand still. Honestly, between the missing wigs and now this, how many more things can go wrong tonight?" That last part was spoken to Rosamunde, who'd snapped a corset string. Mistress Culpepper was frantically trying to replace it.

Cedric stood frozen for a few moments, holding the necklace in his hand. It was made of teardrop-shaped diamonds, which I found appropriate. Not wanting to draw attention, he finally stepped behind me and placed the circlet around my neck. I held my breath, amazed that the whole room couldn't see the effect he had on me. His body was right up against mine, and his hands trembled as he tried to fasten the necklace's clasp. When he finally managed it, he smoothed the chain and brushed a few wayward tendrils of hair out of the way. His fingertips were as light as a feather, but I felt goose bumps break out along my skin. I didn't exhale until he backed away.

At the end of the week, I finally had an opportunity to meet this lawyer at a party hosted by the Thorns. Several girls had offers now, and although Jasper wasn't particularly concerned about the others, he'd decided to gather some of his favorite potential suitors all in one place as a way to further interest. A number of the most prominent Cape Triumph citizens had been invited, in the hopes we'd impress them and increase the buzz.

The guests began arriving at Wisteria Hollow well before dinner, and we were ready to charm them. Well, at least the others were. Although I'd been nothing but proper and pleasant at recent functions, developments with Cedric had made me even more uninterested in others than usual. I offered up no more than was expected of me and had once overheard a gentleman say, "That diamond girl is a lot duller than I expected."

In another act of absentmindedness, I'd forgotten to put on rouge tonight. It seemed a minor thing, particularly since I wore so little anyway, but an already-stressed Mistress Culpepper acted as though the ruin of modern civilization was upon us. She ordered me back to my room, telling me to take the servants' stairs in the back, lest anyone see my terrible breach of fashion.

As I moved through the kitchen, I overheard two men arguing in one of the food storage rooms. The kitchen staff was busy and barely noticed me as I lingered outside the door to eavesdrop.

"What do you mean he's coming? He wasn't put on the guest list!" Cedric exclaimed.

"You mean *you* didn't put him on the guest list," Jasper snapped. "I don't know what you're playing at, but don't think I haven't noticed you cutting him out of her calendar! If you're going to ruin this deal for us, then I need to take charge and fix things."

"He's not a good match for her," Cedric said. "And she doesn't like him."

"How could she, when she's barely gotten a chance to talk to him? Now get out there and be a charming host, and don't screw this up any further!"

Jasper came storming out, and I shrank off to the side before he could see me. I stepped forward when Cedric appeared.

"I assume you were talking about Warren?"

"Yes," he growled, anger sparking in his eyes. "I'm sorry. I didn't have anything to do with it—but don't let it bother you. You don't have to talk to him tonight, and if he tries to monopolize you, I'll distract him."

"Well, as friendly as things have been between you, I'm sure that won't be hard," I said.

"I'll take care of it," he insisted. "You just worry about getting to know Mister Adelton."

He waited for me to get my rouge and then walked with me to the drawing room. We came to an uncomfortable halt at the doorway. Etiquette dictated a gentleman in his position—one who was my guardian, of sorts—escort me into the room. He offered his arm, and I slipped my hand through it. As soon as I did, I felt that jolt of electricity go through me. Cedric took a deep breath, equally affected.

"We can do this," he said. "We're both strong. We can do it."

To my dismay, I saw Warren hadn't come alone—his mother was with him. When he spied me from across the room, he lit up and began working his way toward me through the crowd. Cedric immediately made an abrupt turn and hurried me over to a corner where a thin man with sandy-colored hair stood sipping brandy. He was nice enough looking, though not as dashingly handsome as Cedric—but then, who could be?

"Mister Nicholas Adelton," announced Cedric. "May I present Miss Adelaide Bailey."

Nicholas took my hand with a smile. "Miss Bailey, the reports I heard of you don't do you justice—which is astonishing, considering how effusive Mister Thorn was in his description."

I smiled back. "He's a salesman, Mister Adelton. It's his job."

"Most of the salesmen I've met sell nothing but snake oil. Something tells me that—"

He was interrupted when Warren finally made his way to us. "Adelaide! I feel like it's been forever since I've seen you."

The charm I'd started to turn on for Nicholas instantly faded. "Mister Doyle," I said, responding formally to his use of my first name. "How nice that you could come."

He glanced over at Nicholas. "I'm sorry to interrupt, but it's imperative that I—"

Cedric swiftly stepped forward and moved to Warren's side, blocking me from him. "Mister Doyle! I'm so glad you're here."

Warren gave him a wary look. "You are?"

"Yes. There are all sorts of rumors about the Lorandians amassing soldiers on the borders of the northwestern colonies—some even harassing the forts up there. I was hoping you could provide some insight—after all, I've heard that no one in town is more knowledgeable about the Lorandians than you. You stayed with them back on the continent, didn't you? I assume you must still know something of their affairs—unless you've let yourself get out of date."

"Well, I . . ." Warren grew uncertain, torn between his ardent pursuit of me and the irresistible lure of Cedric's suggestion that Warren might be lacking in knowledge. Cedric pounced on that indecision and physically steered Warren away.

"Come, let's get a drink and discuss it further. We don't want to bore these two with politics." And within moments, he had Warren halfway across the room.

Nicholas watched them with amusement. "He's *very* good at his job. I imagine it's tougher than it looks."

"Yes," I agreed a bit sadly.

He focused back on me. "But I imagine this is a tough job for you too. It must be like being on stage, right? Always on display, never showing weakness. Looking at you all tonight . . . it's kind of incredible. Every detail perfect. But do you ever feel like . . . well, forgive me if this is offensive, do you ever feel like commodities for sale in some shop window?"

It took me a moment to answer. We were coming upon the third week of our social season, and no man had ever thought to ask me anything like that. "Yes," I admitted. "All the time."

That honesty unlocked an ease between us, and we fell into avid conversation. I saw that Cedric was right about Nicholas being candid and funny, and he seemed to appreciate those qualities in me as well. We even talked a little about his legal practice, and I could tell he was surprised that I was so informed about law and politics. Under any other circumstances, I could have easily been this man's friend. Because despite how interesting he was, he mustered nothing more than fond feelings within me. But he was the most appealing of all the suitors I'd met so far. I shouldn't have been surprised, considering Cedric had handpicked him. Cedric knew me that well. And as the night progressed, I tried to decide: If I couldn't give Nicholas my love, could I give him a happy enough marriage? It would be unfair otherwise.

At dinner, Cedric contrived to have Nicholas sit beside me—with Warren far down at the other end. He would occasionally shoot me pining looks, while Viola simply glared daggers. On the other side of me was an older gentleman, grumbling about how Cape Triumph was "falling into chaos."

"Anarchy," he told Nicholas and me. "That's what's happening here. The governor needs to get control before these miscreants take over. Did you hear that those Alanzan heretics they caught last week have already escaped from jail? And where is the army? Why are more and more soldiers going to other colonies? Icori are amassing in the west—they haven't left, no matter what those fools say. Then there's the pirates. A royal tax ship bound for Osfrid was taken last week. The nerve."

"I don't think anyone was too upset," remarked Nicholas. "At least not in the colonies. Too many think we're overtaxed as it is."

"It's about the larger picture," the man insisted. "If the king's ships aren't off-limits, then what is? Pirates don't even stick to the seas anymore. I hear those devils walk the street now. Billy Marshall. Bones Jacobi. Tim Shortsleeves."

"I believe his name is Tom Shortsleeves. And don't forget there are some lady pirates as well," I said. Mira lived for the stories of Cape Triumph's pirates and kept me informed. If one of them had made an offer to her, she probably would've been married by now. "Joanna Steel. Lady Aviel."

"And if the stories are true, they've saved a number of innocents," added Nicholas. "From thieves and whatnot."

The other man frowned. "Yes, and that's all well and good . . . but they're still outlaws! And having *women* involved . . . with swords? Can you even imagine such a thing? What's to become of this world if such a thing catches on?"

"Indeed," said Nicholas, deadpan. "If women start defending themselves, what use will they have for us?"

I had to cough to cover a laugh. This drew my neighbor's attention to me, and I groped for a response. "Well . . . at least I hear they dress well. They aren't shoddy pirates. What is it they say? Golden cloaks, peacock feathers. It all sounds very flashy to me."

"I've never trusted peacocks," growled the man. "Everyone goes on about how beautiful they are, but have you ever seen one up close? There's a look in those beady little eyes of theirs. They know more than they're letting on." He closed the conversation by downing an entire cup of wine in one go.

When dinner ended and we retired for drinks, Nicholas couldn't entirely monopolize me. Courtesy dictated I speak to others—but none of them were Warren. With whatever magic Cedric worked, Warren remained occupied. Once, I saw Mira avidly engaging him in conversation. Well, she was engaged. He looked trapped. I wondered if Cedric had sent her.

As the evening wrapped up and guests departed, Cedric caught me for a private moment.

"Well?" he asked.

"He's everything you promised. I actually had a nice time."

"Excellent." Normally, Cedric would've looked smugger over such a triumph. Not so tonight. "I'll have to work on him a little more, but if all goes well, I think I could expedite an offer and manage a covert wedding before the Doyles catch on. Unorthodox, but so long as I've handled the paperwork correctly and he pays your minimum, there's nothing that goes against contract."

"That's great. That's really . . ." The words caught in my throat, and I couldn't finish. I couldn't pretend gladness over a wedding I didn't want, not when Cedric was standing in front of me. I rarely cried, but tears started to form in my eyes. Angrily, I blinked them away.

"Adelaide . . ." In his voice, I heard the same anguish I felt. His hand started to move toward me, and then he sharply pulled it away, clenching it as I'd done with mine earlier.

"There you are!"

Jasper strode up to us, and he was fuming. It was a rare sight, compared to his genteel public persona. "Adelaide, Mister Doyle and his mother are about to leave. You will go over to them now and bid them a proper farewell, with a promise to see them at another time."

"Father—"

"No." Jasper held a warning finger up to Cedric. "I don't want to hear another word. You've already ruined this night by throwing her together with that lawyer! Do you think he can pay her minimum? He's certainly not going to bid more if others are interested. I told you before, I will *not* let you ruin this." Jasper fixed his hard gaze on me. "Now. Go."

Cedric started to protest, but I waved it away. I didn't want him in any more trouble. I gave Jasper a small curtsey. "Of course, Mister Thorn."

Across the room, Warren and Viola were indeed making their exit. "Adelaide," said Warren. "What a pity we couldn't talk more. I wanted to tell you about some developments with the gold fields in Hadisen."

"How fascinating," I said, conscious of Jasper watching me. "Perhaps we could do it another time. I would *so* love to hear more."

"Oh?" asked Viola archly. "I thought you were more interested in the law."

I smiled sweetly. "Oh, Mistress Doyle. You know how these things are. They have us make the rounds—meet new people. It's just a formality."

"I'm glad to hear that," she said. "It'd be a shame for you to be singling anyone out this soon."

I nodded, even though it really wasn't early in the season anymore, especially with so many girls having made contracts already. "Indeed. I'm just trying to be courteous."

She narrowed her eyes. "Well then, perhaps you will soon be motivated to show Warren the courtesy of a private visit. We wouldn't want anyone to think you were putting on airs or behaving *above your rank*."

I swallowed. "Certainly not."

The party didn't run as late as many of our others, but when morning came around, most of us were exhausted. It had all been wrapped in glitter and decorum, but these last few weeks had been grueling. As Nicholas Adelton had said, it was a tough job, no matter the surface appearance.

Some of the engaged girls still attended parties; others had opted out and now busily planned their weddings. The Glittering Court had no involvement in the wedding once the paperwork and payments were settled. Each girl was allowed to keep one dress, which she usually was married in. The extent of the rest of the wedding depended on the prospective husband. Some threw grandiose affairs. Some were too wiped out financially to afford much more than a magistrate's fees.

Mistress Culpepper maintained a strict schedule and required all of us, engaged or not, to eat breakfast at exactly the same time each day. I didn't mind the early wakeup, if only because breakfast was a brief reprieve from our social whirl. The Thorns, able to eat at their leisure, strolled in near the end of our meal, as was typical. Mistress Culpepper quickly found them chairs, seating Cedric next to me. I didn't dare look at him, but the proximity made our legs touch under the table. At first, I kept my leg tense, but then I let it relax against his. I felt him do the same. For the remainder of the meal, I had no idea what I ate or said. My entire world focused on that touch.

One of the men who guarded the door called out that we had a guest. Mistress Culpepper hurried out of the dining room to investigate, and none of us reacted with much interest. Servants and messengers came and went at all times. Men with more serious intentions were politely told to come back later if they didn't have an appointment.

So, it was a surprise when a pale Mistress Culpepper returned to us with a tall man following her. He wore a cheap, ill-fitting suit in plain worsted wool, which had to be uncomfortable with the recent spring turn our weather had taken. Gray streaked his thinning hair, and hard lines were etched into his face. Clearly, this was no enterprising suitor.

Everyone around the table looked puzzled—everyone except Mira, oddly enough. She straightened up in her chair, eyes sharp. I couldn't entirely decipher her expression. Shocked? Calculating? Maybe a little of both.

Charles rose from the table, straightening his jacket. He was as clueless as the rest of us, but he knew there had to be a reason Mistress Culpepper had admitted a guest at this hour. "May I help you, sir?"

The stranger gave a curt nod. "My name is Silas Garrett. I'm with the McGraw Agency."

If anyone had thought this would be a boring morning, those notions were quickly shut down. The McGraw Agency was a group based out of Osfro who investigated all sorts of matters for those who could pay well enough. Technically, they were an independent organization, but we all knew they had royal authority to enforce the law. Their agents were notoriously ruthless and determined in their missions, going to great lengths—covert or overt—to achieve their goals. They investigated everything from infidelity among minor nobles to espionage for the king. There had been rumors of them being active in the New World, but no one knew for what, or who had employed them.

Jasper strolled up beside his brother. "My goodness. We rarely entertain gentlemen of such standing. I don't suppose you're looking for a wife?"

Silas Garrett didn't crack a smile. "No, but I'm here looking for a woman."

I don't know how I knew then, but suddenly, I just did. My whole body stiffened, and I felt Cedric's hand clasp mine under the table. I didn't dare look at him, but I understood the message: *Stay calm*.

"I'm here on undisclosed business of my own, but I have a colleague up in Archerwood who was hired last summer to investigate the possibility that a runaway noblewoman had fled here from Osfrid," Silas explained. "He's had little luck—not surprising since Adoria's such a big place, and he had no real clues about which colony she might have gone to."

"Understandable," said Charles. "Forgive me, but what does that have to do with us?"

Silas glanced between Charles and Jasper with hard eyes. "Well, I was recently given a tip that the lady in question might very well be in Cape Triumph—and that your household might have information about her whereabouts."

"Us?" asked Charles. "How in the world would we know anything about a missing woman?"

"A noblewoman," corrected Silas. "Lady Witmore, Countess of Rothford."

Cedric's hand tightened its grip.

"Countess . . ." Jasper's brow knitted into a frown. "You don't mean that business that stopped us in Osfro that night?"

"What night?" demanded Silas.

"Cedric and I were bringing a group of girls out last spring. They were stopping everyone at the city gates. We were searched and sent on our way." Jasper glanced at his son. "You remember that, don't you?"

Cedric nodded, wearing the open expression of someone who was simply pleasantly curious. "I do. It was causing quite a stir. Why's it coming up again?"

"As I said, we received a tip that there might be some lead on the lady here in your household." Silas glanced around those of us gathered at the table. "You have a great many girls here—the same age as Lady Witmore."

Jasper's smile stiffened, but only a little. "Yes, we do. Just as we do every year. It's our business, Mister Garrett. We bring girls of marriageable age here from Osfrid. I can't help it if your countess is the same age."

"How would you even expect to find her?" asked Charles. "Surely you aren't going to go blindly accusing my girls."

"No, sir. I wouldn't dream of it. I'm merely following up on this lead and will send a letter to my colleague up north. All I know is that the lady has brown hair. He has a small portrait." Silas's manner was perfectly polite, but I saw his gaze linger briefly on every brown-haired girl at the table, including me. It was a relief that there were three others. "If he comes here, I'm sure he'll bring it to confirm her identity. Can you verify that all of these girls come from the places they say?"

"These girls are from common backgrounds," said Jasper. "Illiterate laborers don't exactly keep extensive paperwork on their daughters. But I can tell you either my son or I saw the households each one came from. No countesses."

"If we did have one," quipped Cedric, "we could certainly charge a lot more."

Silas turned his stare on Cedric, clearly not appreciating the joke. I could tell Cedric was going out of his way to be relaxed and affable, so as not to appear suspicious. But he would have been better off imitating his father and uncle, who were polite but both somewhat affronted.

"Mister Garrett," said Jasper. "I respect what you do—I really do. But we already went through this in Osfro a year ago. I don't know what it is that causes the eye of suspicion to keep falling on us, but please, until you have something more concrete than a 'tip,' I'd thank you to remember we're trying to run a respectable business."

"Of course," said Silas, turning toward the doorway. "I'll most certainly be back if I know more."

"Before you go," called Cedric. "I'm terribly curious about where you got this tip."

"Anonymous," said Silas. "Showed up late last night."

It was hard to keep my panic down until Cedric and I caught a quick moment alone later in the day, just before some suitors were coming for afternoon tea.

"His partner has a portrait!" I hissed. "No doubt supplied by my grandmother when she hired him to come to Adoria."

Cedric's face was grim. "And Mister Garrett's 'tip' was most certainly from the Doyles."

"Viola. Warren still seems so . . . I don't know. Hapless. She suggested that I might become 'motivated' to pay more attention to him."

"And thus the motivation is possible exposure and capture—assuming you don't get married first."

I briefly closed my eyes. "And no doubt she's hoping I'll panic and use Warren for the marriage that will save me."

"No." Cedric stepped toward me and held my hands, a dangerous gesture when anyone in the house might walk right into this parlor. "I told you before, you won't be forced to do that. We'll get things settled with Nicholas Adelton and get them settled quickly. But while we do . . ."

I eyed him carefully. Tenderness filled his face, but I could tell there was something he was hesitant to tell me. "Yes?" I prompted.

"We're going to need to make sure the Doyles don't take any more action. We need to pacify them." He sighed. "I'm sorry, Adelaide. But you're going to have to make it look like you want him."

CHAPTER 18

"THE ICORI DIDN'T KNOW HADISEN HAD SO MANY GOLD deposits. But why would they? They're savages. They don't mine. They don't have the technology for it. It's a wonder they ever got across the sea. So we got a deal on it in the treaty."

Warren looked at me expectantly, and I mustered what I hoped was an impressed smile. "Was it really for sale, exactly?" I asked. "I mean, it was where they lived."

He frowned. "I don't understand what you're asking."

"It wasn't like it was a commodity they had lying around. It was their home. When they made the treaty, where were they supposed to go?"

"We didn't take all their lands," he said. "They had plenty left."

I'd seen the maps in my studies. "Plenty" was an overly optimistic way to describe it.

"And," he continued, "they can always move over to the western tribes' territory."

"Won't that cause friction with those tribes?" I asked.

"Not our problem. We're the conquerors."

I opened my mouth to protest and then thought better of it. It had been this way for the last week, during which I'd had three visits with Warren—two public and one private. He wasn't exactly offensive, but there were a number of times I'd had to bite my tongue, lest I counter his opinions. *Be charming,* Cedric had advised me. *Give him no reason to suspect anything.*

"How wonderful," I said, switching to something less controversial. "To have all that gold."

Warren nodded eagerly. "Yes. It's practically just lying around, waiting for anyone to take. We've got too few men to help get it out, but I think once we put the call out, and I arrive with a more established presence, settlers are going to flock to it." He regarded me meaningfully. "I'm leaving in two weeks."

I knew that. He reminded me of it every time we were together. Putting him off this long had saved me from a wedding before his departure, but I knew he and Viola were hoping to have a marriage contract sealed before then. My friendliness this week might have bought me some time, but soon, the Doyles were going to demand more.

"Pardon me," I said, rising from my chair. He immediately stood as well. "I must check my hair." It was a polite way of saying one had to visit the bathroom, and it provided a guaranteed escape.

This party at the Doyle estate had lasted for three hours, and I hoped we'd be going soon. Cedric was our chaperone, and our exit was in his hands. I might normally have persuaded him to an earlier time, but he'd been watching Caroline all evening. She seemed to have ensnared a respectable landowner who wouldn't leave her side. She'd had some difficulty with offers, and Cedric didn't want to ruin it.

He did, however, intercept me as I turned down the hall leading to the facilities. We rounded a corner and stopped, waiting for two men grumbling about taxes to walk by us. "We need to talk," Cedric said in a low voice.

I glanced around. "Here?"

"There's been no other chance." It was true. With fewer girls left, our social schedule had significantly picked up. He took my hand to pull me around a corner. "I have good news and bad news."

"I hope the good news is that you've somehow acquired ten times more money than you need for the Westhaven stake and that the bad is you just don't know how to spend the rest."

"I'd give it to you, of course, to keep you in the lifestyle you're accustomed to. But no, I'm afraid that's not it." He checked our surroundings one more time before continuing. "There's a man here interested in the painting."

That *was* good news. "How much?

"Four hundred."

"That's most of your stake! What's the bad news?"

"He wants it authenticated." Cedric shook his head. "But, as you can guess, there aren't that many people in the colonies who are qualified to judge Myrikosi art. So, he's willing to wait—which means *we* wait. Unless we can find another buyer."

"There aren't too many of those either."

"Not in Denham, no. But my agent is going to send out feelers to some of the southern colonies. In the meantime . . ." His manner told me there was more news—and not necessarily good. "There've been some developments with Nicholas Adelton."

"Oh?" I tried to keep my tone light, knowing I should be glad for this.

"He's been up in Thomaston this week—helping someone settle a trade dispute. I hear he took the case pro bono."

"Very kind of him."

"Yes," said Cedric. He also appeared to be struggling with an upbeat tone. "He's a very kind man. And he'll be back the day after tomorrow—in time for the Flower Festival, for which I've gotten him an invitation. I'm positive we can settle things then."

"So I just have to string Warren along a little longer."

We'd had no more visits from Silas Garrett, but the threat he'd presented still hung over my head. He'd looked as though he was memorizing every girl's face, and I knew if he saw that portrait, he'd immediately identify me. I needed to secure my position quickly.

"I'm sure that won't be hard for you," Cedric replied. I met his eyes and wished I didn't see such longing. This would be a lot easier to deal with if he'd been indifferent to me. "Go now—before Warren and his mother wonder what happened to you."

"Okay. As soon as you let go of my hand."

He looked down at our laced fingers and said nothing for several moments. Then, with great care, he brought my hand to his lips and pressed a kiss onto the back of it. I closed my eyes, wishing I could freeze that moment in time. When he released my hand, I could still feel the warmth of his lips on my skin. And neither of us moved. It took the loud laughter of a tipsy group walking down an adjacent hall to jolt us back to reality.

I returned to the main party, bracing for more of Warren's self-important conversation. To my surprise, Mira was speaking to him, giving me a temporary reprieve. I eyed her curiously, wondering what had sparked this. She'd yet to show any particular interest in a suitor. She hadn't even mentioned any offers, though I knew she'd entertained callers just as the rest of us had. This wasn't the first time I'd seen her actively pursuing Warren. Was it possible she was interested in him?

I enjoyed a few precious moments of alone time, listening as Warren's father chatted nearby with some magistrates, assuring them the rumors of Icori marching to Cape Triumph had no basis. I was curious as to what had triggered these fears but never found out. Once Warren spotted me, he hurried away from Mira and trailed me again. The slightest slip of her serene expression showed she was more frustrated than heartbroken, but distraction soon came as another young man tapped her on the shoulder. She turned to him, her smile instantly returning.

The party's end couldn't come too soon for me. After assuring Warren I'd be at the Flower Festival, I gratefully joined the others in heading to the carriages awaiting us outside. We only required two now to transport us. As we loaded up, I suddenly noticed something.

"Where's Mira?" I asked. *Not again,* I thought. A check showed no sign of her waiting outside with us. Cedric went back into the house, and I waited by the carriage's door, despite the driver's offer to help me. My unease grew as Cedric remained inside for far longer than I would've expected. She left all the time at home, but how could Mira disappear here?

At last, I saw them come out. He helped her into my carriage, and we were on our way.

"What happened?" I asked.

She rolled her eyes. "I got trapped in conversation by one of those men who wanted to know if he could get a 'deal' on me."

I studied her carefully. Her tone and expression seemed honest enough, but I couldn't shake the feeling that she was holding something back.

The next day, we found out that Caroline had finalized a contract, bringing our numbers down further. Jasper, though excited by the progress, felt the need to give the rest of us a pep talk.

"Although your contract gives you three months to choose," he said at breakfast, "it rarely takes any girl that long. Most are settled in a month's time. I'd be very surprised if the rest of you didn't have many offers at the festival tomorrow night." His gaze lingered on me the longest. "Very surprised."

The Flower Festival, dedicated to the glorious angels Aviel and Ramiel, was the biggest spring holiday in the Osfridian calendar. It coincided with the Alanzan Spring Rites, and there was some controversy over the holiday's true nature. Devotees of Uros claimed the heretics had taken the traditional holiday and corrupted its veneration of healing and pure love by adding in worship of the wayward angels Alanziel and Lisiel. The Alanzans believed it was an ancient celebration of passion and fertility and that the orthodox worshippers had sanitized it.

Regardless, it was second only to Vaiel's Day as our most celebrated holiday. Elaborate parties and banquets were commonplace, even here in Cape Triumph. We'd be at the large town hall again, in a splendid ball paid for by the governor and several other politicians. Even the engaged girls were going. Jasper claimed he didn't want them to miss out, but I suspected he wanted to show off the girls with their fiancés to any undecided men. The gala would have a masquerade theme, which was common in Osfrid, less so here. Mistress Culpepper hadn't been prepared for that and had to hastily make the necessary arrangements.

As usual, her "hasty" work was meticulous, no matter her grumbling. I had a delicate half-mask of silver filigree adorned with crystals. It was more of an enhancement than a true mask, since Jasper wanted us readily identifiable. The mask was the perfect accompaniment to my gown, an off-the-shoulder vision of white satin embellished with silver roses and ribbons.

"You know," Mira told me slyly, adjusting her own glittering red half-mask, "the tradition of masquerades goes back to the Alanzans conducting Spring Rites in masks. They put on masks of leaves and flowers, or dress like animals of the forest. Men and women dance without even knowing who their partner is."

I hadn't seen Cedric all day but had heard him speaking about the ball, which I assumed meant he'd be skipping any Alanzan rites—unless he'd be joining them extremely late. Had he ever participated, I wondered? And to what extent? The whole notion of dancing with a mysterious partner was pagan and improper, of course, but after the Star Advent, I felt a flush spread over me as I thought about him pulling me against him in some dark, wild place.

We entered the hall amidst much fanfare, and I was impressed to see it had been decorated to levels rivaling our initial gala. Flowers, of course, were the main décor, though not all of them were real. Some had been crafted of silk and jewels, hanging in elaborate wreaths and garlands that sparkled in the candlelight. The attendees consisted of more than just potential suitors, the occasion drawing out the finest citizens of both Cape Triumph and Denham at large. I felt certain my companions and I were the grandest in the room, simply because of our greater access to luxury fabrics, but all of the masked guests were fascinating to behold.

Cedric arrived right as things started and, rather than send me off to a scheduled partner, he swept me into the first waltz himself. "Your father won't like this," I teased.

"Oh, don't worry, he'll soon have a lot more to be upset about," Cedric told me. "Besides, from a distance, he might not even know it's me with the mask. It'd require him paying attention to something besides himself."

I recognized the tone, the lightness. It was my cue to throw a quip back. But instead, I found myself saying, "I'd know you anywhere, even with your face covered. It's in the way you move and smell. The way you feel . . ."

His hand tightened around my waist, bringing me fractionally closer. "You're not making this easy. Especially since I'm here to tell you that Nicholas Adelton has agreed to marry you tomorrow."

"I'd hope there isn't *any* way to say that that's easy."

"No, there isn't."

We fell into silence and let the music and the hum of conversation surround us, our eyes locked on each other as we glided through the room. I had the overwhelming urge to rest my head against him, but that wouldn't really help maintain our disinterested cover. Also, that wasn't an appropriate action in a waltz.

As the song wrapped up, Cedric lifted his eyes from my face. He'd been contemplative while watching me, but now his brow furrowed. "The governor-to-be has just spotted you. Let me get you over to Adelton for the next song. He's on board with everything but wanted to ask you something first."

Puzzled, I let Cedric lead me to Nicholas, just in time for the next song. Cedric was all politeness as he spoke to the attorney but cast me a lingering look as he walked away.

"I'm sorry I've been out of touch," Nicholas told me as we moved into the new dance. His half-mask was a simple one of blue fabric. "My client is a cousin's friend, and he'd been greatly wronged in a trade matter. I couldn't abandon him."

"I think it's admirable," I said truthfully.

"I can't fight all the injustice in the world, but I try to do what little I can. But enough business." He smiled down at me. "Mister Thorn has explained to me there's, ah, some urgency in what we have planned and that we'd have to manage a few tricks to make a wedding happen in time. We should be able to pull it off, but first I need to know . . ." His expression turned uncertain. "Are you sure you're willing? I don't want you rushed into this. I don't want you doing something you're not absolutely sure about. You should choose who you want."

I felt a pang in my heart, not only because of his consideration but also because of the truth it skirted around. Who did I want to choose? Cedric, of course. But he couldn't afford even the stake that would keep him alive, let alone my price. Anything else would be a breach of contract and create a great deal of scandal.

You could do a lot worse than Nicholas Adelton, I told myself. *Even if it means becoming Adelaide Adelton.*

Viola, across the room, caught my eye just then. It only strengthened my resolve, and I turned back to Nicholas. I pushed away my heartache, trying to ignore the way every part of my being cried out for Cedric. "Yes," I said to Nicholas. "I'm certain. If Mister Thorn can take care of the technicalities, I want to do it. And he will. He always does what he says he will."

I finished the dance with a heavy heart and expected my next one to be with Warren. Instead, it was Viola who swept me to the side of the room. "Adelaide, dear, I feel like we haven't spoken in ages."

That was true. While I'd dutifully spent time with Warren, I'd gone out of my way to avoid her.

"It's been a very busy time," I said.

She smiled, her lips thin and tight like a snake's. "Yes, I'm sure. But a pleasant time, no doubt. Warren can't stop talking about how much he's enjoyed your company. I'm sure the feeling is mutual."

"He's every girl's dream."

"Indeed. And yet, he remains unwed. Not even promised. You can imagine how distressing this is to me, especially with his departure for Hadisen coming so soon." She sighed dramatically. "I'd feel so much better if everything was settled. I hate loose ends, don't you? I hear

Silas Garrett does as well. His partner is en route to Cape Triumph. Should be here any day."

I kept a frozen smile on my face as I scrutinized her. Was she bluffing? Hard to say. "I'm sure it'll be a great relief to them to figure things out once and for all."

"And I'm sure it'll be a great relief to *you* to no longer worry about what they do or do not figure out." When I didn't answer, her sickeningly sweet expression dissolved. "Stop delaying. You can do no better. You'd be in no danger of returning to Osfrid. Do this, and make everyone's life easier—because I assure you, dear, I can make yours much more difficult."

Warren came up to us just then. "Mother, I didn't expect you of all people to steal Adelaide away."

Viola's smile turned beatific. "Well, we didn't want to bore you with details . . . you know, the sorts of details that really only matter to women when nuptials are involved."

He looked between us both incredulously. "Nuptials . . . you don't mean . . ."

"I think our dear Adelaide has stopped teasing us at last," said Viola.

"Is this true?" Warren caught hold of my hands. "You've accepted? We should announce it right now! It's the perfect night."

That anxious tightness in my chest returned, and I had to remind myself to breathe. "No—no. No announcements tonight. I mean, your mother and I have been speaking informally, but nothing can go forward . . ." I trailed off, staring across the room to where I could see Cedric speaking impassionedly to Nicholas. Nicholas was beaming, so I hoped that was promising news. "Nothing can go forward until all the details are drawn up with the Thorns. The marriage price, contracts . . . it wouldn't be proper to announce before the rest is official. I wouldn't feel right about it."

Viola's eyes narrowed, and Warren looked a little crestfallen but not too terribly put out. Meanwhile, my thoughts were racing. What would this do for me? How much time would it buy? No doubt the Doyles would be knocking on our door tomorrow to settle the deal. Could I put it off perhaps another day? Maybe even two? Cedric and Nicholas had become lost among the revelers, so I had no idea how that plan was developing. What had I just unofficially agreed to?

"Come," said Warren. "At the very least, let's have a celebratory dance—even if it's only the two of us celebrating."

There was no escape for me here. No allies. Only a sea of masked dancers, chattering and laughing about springtime and the renewal of life. I felt like darkness was closing in over me.

"Of course," I said stiffly. "I'd love to."

We danced for most of the rest of the night. A couple of bold suitors took a turn, but Warren moved in such a confident, almost proprietary way that most men simply steered clear of us. When Aiana told me our group was leaving, I barely even heard his words of farewell and promise to stop by tomorrow. I gave a polite nod and then rushed out to join the others. The night was fair and warm, and I needed air to think clearly. Before I could scarcely draw breath, I was led into a coach and then taken straight home to Wisteria Hollow.

I threw open the window when I reached my bedroom and sat there gulping in deep breaths, trying to steady myself. It wasn't enough. That trapped feeling I'd had at the ball wouldn't leave me. I needed to be out of this room, out of this house—out of this life. I felt like I had back in Osfro, locked in a glittering cage that so many admired, little knowing it was suffocating me. Not caring what trouble I got in, I left the room still in my gala clothes, pausing only then to realize Mira should have joined me. All the other girls were back in their rooms. I kept moving. Mira was out making her own choices, whatever they might be. I couldn't fault her for that.

I headed down the hall to the small closet that led to the back staircase. I took it up to the attic level, nearly tripping over my long skirts in my haste. When I reached the landing, I flung open the window and was fully ready to climb down when a voice behind me said my name. I spun around and cringed when a masked figure stepped forward. Half a second later, just as he removed the mask, I realized it was Cedric.

"What are you doing?" he asked. "I was hoping to sneak into your room and talk, when I saw you go through this door."

"I'm getting out. I have to think . . . I can't think here. I can't breathe here. I have to get out for a while. Somewhere. Anywhere but here." I started to lift my foot up onto the window seat, and he grabbed hold of my arm, shutting the window behind me.

"Calm down. You can't climb down that damned trellis in those shoes." He urged me down to the window seat. "Sit, and tell me what's wrong."

I turned to him in amazement. "What's wrong? How can you ask what's wrong? Everything is wrong! I just more or less agreed to marry Warren Doyle tonight!"

"More or less?"

I found myself rambling, scarcely drawing breath. "His mother—Viola—she forced my hand. I couldn't say no. All I could do was delay. Told them I would but that nothing was official until it had been settled here. Paperwork and all that. I don't know what it bought me. Maybe a couple of days? But you know they'll be vicious; they aren't going to—"

"Okay, okay," said Cedric, lacing his fingers through mine. "It's okay. Nothing's settled yet. They don't have you, not yet. And you don't need to stall a couple of days. You only need to stall until tomorrow morning."

His words jolted me out of my near-hysterical state. "What do you mean?"

"Nicholas Adelton is willing—you must know that already after talking to him. The trick was making it legal, but I found a magistrate who'll marry you tomorrow morning in a private ceremony. Most, knowing your involvement with the Glittering Court, wouldn't have done it. He doesn't care so long as you're eighteen and a free citizen of

Osfrid. I'll draw up all the paperwork tonight, log the payment, and you'll be married in the morning."

I was dumbfounded. "In the morning."

He squeezed my hands. "Yes. It's going to create a lot of upset . . . to put it mildly. My father and Uncle Charles. The Doyles—especially if they're clinging to this soft promise you made them. But we'll have the law on our side. We'll even have the Glittering Court's technicalities on our side. No matter how much the others complain, they won't be able to do anything about it."

I had a feeling that "complaining" would be putting it mildly. "You'll be lucky if your father lets you stay on and collect any commissions. Whether it's enough for Westhaven will be irrelevant."

"Let me worry about Westhaven," Cedric said adamantly. He leaned into me, his presence steady and secure. "All you have to do is get to your wedding in the morning. I know it's not the luxury arrangement you imagined, but he'll be good to you. You'll be safe."

"I don't need luxury." My response came as fiercely as his. "I can be a mistress of a modest household. I can be a charming companion on his arm at social gatherings. I can be his friend. I can go to his bed and—"

The words caught in my throat, and I couldn't finish. Everything else I could do with Nicholas Adelton—but not that last one. Maybe I could have once—before Cedric—but not anymore. I couldn't even give voice to it.

Cedric turned me so that I faced him and gently lifted the glittering mask off my face. I'd been in such a frenzy upon leaving the gala that I'd never noticed I was still wearing it. It had hidden the tears welling up in my eyes. He wiped them away and cupped my face in his hands, leaning close so that our foreheads touched. Gone was the satisfaction of his victory with Nicholas. Now there was only melancholy left—and a longing that matched my own.

"El—"

"Don't." I pressed a finger to his lips. "Don't call me that. That's not my name anymore. I'm Adelaide. This is my life now—the one that began the day I met you."

He caught hold of my hand so that he could kiss each of my fingers. A tremor went through him, and he looked away. "You shouldn't say that. Not when you're getting married tomorrow."

"Do you think that changes how I feel?" I reached out and turned his face back toward mine. "Do you think my being someone else's wife will change anything? Don't you know that I'd lie with you in the groves, under the light of the moon? That I'd defy the laws of gods and men for you?"

I couldn't even say who started the kissing then. Maybe there was no true start. Maybe it was just a continuation of what we'd begun that night among the stars. Wrapped in his arms, wrapped in *him*, I couldn't believe I'd somehow gone the last week without touching him. *Really* touching him—not those stolen brushes of fingertips and legs. I had danced with dozens of men in this month and never felt a flicker of what I felt when Cedric simply looked at me.

He shifted so that my back was pressed against the window, and I pulled him as close to me as I could. I undid the tie that held his hair back, releasing it around his face. He delicately ran his hands along where the dress exposed one shoulder and then brought his lips down to it. The heat of his mouth against my bare flesh undid me, and I arched my body against his. He pulled back abruptly, breathing ragged.

"You told me once—"

"That I planned on staying virtuous until my wedding night?" I guessed. "That's true. It's a principle I believe in. But, well, I have a very creative definition of 'virtuous.' And if this is the last night I can be with you, I plan on pushing the limits of that definition as far as they can go."

His mouth was on mine again, filled with a demand that made me shudder. His hands slowly moved up my hips—up, up until they reached the top of the dress's low-cut bodice. He traced the edge of the neckline and then began untying the intricate silver laces that held it all together. I'd nearly pried his suit coat off when the door to the attic landing suddenly opened.

Mira had warned me she thought someone else was using this window as an escape, but I'd never really expected to cross paths with that person.

And I'd certainly never expected it would be Clara.

Chapter 19

To say there was a lot of fallout would be something of an understatement.

I'd feared many things since coming to Adoria. I'd worried I'd be forced into a marriage I didn't want. I'd been concerned the discovery of my identity would get me dragged back to Osfrid. And most of all, I'd always, always feared for Cedric being hung as a heretic.

But being hauled into Charles and Jasper's office for "indecent behavior" had never crossed my mind.

"Do you know what you've done?" Jasper cried. "Do you have any idea what you've done? This will ruin us!"

Cedric and I sat side by side in hard-backed wooden chairs while Jasper paced in front of us with hands clasped behind his back, very much like some sort of courtroom attorney. Charles stood against the opposite wall and looked as though he was still having trouble coming to terms with these new developments. It was the morning after "the incident." We'd both been sent back to our respective rooms last night, with hired men on watch, in case we attempted to flee.

"I think 'ruin' is kind of a strong term," said Cedric calmly.

"Oh, really?" Jasper came to a halt in front of us. Fury smoldered in his eyes. "You don't think this is going to get out? Because I assure you, it's *already* gotten out. The rest of the girls are under lockdown, but the servants and the hired men know. This will be all over Cape Triumph by the end of the day, and no man will come near us. I'm not naïve. I know some of these girls didn't come to us as blushing maidens." Charles looked startled by that revelation. "But we've always preserved that image of purity, letting our prospective clients believe their wife's virtue is still intact. Now, there's hard proof that that's not the case."

The mention of virtue reminded me of my own glib words last night: *I have a very creative definition of "virtuous."*

"Nothing happened." Cedric was remaining remarkably coolheaded, given the situation. Maybe it was the result of years of dealing with his father's moods. "Her virtue *is* still intact."

Jasper fixed me with a look I didn't like. It made me feel . . . unclean. "Oh? I have a hard time believing that. From what I heard, her clothes were scattered across the floor."

A deep blush filled my cheeks. "That's a lie. That's Clara trying to make things worse."

"Well, at least you're acknowledging things are bad to begin with," snapped Jasper. "The truth doesn't matter. It will get twisted—for the worse. By the time this story's told enough, you'll be as brazen as some Alanzan harlot sprawled in the grass. Everyone's going to know my son had his way with one of our girls. And everyone's going to think that's how it is—that all the men here are sampling our goods."

I didn't like being referred to as "goods," but the rest of his words struck me in a way I hadn't expected. Cedric's silence told me they'd affected him as well.

Seeing he'd gotten through to us, Jasper added, "I know you think I'm ruthless—that I go too far to make a profit. And maybe that's true. But one thing I've always done is maintain a reputable business. Now that's all been called into question."

"Then I'll make it right," said Cedric. "I'll marry her."

"Cedric—" I began. I had no problem with the idea of marrying him, but he had to know the obstacles standing in our way were nearly insurmountable. Jasper knew that as well.

"Do you have a fortune set aside that I don't know about? A stash of gold under your bed that will cover her price?"

Cedric's jaw clenched. I hated seeing him humiliated, but Jasper's point was valid. Cedric didn't even have the funds to buy his stake yet, not until the painting deal went through—*if* it went through. And clearly, my commission was off the table.

"She still has time left on her contract," replied Cedric. "I'll earn the fee." I was about to say Cedric had better things to spend his money on—hoping he'd pick up on the hint about Westhaven. But then he said something that sent me reeling: "I love her."

A bright feeling blossomed within me. It was the first time the subject of love had ever come up between us, though I don't think either of us had ever doubted it was there. Uncaring of Jasper's disapproval, I found Cedric's hand and clasped it. "I love him too."

Jasper rolled his eyes. "This is all very touching, but unfortunately, we live in the real world—not some cheap copper romance novel."

Charles cleared his throat, expression uncertain. "Perhaps . . . perhaps we could lend him the fee. He *is* family, after all."

"No," said Jasper swiftly. "No special treatment. He violated our policies, and he'll live with those consequences. If others know he received a favor, it'll only worsen things—confirm the idea that we're taking liberties here. He'll deal with this disaster the same way anyone else would have to."

"*We* will deal with this," I corrected.

A knock at the door stopped Jasper from rolling his eyes again. He nodded for Charles to open the door, and sighed. "This had better not be another one of those girls finding some excuse to get a peek in here. I'm sure they're all gathered outside the door trying to listen."

But it was no eavesdropping girl. Instead, it was Mistress Culpepper who stood there when Charles opened the door. "Forgive me," she said, face contrite. "But Mister Doyle and his mother are here. I wasn't sure if I should send them away or not."

Jasper groaned and briefly covered his eyes with his hand. "And there's another thing destroyed by this debacle. I told you this would spread." He deliberated a moment and then gave a nod to Mistress

Culpepper. "Yes. Bring them in, and let's get their outrage over and done with. It's no more than you two deserve."

Warren and Viola soon entered. Both were dressed exceptionally formally for a morning call, the dark color of their clothing seeming to emphasize the gravity of the situation. I could tell immediately they knew what had happened. Jasper personally escorted Viola to a seat, and Charles hastily arranged the office chairs in a semicircle, as though this were some friendly social occasion in a parlor.

The exasperation Jasper had displayed before was wiped away. He was in performance mode and wouldn't show any weakness to the Doyles. "Mistress Doyle," he began. "It's always such a delight to have you in our home. I swear, you grow lovelier each time—"

She held up a hand to silence him. "Oh, stop with your con man's prattle. You know why we're here." She pointed an accusing finger at me. "We demand justice for the appalling, deceitful way she—"

"Mother," interrupted Warren. "That is *not* why we're here. Although I'm sure you can all imagine our shock when a messenger showed up at our house this morning with the, uh, news."

Jasper put on a look of perfect contrition. "And I'm sure you can imagine how truly sorry we are for any miscommunication that may have happened in our recent interactions."

"'Miscommunication?'" Viola's eyes widened. "*Miscommunication?* That girl said she'd marry my son last night. Then we hear this morning that she went straight into *your* son's bed. That doesn't really seem like a laughable misunderstanding."

"Again," said Jasper, "we are truly sorry for the inconvenience this may have caused you. You have every reason to be upset."

"Upset, certainly . . ." Warren grew hesitant as he glanced between Cedric and me. "But not necessarily surprised."

Even Jasper faltered. "You knew?"

Warren gestured toward Cedric and me. "About this specifically? No, no, of course not. But I could always tell there was something holding her back. No matter my entreaties, no matter how faultless

I thought my logic . . . well, none of it worked. And I kept thinking, 'What good reason could she have for not accepting?' Now I understand."

"She's a conniving little—"

"Mother," warned Warren. His civility toward us incensed her, and honestly, I was surprised by his attitude as well. "Tell me, Mister Thorn. What's going to happen now?"

Jasper was back in comfortable territory. "Well, the first thing that's going to happen is that you will have top priority in socializing with any of our remaining girls. And of course, there'll be a substantial discount—"

"No," said Warren. "I mean to *them*."

I could practically see the wheels spinning in Jasper's head as he tried to figure out how he might best get out of this situation with his business and reputation intact.

"Well, Mister Doyle, we run a pristine establishment. Honor and virtue are values we hold very highly. You've no doubt heard some sordid exaggerations about what happened last night—when the truth is much blander, I'm afraid. My son and this young lady, of course, plan to marry."

Cedric and I exchanged only the briefest of amused glances at Jasper suddenly signing on to that plan.

"How kind." Ice filled Viola's voice. "You're giving your son a beautifully wrapped, glittering gift. An expensive one at that, considering what you were trying to charge the rest of us."

"And he'll be paying the same," said Jasper. "There is no special treatment around here when it comes to our girls. No gifts. Before they're married, he'll pay the base fee that any other man would have."

Viola regarded Cedric incredulously. "And pray tell, young man, where will you be getting such funds? Are your father's wages that good?"

"Many things are still being worked out, Mistress Doyle," Cedric replied.

Warren gave us an indulgent smile. "Well, perhaps I can help them work a little more easily."

From the way Viola's head whipped around to look at her son, it was clear this was an unplanned turn of events. No one in the room really knew what to expect, and I had no reason to believe anything altruistic was to come, despite the smile Warren gave me.

"Adelaide, you've heard me speak many times about the gold claims in Hadisen and how we don't have enough men to work them. I personally own a number of them, and they're simply lying around. What I'd like to propose is that Mister Thorn take on one of those claims and mine it for me."

That stunned us all to silence. After almost a minute of processing, Jasper unsurprisingly spoke first. "You want my son—*my* son—to mine a gold claim for you? You know he was a university student, don't you? Studying business? He's never done real manual labor in his life. He doesn't even like the outdoors."

I wondered what Jasper would think if he knew the truth about his son's spiritual practices.

"Forgive me if I sound ungrateful, but can you elaborate on how this would help me?" asked Cedric.

"I own the land, and you would own the right to work and control it," explained Warren. "And you keep whatever gold you can mine out of it—after paying me an owner's commission, of course." He beamed. "If you get lucky, you could strike it big right away and solve all your financial problems!"

"But most people don't strike it big right away," pointed out Jasper. "Otherwise, Hadisen and the other gold colonies would be filled with mansions instead of shantytowns. Your offer is very kind, but Adelaide's fee must be paid in less than two months in order for her to meet the terms of her contract. There are no guarantees of that."

"I'll guarantee the fee," said Warren. "Should he not mine enough within the time frame, I'll cover the fee to meet her contract, and his debt will switch over to me."

Warren's face was open and guileless, but I felt a chill run down my back. I didn't like the idea of Cedric being indebted to someone, especially this someone. And I certainly didn't trust Warren's being so generous about all of this. His mother, as it turned out, didn't like it either.

"Warren," she scolded. "This is preposterous! You have no business giving him a claim title. You don't owe him anything. We were supposed to come here to express our outrage and hire an attorney to file a formal grievance! Helping him further this illicit relationship was never part of our discussion this morning."

Warren turned to her, exasperated. "What good would any of that do, Mother? Soothe your hurt feelings? Or do you expect me to bully them into letting me marry a woman whose heart belongs to another?"

"Well, not anymore! Not now that she's used goods."

I shot to my feet, angered at being referred to as "goods" again—and in a much less flattering way. "I beg your pardon, Mistress Doyle, but there's nothing 'used' here. I'm still a virgin and will stay that way until my wedding night. It's true this situation has gone in a direction none of us expected, but my morals have remained the same."

Viola crossed her arms. "I don't like it, Warren. I don't like it at all."

"And I don't like it that I have gold just lying around in Hadisen! Squatters have already started moving in. I want honest, hardworking men I can trust on those claims—law-abiding men who follow the rules. Would I have liked to marry Adelaide?" His eyes held me for a fraction of a second as I sat back down beside Cedric. "Yes. But as I said, I could hardly marry her knowing she loves someone else. And so, instead of a wife, I have a potential settler. Mister Thorn here is exactly the kind of person I'd like to help build Hadisen into greatness—assuming he wants to stay. Once your debt is paid, you'd be under no obligation, Mister Thorn. But our colony is going to need people like you—like both of you—to become a civilized place."

Considering Warren's attitude toward the Alanzans, I found it unlikely Hadisen was the kind of place we'd want to stay. Not that it mattered. There was no way we could accept this offer.

"I accept," said Cedric. "I'll work your claim as part of a larger arrangement to pay Adelaide's fee."

I forcibly clamped my mouth shut so my jaw wouldn't drop. In the given circumstances, I had no intention of showing anything but perfect unity between Cedric and me. Once we were alone, I planned on telling him exactly how terrible this plan was. Jasper expressed my thoughts for me.

"Are you out of your mind? What do you know about mining?"

"No more than most of the adventurers who set off for the claims. I'm sure I can learn," said Cedric.

Warren nodded. "Absolutely. We'll get you started. Panning is the most basic type of gold extraction, and you can move on to other techniques from there."

"There's one condition," added Cedric. He took my hand again. "Adelaide comes too."

"First," snarled Viola, "you're in no position to set conditions. Second, you don't get to marry her before the financial details are fulfilled. Unless you plan on some sort of sinful arrangement."

Cedric shook his head. "Of course not. But considering all the rumors and slander that will spread around Cape Triumph, I think it'd best for her to be removed from that—somewhere far away."

Our eyes met briefly, and in that way we had, I understood his true motivations. Taking me from Cape Triumph would offer an added level of protection, should Viola decide to take any sort of revenge and reveal my identity. It would be a lot easier to elude bounty hunters in the wilderness than the city.

"I'll help him mine it," I said. "I've read about the panning process—it's something I could do."

"Living on the claim with him would only stir up more rumors, regardless of your virtuous principles," Warren told me. "But there are a number of families traveling with children, and I'm sure many would appreciate a governess with your education. We might be able to set up a boarding arrangement—though there might be some household labor involved. And the conditions would be rough."

"I'm sure household labor wouldn't be a problem, considering her humble background," quipped Viola.

"I'm not afraid of hard work," I said resolutely.

Jasper looked me over. "You're as naïve as my son. However hard you think you worked as a lady's maid, it is nothing compared to what you'll face on the frontier."

"I'll do whatever it takes."

Warren clasped his hands together, face alight. "Well, then it's settled. We leave in a week, and I'll make the appropriate arrangements."

Despite my declaration, I was still uneasy about all of this. It wasn't exactly too good to be true—but nearly. I needed to talk to Cedric more extensively, assuming we were ever allowed to be alone again. Jasper seemed to be undecided on this deal. He didn't really believe we could handle frontier life. I also suspected he didn't want us to have a happy ending after the trouble we'd caused him. On the other hand, painting this in a seemingly honorable way—one sanctioned by a man of Warren's repute, who'd been courting me—might save face and ensure no future business fallout.

"Thank you," I said to Warren. "This is all very considerate of you."

A wistful look crossed his face. "It's my pleasure to—"

The door burst open, and amazingly enough, it was Mira who entered. Jasper glared. "I told you lot not to—"

"They're here! They're here! I don't understand it, but they're here." Mira was breathless, her eyes wide.

"Who?" asked Jasper. I think he expected a flock of angry suitors.

"The other girls! The other ship." Mira turned to me. "Adelaide! Tamsin's alive!"

CHAPTER 20

I RUSHED OUT WITH THE OTHERS, ALL OF US NEARLY tripping over one another as we tried to get through the doorway at the same time. In the foyer, we found chaos. A group of at least twenty people mingled in the room, and our girls were running down the stairs into the throng, adding to the disarray. The noise of a dozen conversations filled the air and mostly came through as an indecipherable buzz. I stared around for a moment, unable to make sense of it all, and then I spotted it across the room: a head of bright, golden-red hair.

"Tamsin!"

I pushed through the crowd, uncaring of who I ran into. She turned at the sound of my voice, and my heart sang at the sight of that familiar face. I barreled into her, nearly knocking her over with a giant hug. I didn't care if she hated me and pushed me away. All that mattered was that she was alive and that at this moment, I could hold her in my arms. She was real and solid. My friend had returned to me.

And she didn't push me away. She returned the hug, clinging to me fiercely. "Oh, Adelaide . . ." she began. Sobs choked her words. A moment later, Mira appeared, throwing her arms around the two of us. We stood there like that for a long time, the three of us locked together, full of joy despite our tears.

"Where have you been, Tamsin?" I whispered when I could finally bring myself to pull away. "Where have you been? We thought . . . we thought . . ."

Her brown eyes sparkled with tears. "I know. I know. I'm sorry. I wish we could have sent word sooner, and I'm sorry for everything back in Osfrid—"

"No, no." I squeezed her hand. "You have nothing to apologize for."

Until that moment, I'd only been looking at Tamsin's face, taking in the features of this friend I loved so much. But now, after a chance to catch my breath, I could see so much more. She wore a dress of deep blue-gray, made of some plain fabric. It had no ornamentation or frills. Her hair spilled across her shoulders without any obvious styling and was covered by a simple kerchief. Glancing around, I saw the other missing girls dressed similarly.

"What happened to all of you?" I asked.

Before she could answer, a loud stomping on the floor drew our attention. Gradually, others began to notice, and the din of conversation faded. Jasper, seeking to be heard, stood on top of a chair. I was pretty sure I had never, ever seen him look so genuinely happy.

"Friends! Friends! You're witnessing a miracle right before our eyes. Something none of us thought possible. I've just learned that—as you can no doubt tell—the *Gray Gull* wasn't lost at sea! It sustained great damage in the storm and was blown off course—far, far north to the colony of Grashond."

I turned to Tamsin in disbelief. The northern colonies were known both for harsh conditions and a harsh population. They were also nearly four hundred miles away.

Jasper peered around. He looked as though someone had just dropped a giant bag of gold at his feet. Which, I supposed, someone had. "Who do I have to thank for this? Who do I have to thank for saving my girls?"

For a moment, nothing happened. I could see now that along with our missing girls, there were some men who looked like sailors. A few other strangers were dressed in plain clothing like Tamsin, and one of these got pushed forward. He was a young man with tawny blond hair and a surprisingly calm countenance, given this bizarre situation.

"I wouldn't say any one person saved them, Mister Thorn," he said.

"Our whole community came together to care for them until the roads were clear enough for travel."

A Glittering Court girl I didn't know spoke up. "But Mister Stewart was the one who advocated for us. Who made sure we had places to stay and . . . and vocations to keep us busy."

"I'm in your debt then, Mister Stewart," said Jasper, offering a showy bow. "You have saved not just them—but all of us. Thank you."

A bit of the young man's coolness faltered at all the attention and admiration. "You can call me Gideon. And there's no need to thank me. It was simply our duty under Uros. My only regret is that you had to worry about them for so long. The roads made no travel or communication possible until recently."

"Well, they're here now, and say what you want, but we still owe you a great deal—something I'd love to talk more at length about. But first, I need to speak to these gentlemen about certain commercial matters." He nodded toward the sailors. "While I do that, Gideon—my brother and son would be happy to entertain you and your colleagues in our parlor. I'm sure you'd appreciate some refreshments after your journey. I have an excellent brandy I've been saving."

"We don't drink spirits," said Gideon.

Jasper shrugged. "Well, we'll find a beverage you can drink. Water or something. Mistress Culpepper, will you see that our new girls are taken care of? I'm sure they need refreshments too." He eyed some of them askance. "And now that their journey is over, I'm sure they'd like to change out of traveling clothes and into their finer wares."

A few of the girls exchanged uneasy glances. "We don't have those, uh, finer wares anymore," said one. "They're gone."

Jasper allowed himself only a brief flicker of surprise. His miraculous pile of gold had just gotten a little smaller. "Well, then, I'm sure we can put together a wardrobe from the other girls—especially the ones who are engaged."

"I'll see to it," said Mistress Culpepper. "And that they're roomed properly."

I pulled Tamsin close. "She's staying with us," I said.

No one seemed to mind who stayed where, so long as there was room for all of us. The second floor of the house became a frenzy of activity as girls were shown to their rooms, and everyone scrambled to provide the newcomers with clothes. Mira and I were raiding our own closets when Heloise popped into our room, her arms full of green dresses. She smiled warmly at Tamsin.

"You were the emerald, right? I inherited your spot, but I don't need these anymore. Not now that I'm engaged."

"Congratulations, and thank you." The smile Tamsin gave her in return was genuine but tinged with weariness. After Heloise had left, Tamsin sat heavily on the bed, putting the dresses in a heap beside her. "To tell you the truth, I don't care what color I wear anymore, so long as it's not this blasted cheap wool."

I sat down next to her. "Was it awful up there?"

"Not awful, exactly." Tamsin frowned, lost in some memory. "But very, very different than what we're used to. Gideon was right that they took care of us, and really that's all that matters."

I wanted more details about her time away, but Tamsin seemed reluctant. The Grashond settlers—who called themselves "the Heirs of Uros"—just barely escaped the designation of heretics in the eyes of the orthodox church. The Heirs kept the same liturgies and stressed the importance of priests and churches as the way to Uros, but they did so in a very simple way. No grand cathedrals. No gifts or decorations at holidays. No excessive food and drink. No elaborate clothing.

When Mira suggested cleaning up, Tamsin jumped at the chance. While she was away, Mira explained to me, "Maybe it wasn't awful, like she said, but it couldn't have been easy. And she must have been terrified. Sometimes, when you go through something like that, it takes a while for you to want to talk about it."

Once Tamsin returned, cleaned and dressed in one of Heloise's silk poplin dresses, she seemed like her old self again—*very* much like her old self again.

"Well, I'd better remember all my manners and get used to doing my hair and face again," she said briskly. "It's late in the season, but I plan on making up for lost time. I hope you've left some men for the rest of us. You must have both gotten slews of offers by now."

"Not that many in the way of, ah, official ones," said Mira. "But I feel optimistic about my future."

Tamsin turned to me. "What about you? There's no way you haven't have had all sorts of offers. Have you settled on some promising young man?"

When I didn't answer, Mira laughed. "She's settled on someone all right. In fact, I think your arrival interrupted the marriage negotiations."

Tamsin brightened. "Excellent! What kind of man is he? What's he do? Is he in government? Shipping?"

"He's the son of a crafty businessman who ships brides and other luxuries to the New World," I said.

"What are you . . ." Confusion filled Tamsin's pretty face. "But that doesn't make any . . . you don't mean . . ."

I sighed. "I mean Cedric."

When Tamsin couldn't formulate a response, Mira said, "It's true. Adelaide's caused quite a scandal around here. Your arrival might have been the only thing that could top this drama."

I explained the situation as best I could, including the arrangement in Hadisen. Mira hadn't heard that part yet. She kept her face neutral, but Tamsin's expression filled with greater incredulity as the story went on.

"What were you thinking?" she exclaimed. "You turned down a future governor for . . . what, an impoverished student?"

"Well, he dropped out of the university. And he's not impoverished." I reconsidered for a few moments. "He's just . . . um, without assets. But I'm sure that will change."

"This," declared Tamsin, "would have never happened if I'd been around to look after you. Mira, how could you have stood for this?"

"I had no idea," Mira admitted.

"You're her roommate! How could you not?"

A moment of awkwardness fell over us. A chagrined look crossed Mira's face, and I could guess her thoughts. Under normal circumstances, she might very well have noticed something amiss with me. But we both knew Mira had been preoccupied by her own clandestine activities, though I still didn't know what they were.

A knock at the door startled us, and I opened it to admit Cedric. "You're not supposed to be in here," I said, glancing behind him in the hall. "Are you trying to get us in even more trouble?"

"I think that's impossible." He shut the door behind him. "And with everything going on, no one's going to notice. I had to take the chance to talk to you. Welcome back, Tamsin. It's good to see you."

She eyed him disapprovingly. "I wish I could say the same. I've heard you've caused all sorts of trouble for my friend."

He grinned back at her, unfazed. "Well, she's caused all sorts of trouble for me too."

"Cedric," I said, "you know this Hadisen plan is a terrible idea, don't you?"

"It could solve our financial problems. And," he added pointedly, "it gets you out of Cape Triumph."

"I just can't believe Warren would fold so easily. It's an embarrassment to him. He should be outraged."

"He probably is," Cedric agreed. "And I'm not naïve. But maybe this saves face if he acts like it doesn't bother him. Could be there is some ulterior motive, but I'd rather take my chances out in Hadisen."

Tamsin straightened up. "So. This Warren. He's available then, right?"

"I suppose so," I said in surprise. "And he's motivated to find a wife . . . but he's only got a week left before he leaves."

"That's all I need." Tamsin glanced at Cedric. "If you can arrange some meetings for me."

"It's too soon," I said. "Even for you."

Mira nodded in agreement. "Tamsin, you need to rest and recover this week—not chase after some man on your first day back. Take it easy. Let Warren go. There are others."

I studied Mira curiously, but as usual, her expression betrayed nothing. I remembered her various efforts to engage Warren. Now that he was available, was it possible she was trying to push out Tamsin as competition?

"Something tells me I'm not going to be part of the family business anymore," Cedric told Tamsin. "But if you want to throw yourself right into the thick of things, my father's not going to object. I know he'd like to close a deal with Warren—if you really want him."

Tamsin glanced between Mira and me. It was obvious Tamsin was going to ignore our suggestions about resting. "Is there a reason I wouldn't want him?" she asked.

No one answered right away. At last, I said, "He seems nice enough most of the time . . . sometimes he's closed-minded . . ."

"Closed-minded in what way?" Tamsin asked with more interest than I'd expected.

"Religion. The Icori. No more than most around here, I suppose. But his mother's the really terrible one. She's the one you have to watch out for."

"Mothers-in-law are *always* terrible," said Tamsin airily. "Let me meet Warren, and I'll decide if he's worth my time."

Cedric turned back and took both of my hands. The open gesture startled me. "Things are going to move very quickly now," he said. "We have one week. Most Hadisen settlers have had months to prepare."

I squeezed his hands back. "Well, if we're doing it, we'll do it right. How can I help?"

"Most of it's going to be on me—equipment, figuring out the claim." He reached into his pocket and handed me a bag of silver. "You can help by taking care of your clothes."

"What do you mean, take care of?"

He gestured to my organza dress. "This isn't going to really work in Hadisen. You need something that can withstand some wear and tear."

"I figured you'd just mend anything I needed."

A little of his tension faded. "Well, I *did* enjoy that the first time."

"I knew it! You're not as good at hiding your thoughts as you think you are."

"Well, actually, you were the one who wasn't hiding that much—"

"Ugh," groaned Tamsin behind me. "Will you stop already? I just endured one agonizing situation. Please don't put me through another."

Cedric flashed her his winning smile, only to be met with a scowl. Turning back to me, he closed my hand over the silver bag. "I mean it. You're going to need a whole new wardrobe out there. I'll ask Aiana to help—she'll know what to get."

"Where did this silver come from?"

"I have some savings of my own."

I knew what those savings were for. "Cedric, you can't—"

"I can." He rested a hand on my cheek. "If this all works out, it won't matter."

There were no more protests to make. We'd signed on to this plan, and I wasn't going to argue with him anymore. We would stand by each other and make this work. Hopefully.

"Just tell me this," I said. "If things go horribly awry, can we just go run off into the wilderness together?"

"Sure. But we'd have to leave all civilization behind. Sleep under the stars. Wear animal skins."

"Hey, watch it," warned Tamsin.

Cedric looked at her in surprise. "There was nothing improper about that at all."

"I know what you were thinking."

"Can I at least kiss her goodbye?"

"No," said Tamsin.

"And here I thought things were difficult before you got back." Cedric dared a kiss on my cheek. "We'll talk later. I've got to go break the news to Nicholas Adelton—assuming he hasn't already heard it from some gossip."

After Cedric was gone, Tamsin shook her head. "I don't know how you got by without me."

Despite the complications with Cedric, I still couldn't get over the wonder of having her back. I gave her another fierce hug.

"Me either," I said. "Me either."

Chapter 21

Tamsin wasn't kidding about jumping right into the Glittering Court's busy world. Some of the new girls were clearly still in shock from all they'd endured. But for those, like Tamsin, who were ready to get back on track, Jasper had no problem helping them. A new wave of parties and one-on-one meetings were arranged for that week, and in no time, Tamsin's reputation had spread, making her one of the most sought-after. Mira and I helped prepare her as best we could for life in Cape Triumph, but she seemed to need little adjustment. The settlers from Grashond were still around, and while Tamsin was polite to them, I noticed she went out of her way to avoid them. They were a disapproving lot, and Gideon—the young minister who'd helped save them—seemed especially troubled by the Glittering Court's social whirlwind.

Meanwhile, I dropped out of the public eye and began preparations of an entirely different nature. As Warren had predicted, there were a number of families who were interested in having an interim teacher while Hadisen became established. I made an arrangement to help the children of multiple families with their studies. One of the families, the Marshalls, had a claim within riding distance of Cedric's and offered to give me room and board.

Mistress Marshall was a stout, pleasant-faced woman with six children. "We'll need the children to help around the homestead during the day," she told me in one of our meetings. "But you can help them with their lessons at night."

"That would be great," I said. "I could help Cedric on the claim during the day—if you don't need me around the house, that is. I want to earn my keep."

"If I need you, I'll let you know. But otherwise, I have no problem with you helping your young man, provided you give me your word nothing untoward will happen. And he'll need to escort you there and back each day. I can't have you traipsing through that wild land on your own."

The arrangement suited me just fine, and I was excited that I'd get to help Cedric and hopefully wrap up this deal that much sooner. I saw little of him that week. He was busy, wrapped up in the logistics of supplies and claim arrangements.

"You realize I'm one of the 'lucky' ones," he told me one day. "There's actually some sort of shanty on the claim they've assigned me. Some prospector built it and then decided he didn't like being in the wilderness. I hear it's in disrepair, so I'll have to buy some things to fix it up. But most of the miners are living in tents and lean-tos."

We were in the cellar, where I'd finished the painting. Our relationship might be in the open, but we attracted too many prying eyes to feel comfortable speaking in public. "To think we first met in that drawing room," I mused. "And now this shanty is the height of luxury."

"Nah. I hear the Marshall family has a cabin. You won't ever want to leave that palace to come see me."

"I'll see you as much as I can," I insisted. "Though Mistress Marshall told me that nothing 'untoward' had better happen."

He leaned back against an iron-hinged chest, hands in his pockets. "Well, she doesn't need to worry about me. I'll be on best behavior."

I stepped toward him and wrapped my arms around his neck. "Who said you're the one she has to worry about?"

I leaned in, not for a true kiss, but just for the barest brush of my lips against his. I lingered for a few tantalizing moments, holding back despite his obvious interest in more. His hands gripped my waist when I pulled away, his fingers curling into me.

"I should probably get going," I said lightly. "I have things to do."

"I could give you a few suggestions."

"Important *frontier* things to do," I amended. I trailed my fingers along the side of his neck. "Sorry if I led you on."

"You are not. You've been leading me on since the day I met you, and I've been dutifully following. One day . . . one day I'll catch you. And then . . ."

His mouth found mine, and I wrapped myself against him. I wanted more than kisses, more than embraces. I wanted to banish all the space between us until it was impossible to know where I ended and he began. When we finally broke away, I could hardly stand, and wondered who was really leading whom.

"And then," I echoed with a sigh. "And then . . ."

I *did* have other things to do, and as we parted ways, I reminded myself that Cedric and I would have more time on our hands on the journey to Hadisen than we'd had together so far.

As he'd suggested, Aiana was the one to take me into town to shop. I'd spent little time with the Balanquan woman and was still fascinated by her. I came down Wisteria Hollow's main staircase and was surprised to see Mira waiting with her by the door.

"What this?" I asked, not that I was unhappy to have Mira there. Although she wasn't the busiest of the Glittering Court's girls, she'd still been caught up in the routine of it all while I simply cooled my heels.

Mira looked far happier than she ever did about going out to a party. "Who knows when we'll see you again, once you leave? We wanted to come along and get a little more Adelaide time in."

"We?"

"Tamsin should be down any minute. She was finishing a letter."

"She's still writing them?" I asked. Tamsin had been in my thoughts constantly since the storm, but her obsessive letter writing had slipped my mind.

"She had a whole bundle of them that she brought back from Grashond. I guess she was still writing them there. And I heard her making inquiries about courier services back to Osfrid."

Tamsin came down the stairs just then, radiant in a gown of deep emerald taffeta that bared her shoulders. "You know we're going to buy wilderness supplies, right?" I asked. "There's no formal luncheon planned."

Tamsin lifted her chin. "It doesn't matter where we're going. I won't look anything less than perfect—you never know who'll be watching. Besides, I have a dinner engagement afterward. Warren's mother has invited me over."

"Well, I'm sure that'll be very interesting," I said, in as neutral a tone as I could manage. Tamsin had immediately honed in on him, and thus far he'd seemed to return her interest.

Aiana said almost nothing as a carriage took us into the heart of Cape Triumph. She strode comfortably through the streets in her trousers and a long tunic, uncaring who gave her curious looks. It was hard to say if it was her attire or ethnicity that attracted attention. But in the diverse culture of Cape Triumph, I didn't think she stood out that much. Tamsin certainly stood out as well, but those who looked her over said nothing impolite. I think the sight of fierce Aiana at her side kept them at bay.

This was the first time I'd really been out in the crowds, rather than just viewing them from a carriage. It was hard not to stop and stare at everything. The shops and restaurants offered nearly as much as I might find in a busy district of Osfro. Like everything else in the New World, though, there was a tentative feel to it—none of that old, established solidity. Some of the businesses had made good attempts at respectability, with glass windows and well-fortified buildings. Others could have been thrown together that day, with hastily written signs and a fragility that suggested they might fall over at any moment. It was all fascinating and overwhelming at the same time, and despite her show of confidence, I could tell Tamsin was daunted too. Mira moved effortlessly, as though she walked the streets all the time. For all I knew, she did.

We passed fishermen and lumberjacks doggedly going to their jobs.

Adoria's aristocrats strode haughtily through, flanked by servants. One young man, with a long wig and flamboyant purple coat, stopped to bow and take his plumed hat off before us in a gallant gesture. Aiana rolled her eyes when we moved past him. "One of the 'idle elite,' as we call them. The sons of wealthy settlers with nothing to do, so they dress like that and think they're pirates or some such nonsense. Except pirates do more work than they do. They need to spend a day with Tom Shortsleeves or one of the others."

"Are all those pirate stories real?" I asked. "The heroic ones and the cruel ones?"

"Embellished, but real. All stories have a seed of truth."

She took me to one of the more reputable-looking shops, with WINSLOW & ELLIOTT OUTFITTERS etched on the glass window. Stepping inside, I saw all sorts of gear and supplies that one might need in setting off on an adventure to unknown lands. Two young men spoke to another man behind the counter, and when I caught a glimpse of him, I was surprised to recognize his face.

I nudged Mira, who was studying a pair of leather boots. "Hey, remember Grant Elliott from the ship? He's working here."

"Who?" she asked, not really paying attention to me.

Grant walked through the store to fetch a saddle for his customers, his eyes sliding over us in surprise. He nodded a greeting to Aiana.

"*Qi dica hakta,*" she said.

"*Manasta,*" he replied gruffly. Aiana meandered away from us to study a display of canteens, and I hurried after her.

"What was that you said?"

"My native tongue. Mister Elliott is half-Balanquan."

"Is he?" I looked back at him, hoping my scrutiny wasn't obvious. Although he had black hair like Aiana, there was nothing about him that would've suggested he wasn't an ordinary Osfridian. "I wouldn't have guessed it."

"I think he prefers it that way. It'd be much harder to run a business in Cape Triumph if people knew the truth about his background."

"How did you end up in Cape Triumph?" I asked. "If it's not rude of me to ask."

"Not at all. I ran away to escape an unhappy marriage. It had been arranged against my wishes. But my wife and I . . . weren't compatible."

"Your wife?" I asked, wondering if she'd had some sort of translation issue.

"My wife," she affirmed. "The Balanquans don't look down on same-sex relations the way your people do."

I didn't answer right away. "Look down" was putting it mildly, since such things were considered a great sin by the priests of Uros. Possibly more so than being an Alanzan.

"Did you leave because . . . um, because you didn't want to be with a woman?"

She grinned. "I have no problem being with women—just not that one. She was unkind, to put it mildly. I came to your colonies, wanting to learn about your culture firsthand, and eventually fell in with the Thorns. Jasper offered me a job, and as you might imagine, I had a particular interest in looking after girls who were being sold off to men they hardly knew."

"Is that . . . is that why you dress like you do—like a man? Because you . . . prefer women?" As soon as the words left my mouth, I felt like an idiot. Aiana's laughter only intensified that feeling.

"I dress like this because it's more comfortable than all those ridiculous skirts and petticoats the rest of you prance around in. And, as you'll soon see, you'll be dressing the same. You aren't going to work a gold claim in a ball gown."

With that, she left me gaping and went to the counter to speak to a now-free Grant. I found Tamsin and Mira on the other side of the store, sifting through bolts of fabric.

Tamsin held up a piece of coarsely woven linen. "I wouldn't use this to scrub a floor."

"I remember the dress you came in wearing," said Mira. "It wasn't nearly in such good condition."

"Even so, I'm not going to start wearing this stuff again for the sake of nostalgia." Tamsin regarded me sorrowfully. "Damn, Adelaide. I hope you can at least get something in organdy."

"Adelaide," called Aiana. "We need to measure you."

Tamsin came with me out of curiosity, but Mira stayed to further examine the loose fabrics. Grant looked much as he did on the ship—handsome, decently dressed, but messy around the edges. When we reached the counter, he looked us over. "So who's the lucky explorer?" he asked.

"Me," I said.

"Off to Hadisen with Doyle, eh? Quite an adventure ahead of you."

Tamsin fixed him with an imperious look. "That's *Governor* Doyle. Please address my fiancé by his proper title."

We all looked at her in astonishment, and she turned sheepish.

"Well, I mean, he's not my fiancé. Not yet. I'm going to work on that."

"And not really governor yet either," Grant pointed out with a smile. "But who's keeping track?"

Aiana snapped at him in Balanquan, which he responded to good-naturedly. I thought back to how he'd always spoken so politely during shipboard encounters and then been so gruff during the storm. I supposed stress could bring out the worst in everyone, because he seemed perfectly fine now as he gauged my size, keeping a proper distance with his measuring tape.

There was no time to have custom clothing made from the raw materials he sold, but there was plenty of ready-made attire in the store. The sizes were close enough to get me by for now, and adjustments could always be made later. I didn't end up with an exact replica of Aiana's attire, but it was pretty close. Wide-legged pants of soft suede that almost looked like a skirt when I stood. Plain, serviceable blouses and a knee-length leather coat to go over them when the weather turned cold. Sturdy gloves and boots with no embellishment.

"Sorry I can't match the dresses you're used to, but these'll keep you a lot more comfortable." Grant studied me a few moments more. "And a hat. You'll want one for your skin—but I'm afraid it might not help much." He produced a wide-brimmed leather one from behind the counter.

"Why not?" I asked.

"The weather's more extreme. Those summer days'll scorch you. What are you going to be doing out there? You might be okay if you're doing chores inside."

"I'm going to help pan for gold."

He pondered this for a long moment, saying nothing. Finally, he took the hat back and produced one with a wider brim. "It'll be brutal. Good luck."

Once we were outside, Tamsin immediately asked, "What he said about it being brutal . . . Adelaide, are you sure you want to do this? Are you sure you want to go to Hadisen?"

"I'm sure I want to be with Cedric," I said simply. "And I'll go down whatever path that involves. Besides, don't *you* want to go to Hadisen?"

"Yes. And live in the governor's mansion. Not a riverbed."

Mira touched my arm as we were about to turn down the road that would lead us out of the city center to our carriage. "Look over there. By the bank."

I followed her gaze. "Oh. Excuse me a moment." I hurried across the thoroughfare and called, "Mister Adelton!"

Nicholas, who'd been about to walk into the building, turned in surprise. "Miss Bailey. I didn't expect to see you here. I thought you'd be on your way to Hadisen."

"Soon," I said, feeling my cheeks flush. "I know Cedric talked to you, but I just had to come myself and say . . . well, I'm sorry. I'm sorry for what we put you through. You must feel so . . . I don't know. Deceived."

He grew thoughtful. "Not exactly. A little disappointed, perhaps . . . but honestly, I was more dazzled by you than in love with you. If you don't take offense to that."

"Not at all . . . we had only a few meetings."

"Exactly. If I'd felt more, my reaction might have been different. But I could always tell there was something preoccupying you. So long as you were entering of your own free will, I didn't mind. I figured it was the nature of these sorts of arranged marriages."

"I would have done it of my own free will," I said adamantly. "You're a good man—the best I've met here."

"Excepting young Mister Thorn, of course." He smiled at my chagrin. "Don't feel bad. I'm happy for you."

I sighed. "That's kind of you . . . but I can't shake the feeling you've been used. You know, there are a number of other Glittering Court girls I could recommend—"

He held up a hand to silence me. "Thank you, but I'm done with making matches that sound good on paper. The more I think about your grand romance with Mister Thorn, the more I think I'm better off finding one of my own. No contracts."

"I hope you find one," I said earnestly.

He shook my hand. "Me too. And I wish you well. If I can ever be of service, let me know."

"Who was that?" Tamsin asked when I returned to my friends.

"The man Cedric nearly married me off to."

Tamsin peered behind me to get a better look. "Is he available?"

"Yes. But not that well off. Or really interested, after what Cedric and I put him through."

I fell into step with Aiana while Mira trailed behind with Tamsin. "Mister Adelton seems to be taking things reasonably well," Aiana said to me quietly.

"Everyone has. Well, not Jasper. And some of the girls are still holding it over me." Clara in particular enjoyed telling the story of how she'd found Cedric and me in the attic to everyone she met. "But most people have been understanding, even when they probably shouldn't be. Including Warren Doyle."

Aiana took a long time to answer. "Yes. It certainly was understanding of him—making such an offer to you."

I thought back to the shop and then cast a quick glance back to make sure Tamsin was still engaged with Mira. "His mother isn't the most, ah, upstanding of women, but as for Warren, do you think he's—well, I mean, should we—"

"I don't know," said Aiana. "I really don't know much about Warren Doyle, short of gossip. What I do know is that when things sound too good to be true, well, they usually are."

Uneasiness settled over me. "I tried telling that to Cedric. But he said even if there's some ploy going on, we were better off taking our chances in Hadisen."

"He may be right." Aiana stopped walking to look me in the eye. "There's more freedom there—but more danger too. It's a fledgling land. An untamed land. And that makes it easier for people to break the rules. I wish you two the best, but . . ."

"But what?" I prompted.

"Trust each other there," she said at last. "But no one else."

CHAPTER 22

I'D HOPED TO SEE BOTH TAMSIN AND MIRA THE NIGHT before I left for Hadisen. A party kept them late, however, and I found myself sitting alone in our bedroom, pondering whether I should get some sleep or not. I knew the journey ahead was going to be tiring, but I couldn't stand the thought of missing out on seeing my best friends. That, and I wasn't sure my nerves would let me sleep anyway.

The two of them finally came in after midnight, catching me mid-yawn. Both put on smiles upon seeing me awake, but I could instantly detect a difference in their moods. Mira seemed subdued, while Tamsin was exuberant.

"What happened?" I asked her.

She began unlacing her emerald-green satin overdress. "Nothing official—but something pretty unofficially serious."

"Isn't that a sort of contradiction?" I asked, shooting a conspiratorial look at Mira. She didn't share my amusement.

"Warren asked me to wait for him," said Tamsin proudly. "He didn't promise an engagement—yet—but said I was by far his favorite and that he'd like to make things official with me when he returns. So I promised not to enter into any arrangements until then—though of course, I'll still go out. No point in sitting around here bored."

I frowned, troubled by a number of things. "When he returns . . . but that could be a very long time."

"It'll be in two weeks, actually." Tamsin had wiggled out of the dress and now sat in her chemise and petticoats. "He'll go with your party tomorrow, get things established, and then sail back to report on Hadisen's affairs and solicit any other help."

"I suppose that makes sense, but he won't be in Hadisen for long."

Hadisen's inhospitable coastline made it difficult for large ships to get close. So, any substantial shipments of cargo, animals, and other materials needed to be moved overland. That was the way my party would be traveling tomorrow, circling the bay through Denham's territory and then into Hadisen. The trip took a little over a week. Individuals sailing straight across the bay in small boats could do so in a day. It was useful for messengers and those without cargo, but little more.

"Well, I'm sure he'll be back soon—possibly with a wife in tow." Tamsin was shining with pride. "I hope it won't be awkward if you're one of my citizens, Adelaide."

I laughed at that. "Not at all."

"You must be excited," said Mira. She looked eager to change the subject. "A great adventure ahead of you."

"I don't care about the adventure. I just want everything to be settled with Cedric."

I spoke boldly and earned looks of admiration and wistfulness. Tamsin might treat marriage pragmatically, and Mira might treat it with indifference, but I frequently had the sense that both were fascinated with—and even a little jealous of—the romantic love I'd stumbled into. The three of us stayed up late and talked about the future. I didn't want to tell them the truth: that I was a bit terrified of what was to come. Not with Cedric, of course. Leaving a noblewoman's life for that of an upper-class colonial citizen in a well-established city wasn't as big a leap as it might seem. But going from nobility to a commoner in a vast, unsettled wilderness? That was something altogether different, and I had no idea what to expect.

Mira and Tamsin were allowed to see me off the next morning. The party leaving for Hadisen was far bigger than I expected. They gathered on the edge of town, a vast cavalcade of horses, wagons, and people in seeming disarray. Warren was near the front, looking splendid on a white horse as he spoke to several other men who seemed to be advisors. Another rider trotted up to us, and I did a double take when I saw it was Cedric.

"Are you on a horse?" I exclaimed.

He shot me a wry look. "You don't have to make it sound *quite* so outlandish."

"I just didn't even know you could ride." I looked the horse over. She was a shaggy brown mare who seemed to be bored with everything going on around her. "I hope you didn't pay a lot for her."

"I wasn't aware you were such an expert." I understood the cautioning tone in his voice. Horseback riding was a common pastime for the nobility in Osfrid when they were at the country manors. Here in Adoria, many settlers rode horses for survival. But a city commoner, like my Adelaide identity, would never interact with a horse outside of practical transport. I would've expected the same for someone like Cedric.

"I've seen them around, that's all," I said. I had to restrain myself from correcting the awkward way he sat his saddle and held the reins.

"Well, she's tougher than she looks," he assured me. "I call her Lizzie."

I tried not to roll my eyes. "Great choice."

Looking around, I saw that Tamsin was up talking to Warren, her face shining. Mira too had disappeared, and moments later, I spied her listening to some men making plans to explore Hadisen. Not far from her was Grant Elliott, who appeared to be delivering some last-minute supplies.

"My allies have abandoned me," I remarked.

Cedric leaned down and brushed some wayward tendrils from my face. The intimacy startled me until I realized we had nothing left to hide. "You've still got your number-one ally," he said, although he frowned when he saw whom I'd been watching. "Grant Elliott seemed decent enough on the ship, but it turns out he's joined Warren's group of heretic hunters."

"Heretic hunters?"

"Yeah, there's a group of them promising to 'keep order' while Warren's away, and find the Star Advent Alanzans who escaped from jail. Grant's among them."

"Well, then I'm sorry I gave him my business." I touched the wide-brimmed hat on my head. "Maybe I should try to return this."

"Don't," said Cedric. "It's cute."

I wished I could ride too, but the meager funds he and I shared couldn't cover a second horse. That, and my riding skills would have raised suspicions. Instead, I'd be riding in the Marshalls' wagon, something that sounded more luxurious than the reality. It was a plain, rough-planked contraption packed with various supplies that the children and I would have to squeeze in around. It had no top, and I hoped we wouldn't run into any rain.

At last, Warren called for everyone's attention. "It's time," he called, his voice ringing above the throng. "Time to claim our destiny!"

Settlers and well-wishers alike cheered, and even I couldn't help getting caught up in the spirit of adventure. I hugged Tamsin and Mira goodbye and then climbed up into the back of the wagon. I was saving the split skirts for when we reached Hadisen. For the journey, I was in a calico dress that was as barebones as one could get. No chemise, no petticoats—just a simple lining underneath. If not for the floral print, it could have passed for one of the Grashond dresses.

My spot in the wagon was a cramped and narrow one between two bundled crates. The planks I had to sit on were dirty and worn, and trying to clean them only resulted in getting splinters. Five minutes into the ride, I learned that there was no shock absorption of any kind.

I leaned back against the wagon's side, thinking of what we'd always called the "rose parlor" back in my family's Osfro home. Elaborately designed rugs covering every inch of the floor. Velvet-covered wallpaper. One-of-a-kind paintings. Vases imported from the Xin lands far to the east. Chairs and sofas with padding so thick, you would sink into them. And of course, everything was meticulously cleaned on a daily basis by a flock of servants.

"What's wrong?" asked one of the Marshall girls. Her name was Sarah.

I glanced over at Cedric riding that ridiculous horse. "Nothing. Just thinking I've come a long ways."

Within an hour, we were out of the city's limits, past the fort and its skeleton crew of soldiers. A few hours after that, we'd moved past all of Cape Triumph's small outlying settlements. I'd thought the wilderness had a claim on that town, but I was wrong. The far reaches of Denham Colony looked as though no human had ever touched them. The towering trees that had stood like sentinels in Cape Triumph now formed a veritable army, side by side, at times making the rough road difficult to traverse. It was fascinating. Breathtaking. Terrifying. The *real* New World.

My starry-eyed enthusiasm didn't last long. When we called a halt for the night, my legs nearly collapsed underneath me when I got out of the wagon. The constant shaking and close quarters had cramped my muscles, producing a soreness I would have expected only after running uphill for five hours. Dinner was dried biscuits and jerky, little better than the ship's fare. Fires were built for heat and boiling water, and I was sent to gather wood from fallen branches. Mostly I seemed to gather splinters.

Cedric, like most of the younger men in the party, was kept busy with various jobs, so after a quick smile at dinnertime, he disappeared for the rest of the evening. When bedtime came, Mister and Mistress Marshall slept in the wagon while the rest of the kids and I made beds of blankets on the ground. The earth below me was hard and uneven. The blanket couldn't keep me warm as night's chill deepened, so I'd added my long leather coat. I was still cold. And I was pretty sure every mosquito in the colony had found me.

I tossed and turned, my frustration keeping me awake almost as much as the harsh conditions did. I found myself again thinking of my Osfro town house. This time, I was obsessed with memories of my bed. A mattress big enough for five people. Silk sheets scented with lavender. As many blankets as you needed on a cold night.

I didn't realize right away that I was crying. When I did, I quickly got up before any of the children sleeping near me woke and noticed. Wrapping the thin blanket around me, I hurried away from the wagon, slipping through groups of other sleeping settlers. A few still sat by fires, dicing and telling stories, but they paid little attention to me. I moved as far to the camp's edge as I dared, enough to give me privacy but not venture into the wild unknown.

There, I sat down miserably and buried my face in my hands, trying to keep my sobs as quiet as possible. I couldn't stand the thought of my weakness getting back to Warren. I had this horrible image of him looking down at me with a too-kind expression, saying sympathetically: "You could have been my wife. You could have traveled in the padded carriage and slept in my tent." I'd seen one of his men haul a mattress into it earlier.

A hand touched my shoulder, and I jumped to my feet. Cedric stood there, shadows playing over his startled face. He'd been busy with his own chores, and I hadn't seen him all evening. "It *is* you. I didn't mean to scare you."

I furiously wiped at my face. "What are you doing here?"

"I went over to the Marshall wagon hoping to steal you for a quick word. When you weren't there, I started searching around." He reached for my face, but I pulled back. "What's wrong?"

"Nothing."

"Adelaide, I'm serious. What's wrong?"

I threw up my hands. "Pick something, Cedric! Using my skirt as a napkin at dinner tonight. No bathrooms. I keep swallowing gnats. And the smell! I get that bathing will be limited on this trip, but didn't any of them do it before we left? It's only been one day."

"You knew this wouldn't be easy," he said quietly. "Do you regret it? Do you regret . . ."

"Us?" I finished. "No. Not for an instant. And that leads to the worst part of all: hating myself for feeling this way. I hate listening to myself whine. I hate that I'm too weak to put our love above these conditions."

"No one said you had to love it out here."

"You do. I saw your face once we were truly clear of the Cape Triumph settlements. This is some kind of spiritual experience for you."

He held up his hands. From the glow of scattered fires, I could see dirt and cuts. His face was dirty too. "This isn't that spiritual. Neither is the guy who keeps saying my face is too pretty and he wants to break my nose. And you wouldn't believe how sore I am after being on that horse all day."

"Oh, I can believe it. But you aren't letting it get to you. You're not that weak."

He drew me to him, and this time, I didn't resist. "You aren't weak. But for the first time in your life you aren't good at everything. The world rotated around you in Osfro and told you that you could do no wrong. At Blue Spring, despite some mishaps, you were still the best in all your studies. And in Cape Triumph, you were the star of the Glittering Court. Out here, you're . . ."

"Miserable? Useless?"

"Adjusting. This is the first day, and it's a shock. You'll get used to it as the trip goes on, and once you're in Hadisen with a roof over you, you'll think you've gone back to an Osfridian palace."

I let those words sink in. "Speaking of roofs, what happens if it rains out here?"

"One worry at a time."

He smiled in that bewitching way he had, that way that said he could take care of everything. But could he this time? "I'm tired, Cedric. So, so tired. It was a long day, but I can't sleep. The ground's horrible. And I'm cold. How can it be this cold? It's spring."

He took my hand and pulled me down. "I can't do anything about the ground, but I can help with the cold."

He had a thin blanket of his own, and he spread both of ours on the ground. Lying down, he urged me to do the same, and we snuggled together, each of us trying to wrap the other in our respective coats. The ground was still bumpy, but with his body against mine and the sound of his heartbeat by my ear, I didn't mind as much.

"We can't stay like this," I said. "We'll get in trouble if we're caught."

"We'll go back before dawn."

"How will we know?"

"I'll know."

I felt warmth settle around me and the first glimmers of drowsiness seeping in. "I will do anything for us," I said through a yawn. "I hope you know that."

"I've never doubted it." He kissed the top of my head.

"You can give me a better kiss than that if you want."

"I *do* want to, but you need to sleep. Maybe tomorrow night, when you're better rested."

I fought another yawn. "Some things don't change. You're so full of yourself, Cedric Thorn. Certain I'll just sleep next to you again tomorrow. We're not married yet. I haven't taken any vows to lie with you under the moon."

He kissed the top of my head again. I melted into the security of his body and felt true happiness burn through me. After several minutes, I asked, "Cedric?"

His breathing had grown steady, and I wondered if he was asleep. Then: "Yes?"

"You smell good. You're the only thing that smells good out here. Is that from putting on the vetiver this morning, or did you bring it with you?"

"I brought it with me."

I moved closer to him. "Thank Uros."

As promised, Cedric woke up just before sunrise so that we could each go back to our respective places before we were missed. My body still ached, but waking up next to Cedric made me not notice the pain as much.

"Is that some Alanzan thing?" I whispered before we parted. "Are you synced with the sun?"

"It's something I've done since childhood. I've always been a restless sleeper." He squinted over at the eastern sky and raised a hand in salute. "But maybe it's some gift I didn't even know I had, right from Alanziel herself." Seeing the golden dawn play over Cedric's features and cast a fiery hue to his hair, I could very well believe he was favored by the patron angel of passionate love.

As I returned to the Marshall wagon, I felt better than I had the previous night. Both venting and getting rest had given me new perspective. Cedric had been right. There was no question these were harsh conditions. Anyone would have difficulty. But it was truly the most out of my depth I'd ever felt in my life—which was saying something, after assuming someone else's identity. I had to be patient with myself as I figured this out.

And I did, in the days to come. I still didn't like the food or sleeping on the ground. But at least it didn't rain. Cedric and I continued spending our nights together at the camp's edge, and as the caravan fell into a routine, he spent more time with me in the day. Having such a large party, we moved pretty slowly. He and I could walk together, leading the horse, and easily keep pace with the others. The rough terrain and increasing elevation made it tiring, but I gradually toughened up.

"Grant Elliott was right about the sun," I told Cedric one day. It was a few days into our trip. We were on a lunch break, sitting off by ourselves in the shade.

"What did he say?"

"That it was brutal." I held up my hands for examination. "Look how tan these are already. I can't even imagine how my face must look."

"Beautiful, as always," said Cedric. He tore apart a piece of jerky and handed half to me.

"You didn't even look."

"I don't have to." But he did glance up and study my face. "I think you're getting a few freckles. They're cute."

"Don't tell Tamsin that—she's always trying to hide hers. And my grandmother would faint if she could see me." I'd started off flippant but felt my heart sink as I thought of Grandmama. "You know, when I heard she was looking for me, I first worried because of the obvious trouble I could get in. But what really bothers me about it now is knowing that she's still searching. She doesn't know what happened to me but still wants me. She hasn't given up."

"Of course she hasn't. It isn't in the Witmore blood. Er, I mean Bailey blood. At least I assume it isn't in the Bailey blood to give up."

I thought about my former maid. "Well, Ada kind of gave up . . . or did she? If she's at the dairy farm she wanted, I suppose it all worked out for her."

Cedric put his arm around my shoulder, letting me lean against him. "Once we're married and everything is stable, you can send word back to your grandmother. Let her know you're all right."

Afternoon sunlight shone down on us through the branches of the great maple behind our backs. If I weren't feeling so melancholy about Grandmama, I could have thought of it as an idyllic setting. "I just hope she can forgive me for—"

"There you two are," snapped a harsh voice. We both looked up to see Elias Carter, Warren's chief assistant in Hadisen, striding toward us. "The party's getting packed up and nearly ready to move again. I should've known I'd find you two off here doing immoral things."

"Eating lunch?" I asked.

Elias fixed me with a beady glare. He'd made it clear many times on this trip that he disapproved of us. "Don't be impertinent with me, Miss Bailey. How the governor ever found it in his magnanimous heart to forgive you and offer you this chance is beyond me. I wouldn't have. But then, he is a great man. I am not."

"That's certainly true," said Cedric, deadpan.

Elias's brow furrowed, as he seemed to realize he'd inadvertently insulted himself. Before he could respond, we heard a scream coming from the direction of the main camp. Without a backward glance at us, Elias ran off toward it. We followed close behind.

The first thing I saw was that the party hadn't been "nearly ready to move again," as Elias had told us. There were signs all around that others had been in the middle of their lunches too. But no one was eating now. Everyone was on their feet. Some people, particularly those with children, were rushing toward the back of the camp with their little ones. Others—mostly men—were stalking toward the front. Until now, I hadn't realized how many weapons were in this caravan. Guns and knives abounded.

"What's going on?" I asked one woman.

"Icori," she said. "Best hide with us."

Cedric and I looked at each other in disbelief. "Icori haven't been in Denham in nearly two years," he said. He put out an arm to stop me when I started to move forward. "You don't have to hide, but we probably shouldn't go bursting into the middle of this until we know what's going on."

"I just want to see."

Cedric reluctantly moved through the crowd with me. He wasn't the type to try to tell me what I could or couldn't do. But I had a feeling that if there was any sign of danger, he'd toss me over his shoulder and carry me away kicking and screaming.

We stopped near the edge of a group of would-be prospectors, all with guns drawn. It gave us a clear vantage down the dusty trail through the woods. There, Warren and several other armed men stood in front of two men on horseback who met every description of the Icori I'd ever read or heard. Well, except for the part about them being bloodthirsty demons.

Dress and styling aside, these two looked pretty human to me. One was an older man, late fifties perhaps, with a bushy red beard and a tunic of green plaid. He was the size of a bull, and despite his age, something told me he could hold his own against a younger man in a fight. Probably a dozen younger men. The rider beside him didn't look much older than Cedric. His bare, muscled chest was painted with designs of blue woad. A tartan in that same green plaid was draped over one shoulder and held with a copper pin. White-blond hair hanging loosely to his shoulders contrasted with his skin. He was the one Warren seemed focused on while speaking.

"And I told you, you have no business here. Icori are not welcome on Denham lands—or any civilized Osfridian lands. Go back to the territories you were ceded."

"I would gladly do that," the blond man replied, "if your people would stop trespassing onto our lands." There were two notable things about the way he spoke. One was that he was remarkably calm, given all the guns pointed at him. Second, his Osfridian was nearly perfect.

"No one wants your lands," said Warren, which seemed slightly inaccurate given all that Osfrid and other countries across the sea had taken. "If anything, I've heard rumors of *your* people harassing our lands up north. Should that be true, you'll have real visitors in your lands in the form of our soldiers. A little more serious than these delusions you're prattling on about."

"The burned villages I've seen aren't delusions. We demand answers."

Warren scoffed. "Forgive me if I don't really feel the two of you can make demands. There's a lot more of us than there are of you."

"Shoot 'em!" someone called from the crowd. "Shoot the savages!"

The Icori man remained unfazed and never looked away from Warren. "I'd hoped we wouldn't need shows of force to open a dialogue on protecting innocents. I'd think that's what civilized men do."

"Civilized," sneered Elias. "Like you're ones to talk."

"This civilized man is going to give you the chance to leave with your lives." Warren's words suggested generosity, but his tone was pure ice. "Not far ahead is a northward trail that cuts through the corner of Denham and leads over to the western territories. I'm sure you know it. I'm sure it's what you took to get here. Turn around right now and go back. If you move fast enough, you should be out of Denham by sunset. I'm going to leave a group of men to guard that trail's intersection and scout it out in the morning. If there's any sign that you are still in our lands, you will die."

"Shoot 'em anyway!" someone yelled.

The Icori murmured something to his companion. The bearded man scowled and answered back in their own language. The blond man turned back to Warren. "We will take our conversation elsewhere. Thank you for your time."

The Icori turned around on their horses, and I held my breath as several men held up their guns and aimed at the Icoris' backs. Warren noticed this too and held up a hand of warding. The Icori horses quickly moved from a walk to a gallop and were soon out of range.

The Icori encounter was all anyone could talk about for the rest of the day. Opinions were understandably mixed. Plenty were in the "shoot 'em" camp. Others thought Warren's act of compassion only showed what a noble spirit he had.

"It was all a bluff," an older man told Cedric and me at dinner that night. He paused to turn his head and spit. "He had no other choice. If he'd killed him, there's always the chance of triggering another war. No one knows how touchy the Icori are these days. And that whole nonsense about men guarding the trail is . . . well, nonsense. Icori don't need trails. If they want to slip away and melt into the woods, they can."

I looked across the heads of the other settlers, off to where Warren sat on the opposite side of camp. He had a bigger group of admirers than usual, all lauding him on his masterful act of diplomacy. I'd thought it was well done myself until I heard our companion's commentary.

"The Icori were much more composed than I expected," I remarked. "I'd be a lot more hostile if I'd been forced from my land."

"Twice," the old man reminded us. "Don't forget the heroes

who threw them out of Osfrid in the first place. Good King Wilfrid. Suttingham. Bentley. Rothford."

I tried not to wince at hearing my ancestor's name. The settlement of Osfrid had taken place so long ago that it was easy sometimes to forget that the savages Rupert had fought there were the ancestors of those who'd fled across the sea and made new lives for themselves in these lands. Or tried to, at least.

"This place is so vast," I told Cedric later. "Adoria's a hundred times the size of Osfrid. Shouldn't there be enough room for all of us this time?"

He gazed around us. Nightfall was upon us, but we could still make out the enormous trees as they reached up to the stars. "Greedy men never have enough room. I don't know what'll happen to the Icori—or this land. Osfrid was once this wild too, and now it's clear-cut and parceled." He looked back down and slipped his arm around me. I caught the scent of his vetiver, reassuring me not all civilization was lost. "One thing I do know is that they've increased nighttime watches. You and I are going to have to go separate ways tonight."

"Are you sure?" But even as I spoke, I knew he was right. I could already see patrols assembling. "I won't sleep nearly as well."

"I'll actually sleep better," he muttered.

"You don't like sleeping by me?"

"I like sleeping by you too much. I spend half the night thinking about—"

"Hey," I warned. "There are children nearby."

Cedric gave me a look of mock chastisement. "What I was *going* to say is that I spend half the night thinking about when we're getting married. The places your mind goes. Someone should have sent you to finishing school."

"Technically, *you* sent me to finishing school. So you've got no one to blame if you want me to behave differently."

He drew me in for a kiss. "Now why would I ever want that?"

So there was no more shared sleep between us for the remainder of the trip. I missed it—achingly so—but I kept reminding myself this was all just another step along the path to our future. We would endure.

"You and your young man didn't have a fight, did you?" Mistress Marshall asked me one day. We were both riding in the wagon, and I was wondering if I should be concerned that I no longer noticed the rattling.

"Why do you think that?"

She gave me a knowing look. "Just noticed you've been sleeping by our wagon again these last few days."

I felt a flush sweep over me. "Mistress Marshall—it's not—it's not anything like that. Nothing happened. We were just sleeping together. I mean, like, actually sleeping. Then we decided it'd be best to stop after the watches increased."

"Very sensible of you," she said. I couldn't tell if she really believed me.

"I mean it," I insisted. "We've behaved—that is, well, exactly as we should. And we'll keep doing that."

Her smile was kind, despite a cracked tooth. "Perhaps. But you're very young. And I know how hot young blood can run. While you're under my roof, I'll make sure you're respectable and keeping with the virtues dictated by Uros. But when you're not under my roof . . ."

I couldn't meet her eyes. "Mistress Marshall, we intend to behave with the utmost decorum until we're married."

"Intentions and actions rarely line up. And in the event your intentions go awry, I don't want you to get in trouble." She handed me a small burlap bag with a spicy smell. "These are cinnamon thorn leaves. You know what these are for?"

I gulped and, impossibly, felt my blush heat up even more. "Yes, ma'am. Our teachers at Blue Spring Manor—back in Osfrid—told us."

"Well, that's good," she said. "Saves us both from an embarrassing conversation."

I wasn't so sure about that. As it was, I really didn't think my mortification could get any worse at that moment. I tried to hand the bag back to her.

"Thank you, but I really don't think I'll need these."

She refused the bag. "I've got plenty. They've kept me at six kids. If they keep you from having one before you're ready, it'll be well worth it."

I might have tried handing it back to her again, but then I heard a shout from farther up in the caravan. "The eastern tributary! We're at the eastern tributary!"

Cheers sounded, and I looked back to Mistress Marshall. "What does that mean?"

"It means, my dear, that we're about to cross into Hadisen."

Chapter 23

Aside from the tributary itself, there was no ostensible difference between Hadisen and the far reaches of Denham. We crossed the shallow water and continued on. Certainly, the land had shifted from what we'd left in Cape Triumph and its outskirts. Vegetation had thinned out, and the peaks of a low mountain range grew clearer in the distance. The famous gold mines were located in the foothills of those mountains. The lowlands contained greener farmlands, such as those the Marshalls claimed.

We'd been traveling for just over a week when we arrived in White Rock—Hadisen's capital city, such as it was. Excitement and a renewed sense of energy filled our party as we crossed into the town's limits. Had I seen it immediately after Cape Triumph, I would've been disappointed. But after days and days of trees, it felt as urban as Osfro. In reality, it was still a city in its early stages, with dusty tracks for roads and at least half the businesses being run out of tents. As in Cape Triumph, a mix of people walked the streets, but there were no elite well-to-do in this group. All belonged to the rough working class.

There was one fairly large house noticeable on a hill in the distance, almost as nice as Wisteria Hollow.

"That's the governor's house," Warren said, riding up on his white horse. He dismounted effortlessly. "Where I'll be staying."

The words hung between us a moment, and I regarded the fine house with a moment of envy. "Tamsin will be pleased," I said at last.

He gave me a small smile. "I hope so."

In White Rock, a new sort of chaos ensued. This was the launching point for all the settlers. Some already had claims and plots assigned to them. They looked over maps and surveys, trying to determine where their lands were and how long it would take to get to them. Other settlers had come here blindly, carried along by a dream. They either solicited Warren's agents for land to buy or lease, or else they sought work among those more established. Residents of White Rock, seeing new blood, were eager to come and sell their wares.

"I'm going out to my claim tonight," Cedric told me later. He'd been consulting a map with several other men. "Ours are near each other, and we'll go together."

"I wish I could go too," I said.

"I saw where the Marshall place is. It's only about two hours' ride by horse."

"A regular horse or Lizzie?" I asked.

"Lizzie will do just fine. Let me see what shape the claim is in, and then I'll bring you by." Seeing my disappointment, he touched my face and drew me close. "It'll only be a day or two."

"I know. I just hate parting again after everything that's happened."

"Cheer up, you lovebirds aren't parting for long," said Mistress Marshall, striding up to us. "And he's right—we are relatively close by. You'll get there soon enough, though you might not want to after you've stayed with us. A wild claim isn't going to look nearly as comfortable as a well-to-do homestead."

Mister Marshall had been out to Hadisen a number of times, overseeing the construction of a house before bringing his wife and children. I wanted to be with Cedric, but a secret part of me was eager to sleep under a real roof in a real bed—especially since the sky was finally threatening rain. I also wondered what the odds were of taking a bath. There was so much dirt under my fingernails that I could no longer see the whites.

Cedric and I parted with a kiss, and I watched him for as long as I could as I rode away in the Marshalls' wagon. The scrappy little town grew smaller and smaller, and I caught one last sight of Cedric holding up his hand to me before all was lost in dusk's shadows. When we reached the homestead, night had fallen completely. I could just make out the house, a cabin built with crosswise logs. From the outside, it didn't look very big.

As it turned out, it wasn't that big on the inside either. We had a large common room to be used for pretty much every household task: cooking, eating, sewing, entertaining, and so on. A tiny bedroom to the side was reserved for Mister and Mistress Marshall. Upstairs, in a loft, a partition separated out two bedrooms—one for the girls and one for the boys. I was sharing a large bed with the three girls. I hoped none of them kicked.

We spent the rest of the evening hauling in supplies before the rain came. Cape Triumph's sheltered position protected it from storms, but they could sometimes blow through to Hadisen with a vengeance. Most of the journey so far had been about endurance, and this was my first real taste of hard labor. Mister Marshall and a couple of the boys helped put the livestock in their barn. We finished just in time, and Mistress Marshall cooked us a pot of millet and dried meat for dinner over the hearth. We sat on a long bench at the table to eat. It wasn't comfortable, especially with my aching muscles, but it saved us from sitting on the hard-packed dirt floor.

"It won't stay like that forever," Mistress Marshall said, pointing down. "We aren't savages. We'll soon have straw to cover it."

When it came time to sleep, I picked a spider out of the bed and hoped there weren't any more. We blew out the candles and listened to the rain pound against the roof as we lay huddled together in the large bed. It turned out to be a steady downpour, not a fierce storm. The roof didn't leak, so it had that going for it at least.

Lying there in the dark, I remembered that I was a countess of the blood, a peeress of Osfrid. The anxiety I'd felt on my first day on the Hadisen journey rose within me, and I tried to think of Cedric's words, that my difficulty came in simply adjusting to a situation I wasn't perfect at. It was comfort enough to help me fall asleep, though I had to wonder how anyone could feel like an expert at living in a cabin on the brink of civilization.

Cedric didn't come the next day as he'd said he would. Or the day after that. At first, I was annoyed by the delay. But as more days added up, I began to worry. The Marshalls told me all was probably fine, but the fear gnawed at me. I had plenty of time to think about all sorts of terrible possibilities because I was constantly engaged in manual activities that taxed my body more than my mind. My academic lessons wouldn't begin until the homestead was set up, and I didn't mind pulling my share for the Marshalls. But I was hopelessly underprepared.

The skills I'd learned as a noblewoman were useless. And most of the Glittering Court's lessons were as well. No marriage possibility had ever ended in a scenario like this. We'd practiced tasks that the mistress of a modest household—like Nicholas Adelton's—might need to supervise or even help out with if the other servants were busy. But there'd been no preparation for the chores that met me out here. I learned to milk cows and churn butter. I ground hard corn into fine grain. I dug in the earth to plant seeds for vegetables and herbs. I cooked batches of simple, hearty fare that was low on taste but could feed a large crowd. I made lye soap—which was pretty much my least favorite job of all.

There was no party planning. No dancing. No sugared glass plates. No music in the conservatory. No conservatory.

And my hands were . . . well, not what they once were.

When Cedric finally showed, I was sweeping the cabin's earthen floor—something that seemed completely pointless to me. It mostly felt like I was moving dirt around. I'd been up since sunrise, and it was only one of many grubby chores I'd performed. I looked up to wipe my brow, startled to see Cedric standing in the doorway, regarding me with an astonished look. I let the broom drop to the floor and threw myself into his arms, nearly knocking him over in the process. He used the doorframe to steady himself and then wrapped me to him more closely. I rested a hand on his chest, taking in how real and solid he was.

"You're not dead," I breathed.

He choked on a laugh. "Nice to see you too, dear."

I wanted to make a joke to hide my true feelings. I didn't want him to know how afraid I'd been these last few days, that I'd imagined terrible things happening to him, that I'd feared all these dreams we'd built would be lost. But as Cedric looked me over and his smile faded, I knew he could see it all in my eyes.

"I'm sorry," he said softly.

"Cedric, where have you been?" I tightened my hold on him and could see now that he was as dirty and worn as I was. "I've been so worried."

"I know, I know. I should've sent word, but there's been so much to do. More than I expected. You'll see soon enough."

"We just finished breakfast, but you're welcome to some porridge," Mistress Marshall said from behind me. I'd forgotten she was there. Her tone was friendly, but there was an edge to it Cedric and I both understood. We quickly sprang apart.

The aforementioned porridge had been one of the blandest things I'd ever had. Cedric had always been picky at Blue Spring Manor and Wisteria Hollow, insisting his eggs be poached and his pastries warmed. I figured he'd turn down such a mundane meal, but to my surprise, he accepted and ate two bowls. When he finished, he asked the Marshalls if he could bring me to his claim.

"I know she must have all sorts of things to do here, but I'd like to show her the land," he said. "I'll return her by dinnertime."

"Certainly," said Mistress Marshall. "And then you can stay and eat with us."

Cedric looked immensely pleased by that.

Another rainstorm had made for a cool morning, and I donned

my suede pants and coat, along with the wide-brimmed hat. It was as much for practicality as to put on something clean. I tended to wear the same work dress each day, and the Marshalls took baths only on weekends.

"Don't you look like a proper frontier woman, ready to ride off and tame the wild," Cedric said.

"Makes sense, since I'm a better rider than you." I walked up to Lizzie. "Are you sure she can carry two of us?"

"You tell me, horsemistress."

I patted the old mare's neck. "Sure she can. Just no hard gallops."

We'd been too fresh out of Cape Triumph to even think about riding a horse together on our initial journey. Here, on the edge of civilization, the rules were more relaxed. Customs were dictated by expediency, and if we'd travel faster by horseback, so be it. He helped me up to the front of Lizzie and then jumped up behind me, much more gracefully than other times I'd observed him while traveling.

We followed a narrow, nearly overgrown trail through a wood of mixed trees. The morning soon warmed up, and I shrugged out of the coat. Our relationship might not be exactly forbidden anymore, but that didn't change the electric connection between us. My body still buzzed with awareness of his, and as we made the two-hour journey, I realized I'd never had his arms around me for so long—aside from our nighttime getaways on the road to Hadisen.

The land sloped upward rapidly, but Lizzie plodded on. The claim was perched on a foothill that had been given the fanciful name of Silver Dove Mountain. A wide river flowed through it, and the view was breathtaking, revealing other mountains as well as the fertile lands we'd just ridden out of. I was so transfixed by it that took me a moment to really take in the rest of the claim.

"Wasn't there supposed to be a house here?" I asked.

"There," he said, gesturing to a small rise of land.

I followed him over and made out what I'd mistaken for a storage shed. It had a significant slant to it, and it was unclear to me if that was intentional or not. The outer planks were a mix of woods—some old and weathered, some new and yellow. The roof looked aged but sturdy, except for one corner that was covered by a tarp.

Cedric followed my gaze to it. "I still have to work on that."

"Have you . . . have you been working on the rest of it?" I asked delicately. I didn't want to offend him, but it was really hard to tell.

"It's why I was so late. When I got here, this thing was barely standing. I spent that first rainy night on the ground, huddled under the tarp. I've made trips into town for supplies and did a lot of the repairs myself. The prospector on the next claim over helped me with some too." Cedric looked over the shack. "I didn't want you to see it—or even this whole place—in such a state. There's so much work to do. But I knew I couldn't stay away any longer."

I found his hand and laced my fingers with his. "I'm glad you didn't. And you can't be ashamed of any of this, not if we're going to share a life together."

He lifted my hand and studied it. The skin was cracked and raw from the lye. Dirt was everywhere, especially under my nails. There was a long cut I didn't even remember getting. Releasing the hand, he sighed.

"Hey, now. Don't so sound so dejected," I told him. "It's nothing some moisturizer and a little soap—real soap, not that cursed stuff Mistress Marshall made—won't fix. I'll be back to my same old beautiful self in no time."

He turned me to face him. The afternoon sun lit him up, turning his dark auburn hair to fire. "You're already your same old beautiful self. Maybe even more so than when I first met you. I think about that day a lot, you know. I remember every detail. I remember that dress you wore—blue satin with rosebuds on the sleeves. And every curl perfectly arranged. I'd never seen anything like you. Lady Witmore, Countess of Rothford." He sighed again. "And now look what I've brought you to. If I hadn't darkened your doorway that day, where would you be now? Certainly not in the middle of nowhere, scrubbing some farmwife's house while desperately hoping your heretic husband can scrape together enough money to buy us both out of suffocating contracts. You'd have been married in silk, on the arm of someone whose bloodline matched yours. You're still like nothing I've ever seen, and you're the first thing I think of when I wake up each morning . . . but sometimes, well, I'm just not sure if I've improved your life or made it worse."

I looked him over. Like me, he was dirty and disarrayed, his workman's clothes a far cry from the brocade vest and amber pin.

"You *saved* my life," I told him. "And I don't need silk." I pulled him toward me, and we met in a kiss. The world around me was golden. I was warmed by the sun, his embrace, and the joy building up within me. There was no dirt or fear or complication—only this perfect moment with him. "Now," I said. "Show me around your house."

His house consisted of one room. A battered, tiny stove in the corner provided both heat and cooking, though he didn't have much in the way of food. There were two chairs and a table about the width of a bookshelf. His bed was a hay-stuffed mattress on the floor—which was packed dirt, just like the Marshalls'. I tapped my foot on it.

"I know how to sweep this if you need help."

He shook his head. "This whole place needs help. Do you want to see the rest of the property? I can even show you the basics of panning. I haven't been able to do much with it while working on this place."

I hesitated. I did want to jump in and start earning the money to pay back Warren. And desolate or not, this claim and its view were beautiful. I wouldn't have minded exploring them.

"Mostly I just want a bath," I blurted out. When he started laughing, I put my hands on my hips and attempted an affronted look. "Hey, some of us haven't been able to sleep out in the rain. Apparently baths are only for Saturdays at the Marshall house."

It was worth the teasing in his eyes to see the old, genuine smile back.

He caught my hand again. "Come on. I think that can be arranged."

"Is there a luxury bathhouse on your property?" I asked hopefully.

There wasn't, but there was a small pool—more of a pond, really—not far from a bend in the Mathias River. It appeared to be fed by some underground source, which wasn't surprising given the river's meandering and branching nature. A few trees grew around the pond, offering a little shade on the increasingly hot day.

"I know it's not what you're used to," Cedric said apologetically. "But given the circumstances, I figured—wait, what are you doing?"

What I was doing was stripping off my clothes. I didn't care that I couldn't see the bottom of the pond. I didn't care that I had no soap. I didn't care if the neighborly prospector came strolling by and saw. And I certainly didn't care if Cedric saw.

I left my clothes in a pile on the thin grass and waded into the pond. The afternoon might be warm, but the water was still cool and welcome after days of grime and sweat. I didn't stop until the water was just below my shoulders, and then I dunked my head under in a feeble effort to clean my hair. When I emerged, I pushed the tangled mess back and looked around. Cedric still stood on the grass, his back to me.

"What are you doing?" I asked. "Come in here."

"Adelaide! You're—"

"—perfectly respectable, I swear."

"Is that a creative definition of respectable?" But he dared a peek back, looking relieved that I was mostly submerged.

"Come in here," I said again. "You could use a bath too. Besides, didn't you see all this that day in the conservatory? Look, I'll even turn around." I did and waited until I heard the sound of splashing as he too entered the water.

"You know," he said, "you keep bringing that up, but I actually didn't see anything that day. I was so terrified that I pretty much looked everywhere but at you."

I turned around and grinned, seeing him just a couple of feet from me. "And here I thought I'd been feeding your imagination for months."

"Oh, it's had plenty to feed on, don't you worry." He dunked his head too and then brought it back up, scrubbing at his hair with his hands.

"For my last bath back at Wisteria Hollow, I used lavender cream soap from Lorandy. If I'd had any idea what I'd be facing here, I would've smuggled it with me."

"I'll be sure and pick some up for you the next time I'm in White Rock," Cedric said. "I think they sell it between the jerky stand and the ammunition tent." I moved toward him, and he took a step back. "Adelaide . . ."

"We can't kiss? I thought we established you can't see anything."

"I can feel plenty."

I stepped toward him again, and this time he didn't retreat. "I thought you were the dark, wild rebel who leads maidens into unspeakable acts in moonlit groves."

"That sounds like me," he agreed. "But only if one of the aforementioned maidens is my wife."

Mira's words came back to me. "The Alanzans do have morals."

"Of course. Some do. Some don't. That, and I want to maintain something honorable and . . . I don't know . . . exalted with you."

"I want that too." I moved closer again. "But I also want to kiss you now."

Cedric shook his head. "You don't make it easy. But then, you never have."

He leaned down and cupped my face, kissing me without any more fear or hesitation. There was only the scantest breath of distance between us, a distance I knew we were both acutely aware of and struggling to maintain. Despite my bold words, I found myself shaking. I no longer felt cold in the water. I had that sense I always did with him, that the two of us were standing on some kind of precipice, always on the verge of some drastic outcome. I knew if I closed the space between us and wrapped myself in him, all his honorable and exalted intentions would fall away—probably landing right beside my fine words about going to my wedding bed a virgin.

But we didn't close that distance. When we finally managed to part, we were both breathless and aching, starving for something we couldn't have.

Long, tension-filled moments hung between us as our gazes locked, and we both tried to gain some control of ourselves. "I think," said Cedric, tucking a wet lock of hair behind my ear, "we should get married sooner rather than later."

"I agree." I was still reeling, still heady from how tantalizingly close he was. I took a few steps back, just to be safe, and then gestured around us. "But in the meantime, if we don't have anything better to do . . . well, do you want to go pan some gold and strike it rich?"

CHAPTER 24

WE DID NOT, AS IT TURNED OUT, STRIKE IT RICH THAT day. Or the next day.

And soon, one day merged into another as we settled into a routine. Cedric was up at sunrise each morning to make the two-hour trip to the Marshalls'. He'd bring me back to his claim, and I'd help him until late afternoon. Then, it was another ride back to have dinner with the family. Cedric would return to his claim, and I'd tutor the children until we went to bed. I had no trouble falling asleep anymore.

I felt especially bad for Cedric. He spent half his day bringing me back and forth. But he said he liked having me around, and a lot of tasks went more smoothly with two sets of hands. Every little bit helped.

And really, we were just dealing with "little bits." Panning for gold wasn't that difficult once I got the knack of it. The river was wide and shallow in some places, and it was a simple matter to wade out and sit on a rock. I could pan all day and end up with a handful of tiny, glittering gold pieces. Dust, really. A handful each day wasn't going to pay out what we owed Warren, certainly not in a month.

"It adds up," Cedric told me near the end of one day.

I eyed our carefully protected hoard of gold dust. "Will it be enough?"

"It's worth more than you think. I mean, I'm sure back in Osfro, your servants swept up and threw out this much gold dust every day from your house. But in the real world, this is a lot of money."

It was enough money, in fact, that Cedric announced he was going to take a trip into White Rock and spend it on something called a sluice.

"You're going to spend what little we have?" I asked. "Or are you using credit?" That would have been worse. I didn't want to owe Warren any more than we did.

Cedric shook his head. He didn't shave very often these days, and an auburn shadow covered his lower face. I didn't mind it, though it made for itchy kissing. "We've got enough in the gold we've panned so far to get what I need."

"All that work gone." The very thought made me weary, considering how many hours I'd spent standing in the river. Both of us had toughened up considerably in the last couple of weeks. I had calluses on my hands, and when I'd finally found a mirror, I'd discovered the hat had done only so much to keep the sun off me, as I'd feared.

"It'll be worth it to get what I need," Cedric said. "Sluices sit in the river and essentially pan for us. We can get more gold in less time."

"That's promising," I admitted. "But sometimes, I feel like this claim has just enough gold to give us false hope but not enough to pay out. And I think Warren knew that."

"There's a very real possibility of that." Cedric's face started to fall, but then his optimism quickly returned. "But we're not going to make that call until we've exhausted all our options. If he expects us to give up at the first sign of trouble, he's in for a surprise."

So, I spent the next day helping around the homestead. There was never any end to the chores needing to be done, something I thought about quite a bit. If Cedric and I were able to settle in Westhaven, life wouldn't be very different than in Hadisen. We'd be living on the frontier in modest accommodations. There'd be no servants to help. When I'd come to Blue Spring Manor, I'd been naïve about the labor ordinary people did. Now, I was rapidly becoming proficient in all sorts of tasks I'd never imagined.

I also found that all of my fancy education meant little to my students. These were children who'd grown up without a school of any kind and had been sent to work early. The things I taught them were basic: reading and simple arithmetic. It gave me a new understanding of the world and the variety of people who lived within it.

These thoughts were on my mind when Cedric came for me the day after his White Rock trip. Noticing my thoughtfulness as we rode on old Lizzie, he asked me about it.

"It's hard out here, harder than I ever imagined," I said, trying to explain. "But I don't always mind. I'm coming to love this land. I like the quietness. The openness. And I like the way people have come to better themselves—and not in the way the Glittering Court bettered us. It's hard to explain, but I realize the 'common' people out here aren't going to be common forever. It's all survival now, but one day, arts and education could flourish here like they have in Osfro. And . . . I'm excited to be a part of it."

He leaned forward to kiss me lightly on the neck. "It'll be even better in Westhaven. The determination they show here is a great thing, but it's even greater when paired with the freedom of thought and belief Westhaven'll have. Mind *and* body have to survive out here. Oh." He shifted around behind me, reaching into his pocket. "I picked up a letter for you while I was in town."

I read it as I rode. It was from Tamsin:

Dear Adelaide,

They tell me you can get letters out there, but I'm skeptical. I hope this actually reaches you and doesn't get eaten by a bear.

Life here is beautiful. I've gone to a different party every night. There've been a few gentlemen with potential, but I'm still holding out for Warren. His position, both in finances and in power, is exactly what I need. Plus, I'll be nearer to you! Now, if I could just get him to fall hopelessly, madly in love with me, things would be perfect. It's a good sign that he told me to wait for him, but I could use a little bit more.

Some of the Grashond settlers are still hanging around, and I wish they would go. I'm tired of seeing them. The only upside of them being here is that it reminds me how nice it is to wear color again.

Mira's been behaving very strangely. Did she do that while you were here? The last couple of days in particular, she's been off. Sometimes distracted, sometimes irritable. Since she's always been the least moody out of all of us, you can imagine how weird that is.

I found out she's only received one legitimate offer. Did you know that? I guess plenty of men like to dance with her and talk to her, but they leave it at that. The offer is from some ancient plantation owner. And I do mean ancient. He's at least eighty. I suppose that would make me irritable too, but it's a very respectable position. He's well-situated, and she'd have a lot of control of the house, which I think she'd like. And since he is so old, I don't think he'd ask much of her, if you know what I mean.

I wish I could write more, but that would take time away from doing my hair for tonight's party. It's at a shipping magnate's home. He's not as good a catch as Warren, but he's a solid backup—just in case.

I don't know how you could have given this up for digging in the dirt all day, but I hope you are happy and well.

All my love,
Tamsin

I smiled as I folded up the letter. I could practically hear every word of it coming from Tamsin's mouth. "She's always writing letters," I told Cedric. "It's nice to finally get one of my own."

The day was already heating up when we reached the claim, but I hardly noticed anymore. I worked in rolled-up sleeves and a split skirt of light cotton that Mistress Marshall had helped me make, since the suede one was too warm these days. I'd done a lot of the sewing myself, and while my stitches still weren't great, they were significantly improved.

Also improved was our efficiency once the sluices were set up. A sluice was a wide box that water could run through, filtering through a screen that trapped heavy minerals—ideally, gold. We decided on a few good spots in the river and placed them there, watching for several minutes as though we expected huge gold boulders to immediately get trapped.

"Not an instant gold strike," I said. "But faster than panning."

Cedric handed me my pan. "Which we still have to do."

We'd been out panning in the river for a couple of hours when we heard a voice call, "Thorn, are you here?"

We looked up. Several riders were cutting across the claim and waved their hands in greeting. Cedric waved back and began wading through the water toward them.

I followed close behind. "Who are they?"

"Alanzans. I saw them in town the other day. They just finalized the paperwork on a claim on the far edge of Hadisen—far by design. I know a cousin of theirs. He was one of the Alanzans arrested at the Star Advent that later managed to escape. He's waiting for them at that claim, and I told them to stop by when they made their trip out."

Although I'd grown used to the idea of Cedric as an Alanzan, I'd yet to truly meet any others. This group looked perfectly ordinary, not much different from the Marshall clan. They wore rough, working-class clothes and hauled a wagon loaded with supplies. Cedric introduced them as the Galvestons, consisting of a middle-aged couple and their four children. Their oldest son was married and had his pregnant wife with them.

No sordid rituals or prayers followed. The Galvestons had been traveling that day and appreciated the break, especially from the younger children, who ran off to play. We sat with the adults and shared our water, mostly trading news. After a few weeks in Hadisen, Cedric and I felt like veterans and offered what expertise we had. The elder Mister Galveston, named Francis, proved to have more expertise as he surveyed the shanty.

"Why don't you have anything to seal this roof?" he asked.

"There's wood there. I nailed the boards in myself." Cedric's pride in that feat was obvious, and I couldn't help smiling. I'd been there that day, and he'd hit his fingers with the hammer at least half a dozen times.

"And it's going to let in a deluge as soon as this place gets one of its famous storms. You need to get some canvas to cover the gaps. We got the last of it from the supplier in town. You'll have to wait until his new shipment comes in, or head back to Cape Triumph."

"I don't think we'll be back there anytime soon," Cedric said. "I'll have to take my chances with the rain."

Francis gestured for his older son and Cedric to follow. "We might be able to do some patches. Let's take a look."

That left me sitting with the women in the grass. Alice, the daughter-in-law, stretched and rested a hand on her swelling belly. "Are you uncomfortable?" I asked. "Can I get you anything?"

"No, thank you." She shared a knowing smile with her mother-in-law, Henrietta. "When we read my destiny card at the beginning of the pregnancy, I drew the Keeper of Roses."

When they saw my blank look, Henrietta asked, "Aren't you familiar with the card?"

"I'm not familiar with any of the cards," I admitted. I realized they were talking about the Deanzan cards, like the pack Ada had had. Ordinary people used them for games and fortune-telling. For the Alanzans, the cards had a more sacred meaning and were holy to Deanziel, the moon angel who governed inner wisdom.

Alice's frown smoothed out, but her confusion remained. "When Cedric introduced you as his fiancée, I just assumed . . ."

"That I was Alanzan?" I finished.

Both looked embarrassed, and then Alice asked, "Are you going to convert after you're married?"

"I hadn't planned on it."

"Then why go to the trouble of raising money for Westhaven now?" asked Henrietta. The Galvestons would've liked to go there as well but were waiting until the colony was more settled and required no charter fees. They hoped to earn money in gold in the meantime.

"For Cedric. I want him to be able to practice safely. And he's very interested in taking up a leadership role there," I explained. "Being a charter member would help with that." Awkward silence fell, and I tried to fill it when it was clear they wouldn't. "So. What does the Keeper of Roses mean?"

For a moment, I didn't think they'd tell me. "It shows a man who works hard in his garden, protecting delicate flowers against harsh conditions. He's ultimately rewarded with beautiful blooms," said Henrietta.

I turned to Alice. "So for you, it's symbolic of the pregnancy. You're going through a lot of tough times now, facing a lot of hardships on this journey . . . but your baby will be born healthy and strong, ultimately flourishing as the roses do. I'd hope the card's message could be extrapolated to your family's all-around prosperity in Hadisen."

Both women stared at me in astonishment.

"Was I close?" I asked.

"Yes," said Henrietta at last. "Something like that." Her eyes lifted beyond me. "Glen! Get down from there before you break your neck."

The two young Galveston daughters were splashing in shallow water, but the younger son was trying to climb some of the rocky outcroppings that marked the beginning of the foothills and mountains. He wasn't going to get very high free-handed, but I could understand her concern. He didn't seem to hear.

"I'll go get him," I said. I rose, both wanting to be helpful and get away from the stares.

Glen had made impressive progress getting up, which only meant he was in more danger if he slipped and fell.

"Glen," I said. "Your mother wants you. It's too dangerous up there."

He didn't even look at me. "Just a minute. I've almost got another one."

"Another what?"

He stretched his arm up to a small jutting of stone and whooped triumphantly. Then he scrabbled down like some kind of rock lizard. The front of his overalls had a huge pocket that was filled with rocks. He slipped his shiny new find in with the rest.

I beckoned him back toward his family. "Isn't that heavy to carry around?"

"It's for my collection. I've got dozens more. Did you know there are people—special smart people—back in Osfrid who study rocks all the time?"

"I do know that. They're called geologists."

"Geologists." He said the word like he was tasting it.

"The king commissions them to travel and learn new things about rocks and minerals."

"I'd like to do that. But once we've got enough gold for a farm, they say I'll have to help work it."

I patted his head. "Never assume you'll have to follow the destiny someone else has planned out for you. And I'll show you some other neat rocks."

I walked him over to the shaded pond, where I'd previously noticed some small mottled pebbles. Glen was fascinated, and I left him to it, figuring he couldn't get in much trouble. As I approached the others from the back of the shanty, I overheard Henrietta speaking to Cedric.

"—not my place, but are you sure that's the best idea?"

"Of course it is," said Cedric. "I love her."

"That's fine and well, but you're letting yourself get charmed by a pretty face. Once you're out of bed, you'll see the real consequences. What are you going to do when you have children? I hope you're at least going to make her convert."

"No one makes her do anything. As for children . . ." Here, Cedric hesitated. "Well, we'll get around to discussing it."

"You'd better discuss it now," said Francis. "It's a serious matter. You're an educated man with a business background—exactly the kind the Alanzans need to go forward and build respectability for the future. Founding Westhaven is the right way to do this. But how will it look if your own wife isn't a member of the faith?"

"It'll look like she has her own opinions and goes with them—just as we've been telling the orthodox we have the right to do. And the point of Westhaven is to welcome people of all beliefs. Alanzan or otherwise."

The Galvestons weren't convinced, and Alice finally concluded with, "Well, there's a magistrate in White Rock who's one of us. You should seek his counsel before you do something stupid. She's a threat to your faith and a threat to our success."

When I rejoined them, they all tried to act like nothing had happened, but didn't do a very good job. It was time to wrap up their visit anyway, and we were all a little relieved.

"Oh, Glen," exclaimed Henrietta when she saw his bulging pocket of stones. "What did I tell you about those rocks?"

"They're for my collection," he stated. "I'm going to be a royal geo-geologist."

"A what? Never mind. We aren't going to keep hauling rocks around. Leave those here."

Glen obstinately stuck out his lower lip, and I quickly knelt down before him. "It *is* a lot to carry around. Why don't you leave them here? I'll keep them safe until you're able to come back for them."

He didn't look as though he liked that idea, but he also didn't like crossing his mother. So, the rocks were left in a small pile by the shanty, and we waved the Galvestons off.

"Don't say it," Cedric said, as soon as they were gone. "I know you overheard, and you just need to forget about it."

"It's kind of hard to forget being called a threat to you. Or hearing that our marriage would be 'something stupid.'"

"No religion is truly enlightened. There are closed-minded people in all of them."

I looked him in the eye. "What *are* we going to do when we have children?"

"Marvel at their perfection?"

"Cedric! Take things seriously for once."

His smile faded. "I am. And as for kids, I don't know. We'll teach them my beliefs, and . . . whatever it is you believe . . . which I still don't really know. And they can make their own decisions."

"I don't think your Alanzan friends will like that." It was strange. There'd been so many complications in our relationship. The scandal of it even existing. Our money troubles. The danger surrounding him. But never had I imagined that *I'd* be the complication in his life. "I haven't gone through all this—given up so much—just for you to get out of bed one morning and realize you made a mistake."

"In that scenario, the only mistake would've been leaving your bed in the first place." He took my hands and pulled me to him. "In all seriousness, this issue—our difference of belief—isn't one that's taken me by surprise. I knew from the instant I fell for you that we'd have this looming beside us. *Beside* us. Not between us. We will deal with it, and we will overcome it just like we have everything else."

I closed my eyes briefly and then sighed. "I just wish . . . I just wish there wasn't so much we had to keep overcoming. Probably when it's all over, we'll just be bored."

"The two of us? Never."

We kissed, and he pressed me up against the side of the shanty. Somehow, the argument had made me want him even more, and heat shot through me at the feel of his body on mine. One of his hands tangled in my hair, and the other played dangerously with the edge of my skirt, pushing it up my leg.

"Be careful," I said, unable to resist. "I don't think this shanty wall can withstand very much."

He pulled back, his breathing rapid and eyes hungry as they looked me over. Not hungry. Ravenous. "*Now* who doesn't take things seriously?"

"Hey, it's a credit to your prowess that I'd even think—"

I lost track of what I was saying as a flash of sunlight caught my eye.

I pushed Cedric aside, confusing him even more, and knelt down to where I'd seen the sparkle. It was in Glen's rock pile. Sifting through them, I found one that glittered golden in the sunlight. I held up for Cedric to see.

"Is it real?" I asked.

We'd heard plenty of stories in White Rock about prospectors being deceived by look-alikes. Cedric got down beside me and held the rock up. It was only a pebble, but it was solid gold.

"It's real," he confirmed. "Where did this come from?"

"The future royal geologist found it over by the outcroppings, heading toward the foothills. I saw it shining but thought it was some kind of crystal."

We walked to the far side of the claim, opposite the river. The sparse vegetation thinned out even more here as the rocky land took hold. I pointed to the base of the outcropping in question. It was no mountain, but the large formation was still high enough to make me uneasy when I thought of how high Glen had gotten. And that wasn't even near the top.

Cedric stared up at it for a long moment. "You need to meet my neighbor. Sully. Nice old guy. He's helped me figure a few things out. His claim has some rock formations like this, and he said he nearly ground them to dust looking for gold. Apparently, there was some early Hadisen explorer who found big deposits of gold in things like these—massive deposits. Larger than anything gleaned from the river."

I followed his gaze, and let those words sink in. "How would you be able to find out? Just start chipping through?"

"Kind of. Look, there's a crevasse at the top. Digging into it might show something. If I can get up there—"

"Get up there?" I stared at the tallest cliff. "That's pretty high."

"I'll need some equipment to climb up and check. Come on, Adelaide," he added, seeing my face. "It's safe with the right gear. And if there is a deposit in there, we're set."

"Where are you going to get that equipment?"

He held up the pebble. "This'll buy what I need for the initial inspection. If there is gold in there, that's going to be a much more serious excavation. One we'll need to talk to Warren and Elias about. We might need to talk to them anyway. The sooner we can move on this, the better."

The smile on his face was radiant as he looked back at me. The sunlight lit up his tanned features, turning his auburn hair molten. He looked like some sort of ardent young god. A dirty one. But despite all the doubts I had in the world, I believed in him.

"Adelaide," he told me. "You might just be married in silk after all."

CHAPTER 25

I STAYED BACK WITH THE MARSHALLS THE NEXT DAY while Cedric went to buy the climbing gear. It was hard to hide my excitement as I helped with the chores, but I couldn't risk tipping my hand yet.

"Well, you're in a good mood," Mistress Marshall remarked. "Haven't complained once about the lye."

"Just have other things on my mind, that's all."

"Getting use out of the cinnamon thorn, eh? That's the only thing that could give you a smile that big."

"Haven't even touched it," I said. She obviously didn't believe me.

When Cedric took me out on the claim the next day, I barely waited until we'd cleared the Marshall property. "Did you get the gear?"

"Yes and no. The supply store had only some of the things I needed. And then I ran into Elias Carter."

"Wonderful. Is he smiling yet?"

"No. Especially when he found out what I was there for. He's skeptical about a deposit in the cliffs and says I'm just stirring up trouble. If there really is a substantial amount there, we'd have to bring in more laborers, and there are a lot of men in town jumping at the chance for extra work."

I could picture Elias delivering all of that in his condescending tone. "So, what? He's not going to let you do it?"

"I can survey it, but he wants to see it himself—at least from a distance. He's supposed to come out today and bring some climbing gear from another supplier in town that was closed yesterday. He made it clear, of course, that it was a terrible inconvenience for him."

"Of course." I sighed. "And here I thought this was going to be a nice day."

It *was* a nice day. The work was so second nature now that I could do it automatically and spend time talking with Cedric. We talked about the future, what we'd do in Westhaven, what we'd name our children with their yet-to-be-determined religious futures. The happy mood evaporated when Elias rode up with a few cronies in tow.

"No ball gown today, huh?" he asked. "From a distance, I wouldn't even think you're a woman at all."

"Do you have the gear?" Cedric asked pointedly.

Elias nodded to one of his men, who threw down a pile of ropes and spikes. "The gold you left didn't entirely cover it. We'll be adding it to your account."

Cedric managed a tight smile. "Of course."

Elias gestured impatiently. "Well, then, let's see this fortune you think you've found. I don't have all day."

We went to the far side of the claim, opposite the river. The sparse vegetation thinned out even more here as the rocky land took hold. Cedric pointed to the base of the outcropping in question. It was no mountain, but it was still high enough to make me uneasy. The jagged, uneven surface was equally disconcerting.

"Sully says this is just what Davis Mitchell had on his claim when he made his big strike," Cedric said.

Elias squinted up. "Sully? You mean George Sullivan? I'd hardly consider him an expert. He's been out here a year with no luck."

"But he knew Davis Mitchell," Cedric pointed out. "And saw his claim."

Davis Mitchell was a legendary figure in Hadisen. He'd made a huge fortune in gold and eventually returned to Osfro to live on his earnings. If there was even a remote chance this might yield the same, it had to be investigated.

"And," added Cedric, "this is the edge of my property. If there's gold here—"

"Mister Doyle's property," corrected Elias. "You only work it."

Cedric was undaunted. "If there's gold here, it's likely part of a vein that runs up through those foothills and into that mountain stretch. Those don't have any leases, right? Mister Doyle could hire workers directly and wouldn't have to split it with a claimholder."

"No end of trouble to mine those mountains," grumbled Elias. But I could see the gleam in his eyes as he contemplated the possibility. "Fine. Climb that beast, and see what's up there. Report your findings to me immediately. If there's anything worthwhile there, Mister Doyle will help make arrangements for a proper extraction when he returns from Cape Triumph. And don't start spreading rumors until you're absolutely sure what it's holding."

"Of course," Cedric said, again keeping his tone polite in spite of Elias's snide tone.

An awkward silence fell between us all, and then Elias said, "Well, aren't you going to invite us into your home for some refreshment? We came all this way to help you."

I flinched, remembering that Cedric had an Alanzan diamond on the wall. "It's so cramped in there," I said. "Hardly any room between the bed and the stove. I'll go bring you something and you can enjoy it out here on this beautiful day."

Elias eyed me askance. "How kind of you. And how fortunate you're so familiar with the shanty and its bed."

I smiled sweetly. "I'll be right back."

I walked away calmly, like some dutiful young lady serving the menfolk. Once inside Cedric's shanty, I hastily closed the door and performed a frantic search. I pulled the diamond down and shoved it in a trunk he'd brought from Cape Triumph. It held a pack of Deanzan cards, though they at least were at the bottom of the trunk. I wrapped them in a shirt to make them harder to find and deemed the house safe should anyone come in.

Refreshment options were meager, as Elias no doubt knew. This was a power play. I'd seen canteens on their horses, and he and his men probably had snacks far better than anything we could muster. Cedric's stove was quirky at best, which was why Mistress Marshall's food always seemed so indulgent to him. I wrapped up some corn bread that she'd given Cedric and brought it outside with cups and a pitcher of water. The water had come from a good well on the claim, but it had long grown warm in this weather.

Nonetheless, I served it with all the grace and courtesy drilled into us in all of the Glittering Court's "good hostess" lessons. I even earned a gruff "thanks" from one of Elias's otherwise silent men. A brief exchange of glances with Cedric told him all he needed to know. It was unlikely that Elias would search the shanty, but nothing obvious would point to the Alanzans.

"You should've never had that diamond out," I told Cedric, once our visitors had left. "This is as bad as the open rituals."

He pushed sweaty hair out of his face and nodded. "You're right."

"Did you just agree with me?"

"I agree with you all the time. You're an astute and intelligent woman. Smarter than me."

We both looked up at the stony outcropping. "When are you going up?" I asked.

He leaned down and began sifting through the lines and other gear Elias had brought. "No time like the present."

"What, now? It's the hottest part of the day!"

"It's *always* hot these days." He separated out a couple of ropes and some hooks. "I can't wait to get one of those big storms old Sully's always talking about."

I tried to think of some other excuse to delay his climbing up, but there was none. And again, there was always the pressure of time and money weighing upon us.

"Do you even know how to use any of this?" I asked.

He fastened a leather harness around him. "You doubt me?"

"I've just seen you ride a horse, that's all."

"No need to worry. I've researched it. Talked a lot to Sully and the suppliers in town. It's pretty straightforward."

I was skeptical, but I couldn't deny that he seemed pretty competent as he hooked up the various lines and stakes. I handed him a pick and kissed him on the cheek. "Be careful. Don't leave me a widow before we're married."

He grinned by way of answer and began his climb. I knew little of such matters and was impressed with the way he could pierce the rock with stakes and hooks, creating handholds to scale up. The jagged surface I'd worried so much about actually helped along the way, as it provided extra traction.

"You might be good at this after all," I called up.

"I told you: no need to worry."

A few clouds had moved in. I was still sweating in the humidity, but at least it cooled me as I waited. The climb didn't take that long, really, but I watched it with clenched fists, aware of every second until he finally swung himself up onto the wide ledge at the top. He waved down at me, and I exhaled in relief. He unhooked his pick from the harness and stepped inside the crevasse. Losing sight of him made me tense again, especially since I didn't know how long this part would take. I doubted he'd simply walk into a wall of gold. And how deep did that opening go? Was he entering some cavern that would put him in danger of a rockslide?

A half hour passed before he finally emerged. "Well?" I yelled.

"Catch," was all he answered back. He tossed something down. The throw was wide, and it landed several feet behind me. I scurried back, searching the ground. A flash in the sunlight caught my eye, and disbelieving, I picked up a gold nugget the size of a cherry. Five times the size of Glen's pebble. More gold than from a day of us panning together. I ran back to the cliff's base.

"Are there piles of this laying around?"

He put his hand around his mouth so I could better hear. "No, but it didn't take that much digging to get it out. I think there's a huge deposit running through this. To do it right, they'll want more men and some engineers, I'm sure. But there's more than enough here to pay out your contract."

"And will that 'more' part also cover your Westhaven stake?"

"Definitely."

"Then get down here so I can kiss you." My heart drummed with excitement. Without even using a backup team, we could almost certainly get out what we needed in a relatively short term. If the vein was fully excavated properly, Cedric would have rights to everything pulled out, less Warren's ownership fee. It would not only get us to Westhaven but ensure we didn't have to move into another shanty. Maybe I could live on love, but that didn't mean I didn't want to also live with a solid roof over my head.

Cedric's climb down required some different maneuvers. In theory, it was simpler. He secured a rope in the stone and then swung himself down, gripping the rope with gloved hands as he rappelled over the stony face. It was less work than getting up, but I was constantly aware that a lot depended on his grip. The harness was secured to the rope as well, providing extra security. And despite his outward cockiness, I could see that he was moving very cautiously.

Which was why it was so astonishing when he slipped, suddenly sliding down, with neither hands nor harness holding the rope. I screamed as a brief, terrifying vision flashed through my mind of him crashing to the ground. His hands flailed out, trying to get purchase, and then somehow, amazingly, he managed to stop himself on a piece of rock jutting out about two-thirds of the way down. It was a narrow horizontal ledge that was just barely big enough for his feet to fit if he turned them outward in opposite directions. The rest of his body clung to the cliff's face, spread eagle.

"Are you okay?" I cried.

"Take Lizzie, and get Sully," he called back. "You can probably be back in an hour."

"Are you crazy? I'm not leaving you up there for an hour!" His hold looked tenuous as it was. I didn't even know if he'd last five minutes.

"Adelaide—"

"Be quiet. I'm smarter than you, remember?"

My tone was harsh, but it was only to cover my own fear. Cedric had fallen far from the rope he'd been on; it was too high up now. He'd placed another, lower rope just before his fall, but he could no longer reach it. I had a few extra pieces of equipment at my feet, most of which didn't seem to be of use—with a few exceptions.

That last rope he'd placed was just barely too high for me to reach. Picking up two sharp metal stakes, I practiced plunging them into the rock. To my surprise, I had the strength to embed them and get a secure hold. What was more problematic was pulling myself up. The muscles in my upper body just didn't have the capability to do it with ease. So, I did it with difficulty. I told myself over and over that I only had to go up a few feet. I told myself it was no problem. Most important, I told myself that Cedric's life depended on it.

"Don't do anything dangerous," Cedric said.

"You can't even see me," I yelled back.

"Yeah, but I know you."

With every muscle in my body screaming, I managed to use the stakes to claw my way up enough to reach the rope. I gripped it and was surprised to find it harder to hold on to than the stakes. My hands immediately began to slide, and I yelped in pain as the rope tore at my skin. Using every bit of determination I could muster, I managed to stop my descent and hold on to the rope, bending my body at an angle so that my feet stabilized me on the rock.

I contemplated my next move as a light wind blew strands of hair into my face. I needed to get the rope over to Cedric. If he could reach it, he could climb down safely. Lifting my feet, I hopped to the side, attempting to swing over on the rope. I moved only a little and soon realized the problem. This low on the rope, my weight wasn't enough to move the line a significant distance. I needed to climb up.

Again, all my muscles were pushed to their limits as I raised one hand over the other. I'd seen laborers in Osfro climb ropes my entire life. I'd had no idea how much work it was. Having skinned-up hands didn't help either. When I thought I was high enough to swing myself and the rope over more effectively, I told Cedric, "The rope's coming in on your right. Grab it when you can."

I then launched off again to the side and, as hoped, I moved the rope significantly closer to Cedric. But still not enough. Another ungainly swing got me within grasping distance.

"I can see it," he said. "I think I can do it."

Peering up, I held my breath as I watched him scoot over on that tiny ledge. A few rocks skittered down as he did, and I hoped it would hold him. His hand stretched out and grasped hold of the rope—but now he needed to get the rest of him over. With what sounded like a muttered prayer, he jumped off the ledge, reaching wildly for the rope with his other hand. Once more I had that terrible image of him falling, but he managed to make contact and grip both hands on the line.

The sudden change in weight on the rope made me lose my foothold, and we both swung wildly for several moments. I slid again, doing more damage to my hands, but managed to keep my grip and finally plant my feet on the rock again. Above me, I felt Cedric do the same. Before we could take any comfort in that momentary security, I felt the entire rope shift, jerking me down. I realized what was happening before Cedric spoke.

"The hook on this line wasn't planted deeply enough to hold us both."

In an instant, I knew what I needed to do. I had to get off the rope. I began shimmying down it, which was slightly easier than going up but still required great care. When I reached the bottom of the rope, I felt the whole thing shift again, but it continued to hold. I couldn't reach the spikes I'd used to climb up to the rope. The distance from where I was to the ground wouldn't kill me, but it would probably hurt. Cedric falling from his height would be much worse.

Without hesitation, I let go of the rope and jumped to the ground. I'd feared I'd break my leg or ankle, but I managed to land in a way so that my hip struck the ground first. It was a jolting, teeth-rattling landing, but at worst, I thought I'd have only a bad bruise on that hip tomorrow. Freed of my weight, the rope held as Cedric quickly scrambled down. He made the same jump I had, and his greater height gave him less distance to cover.

"Are you okay?" he asked, helping me to stand.

"I think so." But as I spoke, I looked at my hands and winced at what I saw. Broken skin and blood. I'd ignored them in my frantic attempt to come down, but now the pain hit me full force.

Cedric held my hands gently. I could see small cuts and scrapes on him as well. "Oh, Adelaide. You shouldn't have done that."

"And leave you up there? No way. What happened? You seemed to be doing so well."

"I thought so too," he said, leading me away. The clouds were increasing and growing darker, which seemed fitting given the turn the day had made. When we reached the shanty, he helped me wash and wrap my hands in clean cloths. "Mistress Marshall will have some kind of salve for you. I'll take you back now." He began unbuckling the harness and started to toss it aside.

"Wait, let me look," I said, reaching for it. Cedric might be an amateur at a lot of these frontier tasks, but I knew he hadn't been careless with the harness or disregarded the directions he'd been given. This mishap wasn't his doing. I turned the harness over and examined each part, with a feeling of dread in my stomach that intensified when I found what I'd feared. I pointed to a small metal loop. "Look."

It was one of two that the rope had fed through, wrapping around so that it kept him secured while still letting him move. The loops were made of a single strand that had been bent so the ends met to close the circle. One loop's ends were brought together tightly, leaving no space between them. But the one I indicated had bent ends that appeared to have been strained to a point where they pulled apart and released the rope.

Cedric leaned forward. “It looks like the ends were never attached properly . . . or they were pried apart.”

We both sat there quietly as those words hung between us. “Maybe it was an accident,” I said at last. “But if it wasn’t . . . why? It’s in their best interest to know what’s in there. Warren’s fortune is at stake too.”

“He’s out of town,” Cedric reminded me. “Maybe this was all Elias’s doing. He’s a petty man. I can see him being vindictive. And he’s never liked us.”

“But this is all speculation,” I said. “Maybe it was an accident.”

“Right. Maybe it was an accident.”

But I knew neither of us believed that. *Trust each other,* Aiana had said. *But no one else.*

I pulled out the gold nugget, which I’d tucked into a pocket before my climb. Its glitter was hypnotic. “I don’t think we should wait for Warren to get back to get this gold out.”

“Agreed,” said Cedric. “Tomorrow we’re taking matters into our own hands.”

CHAPTER 26

WE MADE OUR PLANS WHILE RIDING BACK TO THE Marshall place that evening. About two-thirds of the way, we ran into Mister Marshall coming toward us. By that point, the sky was a sickly greenish-gray marked by occasional flashes of lightning jumping between the clouds. The wind rose and fell like someone's breath, as though the world were waiting for something big to happen.

"I was coming to fetch you if you weren't already on your way," Mister Marshall said. "Come on—be quick. This one's going to be bad."

The rain had just begun when we reached the cabin. Mister Marshall urged Cedric to stay the night and put Lizzie in the barn with the other restless animals. "You don't know what these storms are like. I saw a couple when I first came to survey this place. They roll in off the ocean, big swirling beasts that grow and grow, with winds that can flatten houses. They're worse closer to the water, but we'll still catch some of it here inland before it breaks up."

I immediately thought of my friends back at Wisteria Hollow. "Will it hit Cape Triumph? It's right on the water."

"Depends on what direction it's coming in from. Lots of times they're shielded from the coast. If it does hit—don't worry. They know what to do."

Cedric was reluctant to stay at first, but as the rain turned into a nonstop sheet of water and the wind wailed around us, he finally conceded. "You wanted a storm," he told me as we ate dinner. Everyone was tense as the storm grew in ferocity outside. Every so often the little cabin shuddered from a particularly strong blast of wind.

I couldn't sleep when we went to bed. The little girls around me were scared, and I told them soothing things I didn't entirely believe, like that the storm was almost over and the cabin would hold. They eventually drifted off, but I still couldn't manage it and got out of bed. Downstairs, I found I wasn't the only one awake. Cedric sat on the kitchen table's bench while Mister Marshall paced restlessly around. He glanced over but didn't chastise me. "Stay away from the windows" was all he said before resuming his vigil.

I sat down next to Cedric and laced my fingers with his. "Your home won't survive this. You should have gotten that tarp."

"I don't think a tarp could've stopped this. But we'll be okay as long as the gold doesn't blow away."

I stared off as the storm raged and felt old memories consume me. "It's just like the ship."

"No." He squeezed my hand. "You're safe here. Your friends are safe."

I nodded, but it was hard not to shake that unease. I remembered that feeling of being knocked around at sea, my stomach rolling as the world turned on its side. And off on the dark water, the *Gray Gull* tossed to and fro . . .

The storm eventually quieted, but I didn't trust it. "The eye," Mister Marshall confirmed. "We're halfway through."

Sure enough, the lull passed, and the storm renewed its fury. I grew tense again. Cedric sat on the floor (now covered in straw) and put his back to the log wall. He beckoned me down, and I sat between his outstretched legs, leaning back against his chest. Mister Marshall glanced at us but didn't seem particularly interested, even when Cedric wrapped his arms around my waist.

Cedric smoothed my hair back. "Get some rest. We've got a big day tomorrow."

A particularly powerful blast of wind slammed into the cabin, making the walls shake. I flinched, and Cedric readjusted his hold on me.

"The ship," I said. "I just can't stop thinking about it. And you know what else? I can't stop thinking about Tamsin thinking about the ship. I know that sounds weird. But if they're getting some of this back in Cape Triumph, she must be so scared."

"She's in a house better built than this one. And she's with Mira. Surely Mira can fight the forces of nature."

"Mira *is* a force of nature."

Somehow, amazingly, the raging wind and rain faded to background noise over time. I stopped jumping at every loud sound, and dozed against Cedric. I woke to him gently helping me to stand. "The worst is over. It's getting quieter. Let's get to real beds." Stifling a yawn of his own, he guided me upstairs to the girls' room. I climbed into bed with them and fell asleep before Cedric even shut the door.

When morning came, the blue sky and bright sunlight would have made anyone believe the storm had been a dream. Closer scrutiny proved otherwise. Trees and limbs had fallen all over the property, but none had hit the buildings. Mister Marshall's diligent work on the cabin had paid off, though the barn roof had sustained some damage, as had the fence surrounding his fields. He and his family immediately set to work on repairs, and Cedric and I rode off to White Rock.

There, we found a wide array of storm damage. The more hastily thrown-together businesses and homes hadn't fared well, though most of their owners had been able to seek shelter with neighbors whose structures were sturdier. Residents now worked side by side to rebuild, uniting in a way that stirred up that feeling within me about the promise this new frontier held.

With everyone so busy, it was a difficult time to recruit workers for Cedric's claim. When we heard that Warren had fought through the storm and arrived late last night from Denham, we decided to change plans and appeal to him directly. We still didn't know if Elias had been responsible for the harness accident, but Warren had seemed legitimately interested in our success.

The governor's home was a newly built estate, boasting luxuries like wallpaper and brass sconces. Elias's snide words rang in my head as a servant led us to a fine rug in the foyer: *"From a distance, I wouldn't even think you're a woman at all."* My practical attire was worn, my skin darkened from the sun. The only styling attempt I made anymore was halfheartedly tying my hair back.

I felt particularly inadequate when I caught sight of Warren in his typically impeccable attire. He was walking out a man I didn't know, saying, "I assure you, the rumors are just that. There are no Lorandians moving across the western colonies. No Icori either. Times are becoming stable, and so people start creating phantoms."

When the visitor was gone, Warren turned his attention to us. A brief, raised eyebrow was his only indication of surprise at our appearance. "I'm so happy to see you again, Adelaide." Then, belatedly to Cedric: "And you too, of course."

"How was your journey?" I asked politely.

"Rough." Warren's face fell. "The storm blew up while we were crossing the bay last night. We . . . lost a few people." He studied me a few moments before going on. "I would've stayed in Cape Triumph had I known the risks, but here we are. Elias tells me you two have some exciting news."

Like a conjured demon, Elias slinked into the room. Cedric held out the gold nugget. "I found it after only a little digging."

Elias took the nugget but held it at arm's length, like it might be toxic. "Bigger than that last bit you came flashing around. And it *seems* authentic."

"Of course it is," said Warren, snatching it away. Enthusiasm filled his features. "And this could make both our fortunes. Have you told anyone?"

I hesitated. "No . . . but we were hoping to hire some men today now that this is confirmed. Of course, with the storm—"

"Don't," interrupted Warren. "Don't tell anyone yet."

"I understand the need for control of the situation," said Cedric. "But I also need to get moving on this."

"Don't speak to Mister Doyle that way," snapped Elias.

Warren gave him a withering look. "He's right. We do need to move—but I'm not delaying because of any need for control. I'm delaying for your own safety."

"How so?" I asked.

"As much as I want to believe Hadisen is a wonderful, righteous place . . ." Warren shook his head. "Well, the lure of gold is irresistible to some—it makes them do terrible things. There are still raiders and bandits who'll swoop in on prosperous claims to scavenge what they can—and aren't afraid to hurt those who own them. Aside from having the proper workers and equipment, I'd like to make sure you have proper security before this project begins."

It was a hard argument to counter. We'd all heard stories of claim-raiding brigands, but I'd never expected we'd run into them. I'd never expected our claim would have the potential to be so rich.

"That's very kind of you," Cedric said at last.

Warren gave him a wry smile. "And don't worry—I *will* make sure this is done expediently. Don't worry about your timeline."

I hoped he was as sincere as he seemed. "Thank you."

Warren promised he'd have news for us soon. A servant came forward to show us out, but I lingered a moment with Warren, unable to hold back my curiosity.

"How is your search for a bride coming?" I asked softly. "I expected you to be married by now."

"I expected it too," he said with a chuckle. "I'm considering a few possibilities, but . . . well, you're a tough act to follow."

I found it odd he'd be considering any possibilities, seeing as how certain things had seemed with Tamsin when I left. "I'm sorry," I said, needing to say something.

"No need to be. It's over and done." He regarded me speculatively.

"Have you heard any news from Cape Triumph? From the other girls in your cohort?"

"I had a letter from Tamsin that she sent a while ago. Nothing from Mira yet."

"Mira . . ." I'd seen him have several conversations with her, but the confusion on his face seemed legitimate.

"My Sirminican friend," I prompted.

"Ah, yes. Her. Of course. The one interested in books."

Now I was lost. "Books?"

"Whenever we hosted events at my parents' home, she was always asking about books. Mother isn't as . . ." He paused to give me an apologetic look. "She isn't as open-minded as we are, so she was more than happy to let your friend stay in the library as long as she liked."

"Of course she was," I said. Typical Viola, hiding away "unsavory" elements from her party.

Cedric and I returned to White Rock's central district with mixed feelings. "More delays before we can get married. More sleepless nights," I teased.

"Well, I think the sleepless nights will actually come after we're married, but yes . . . it's frustrating." We came to a stop, and he stared off at the busy White Rock residents and their rebuilding. "And he's not wrong about bandits. Sully was telling me about some. It happens."

"I really need to meet this Sully."

Cedric smiled fondly. "He's a character, that's for—"

"Mister Thorn?"

We both turned around at the unfamiliar voice. But when I got a good look at the speaker, I realized he wasn't so unfamiliar after all. I immediately froze up, but Cedric recovered quickly.

"Mister Garrett," said Cedric, extending his hand in greeting. "A pleasure to see you. I didn't know the McGraw Agency had business out here in the wilderness."

Silas Garrett, the royal investigative agent, regarded us speculatively. "His Majesty has business in all the colonies, and I am but his humble servant. You . . ." He frowned, taking in my rough clothes and disheveled hair. "You were one of the girls at Wisteria Hollow?"

I was getting tired of having the difference in my state constantly being reinforced. "Yes. I'm Adelaide Bailey."

I stated my assumed name firmly. I didn't know what had happened with the search for my former self, but if he'd seen my portrait, I was pretty sure he would've identified me immediately. Surely I hadn't changed that much.

"I'm surprised to see you here. I thought you girls married up? Unless you've found some successful prospector . . ." Again, his tone told me he found that hard to believe, given my appearance.

"Things change," I said. "And you never know—anyone can make their fortune out here. But it's certainly a lot of hard work."

"Hard, sweaty, dirty work," Cedric confirmed. "Not like the glamorous life of a McGraw agent."

Silas guffawed. "Not that glamorous. Lots of hard and dirty work there too."

Cedric wore the bright, dazzled look of someone in the throes of hero worship. "Come on, don't ruin it for us. I don't suppose you can tell us anything about what you're working on? The case you mentioned that was so top secret?"

"Still top secret," said Silas. His tone was gruff, but I got the impression he liked the attention.

I picked up on Cedric's lead. "What about your associate's case? That missing noblewoman? You can tell us about that, can't you?"

"Not much to tell, I'm afraid. That other agent got delayed up north, and I'm sure last night's storm hasn't helped things. But I expect he'll arrive soon. He may end up out here, for all I know. Rumor has it the lady in question might have fled to some of the outer settlements." Again, his eyes fell on me, and I laughed.

"I have a hard time believing that—at least if she's anything like the noblewomen I worked around. I remember our household was in an uproar when my lady cracked a nail just before some fancy gala. Someone like her could never handle this." I held out my hands and pulled off some of the wrappings. The bleeding had stopped overnight, but they still looked pretty terrible. Silas actually flinched.

"My goodness," he said, looking away. "That . . . must hurt quite a bit."

"That's life out here, Mister McGraw." Cedric gave him a polite nod of farewell. "And now we've got other things to attend to. Good luck with your case."

We strolled away casually, but I groaned as soon as we were out of earshot. "Why do I have the feeling that the latest 'rumor' he heard came from Viola Doyle?"

"Because, as previously established, you're a smart and intelligent woman. And Viola Doyle is a vindictive one."

I came to a halt in front of some shops where men busily hammered away, making conversation difficult. "If that picture gets shown in Cape Triumph, the other agent doesn't even have to come to Hadisen himself. All it'll take is some enterprising bounty hunter trekking out here to claim his prize."

"You need to get married."

"A conversation we keep having over and over."

He started to respond, but then his eyes fell on something across the dusty road—or, more specifically, someone. "I know that man . . ." Cedric murmured. His brow furrowed and then smoothed out. "It can't be. I need to go talk to him."

I nearly said I'd follow, but then I realized we were standing in front of the courier's office. "Meet me back here," I said.

The office had sustained only a little damage and was still operating. The mail chief recognized me from our first day and produced two letters he'd been holding, one each for Cedric and me. Cedric's was from his associate, Walter, back in Cape Triumph. I tucked it into my pocket and tore into my envelope. It was from Mira.

Dear Adelaide,

I know it hasn't been that long, but life without you feels so strange. I've had you by my side for the last year, and there's an emptiness now that you're gone. Having Tamsin back helps a lot. She won't talk much about Grashond and seems troubled when it comes up. But aside from those moments, she's her same old self.

She kept good on her promise to not accept any offers until Warren's return, but of course, she still entertained plenty of gentlemen while he was gone. That's Tamsin—always keeping her options open. Since Warren came back, it seems as though her loyalty paid off. He was pretty smitten the last time I saw him, and excited to bring her back to show her around Hadisen.

And so, it seems as if both of you are going off to great adventures while I stay here. Only a few of us aren't engaged yet, and I know I'll have to choose soon. None of my suitors have really inspired a burning passion within me, so it may come down to simply accepting the one—the only one—who offers me the most respect and freedom. Surely that's as good as love. I rather liked that lawyer you knew briefly, but he's made it pretty clear he's not interested in the Glittering Court right now.

Write when you can,
Mira

I reread the letter before folding it up. I missed Mira as much as she missed me, and it saddened me that she might be forced into something simply because she had no better options. But I couldn't think too much about that—not with the perplexing information she presented about Tamsin. Warren had given no indication he'd settled on any girl, but Mira claimed he and Tamsin almost had a match, so much so that he wanted to bring her to Hadisen. What was the truth? The letter was dated only a few days ago and must have come with the mail on Warren's ship last night. I supposed anything could have happened. Had they quarreled in so short a time? Had Tamsin decided she didn't want to live on the frontier after all?

Cedric reappeared as I pondered all this. That excited, knowing look was on his face, which meant he had some brilliant plan in place. "Come on," he said, steering me back to where Lizzie was tied up. "Let's go back to the claim."

I'd expected him to take me back to the Marshalls' since part of the day was gone, but I had no objections to this change. I was curious about how his place had fared in the storm.

"What's going on?" I asked, once we were on the trail heading away from the town. "Who was that man?"

"The man the Galvestons mentioned. The Alanzan magistrate."

"Did you talk to him about marrying your heathen fiancée?"

"Yes, actually." Again, I could tell Cedric was bursting with eagerness. "And he's the one who's going to perform our wedding."

"When the contract's taken care of?" I asked. "You're planning ahead."

"Not then. Now. Tonight." Cedric hesitated. "I mean, if you want to get married."

I craned my head back and tried to determine if he was serious. "How is that possible? We aren't allowed to."

"Only in Warren's contract are we not allowed to. Legally, if a magistrate will do it, we can. Robert—that's his name—will do it *and* keep it secret."

"Okay . . ." His enthusiasm was contagious, but I still didn't understand the entire plan. "If it's secret, what's the point? I mean, aside from the obvious joy of us being bound forever."

"The point is that if Silas Garrett's friend shows up and outs you, then Robert produces the documents that prove our marriage," Cedric explained. "It'll create a lot of hassle with Warren and his contract if we haven't settled those financial matters yet, but your grandmother won't have a claim on you anymore as a married woman."

"And that 'hassle' with Warren is the reason we have to keep it secret in the meantime," I realized. "It . . . it's a backup plan."

"Exactly. Assuming you're okay with an impromptu marriage. Once this all works out, we can have another ceremony with our friends. If we find enough gold, Father might forgive us and let you wear one of your Glittering Court dresses."

"I don't even know if I remember how to lace one of those up," I said, laughing. "I don't need it. I just need you."

He leaned forward and kissed my neck, his arms tightening around my waist. "Careful," I said. "We're not married yet."

Back at the claim, things were about what I'd expected. The river had flooded, overturning the sluices. They were still intact, at least, and easy to set back up. The shanty had been completely flattened. Most of Cedric's belongings had been soaked, except for what was in his trunk. The rickety old stove had also survived. It seemed to be impervious.

Everything else was put on hold as we worked to get the shanty put back together. I wasn't very good at that sort of thing, but, as it turned out, neither was Cedric. Now I understood why it had taken him three days to get the shack in the shape it had been. By evening, we'd done as many repairs as we could with what we had. He'd have to replace the bed and a few other items, but at least he sort of had a roof again.

I looked up at the darkened sky. "It's past when we usually go back. I hope the Marshalls don't come looking for me."

"We'll tell them we got caught up in the repairs. And we have bigger things now. Look." Cedric pointed toward the trail that led to his property, and I saw Robert the magistrate riding toward us. He waved a hand in greeting.

A tremor of nervousness ran through me. "I can't believe this is really going to happen."

Cedric slipped an arm around me. "You can still change your mind. And you might want to—I'd hoped to do an Alanzan rite, if that's okay. He could do a civil service if you wanted."

I had only the briefest flash of that old fear, of dark rituals around a fire. Then those thoughts were banished. "The means don't matter. As long as I get to pledge myself to you, I'll be happy."

It was a little surreal when Robert dismounted and donned a robe of black and white, so very different from the glittering vestments worn by the priests of Uros. Equally strange was the thought of an outdoor wedding. It seemed so casual compared to the formal processions and long services performed in the great cathedrals of Uros.

For the briefest of moments, I was taken away from this nighttime wilderness and remembered what it was like to sit between my parents in the pews of the King's Crest Cathedral, the wood hard and golden from years of use. Enormous candelabras. Rainbows of stained glass covering the walls. We'd gone to dozens of noble weddings in my childhood, and I'd see my mother scrutinizing every detail of each bride's attire, from her slippers to the enormous train trailing several feet behind her. And I could always tell my mother was mentally planning my wedding, deciding what would look best on me. Velvet or silk for the gown? Beadwork or embroidery on the train?

That long-ago idea rose up in me that at any moment my parents were going to walk through the door. I found myself looking toward the trailhead, like they might suddenly appear there. But my parents weren't here. Neither was Grandmama. I wasn't even wearing a dress.

"Adelaide?"

Cedric drew my attention back to him. One eyebrow was raised in question. No doubt he was thinking I'd changed my mind. Looking at him, at that beloved face, eased the weight of the ghosts that had settled on me. They weren't gone. They never would be. But they were part of the past, and I couldn't change that. It was the future I looked to now. The future I had chosen. The future I saw in Cedric's eyes.

We held hands as Robert recited the words of the Alanzan ceremony. It was sweet and beautiful, speaking of how the joining of two people was part of the natural order of things. It made our union seem greater than us . . . like we now shared a part of some powerful, heavenly secret. Above us, a full moon shone down, and I remembered Mira saying that was a fortuitous omen for Alanzan weddings.

When Robert had finished reciting his words, it was time for us to recite ours. But first, he placed a circlet of bishop's lace around our clasped hands. We tightened our hold as the frilly white flowers encircled our wrists. Then, I learned the full wording of the vows Cedric had once mentioned:

I will take your hand and lie with you in the groves, under the light of the moon. I will build a life with you upon this green earth. I will walk by your side for so long as the sun continues to rise.

The ending kiss was the same as the ceremonies of Uros, and we savored it, clinging to each other as though afraid this would all slip away when we released each other. Also the same was the signing of various legal papers. It seemed odd to be doing something so bureaucratic in this wild setting, but it meant we were bound both in the eyes of the law and whatever gods were looking down upon us. With that realization, a new lightness suddenly filled me. I was free of anyone else's claim upon me. And Cedric and I were together—truly together—as we'd been meant to be since that first day we met.

He drew me to him once Robert had wished us well and gone his way, promising to keep the documents safe. "How do you feel?" Cedric asked.

"Happier than I ever imagined I'd be at my wedding," I said. "Happier than I ever imagined I'd be in my life. Also dirtier . . . but that doesn't bother me as much as I expected."

He brushed his lips over mine. "Well, it's a good thing I know where there's a luxury bathhouse. Although it's probably going to be freezing."

I grabbed his hand and immediately began leading him toward the shaded pond. "Then I'll keep you warm," I said.

He was right—the water was a lot colder than that day we'd bathed in the heat of the afternoon. And it was a lot harder to see by moonlight. But neither of us looked away this time. And neither of us held back. We helped each other wash, but I don't know how good a job we really did. There was too much kissing. Too much holding. Too much everything.

I felt no chill in the water or when we left it and lay down on his coat in the grass. I felt nothing but heat, like we were both flames merging into something brighter and more powerful. And in what followed, I had that sense again that we were more than just us. We were part of the earth, part of the heavens. I understood why Alanziel and Deanziel had fallen from grace in order to be together. I would have defied Uros a thousand times over to be with Cedric.

Afterward, entwined with him on the grass, I didn't want to go. It didn't seem right to leave him on our wedding night. It didn't seem right to leave him ever.

"Just a little longer," he said. A warm breeze danced over us, but I still shivered. He pulled me closer. "Just a little longer, and then things will be normal."

I rested my head on his chest and laughed. "Things have never been normal between us. And I hope they never are."

And so, with great reluctance on both our parts, we put our clothes back on. Poor Lizzie probably thought she'd had the night off but doggedly took us down the trail. I sank into Cedric as we rode, dizzy and warm with this new connection between us.

At the cabin, we found Mistress Marshall waiting up for us. She sat at the table with a cup of tea but couldn't fight a yawn as we entered. "There you are. Andrew wanted to come get you, but I told him you'd be along."

"There was a lot of damage from the storm," I said. It wasn't an outright lie. "I'm sorry I missed the lessons."

She yawned again. "It's no concern. The children had plenty of cleanup work to do here. But your young man might as well stay over. No point in going back and turning right around in the morning. Just go upstairs and push the boys out of the way in the bed."

"I will," said Cedric. "Thank you."

She headed toward her bedroom, and I asked, "Is the water still hot? I'd like to make some chamomile."

She gestured at the kettle on the smoldering hearth. "Help yourself."

Cedric and I walked upstairs together and then lingered on the landing that separated the boys' and girls' rooms.

"Well, how about that," I whispered. "We get to spend our wedding night together after all." Through a crack in the door to the boys' room, we could hear loud snoring.

"Exactly as I imagined," Cedric said.

We kissed as much as we dared with me holding a hot cup of water and the knowledge anyone might stumble upon us. I went off to the girls' room floating, heady with everything that had taken place this night. I changed out of my work clothes and slipped on a plain nightgown. Before getting under the covers with the other girls, I sat on the room's one stool and finished my tea. I hadn't added chamomile to it, however. Instead, I'd mixed in the cinnamon thorn leaves that Mistress Marshall had given me on our journey.

CHAPTER 27

AND SO, UNBEKNOWNST TO ANYONE ELSE, A NEW PATTERN emerged for us in the next week. The entire world had changed for me.

Each morning Cedric would dutifully ride to the Marshall place and bring me back to help with the claim. We didn't get to work right away, though. We'd fall into the bed—or, well, the straw mattress that passed as one—and linger there as long as we dared. At least the straw was new, having been replaced after the storm. Getting up and starting our day took some effort, but the knowledge that we were that much closer to the life we wanted spurred us on. Equally hard was leaving him at the end of the day, but we did that too. I'd teach my lessons, sleep, and begin it all anew.

"I got you something," Cedric told me one morning.

"More than a gourmet meal?"

That too was something else that had emerged. Cedric would always get out of bed first and make me breakfast. The old stove's options were limited, but he could pull off bacon and simple biscuits reasonably well. He'd serve it to me in bed, teasing that he had to wait on me because he knew that I secretly missed my old noble life and might leave him for it.

"Don't think I didn't notice that sarcasm. And yes, something more."

I sat up cross-legged on the mattress. The only thing I'd bothered putting on so far was my plain white blouse, which was looking a lot less white than when I'd come to Hadisen. "Don't leave me in suspense."

He came over and handed me my morning cup of cinnamon thorn tea, something else he'd taken upon himself to make, and a small metallic object. I looked closer and saw it was a necklace. A narrow linked chain held an oval-shaped pendant of thin glass with a flower pressed in the middle. I'd seen this pressed-flower style before; they were trendy in Adoria right now. I held it up the light and realized what the flower was.

"It's bishop's lace," I said in delight. "Just like the ones from our wedding."

"It *is* one from our wedding. Since you can't wear a ring yet, I saved it so you'd have some kind of token."

"That was resourceful of you." I put the chain around my neck and ran my hands over the glass. "I forgot all about those flowers after . . . well, everything else that happened that night."

He touched my cheek. "Well, I can be pretty distracting. It's a wonder you can remember your name anymore. Any of them."

"Now, now, don't be so humble," I said, elbowing him. "But thank you. I hope you didn't spend too much on it."

"Don't worry, it's brass. I'll do better on the ring."

He leaned down to kiss me, and then the sound of a horse outside made him jerk back. Without speaking, we both jumped up from the bed. Cedric tucked his shirt in while I hastily pulled on my split skirt and boots. I'd just seated myself at the tiny table with my tea when a knock sounded at the door. Cedric opened it casually, putting on a pleasantly surprised smile when he saw Elias's sour face outside.

"What an unexpected delight," Cedric lied.

Elias peered inside. "Hard at work, I see."

"You're just in time for breakfast." I gestured to the bacon before me. "Always a good start to the day. Would you like some?"

Elias stepped inside, studying the shabby room with disdain. He leaned toward my food and sniffed, wrinkling his nose. "Of course not. I'm here on business."

"Now, now, Elias. Don't be rude," said a familiar voice. Warren appeared in the doorway. "May I come in?"

"Certainly," Cedric said with a wave. "Welcome to my home."

Warren's pleasant smile never left his face as he came in and looked around. I'd grown used to the shabbiness, but Warren no doubt thought I'd made a terrible choice. "How quaint," was all he said.

Cedric had left the door open, and I could see Elias's usual henchmen out there, along with a few other unknown men milling about. "Is this for the lode?" I asked.

Throughout the week, Cedric and I had dutifully worked the pans and sluices but had stayed away from the outcropping. Warren and Elias had urged us to wait until the proper men and tools were there, and we'd obeyed, despite our growing impatience. It had been hard, knowing that Cedric could have easily gone up there and, within a week of hacking, gotten what we needed for our immediate debts.

"What else would it be for?" Elias snapped. "Now, if it isn't an inconvenience to your meal, we'd like to get started."

He turned for the door, and Cedric and I exchanged looks behind his back. What else could we do? We both wanted this, and if Elias's attitude was the price we had to pay, so be it.

"I'm sorry," said Warren in a low voice, once Elias was back outside. "I know he's . . . abrasive at times. But he's good at his job, and he's loyal."

Outside, we found more climbing gear and several small crates. One of the men stepped forward, introducing himself as Argus Lane. He was an explosives expert and showed us how the crates were filled with small containers. "These work on a delay," he explained. "There are two components. On their own, they're perfectly stable. When mixed in great enough quantities with each other, they trigger an explosive reaction. Men'll go up there and set them, then hurry down before the reaction occurs."

"It sounds dangerous," I said.

Argus smiled at me. "Not if they're done correctly. Once the components are attached and we're ready, you just pull out a pin that triggers the top one to gradually fill into the bottom. It's designed to be slow enough for a getaway."

"Argus knows what he's doing," Warren said, patting the other man on the back. "He mined in Kelardia before coming to Adoria, and he's already overseen the excavation of several lodes here."

Two of the men began strapping on harnesses and ropes, and Cedric offered to go with them. "You stay on the ground," said Elias. "We need skilled climbers who can get out in time. You can help when we're ready to dig it out—and then you can fall at your leisure."

We'd mentioned Cedric's fall while at Warren's, and Elias had blamed it on Cedric's inexperience, rather than faulty equipment. Anger flared up in me, and I started to speak, but Cedric laid a calming hand on my arm. "We have bigger battles to fight," he murmured.

"Elias," said Warren in a warning voice.

Elias eyed Cedric for several moments, seeming undecided about something. At last, he said reluctantly, "If you want to help, you can fasten the second load of explosive components together. *Just* fasten them. Don't take the pins out. We don't need these going off."

The components were clearly marked, one blue and one red, and Argus demonstrated how to intricately twist the two cases so they clicked into place, one on top of the other. The pin that stopped them from mixing was fixed in tightly between them. "Hard to get out—but still, be careful. Go slow."

"I'll help," I said, starting to kneel with Cedric in the grass.

"In Uros's name, no," groaned Elias. "I just said we don't need these going off. This is men's work, Miss Bailey. Not sewing and mending."

I put my hands on my hips. "I'm aware. And I've been doing 'men's work' for weeks now."

"She's actually better at it than sewing and mending," remarked Cedric, deadpan.

Elias turned to Warren beseechingly. "Sir, I beg you."

"Elias, she *is* a very capable woman, and you'd do well to recognize that," said Warren sternly. He turned to me. "But, in fairness, I know when too many hands are involved in that kind of detailed work, it actually can get more complicated. Would you mind terribly if instead

I took you up on your earlier hospitality? I thought I smelled tea back there, and now I can't stop thinking about it."

Elias's smug smile nearly drove me to refuse. I'd served them willingly last time, but now this felt like proof that I could do only "women's work." But I kept the polite façade and went back to the shanty, grateful that on this trip, at least, I didn't have to hide Alanzan artifacts. I'd used up the last of my cinnamon thorn tea this morning and would have to endure the humiliation of asking Mistress Marshall for more. Not that I would've ever served that to Warren anyway. I instead used some decent black that Cedric had splurged on during a recent trip to town.

By the time it was steeped and ready to go, I found all sorts of progress outside. Warren's men were almost at the top of the outcropping. Cedric was just about finished with his task when Elias unceremoniously set down an enormous pile of rope, as well as a couple more explosives with the components already joined. "Since you're so eager to help," said Elias, "this needs untangling." His tone was as demeaning as ever. I was about to hurry over to help Cedric, but Warren beckoned me over, excitement on his face. He pointed up.

"We could mine what's at the top with picks, but the bottom would be too inaccessible because of the column's narrowness. Once they've assessed what's there, they'll blow off the outer rock on top and then mine what's exposed. They'll keep blowing it off section by section, working their way down until we get everything out. And then . . ." Warren gestured to the foothills beyond. "Then we go after that."

"Where you'll get a lot more than a forty percent commission," I said with a smile.

"Hey, boss," called one of the men on top. He'd been looking in the crevasse. "This place is *stacked*. I can tell just from where he picked at it the other day."

This elicited a few cheers from the men on the ground. Warren looked equally excited but managed to keep his voice dignified. "Well, that is what we're here for. Proceed."

The men on top set to work placing the combined explosive components. Warren took my arm and began steering me backward. "The charges are designed to be strong enough to break through the rock but not *so* powerful they bring that whole structure down. Nonetheless—it's best if we keep our distance in case there's any falling debris."

Other men on the ground were doing the same, and I cast an anxious look over at Cedric. He was on the opposite side of the outcropping from me but farther back than we were. When the explosives were set, the men pulled the pins out and then began quickly rappelling back down. Part of me expected something dramatic—like the explosives going off just as the men made it to the ground. But the mixing of the components had been timed to give a high margin of safety, and the men were back in the safe zone when the top of the outcropping exploded spectacularly.

Even knowing what to expect, I couldn't help a small cry of surprise. Thunder boomed around us, and the ground shook as a flash of fire lit up the crevasse. Warren pulled me to him and put his arm out protectively, but there was no need. We were indeed outside the most dangerous radius, and the rocks and debris that rained down stayed relatively close to the cliff itself. As the smoke blew away, I could see glittering spots on the ground among the rocky debris.

"There's gold there," I said.

Warren smiled. "From the outer layers of the deposit. We can just walk over and pick that up later when the main part of the excavation has wrapped up. A lot easier than panning, huh?"

I started to answer and then caught sight of something in my periphery. I turned and saw a figure on horseback approaching from the side of the claim opposite the one that led to town. "Cedric," I called. "There's someone there."

Cedric rose and put a hand to his eyes to block the sun. A big grin broke out over his face. "Hey, Sully!" Cedric strode away from his task and waved to the approaching figure, who answered with his own wave.

A few things happened almost at once then. I saw Elias shoot Warren a questioning look. Eager to meet Cedric's infamous neighbor, I left Warren's side and hurried after Cedric, going very near where he'd been working on the rope. Elias ran up and grabbed me from behind, literally throwing me back toward Warren so that I hit the ground hard and bit my tongue.

"Hey," I said, struggling to my feet. "What's the—"

The world was suddenly ripped apart. The prior explosion in the crevasse had been loud, but nothing compared to this deafening roar. One successive *boom* followed after another. I covered my ears, but it did little to dampen the sound. The shaking of the ground caused me to fall over again. Plumes of flame rolled up into the air from the equipment pile, soon leaving black smoke in their wake.

A hand on my arm tugged me up, and I found Warren looking down at me solicitously. At first, my ears rang too much to make sense of what he said. Then I finally heard: "Are you okay?"

I gave a shaky nod and looked around. All of his men were grouped not far from us, over by the outcropping and well away from the pile of explosives that had just gone off. Being on open ground like that, the blast had thrown up little debris short of dirt. My real panic, of course, came at seeing Cedric. He stood up on wobbly legs, having also been knocked over by a shock wave, and moved about unsteadily. I started to head toward him, but my own balance was still off.

"Easy there," said Warren, holding me again so I wouldn't fall.

I started to protest, but then Sully rode up to Cedric and dismounted. The older man said something, and Cedric nodded. As I watched, his steps grew surer, and his balance returned.

"Get some water on that!" shouted Elias.

Most of the fire from the explosions was already out. A little of the surrounding grass still smoldered, but all that remained of the initial blast was a shallow crater. Warren's men all had canteens and used them to put out the residual flames. This just created more smoke, and for a few minutes, we all coughed and wiped tears out of our eyes.

"Having a little trouble with your charges?" asked Sully conversationally. He was a stereotypical prospector, long and lanky with shaggy gray hair and an unkempt beard.

Elias turned on Cedric angrily. "This is what comes of letting you near those! You never should have been let near *any* of this! A coddled city boy has no business out here around real work—deadly work for those too stupid to know what they're doing!"

Cedric took an angry step forward, fists clenched at his sides. "I did know what I was doing. I handled every one of those components perfectly, and then I checked them over twice. No pins were out. Something in the explosives was faulty—just like that harness you brought me."

"Don't blame your continued incompetence on me!" exclaimed Elias.

"And don't act like I can't see this sabotage!" returned Cedric. "There was nothing wrong with the canisters I assembled."

I was rubbing my head, still recovering from the blast. Slowly, memories surfaced to the front of my mind. "But you didn't assemble them all," I said. Everyone turned to me, and I pointed at Elias. "When you brought the rope, you added more explosives to Cedric's pile."

"Leftovers that weren't needed in the first wave," said Elias. "Safer to keep them in one place rather than—"

"Leftovers that Cedric didn't put together," I interrupted. "I don't fully understand their mechanics, but they must have been tampered with from the inside to do a slow mix and eventually combust."

Warren placed a gentle hand on my arm. "Adelaide, you need to rest. That blast was harder on you than you realize."

I pulled away from him. "Elias knew! It's why he pushed me away when I started to get close to the explosives. He steered everyone away. He knew they were going to go off. If Sully hadn't arrived, Cedric would've been right there." I choked for a moment, unable to comprehend such a terrible outcome. Then, a new realization hit me as I met Warren's eyes. "And you knew too. Elias turned to you when Cedric left. And you made sure to keep me away too. You were in on it."

Cedric moved forward, putting himself between Warren and me. "What's your endgame been? Why did you bring us out here? Has this really all been some sort of elaborate revenge scheme?"

Several heated moments hung in the air as we all sized each other up. Then Warren gave a simple nod, and two men lunged forward and tackled Cedric to the ground. I screamed and moved forward, but Elias grabbed hold of me. Sully also started to come to the rescue, but Cedric managed to lift his head through his assault and cry out, "Go, get help!"

Sully hesitated for only the blink of an eye before hopping back on his horse. For a man his age, he moved remarkably fast. It didn't hurt that his horse could've run circles around Lizzie. Within seconds, Sully was tearing off across the claim. "Go after him!" Warren shouted at one of the men. Their horses were farther away, tethered near the shanty, giving Sully a respectable lead.

Neither Cedric nor I were yielding easily to our captors. We were restrained in different ways, however. When Cedric resisted, he was met with brutal punches and hits. I saw him gasp as a foot slammed into his ribs, and later, a punch to the face made him spit blood. I fought frantically against Elias, desperate to help Cedric, but he shoved me down onto my knees and use his greater weight to keep me in place.

"Be still, you hellion." To Warren, he asked, "What now?"

Warren looked weary more than anything else. "Take her to that hovel and tie her up for now. As for him . . ." His eye fell coldly on Cedric. "Over to the river, by one of the sluices. That's where he'd most likely be working if raiders came. Then clean out the other sluices and do a little work on the outcropping—enough to look like some hasty, haphazard job. We'll truss up the house later, not that anyone could tell the difference. The rest of you, come with me and see if we can catch up with that old fool." As he started to walk away, Warren paused and added to Elias, "Don't *quite* kill him. I'll take care of that when I'm back. But make sure he doesn't get up in the meantime."

The group dispersed, and I realized they were going to make this look like the work of bandits who'd swooped in to kill whoever they found and seize whatever gold was easily accessible. "Cedric!" I screamed as two men literally dragged him off toward the river.

Elias slapped me, apparently bolder without Warren's watchful eye. "Quiet." He hauled me back to the shanty, and I kicked and fought him the whole time. Once inside, he tied up my hands and feet with climbing rope and left me on the floor. After a moment's thought, he also tied an old cloth around my mouth. "You're getting no less than you deserve," he said coldly. "You could've had everything—now, you're losing it all."

I cursed him through the gag, but he only gave me that infuriating smirk before shutting the door behind him. I immediately began struggling against the ropes, but he'd made the knots tight. I paused, frustrated, and then heard Cedric's scream of pain in the distance. Frantically I renewed my efforts, wiggling and flailing. The knife Cedric had used on the bacon was up on the table. If I could somehow get over to it—

Knife.

The Alanzan tree knife Cedric had given me on the ship was in my belt, concealed in the folds of the split skirt. I wore it every day, mostly out of habit, using it occasionally. My fingertips could just now graze it as I reached toward it. A little farther, and I'd be able to pull it out. The ropes at my wrists were tight, and I felt them chafing and cutting as I strained against them. At last I managed to release the knife from the belt, only to drop it. I rolled over and grabbed it with my hand. Now began the weary task of trying to cut my ropes from such an awkward angle, since my hands were bent in the wrong direction. No more cries from Cedric came, and that terrible silence drove me on more. At long last, I wore away at the ropes enough to free my hands with my own strength. Cutting the ones at my ankles and removing the gag was easy after that.

I sprang up and ran to the door, peeking out just in time to see Elias land a hard kick on something in the river before striding off. I knew what that "something" had to be, and my stomach turned. There were two other men destroying and cleaning out the sluices, and they too were finishing up their tasks. Elias waved them toward the outcropping and barked out words I couldn't hear. Soon, they were all crowded at its base, gathering the fallen gold and picking near the bottom, just as frantic raiders might do in the hopes of making a quick score. As they moved around the back side of the outcropping, I made my move.

I didn't care that I was exposed on open ground. I had to get to Cedric. The men continued working, never turning back to the river, and I splashed into one of its shallow parts unnoticed. There I found Cedric lying on his back, and I nearly fell forward weeping. His face was bloody and bruised, with one of his eyes swollen shut. I couldn't assess the damage to the rest of his body, but there was an unnatural bend to his arm. For a moment, I feared the worst, but a ragged breath from him told me otherwise. And I knew there was no time for tears.

"What . . . you doing . . . ?" he gasped out when I slid an arm around him and raised him up. His good eye fluttered open.

"Getting you out of here." I supported as much of his weight as I could and began leading him down the river. He was able to walk a little, but I did most of the work.

"You . . . you need to get out of here."

"Yes," I agreed. "And you're coming with me."

A glance back showed we were still unnoticed, but we'd never make it to the far side of the claim in time, not at this rate. The grove and pond weren't that far away, and I made that my goal, guiding Cedric one agonizing step at a time. I had no idea if I was worsening his injuries, but I had no choice. When we finally reached the shelter of the trees, I eased him down and reassessed my options. One of the men had moved to the front of the outcropping, but we were concealed, and they all thought Cedric was back in the river.

"Lizzie," I said, turning my gaze to the shanty. She was tethered there, grazing idly. "We need to get her."

"Too dangerous," said Cedric.

"Going on foot is dangerous. I'll get her. Stay here." It was a stupid thing to say, since he didn't have many other choices. I kissed his forehead and then timed another sprint to run back to the shanty. Again, I had to cover open ground, and again, my luck stayed with me. At least until I reached Lizzie.

As I was about to untie her, I saw two riders returning to the claim. One was Warren. I could've released her and rode back to Cedric, but not without being seen. There was no way I'd be able to retrieve him before we were caught. And I wasn't going to ride off without him. Out of options, I dove back into the shanty.

With the skillet in one hand and my dagger in the other, I waited by the door, certain someone would be coming for me. One of Warren's men entered, and I swung the skillet hard over his head, catching him unawares. He fought against me briefly before passing out, knocking my knife out of my hand in the process. Before I could recover it, Warren appeared in the doorway with a gun pointed at me.

"Drop the skillet," he said.

I did, slowly raising my hands up. He shut the door and stepped over his fallen man, nodding at me to back up against the wall. "Why are you doing this?" I asked. "Was this really to get revenge on me?"

"Not on you, exactly," he said. There was a cold, dispassionate tone in his voice, so different from the guileless enthusiasm he'd displayed in Cape Triumph. "Mostly on him. I told you before I was straightforward and go after what I want directly. I wanted you. He took you, so the plan was to eliminate him and then, when your grief eventually subsided, take you back. But then two things happened. Three, actually."

"Your attempts to kill him didn't work?" I guessed. As I spoke, my eyes darted around, looking frantically for some weapon or escape. That gun definitely put the odds in his favor. If it was a newer one, it could have two shots in it.

"Yes, actually," admitted Warren. "And then, this seemingly useless gold claim turned out not to be so useless after all. Not that it would matter in the end—once he's dead, it reverts back to my full ownership. But it did mean he might have had a chance to pay off his debt early."

My knife was the closest weapon to me, but even so, I'd never reach it in time. "What was the third?" I asked, needing to keep him distracted.

He sighed melodramatically. "You found out what was happening. This was all supposed to end with you willingly back where you belong—with me. But something tells me that's pretty unlikely at this point."

My only answer was a glare.

"And so," he said, "it seems you and the unfortunate Mister Thorn will both have died at the hands of vicious claim bandits. But at least I won't feel like I'm leaving empty-handed before you die."

Hope surged in me as I realized he didn't know Cedric was gone. Then, those last words struck me. "What . . . what do you mean?"

Warren gestured casually at the table with his gun. "I've been in houses of ill repute. I know what cinnamon thorn smells like. And I know what kind of girls drink it. So much for all your fine talk about staying virtuous until your wedding night. But—I guess it means I don't have to feel guilty about taking anything of value, seeing as it's so freely offered."

He set the gun down on the table but moved too quickly for me to take advantage of the reprieve. He threw himself on me, knocking me to the floor and pinning his body over mine. I balled my fists and tried striking at his chest. When I realized that wouldn't work, I started poking at his eyes. He cursed and held my hands down with his.

"You were more docile back at the balls," he said. "Prettier too. Cleaner."

He tried holding both my wrists with one hand so that his other could grapple with my clothing. He managed to tear the blouse and then move down to my skirt just before I broke my hands free. He couldn't hold them both one-handed, and he knew it. I clawed at his face again, and frustration replaced the earlier confidence.

"Damn it." He grabbed hold of me and rolled us over so that I lay on my stomach. "Less refined it is."

Positioned like this, with his body keeping me facedown, I couldn't so easily attack or even shift around. He kept one hand on my head to keep it down and began pulling at the skirt again. I called him names that would have made Tamsin blush and struggled as much as I could, knowing it wouldn't save me but would at least make it more difficult for him. Then, I caught sight of what this new position had brought me closer to.

The Alanzan dagger was within my reach.

Without a second thought, I grabbed it and swung backward, not caring what I struck so long as it was him. Warren screamed and fell off me. I immediately scrambled away and made it to my feet with shaking legs. He lay there on the floor, clutching at his leg, which had my knife embedded in his thigh. It wasn't a killing blow, but it had bought me my escape. I moved toward the door, only to have it open from the outside. I braced myself for one of his men and instead came face to face with Silas Garrett. He wielded a gun and looked as surprised to see me as I was him.

"Arrest her!" Warren shouted. "I came to inspect this claim, and that bitch attacked me! She stabbed me—stabbed me with this—" He pointed down and gaped as he got a good look at the knife with its tree design. "With this blade—this *pagan* blade! It's an Alanzan knife! She's a heretic—arrest her!"

"It . . . it's not hers," a voice behind Silas said. "It's mine. I'm the Alanzan."

Silas stepped aside, revealing Cedric leaning on Sully. I couldn't believe Cedric was even conscious after all his injuries. I wanted to run to him and order him to lie down, but Warren was still on the offensive. "He'd say anything to protect his whore."

Sully had the sense to try and keep Cedric back, but Cedric was undaunted. "The knife is mine. I've got more Alanzan items in my trunk. You won't find anything in her possession."

"Then arrest him!" said Warren. "And her for being his accomplice! And for attacking me!"

"He attacked me," I retorted. I gestured to my torn clothes. "He subdued me and tried to assault me! I defended myself!"

Warren was pale and sweating, no doubt feeling the wound and blood loss, but he pushed on. "She invited me here. She's a girl without morals—laid down for Thorn, laid down for anyone. Then she changed her mind and acted like it's my fault. You can't trust the word of some common, vulgar girl!"

Silas looked like he didn't know what to think, and I didn't blame him. But it occurred to me that as improbable as it might be, there could be a chance Warren could get away with all this. He was the governor of this colony. And who was I? A memory surfaced from long ago: Cedric telling me that I didn't know what it was like to live without the prestige of the upper class, that there was a power there I didn't even realize.

I straightened up to my full height and put on as imperious a look as I could manage. "I'm telling you again: He assaulted me. And maybe you can't take that seriously from some 'common, vulgar girl,' but I'm not one. I'm Lady Elizabeth Witmore, Countess of Rothford, and I am a peeress of the realm."

CHAPTER 28

TRAVELING BACK TO CAPE TRIUMPH BY BOAT WAS A LOT easier than the overland journey had been. We didn't return right away—not with Cedric's injuries being what they were. Between us, Warren, and the hired thugs, Silas Garrett had his hands full keeping track of everyone. He finally hired his own muscle from among the various men looking for work in White Rock—deputizing them as temporary agents of the law. Silas used a group of them to help him take Warren and the others back to Cape Triumph. He left a smaller group to keep an eye on Cedric and me at the Marshalls'—not that we were much of a flight risk.

When Silas came back a week later, news came to us by way of the doctor who'd been making regular visits to check up on Cedric. "I told Mister Garrett you're fit to travel now," the doctor said. "And he plans on taking you both back tomorrow."

We were sitting outside in the afternoon sun, with Cedric propped up in a makeshift lounge chair that Mister Marshall had crafted. Cedric's eye was open again, and most of his bruises had faded to a yellowish color. His left arm was in a sling and would need a few more weeks of recovery. He'd also broken a couple of ribs, and there wasn't much to treat them, aside from binding them and taking it easy.

"Fit to travel?" I exclaimed. "Like this?"

"The worst is over," said the doctor. "Your life's not in danger. Will the journey be uncomfortable? Possibly—especially if you're careless. But the boat's nothing compared to the land route."

"I'll be fine." Cedric placed his right hand over mine. "And we need to get back. Warren being there ahead of us isn't a good thing."

It was something we'd discussed frequently: The more time Warren was in Cape Triumph, the more time he had to perfect his story and muster support from his powerful friends.

"One other thing . . ." The doctor looked a bit uneasy and cast a nervous glance my way. "Mister Garrett said to tell you that his partner had arrived in Cape Triumph and that he had your portrait—that it was a match. My—my lady."

I held up a hand. "Please. There's no need. Adelaide is fine."

The doctor gave some advice to Cedric before leaving, as well as various medicines to help with the healing. When he was gone, I leaned my head on Cedric's shoulder. "Well, that's that. The secret's out."

"Exactly which of our many secrets are you referring to?"

"You know which. My identity. Er, my old one." I sighed. "But if Silas's partner authenticated it, then maybe my word will have greater weight. Except that now I've opened myself up to anyone hoping to cash in on Grandmother's reward."

"Do *not* tell anyone we're married," Cedric said in a low voice, guessing what I was about to say next.

"But that was the whole point! To give me protection if I was outed as a runaway countess. And I have been."

He shook his head. "You're key in this case—Silas will protect you now. And our backup plan was created before *I* was outed as a heretic. They're going to put me on trial for that. If you're identified as my legal wife, they're going to cast you as Alanzan by association. I'm not going to have you hanged with me."

"And I'm not going to have you hanged at all," I growled. "Or let Warren go unpunished."

But when we sailed back to Cape Triumph the next morning, I wasn't nearly so confident. As a fledgling colony, Hadisen had no court capable of handling a major case like this, so it was being dealt with in Denham. Warren had a lot of connections there. And the Alanzan faith was illegal in both colonies.

We docked in Cape Triumph in early evening and were promptly separated. Cedric had to stay in custody throughout his trial, and it was only a small comfort that Warren and his henchmen were also in custody.

"I'm not completely insensitive, my lady," Silas told me. I didn't bother correcting him. If my title could strengthen our case, I'd let it be used. "I'll make sure he's looked after. And I'll have a doctor check in."

"Thank you," I said. He gave us a moment of privacy to say goodbye, and I clasped Cedric's hand. It was about as much as I could do, given his injuries.

"We'll get through this," I said. "I'll find a way."

"You always do."

The old bravado was in his voice, but I caught a glint of uncertainty in his eyes. I kissed him fiercely, uncaring of any passersby who saw. And when Silas's men led him away, I stared after them until Cedric had been swallowed by the bustling crowd on Cape Triumph's docks.

"Miss," said one of the hired lawmen. "Mister Garrett said we're to escort you wherever you want to go."

I had no idea where I wanted to go. I'd thought little beyond Cedric's fate and now found myself in an odd situation. After years of feeling constricted and defined by the rules of others, I had no limitations now. I could move and go freely—except I had no place to go. No home, no money, no family.

But I still had friends.

"Take me to Wisteria Hollow."

Unsurprisingly, my reception wasn't that warm. Jasper came striding out of his office as soon as Mistress Culpepper announced me in the foyer. He pointed an accusing finger at me.

"No. *No.* I don't care who you are or what titles you allegedly have.

You cannot come crawling back here after everything you've done to us. You chose to walk away from this life. Don't try to get it back."

"I'm not," I said. "I just . . . well . . . that is . . . I don't have anywhere to stay."

We'd gathered an audience of my beautifully styled peers, making me self-conscious about my bedraggled appearance. Charles was among them. His return to Osfrid to help recruit the next batch of girls had been delayed after all the recent developments. "Jasper, the girl was one of our own, and she may very well be one of our family once this business with Cedric is settled."

Jasper turned on his brother incredulously. "'This business?' He's being tried for heresy and assault! There's only one way that can be settled."

"Assault?" I asked in surprise. "Have you seen him?"

"That's the story going around," Jasper said. "That you two got desperate when it became clear you weren't going to be able to pay off your debt to Warren Doyle. So you staged an attack to make it look like raiders had come after him—only his men got there in time to save him."

My jaw nearly hit the floor. "Is that what they've come up with? It's a lie! Come on. You must know Cedric better than that."

"Actually," said Jasper, face grim, "I really don't feel like I know my son at all. What I do know is that before you came along, he wasn't abducting noblewomen, practicing heresy, or assaulting government leaders. So you'll understand when I say politely as I can: Get out of my house."

"She can stay with me." Aiana strode forward from those gathered, as cool and confident as ever. "And don't look at me like that, Mister Jasper. I rent my own home and can do as I like. Come on, Adelaide."

What else could I do? There was no home for me here. I had to take whatever allies I could get—though I was surprised to find that my two biggest ones hadn't been in the foyer.

"Where are Tamsin and Mira?" I asked, once I was inside Aiana's home. It was a surprisingly spacious suite of rooms above a tavern in the city's busy entertainment district. The soundproofing was good, but I could still make out the faint tinkling of piano music from below.

Aiana had been putting a teakettle on her large stove and turned to me in surprise. "You don't know? About Tamsin?"

"What is there to know? Did she get married or something?"

"Sit down," Aiana ordered.

I obeyed, settling into a chair covered by a blanket with an intricately colored turtle design. I wondered if it was Balanquan, but the look on Aiana's face made me forget all about art. "Where is Tamsin?"

Aiana pulled up a stool and sat across from me. "Adelaide, Tamsin was lost on the day of the storm a couple of weeks ago—the tempest? Part of it hit you too, right?"

I almost thought I was mishearing, that we were somehow talking about our initial sea voyage. "Lost . . . what do you mean, lost in the tempest?"

"She was in Mister Doyle's party—going back to Hadisen. They were practically engaged, and he was going to show her around. They were approaching the bay as the storm was rolling in, and they say she panicked and . . . well, left. No one knows what happened to her."

"Panicked? Tamsin's never panicked in her life!"

"I don't know anything firsthand, only what they tell me." Aiana's calm was impressive. "She didn't want to get on the boat during the storm. She ran away from the party. They tried to find her, but it was too late—especially in those conditions. They searched for her the next day, but there was nothing."

I put my head between my hands, afraid I would faint. "No. That's impossible. You're confused. She was lost once—this can't happen again! She wanted that marriage more than anything. She wouldn't have let a stormy crossing hold her back . . ."

And yet as I spoke, I wondered. Would she? The tempest had upset me with painful memories of that night at sea. What had it done to Tamsin? Maybe the thought of boarding another ship in the storm really had been too daunting. But enough to run off alone into the night?

"I'm sorry," Aiana continued, oblivious to my mental revelation. "I thought word would've gotten to you, especially since Mister Doyle took the blame upon himself and still paid the Thorns her price."

"How nice," I said, lifting my head. Anger was easier to deal with than grief. I still couldn't truly process this. "I'm sure Jasper was glad to make a profit on her after all, especially if . . ." My words gave way to a gasp as I replayed what she said. "Warren knew . . ."

"He was there when it happened."

I jumped to my feet. "Why didn't he say anything to me? I talked to him the morning after that storm! How could he have not mentioned that my best friend disappeared?"

"I don't know." Her face was filled with compassion. "The more I hear about Warren Doyle, the more certain I am that I can't ever guess what he might be thinking."

I felt a sob catch in my throat and swallowed it back, not wanting to cry in front of her. Understanding, Aiana got to her feet. "Mira's at a social engagement. I can get her excused early. I think it'd be good for you to be together. You can make yourself at home, and I'll pay one of the girls downstairs to bring up hot water for the tub."

I could only nod by way of answer, and as soon as she left, I broke down in tears. The stress of everything came crashing down on me, and I didn't even know what I was crying for anymore. Cedric, Tamsin . . . what good was I to the people I loved if I couldn't keep them safe? Was this some kind of divine punishment for running out on my responsibilities in Osfrid?

I was red and puffy-eyed when the girl came to fill the tub, and she politely pretended not to notice. Sinking into that kind of bath was a luxury I hadn't experienced in almost a month. Baths at the Marshall place had been sparse in water. And cold. Really, after my time in Hadisen, everything in Cape Triumph seemed luxurious by comparison. Aiana's rooms were on par with a royal Osfridian estate as far as I was concerned.

The water was dark gray when I finally emerged, and my head felt slightly better. Not good, but functional. I couldn't stand the thought of putting on my dirty claim-working clothes and borrowed a long, thick woolen robe from Aiana's closet. A lot of time had passed, and I wondered if Mira's event had been far away or if there'd been difficulty in getting her out of it.

In the end, Aiana delivered. Mira walked through the door with a bundle of clothing in her arms that she promptly dropped as she ran across the room to me. I pulled her into a hug and felt the tears come anew. Aiana discreetly retreated to the kitchen and bustled around in the cupboards.

Mira was the same as ever. Beautiful. Fierce. But not as dressed up as I'd expected, based on Aiana's comment about a social engagement. The violet organdy dress she wore was well-made but too plain to be anything from the Glittering Court. She wore her mother's shawl over it, and her hair had been tied with a ribbon behind her neck with obvious haste.

"Mira—how did this—Tamsin—"

"I don't know," she said, her own voice cracking. "I couldn't believe it when I heard. Two men came back from the boat to deliver the news—witnesses who swore she wouldn't board the boat during the storm. They say she ran off into the woods and that Warren was devastated."

I found that unlikely, recalling his blasé attitude the morning after. The morning after . . .

The storm blew up while we were crossing the bay last night.

Failing to mention Tamsin's disappearance wasn't the only odd thing from that conversation with Warren. He'd also said the storm had blown up while they were on the water—not when they were boarding. And really, if it had happened beforehand, would any of them have gotten on the ship?

"The storm was bad here," Mira continued, eyes shining. "They said it was bad for you too. And the fact that we haven't heard anything from Tamsin in weeks . . . well, it's hard to know what to think.

If she did survive, where is she? Why hasn't she gotten in touch? I've had some people . . . resources . . . searching, but there's just been nothing to find."

The despair sank back into me. "I can't lose her again."

"I know. I feel the same way. But you have to put that grief aside for now. We'll cry for her later—a lot. I hear you have other things to worry about, Lady Witmore." Her gaze fell on my pendant, which I'd kept on. She lowered her voice. "Or should I say Mistress Thorn?"

I shot a panicked look toward Aiana in the kitchen. "Is it obvious? Is this some telltale Alanzan charm?"

"No, not at all. They're selling that style of necklace all over town with different flowers. I just recognized the bishop's lace and took a guess." Mira hesitated. "But I wouldn't wear it to court if I were you. You can't let anyone think you're Alanzan. And you can't let them think of you as some frontier woman either. You need to walk in and remind them that you're the Countess of Rothford."

She said that last part as she walked across the room toward the dropped clothing. "We tried to collect as much as we could for you around town. There are plenty of dresses not being worn at Wisteria Hollow, but if Jasper noticed you wearing one in the courtroom, there'd be hell to pay."

"You think he'll actually be there?" I asked bitterly. "He didn't seem to care what happened to Cedric."

Aiana, overhearing, strolled up to us. "He cares what happens to his business, and this all reflects on it. He'll be there."

A knock sounded at the door, and we all jumped. Aiana's casual attitude vanished. She grew tense and alert, her eyes narrowed like a cat's, as she slowly approached the door. Placing one hand on the knob, she used her other to pull a knife out of her coat that was as long as her forearm.

"Who's there?" she yelled.

"Walter Higgins," came the muffled response. "I'm looking for Adelaide Bailey—Cedric Thorn's partner."

The name rattled in my head, and suddenly, it clicked. "That's Cedric's agent! Let him in."

Still being cautious, Aiana cracked the door and peered out before finally opening it all the way. A small, wiry young man the same age as Cedric stood there in a smart suit. His face gave away little as he took us all in, but he struck me as someone who filed away every detail he saw.

"Walter," I said, stepping forward. "It's nice to finally meet you. Cedric's spoken very highly of you."

Walter gave a small nod of thanks and tried to pretend I wasn't in a robe. "He spoke very highly of you too. I always thought he admired more than just your artistic knowledge. Now I hear that's true."

I winced. "Does everyone in this city know the story now?"

"Pretty much," said Walter. Mira and Aiana nodded in confirmation. "I'm leaving town tomorrow and had some news I thought I'd best share now. With Cedric, uh, detained, I thought I should discuss my business with you. Is there someplace we can talk privately?"

"You can talk in front of them," I said. Art forgery seemed pretty insignificant now.

He hesitated and then gave a shrug of acceptance. "I have another potential buyer—one willing to pay out a lot more, once he heard there's competition. And he's closer too—about a two-hour ride from here."

"Well, that's sort of good news," I said. "Not that it does us much good with Cedric locked up."

"It doesn't do anyone any good because he too wants some kind of authentication."

I groaned. "And here I thought these colonials would be easy marks."

"Well, the good news is that the other man wanted an art expert to verify it. This new one will settle for 'any knowledgeable and cultured Myrikosi who can tell the difference between dross and gold.' His words, not mine." Walter paused, his gaze falling meaningfully on Mira.

"And I heard you have a Sirminican friend. Sirminicans look a lot like Myrikosi."

Mira glanced between us in confusion. "I have no idea what you're talking about, but if you're trying to include me with art experts, I don't think I'm who you need."

"You're exactly who we need," I said eagerly. Cedric had described Walter as someone who would always figure out a way to close a deal, and now I understood. "You can do a Myrikosi accent. I used to hear you do it back at Blue Spring. All you have to do is meet this guy and tell him the painting he's interested in is an authentic piece from one of Myrikos's greatest masters."

"Is it?" she asked, looking impressed.

"Um, not exactly." After weeks of no movement on the painting, I had a brief surge of excitement over this. Mira in her finery could certainly pass herself off as an upper-class Myrikosi woman, and sell this man on the painting. Then reality hit me again. "But it'll have to wait. I can't chase down the painting sale right now. The money from it was supposed to help us build a life together. It won't do us any good while Cedric's locked up."

Walter cleared his throat. "Begging your pardon, but there's never really a time when money won't do any good."

"He's right," said Aiana. "I don't understand the means either, but if you have access to significant money of your own, it could come in handy. You don't know what you'll need to do while this trial goes on."

I didn't quite follow, but Walter was more blunt: "Never underestimate the power of a good bribe."

"Maybe . . . but there's no time. At least not right away. You said you're leaving town tomorrow?"

Walter nodded apologetically. "For a week, down in Lyford Colony. Other people in need of my services."

"And I need to be at the courthouse in the morning," I said. "No one can go with Mira."

Mira looked between both of us, puzzled. "Why do I need anyone to go with me? I've just got to meet this man and act like I know about art? I can do that."

"It's too dangerous," I insisted. "We'll wait for a better time." Although, as I spoke, I wondered if there'd ever be a better time for anything.

"Actually . . ." Aiana's brow furrowed in thought. "Tomorrow might be the best time. There'll be a lot going on the first day of the trial. Everyone will be distracted. If Mira disappears for part of the day, it's less likely to be noticed."

I still didn't like it. Not because I didn't think Mira could pull off anything—but because I couldn't handle the thought of another friend going off into danger. "I'll be back," she said, knowing what I feared. "Go to court tomorrow. We'll take care of this. You can give me the information?"

Walter produced a piece of paper from his pocket and handed it to her. "Here's his name and address. And that's the location of the man holding the painting right now."

"You don't have it?" I exclaimed. The second address was in a neighboring town in Denham.

"I survive in this business by making sure nothing's ever linked directly to me. The painting's safe, but certainly not hanging in my own bedroom," he said. "If he agrees to the deal, you can complete the transaction yourself or wait until I'm back to do it. Just don't spend my commission."

"We'll help you with the rest," said Mira. "We'll make it work."

"All for money that may or may not help Cedric," I muttered.

Aiana rested a hand on my shoulder, a steely look in her eyes. "Having a backup supply of money isn't just about helping him. You need to accept that there's a chance Cedric may not get out of this. And if he doesn't, you're going to need your own resources to escape."

CHAPTER 29

AIANA PUT TOGETHER A MAKESHIFT PALLET IN THE CORNER of her sitting room. When I woke the next morning, she was gone, and I set about preparing for the day. The dresses Mira had brought were nowhere near the extravagant affairs of the Glittering Court, but they were still something an upper-class Denham woman would wear. The one I chose was made of ivory cambric scattered with sprigs of pink and purple flowers. The dress felt foreign to me after a month in rough gear, the fabric dangerously delicate. I didn't mind being back in something nice, but it was a reminder of how much my life had changed.

I just had finished arranging my hair when Aiana returned. "I thought you were going with Mira," I said.

"I'm going with you. I saw her off—she's on her way."

Again, I felt that nervous pang about losing another friend. "Is she alone?"

"No."

Aiana offered no other information, and I took it that I wasn't meant to ask more about it.

A crowd had gathered outside the courthouse when we arrived. Even in a lively city like Cape Triumph, this was serious drama. The governor's son, an illicit romance, heresy . . . citizens were dying to get a front-row seat. Aiana steered me by them and up to the entrance, where a court official waved us through.

The courtroom was already full, with seating set aside for principal players. One of those seats was for me, and I sat down, noticing that Jasper wasn't too far away. He gave me a cold nod and then pointedly looked in the opposite direction. Over near the front, Governor Doyle sat with Viola by his side and other advisors nearby. Two rows of seats were still empty, and those I watched avidly. At last, a bailiff opened a side door and led in the held men. Warren was first, looking remarkably smug given the circumstances. Cedric came last, and my heart leapt at the sight of him.

He needed a shave, and his arm was still in the sling, of course. But otherwise, he moved well and had lost more of his bruises. I wondered if that was a good or bad thing. It might have helped our case if we'd had proof of how badly he'd been beaten. He scanned the room and caught my eye, giving me a small nod to tell me he was okay. He even managed a ghost of his usual smile, but it was strained.

Everyone rose when the tribunal entered, consisting of seven men. They were magistrates and other prominent Denham figures. Normally, the governor would lead the group, but Governor Doyle had to sit out for obvious reasons. A magistrate named Adam Dillinger had instead been appointed as the lead.

"We're here to rule on a . . . complicated dispute that took place in Hadisen Colony. Here, we will seek out the truth in accordance with the laws of our mother Osfrid. Let us pray to Uros for guidance."

He led us in prayer, and most everyone in the room bowed their heads solemnly. Peeking up, I saw that several people were watching Cedric, as though they expected him to stand up and conduct some black rite then and there.

"Mister Doyle," said Magistrate Dillinger. "Please come up and tell your story."

Warren strode forward. He'd washed and shaved and wore new clothes, which irked me. That came of having supporters here. Cedric looked shabby by comparison, but who did he have to rely on? Certainly not his family. And I hadn't been able to dress myself without charity.

No one needed Warren's background, but he gave it anyway, painting himself as a model citizen who'd followed in his father's footsteps. He made sure to remind everyone of all the good things Governor Doyle had done and how Warren humbly hoped to emulate his father in Hadisen.

"As part of my new position, I knew it was crucial I seek a wife and advocate of righteous family values. When the Glittering Court began its new season, I began courting one of its girls—a young woman who called herself Adelaide Bailey."

Half of the courtroom turned to stare at me, and I kept my gaze focused forward, refusing to meet any of them in the eye.

"By all appearances, Miss Bailey seemed like an honest, virtuous girl. She led me to believe she was interested in me and was on the verge of contracting a marriage. It was then that I found out she'd been . . . *involved* with Cedric Thorn, one of the Glittering Court's procurers." There was no mistaking what he meant by "involved."

"That's a serious accusation," said one of the tribunal members.

"Miss Clara Hayes of the Glittering Court witnessed their indiscretion firsthand," said Warren. "Several others saw the aftermath. You may question any of them for further clarification."

"What did you do next, Mister Doyle?" asked Dillinger.

"What could I do?" Warren spread his hands wide. "I'd hardly push for a woman whose heart was with another. I felt sorry for them, really. So I decided to help."

He detailed the arrangement he'd had with us in Hadisen, again painting himself as an exemplary—and charitable—man. Several spectators shook their heads in a mix of anger and sympathy, clearly showing they thought Warren had been taken advantage of.

"I gave Mister Thorn every opportunity to succeed," Warren said. "Equipment, training. But it soon became clear that he'd taken on more than he was capable of. He's a businessman—a scholar. Hardly suited to the kind of labor needed on the frontier. His ineptitude resulted in accidents, one fall in particular being especially bad. And he'd make grandiose claims of huge gold strikes but never actually unearth said gold, no matter how long we kept waiting for it."

I didn't realize I was starting to stand up until Aiana pushed me back down. "Wait," she murmured.

The true atrocity came when Warren described that last day. "I wanted to believe his stories of gold on the claim—especially since Adelaide's contract expiration was approaching. I brought several men out to the claim with the intent of excavating the gold, though things almost ended before they began when more of Mister Thorn's inexperience nearly resulted in him blowing all of us up. It was clear he and Miss Bailey were growing desperate at this point. There was no way they were going to pay off their debt in time, and things grew worse when we discovered Alanzan artifacts in Mister Thorn's possession."

Scandalized murmurs slid around the room, and Dillinger called for silence.

"I needed to talk things out with them, clearly," Warren continued. "I was certain there was a misunderstanding. I sent my men away for lunch and sat down to discuss how I might better help this couple—and that's when the treachery started. With me alone, Mister Thorn attacked, intending to kill me and make it look as though claim raiders had done it—thus freeing him of the contract. Through the greatest stroke of luck, two of my men returned to retrieve something and were able to save me in time. They subdued Mister Thorn, but the danger wasn't over. Miss Bailey took up her lover's fight and then brazenly offered herself in an attempt to distract me. As I was refusing her, she stabbed me with a knife. I can't imagine what would have happened if Silas Garrett of the McGraw Agency hadn't arrived."

The tribunal asked more clarifying questions, and I was amazed at how Warren had an answer for everything. Each event, each detail was twisted in a way that favored him and supported his lies. When he was dismissed, it was clear he had almost everyone on his side.

Cedric was called next. One of the magistrates held out a holy text of Uros. "Please swear to tell the truth . . . if you're able."

I was shocked at the insinuation from a group that claimed impartiality. More buzz stirred in the room, especially when Cedric placed his hand on the book without it bursting into flames or something equally absurd.

Normally, in cases with conflicting views, Cedric would be asked to retell the story from his point of view. Instead, Dillinger asked, "Mister Thorn, are you an Alanzan?"

Cedric blinked in surprise. I was sure he'd prepared for this question but hadn't expected the irregular order. "I simply had Alanzan artifacts in my possession. But no one saw me worshipping with them."

"Why, then, would you have such items in your possession?"

"Curiosity," said Cedric, keeping his tone mild. "I knew Alanzans at the university in Osfro. They gave me the items, hoping to convert me."

"And you didn't report these deviants?" asked another tribunal member.

"They were young and rebellious. I thought it was a phase they'd outgrow before returning to Uros and the six glorious angels."

Dillinger held up a piece of paper. "We have a signed testimony from a convicted Alanzan—one Thaddeus Brooks—who was caught in the act of worship. He swears you participated with him in some heathen rite called a 'Star Advent.' How do you respond to that?"

Cedric gave no sign of distress. "I think an imprisoned man would say anything to get himself freed."

"Alanzan worship is illegal in both Denham and Hadisen," Dillinger stated. "Illegal religions are punishable with execution if you have no protection from another colony or a royal exemption."

"I am aware," said Cedric.

"Is the young woman who calls herself Miss Bailey an Alanzan?" asked the tribunal member to Dillinger's right.

"No," Cedric replied swiftly. "Miss Bailey made it clear on many occasions that she believes they're misguided pagans. I'll swear to that as much as you like."

The tribunal pushed the Alanzan angle a while longer, but Cedric remained firm on his defense: that no one had caught him worshipping. But Dillinger made it clear that he thought Thaddeus Brooks's testimony was proof enough.

They finally let Cedric tell his side of the story. The tribunal questioned and commented in a way that made the details sound improbable and even silly. The members made no attempts to hide their derision, and the courtroom echoed that sentiment. And as I'd feared, the improvement of his injuries disguised just how excessively brutal his attack had been. One magistrate pointed out that a broken arm wasn't out of line when two men tried to stop a murderer.

Cedric was released, and Dillinger called, "Lady Elizabeth Witmore, Countess of Rothford."

Anyone who hadn't noticed me in the courtroom before noticed me now. I moved to the front with all the haughty confidence of a girl who'd spent her life being told her bloodline was superior to all others. I took my vow to Uros and then met Dillinger's gaze with a coolness that told him he was wasting my time.

He cleared his throat. "Lady Witmore . . . please tell us how you came to be part of the Glittering Court under an assumed name."

I'd expected this and had my answer well prepared. I spoke of how my family's fortunes were fading and that I realized I'd have more opportunity in the New World. I told them my maid had run away, and I saw a chance for myself. "A title is nothing without substance," I declared. "Perhaps I acted impulsively, but others have fought to find a place in the New World with success. I decided to join them."

This earned a few approving nods until Dillinger declared: "So you lied and deceived others to get your way. Did Cedric Thorn know your true identity? Did he help cover it up?"

"No. He'd never met my lady-in-waiting. He didn't learn my true identity until much later in Adoria."

I told my Hadisen story, repeating almost everything Cedric had said in his version. When I reached the point about Warren assaulting me, the men on the tribunal showed obvious skepticism.

"Do you have any proof of this alleged attack?" asked one man.

I regarded him with narrowed eyes. "I have my word."

"Plenty of women make claims like that. It's an easy thing when there are no witnesses. The man says one thing, the woman another."

It dawned on me then that I'd been wrong in thinking my title would give me an edge in this trial. The edge here was in being male. Women were easy to dismiss.

"Also," added Dillinger, "I find it unlikely a woman of loose morals would object so violently to a man's advances."

The statement was so ludicrous that it took me several moments to form my response. "I . . . think any woman—moral or immoral—would object when forced against her will. And I don't appreciate what you're implying about my virtue."

"Weren't you Cedric Thorn's lover?"

I had my imperious mask back on. "Preserving my virtue until marriage has been a principle I've adhered to my entire life. I didn't give up my virginity to a man I wasn't married to, if that's what you're suggesting."

"You swear to that?"

"Yes."

"Then why were you drinking cinnamon thorn tea?" I saw a few whispers at Dillinger's words, which I found comical. Plenty of women drank it to prevent children. Everyone pretended they didn't.

"Do you have proof I was?" I asked. I'd thrown away the dregs before serving Warren his tea, and there'd been none in my possessions at the Marshall house.

"Mister Doyle states he smelled it."

"Just as I've stated he assaulted me. The man says one thing, the woman another."

As more details were examined, I became certain this tribunal had been bought off to cast everything Cedric and I said in a negative light. My virtue was constantly brought up in my examination, as was my allegedly deceitful nature.

We broke for lunch after that, and I told Aiana my thoughts.

"Bribes go a long way," she said.

I watched wistfully as Cedric was led out with the others. He sent a quick parting glance my way, slightly less confident than before. "Our so-called bribe money can't match theirs. If we can even get that money."

Aiana nodded toward the door. "Why don't you find out?"

I turned and saw Mira entering, impeccable in a luxurious riding dress. I hurried over and hugged her, relieved she was safe. "How'd it go?" I whispered.

She grinned. "Easy. I could have sold him on anything."

I hugged her again. "Thank you."

"How'd it go here?"

"Let's just say . . . not as successful as your task."

We caught Mira up over lunch, and then the proceedings resumed. Silas Garrett gave a wonderfully impartial testimony that didn't favor either side but did throw a couple of questions up about Warren's story. I didn't know if it'd be enough, though. Elias gave a predictably convoluted statement after that, and then the tribunal adjourned for the day. Cedric and Warren were escorted out separately, in different directions, and as luck would have it, Cedric was led toward the opposite side of the room and Warren was taken in my direction.

He paused in the aisle next to me, acting as though he needed to adjust something on his jacket. "How sad this must all be for you, Lady Witmore. First you traded security and a title to play house with scullery girls. When you got a chance to salvage your life from that downfall, you threw that opportunity away too for some romantic daydream. And just when you thought things might finally be going your way, *poof*!" He held his hands outstretched. "That crumbles away too. So much you've given up. So much you've endured. And when all is said and done, the only thing you'll walk away with is . . . well, nothing."

I clenched my fists, lest he see how I trembled. I couldn't let him know how his words had struck me. Because in many ways, he was right. I'd made sacrifice after sacrifice in my life over the last year until I was left with one thing, the only thing that mattered: Cedric. And now they were threatening to take him too.

I met Warren's gaze unflinchingly. "Just as you'll have nothing when you walk to the gallows. I'll see you hanged for what you've done to my loved ones. I know you had something to do with Tamsin's disappearance."

I saw the slightest glint of surprise in his eyes, but whether that was from shock at being found out or confusion at the accusation, I couldn't say. The delay had gone on too long, and his escorts moved him along.

"There are only a couple more witnesses tomorrow, but I'm sure it'll all be the same," I said as Mira and Aiana walked with me back to town later. Not being able to talk to Cedric had been the final blow of the day.

Mira slung her arm around me. "Stay strong."

They ate dinner with me at Aiana's place, and then Aiana said she had to take Mira back to Wisteria Hollow before curfew. "I'll be out on my own errands after that. Stay inside, and keep the door locked. There's no telling what this may have stirred up."

I hated to see Mira go, but there was a good chance her absence had been noted. She'd done more than enough for me today, and I didn't want her to get in trouble.

"Your contract's coming up," I said. "What will you do?"

She shrugged. "Something."

I cast a glance over toward where Aiana had gone in her bedroom. "Is the reason you haven't chosen someone . . . are you and Aiana, I mean . . ."

It took Mira a few moments to understand, and she shook her head. "No, no. Aiana's been good to me . . . a, uh, mentor of sorts. But I like men. I just don't like any one of the ones I've met."

Seeing as I'd already embarrassed myself, I figured I should go the whole way. "Before you came to Blue Spring Manor, did anything ever happen between you and Cedric?"

She seemed to find that even more incredible. "No. Why would you think that?"

I flushed. "He's always liked you. And he did so much for you."

Mira's smile was gentle. "He did so much for me because he's a kind man. And we'll find a way to save him."

They left me alone with my whirling thoughts. I'd come up with some brilliant, outlandish idea—like breaking in and rescuing Cedric—and then the reality would hit, plunging me into despair. It was mentally exhausting, and I'd decided to go to bed when a knock sounded at the door.

Remembering Aiana's warnings, I nearly made no response at all. Then, I crept forward and asked, "Who's there?"

"Gideon Stewart."

"I don't know who that is."

"I'm a minister—from Grashond. I helped bring your friend Tamsin back."

Memories of the day of her return stirred in me. Most of the Grashond delegates had blurred together, but the more I thought about it, the more his name began to sound familiar. I was still reluctant to open the door.

"What do you want?"

"I might know a way to save Mister Thorn. It involves the colony of Westhaven, but I'd need your help."

At the mention of Westhaven, I couldn't resist. I opened the door and found the handsome blond man who'd come to Wisteria Hollow. He wore the same drab attire as before. After casting a quick glance down the hall, I waved him in and shut the door.

"Well?" I kept my arms crossed over me. Religious purist or not, I wanted to be cautious.

"I was at the courthouse today . . . and I'm very sorry for what you're going through," he said. "If it makes you feel better, I don't think they'll be able to rule on the dispute. Too many contradictions, no proof. With no one killed, they'll write it off as a brawl."

My heart sank. Of course I was glad that meant Cedric wouldn't be implicated, but I hated the thought of Warren going unpunished.

Gideon made a face. "Unfortunately, I think the Alanzan charge will hold. Even without actual worship, those artifacts are damning. I've seen men convicted for far less. Those in power will accept that witness's statement, and I'm sure Warren Doyle has enough sway to get the full punishment enforced—probably immediately."

"Death." I sank into the chair. I was on a precipice with Cedric again. If he died, I would fall and fall forever. "So what miracle can you pull out? Do the Heirs have some special power?"

He gave me a small smile. "No. But the colony of Westhaven does. Those who've bought a stake would technically be citizens of it. The reciprocal privilege between the colonies allows citizens from outside to practice certain things, even if they're illegal in that colony—so long as they don't break any other laws. This would apply to Cedric. The fight in Hadisen had nothing to do with the Alanzans."

"That's great," I said, "except Cedric's not a citizen of Westhaven. Though it hasn't been for lack of trying."

"There are representatives from Westhaven in the city right now, and they've been selling stakes. If Cedric was able to purchase one, and you found an attorney to go over the paperwork and, how shall I put this, modify the date, Cedric could claim retroactive protection as a citizen of Westhaven. Assuming you could find that kind of attorney. I suppose in this town, you can find anything."

I sat up straight, too shocked by this possibility to even reflect on a righteous minister suggesting something so illegal. "I might . . . might know an attorney who would."

Gideon brightened. "Then you just need to buy the stake."

"There's no 'just' about it. I know how much those cost. And we don't have—" I groaned as the answer hit me. "I know where I can get the money. Maybe. But it won't be easy."

"I'm sure it won't. I wish . . . I wish I could help you on that front. But I've already spent my savings buying my own stake."

I regarded him in astonishment. "Why would a minister from the Heirs of Uros buy a stake in a religiously tolerant colony—one that's already getting a reputation for wild ways?"

He gave me a wry smile. "Because this minister isn't so sure he agrees with his brethren anymore."

"Is that why you're sympathetic to Cedric?" I asked softly.

"Somewhat. If someone's beliefs aren't hurting others, I don't believe they should be punished for it. And . . ." His face fell. "You were her friend. She spoke of you often. I couldn't help her, but maybe . . . maybe I can help you."

"Tamsin," I said. Familiar tears stung my eyes.

"I'm so sorry. I did what I could to find her—to find out what happened to her that night . . ." He looked genuinely distraught, melting my earlier wariness.

"It's okay," I said. "There's nothing any of us could have done." But as I reflected on the bizarre inconsistences around Warren's story about what had happened to Tamsin, I wondered if that was true.

"I don't know if that's the case, but I'll have to come to terms with that later." He shook off his grief and focused on me again. "For now, tell me how I can help."

I thought about it. "Can you get me a horse?"

"I have one downstairs. I rode it out from Wisteria Hollow."

"Well, that's the first thing that's worked out for me in a while. Give me a few minutes." I left him to change out of the dress and into my split skirt and blouse. They'd been laundered and looked a little better. As expected, I also found various weapons hidden around Aiana's home and helped myself to another knife. Then I penned a quick note and gave it to Gideon with instructions to deliver it to Nicholas Adelton.

"He's the attorney who'll help?" Gideon asked.

"I think so." I considered. "I hope so."

We went downstairs and found a perky mare tethered in front of the tavern. Gideon patted her. "Her name is Beth."

I couldn't help a laugh. "Lizzie and Beth. I can't escape my past."

"What?"

"Nothing. Just get that letter to Mister Adelton."

Gideon scrutinized me nervously. "You aren't going to do anything dangerous, are you? Should I . . . should I come with you?"

"No, I'll be fine," I said, hoping that was true. "Just going for a short ride."

My short ride, of course, was actually a two-hour one outside the city to Walter's contact, the one holding my painting. Dusk was falling, and I rode out with my hat pulled low, hoping it wouldn't be immediately obvious I was a woman. Denham was an established colony and certainly not lawless, but it had its dark element just like any other place. And until the world changed drastically, a woman riding out alone in the night was at risk.

But as I left the city limits and rode down the darkened road, I couldn't let the possible threats slow me down. Fear was only another enemy, and I had far too many others to worry about just now. Cedric's salvation was within my grasp, and I would not be defeated.

Mira had given me back the sheet with Walter's names and locations, and I carried it now. I also had a letter he'd written, authorizing his contact to yield the painting. It was a two-hour trip south, then back to the city, and then another two hours up north to the buyer. I'd be out all night, and there was a good chance I might not make the trial's start tomorrow. I urged Beth on, knowing I risked exhausting her.

Amazingly, I encountered almost no one on the road. Those I did pass didn't give me a second glance. It was deep night when I rode into Idylwood, a sleepy village that showed the promise of eventually becoming a flourishing town. Walter's contact was the town's blacksmith, and I found his home easily. I tied Beth up near a trough, which she drank from gratefully.

The blacksmith was surprised to see me—even more surprised that

I was a woman. He read the letter and handed it back with a shrug. "I guess Walter employs all types now. Come with me."

He led me to a locked shed in the back that, when opened, revealed mostly a lot of junk. I worried what shape my painting would be in. He moved things aside and finally pulled out a cloth-wrapped, rectangular object. I unwrapped it and examined it by the light of my lantern. It was my painting, in exactly the same condition as I'd last seen it in Wisteria Hollow's cellar.

"Satisfied?" he asked.

"Very. Thank you."

I wrapped it back up in its padding, and he helped me tie it to the back of Beth's saddle. It wasn't ideal for transportation, but I felt confident the canvas wouldn't tear. A little bouncing wouldn't hurt it much.

Beth and I rode off back on the black road to Cape Triumph. A quarter moon offered little guidance, and I was glad this was a well-worn and traveled road. When I reached the edge of the city, I ended up circling around it. Taking the extra time seemed like a better choice than being recognized.

The road north was narrower than the one south, surrounded by thick woods that made the way even darker. I knew I should go slowly in case of unseen obstacles, but I was growing uneasy about the passing time. It had to be after midnight, and I still had a lot of traveling to do—not to mention finalizing the paperwork back in Cape Triumph. There were only a few more witnesses in the trial. I didn't know how soon the tribunal would make a ruling. It was possible the paperwork might overturn a conviction. But I knew sometimes, especially for heretics, punishment was enacted immediately. I couldn't spare the time.

I urged poor tired Beth into a hard gallop. For all my fine talk about being a great horsewoman, what I was doing was incredibly foolhardy. That was confirmed for me only a few minutes later when Beth suddenly stumbled, nearly throwing me and the painting from her back. She managed to catch herself just in time but came to a quick stop, refusing to go further. I dismounted and tried to see what obstacle she'd tripped on. As it turned out, she'd lost a horseshoe.

"Damn it," I cried into the night. An owl answered in return. Further examination showed Beth didn't seem to have damaged her leg or hoof, but there was no way I'd be able to ride her at the earlier rate. And from her exhausted appearance, she probably wouldn't have let me do it much longer anyway.

I got back on her. Even at an easier trot, every equestrian instructor I'd ever had would chastise me for this. It risked further injury. I hoped that wouldn't happen—just as I hoped the painting's buyer would sell me a horse.

But Beth refused to budge. I was finally forced to go on foot, leading her behind me. Each step down the road was agonizing—not because of the physical toll, but the mental. I was weary and frustrated. The moon was traveling farther and farther across the sky, and all I could think about was how each delay put Cedric at risk. At least two hours had passed when I heard a thunder of hoofbeats behind me. I instantly became guarded, not knowing if this would be a help or hindrance. At the rate the riders were coming, there'd be no chance to divert into the woods, so I simply moved to the side and waited for what was to come. I put my hand on my knife.

Five men rode up, slowing when they reached me. One held a lantern. They all had weathered faces, with worn clothing suggestive of a laborious life. I didn't recognize any of them. But they recognized me.

"Countess," one said cheerfully. "We're here to escort you back to Osfrid."

CHAPTER 30

I TOOK A STEP BACK, TRYING TO CALM MY RAPID BREATHing and pounding heart.

"You've made some mistake, sir," I said. "I'm a common laborer, making a delivery."

"A little late for that," said one of the other men. "Looks more to me like you're trying to run for it before things blow up in Cape Triumph. Not sure I blame you."

"We aren't going to hurt you," said the first man. He dismounted, and a couple of others followed suit. "Just need to ship you back and collect our payday. Come with us, and make it easy on everyone."

I tightened my hold on the knife and took another step back. I was almost off the road and wondered how far I'd get if I took off into the brushy woods. Probably not very. The terrain looked rough, and I'd likely fall over some log before getting ten feet away.

"She ain't going to make it easy." The first man reached for me, and I swung out with the knife, cutting through his shirt and slashing shallowly across his chest.

"Bitch!" he cried. "Get her!"

The other men surged forward, and I knew I couldn't beat those odds. As with Warren's attack, I refused to make it simple for them. If they expected a woman to be easy prey, they'd soon learn otherwise. I dropped to the ground as they reached me, causing them to run into one another. I wiggled away as best I could, stabbing one man in the calf. I had the sense to yank the knife out and scurry away as he fell yelping to the ground. I scrambled to my feet and ran—but was quickly stopped. A hand grabbed my hair and jerked me backward. I fell down, slamming the side of my head against the dirt road.

"Don't injure her!" yelled their leader. "We need her intact."

"She's got two months at sea to heal," countered the man nearest me. He tried to grab me, but a wild swing of the blade kept him at bay. His companions were moving in, and one finally managed to knock the knife out of my hand. Surrounded, I finally slowed down and accepted defeat—for now. They had to get me back to Cape Triumph and onto a ship. Plenty of time to escape.

Sensing their victory, the men came to a standstill and awaited their next order. That moment of silence was suddenly filled with the pounding of more hooves. Everyone turned to stare down the road—everyone except me. I used their distraction to slip through two men and grab my knife.

But when the riders came into view, even I was taken aback. A man and a woman slowed before us. They both rode white horses and wore black masks across their eyes. The man nearest me gasped.

"Pirates!"

"Tom Shortsleeves!"

"And Lady Aviel," said another. He spoke the name like that of a demon, ironic since she bore the name of one of the six glorious angels.

Aiana's words came back to me: *All stories have a seed of truth.*

Legends come to life. I hadn't really believed the stories. So many rumors flew around Cape Triumph, and this had seemed particularly outlandish. But if these intimidating figures weren't really two of Cape Triumph's most notorious pirates, their impressions were so good that it didn't matter. They matched the descriptions I'd heard numerous times at parties and, of course, from Mira, their biggest fan. Tom's sleeves were, in fact, short, and I could just make out the peacock feather in his hat. A mane of golden hair fell down Aviel's back, over a cape stitched with stylized stars. The two of them drew swords at the same time, their movements practiced and efficient.

"You have something we want," said Tom or whoever he really was. "Leave Lady Witmore with us, and go."

Two of the men immediately began retreating, their faces full of fear. The gang's leader faced the riders down. "She and her reward belong to us. Get out of here before we— Ahh!"

Tom charged forward, slamming the pommel of his sword into the leader's head. Aviel moved just as quickly and went after another of the men. They might be outnumbered, but the horses gave them an advantage since all of the other men had dismounted. The fear the twosome inspired was equally effective. Some of the raiders were trying to get away, and the one I'd injured in the leg was having trouble moving at all.

I took it all in as I hesitated on what to do. With the gang in disarray, I could easily join in with my knife and be effective. But as I watched Tom and Aviel swing their swords fiercely, I decided I didn't want to take my chances with this unknown element. It was time to run.

I climbed back on Beth. With all the commotion, she was much more willing to carry me. We set off at a medium trot—not as fast as I'd like, but enough to get me away. My plan was to put some distance between me and the fray, then get off and take my chances with the woods. It would mean abandoning Beth and the painting, but this was the time for hard choices.

I didn't get nearly as far as I'd hoped. In fact, I'd barely gotten started when Tom and Aviel overtook me and blocked the road ahead. I brought Beth to a halt and stared at these new threats. I tried not to get caught up in the mystique of their fearsome reputations, but it was hard not to.

"You don't need to worry about those men anymore," said Tom, almost cheerfully.

"Dead?" I asked.

"Maybe," said Aviel. "Or they ran." She sounded like she had a Belsian accent. Tom's was solidly colonial.

"Well, it doesn't matter. I wasn't going with them, and I'm not going with you." The boldness came automatically, even though there'd be little I could do against them. I'd revert to my plan to find a future escape.

"We don't want to take you away," Tom replied. "Wherever you're going, we'll help you get there safely. We're your escorts for the night."

I couldn't see their expressions in the darkness, but he sounded in earnest. "Why? What do you want?"

"Nothing that you need to worry about. Our interests are our own. All you need to know is that you're safe with us."

I didn't trust them. How could I? None of this made any sense, but then, according to all the stories, it was hard to guess the motives of these two.

When I didn't speak, Tom added, "Your horse is lame?"

"Not yet," I admitted. "But she threw a shoe."

"Then we'll have to take you on ours."

I saw him glance over at Aviel. Something passed between them—something a bit strained—and a moment later, she dismounted. "Mine won't have trouble carrying two," he said. "You can ride hers."

Eyeing Tom's large destrier, I suspected the beast could carry ten. The smaller mare had seemed lively and energized back by the lantern, and I felt encouraged by the idea of having my own horse. It increased my getaway odds. "Okay," I said, walking over to her. "We're going to Crawford."

Aviel moved to the destrier, hesitating only a moment before effortlessly climbing on with Tom. I tethered Beth to a tree. "Sorry, girl." I patted her neck, feeling guilty about abandoning this gift. "Hopefully we can get you back to Gideon. Or maybe some new owner will get you a shoe."

I bound the painting to my new mount, and then we were off at a dizzying pace. The speed was exhilarating after Beth's slow gait, and I allowed myself to hope that this might work after all. But I hadn't even made it halfway to Crawford, and time was still my enemy.

When we finally reached the edge of Crawford, Tom and Aviel slowed. "You have the address?" he asked.

"Yes."

"Then it's probably best we wait here. Seeing us in the middle of the night might be . . . alarming to some people."

I could believe that. Crawford was bigger than the last village, and it took some doing to find the right place. When I did, I could understand how this buyer could afford my painting. His house was by far the largest in town, a beautiful manor on the opposite side of the center green. Lanterns hung outside, but the windows were dark. Taking a deep breath, I retrieved the painting and knocked on the door.

It took two more knocks before someone answered, a sleepy servant who eyed me askance. "I need to see Mister Davenport."

"Madam," said the servant, his tone suggesting that title was generous, "it's the middle of the night."

"It couldn't be helped." I held up the wrapped painting. "I have something he's very interested in buying. A painting. I think he'd be upset if he learned you turned me away, and I sold it to someone else."

The servant's change of expression told me he was familiar with the painting negotiations. He brought me into the foyer and warned me not to touch anything while he was gone. Minutes later, a gray-haired gentleman entered in a house robe. His eyes widened at the sight of me. "You're . . . you're delivering the Thodoros?"

"If you still want it," I said. "There's a Myrikosi lady in Cape Triumph who's very interested." I unwrapped it, and he hurried forward, leaning close to the canvas.

"Magnificent. I saw it three weeks ago and couldn't get it out of my mind. I saw one of his other works in this series back on the continent. I was struck back then too." He gently touched the canvas. "See how the sun illuminates her? Thodoros knows his lighting."

A pang of guilt hit me. This man was a legitimate aficionado, and I was deceiving him. But was it so wrong if it could give him joy and save a life?

We completed the transaction, and I left his house with a heavy bag of gold. It occurred to me as I walked back to the road that Tom and

Aviel might somehow know what I was doing and plan on taking my money. They materialized out of the shadows before I could consider any alternative courses of action.

"All done?" Tom asked, making no threatening moves. "Then let's get you back. Dawn is coming." Aviel remained quiet. In the light of the lanterns hanging in town, her hair glittered gold.

Our journey back was frenzied as we tried to beat the sunrise. We were going too fast for me to see Beth, but I did notice the point where we'd had the altercation. The lantern still burned on the road, and two men lay prone nearby. I wasn't sure if they were dead or unconscious, and no one stopped to find out.

Our speed was good—but not that good. The sun was touching the eastern horizon when we reached the outskirts of Cape Triumph, and here Tom and Aviel left me. "We disappear with the dawn," he said with a smile. "But I hope you can handle things now."

I got off the mare. My legs were so stiff from all the riding that I nearly fell over. "Thank you for your help. I couldn't have done this without you." I glanced at Aviel. "Either of you."

"Our pleasure," he said. She simply nodded in acknowledgment as she mounted her horse. He sketched me a bow from his saddle. "*Que Ariniel te garde*, Lady Witmore."

I couldn't help a smile, both at hearing a pirate perfectly deliver an old Lorandian proverb and at having Ariniel invoked on my behalf. Back at my parents' crypt, I'd dismissed the glorious angel who helped with safe passages, but I could certainly use her help now. I waved to the pirates, and their horses soon thundered out of sight.

I walked into Cape Triumph alone. I didn't know the exact time, but seeing so many businesses open didn't bode well. The trial would be starting soon. What would Cedric think when he didn't see me among the spectators? That I'd abandoned him. No. He knew me too well. He'd know I was working to save him. I just hoped I could do it.

I went to Nicholas Adelton's home and found him walking out

the door. He sized me up from head to toe. "I'm running late and had planned to go to the courthouse—but it looks like you need me more."

"Gideon Stewart talked to you?"

"About his tenuous plan? Yes. And I really didn't think it could be pulled off in time . . . especially the part about the woman with nothing coming up with five hundred gold."

I pulled back my coat and showed him the money bag.

He shook his head and laughed. "Never a dull moment with you."

"Will you help us? I know it's a lot to ask after everything we—"

"Miss Bailey," he interrupted. "Let's go find the Westhaven representatives."

They were staying at an inn in town, one of the nicer ones. The common room here was quiet and orderly, and Nicholas and I sat at a table while the innkeeper fetched the Westhaven representatives. I yawned once, then again.

"You look like you're ready to fall asleep," Nicholas said.

"Just need a quick break," I said. "Then I'll get a second wind. Or maybe I'm on to my third or fourth at this point."

I could tell he was struggling to say what came next. "Adelaide . . . you didn't do anything, uh, illegal to get that money, did you?"

"No." I reconsidered. "Well, not exactly. Maybe kind of. I don't know. No one was hurt, if that makes you feel better."

"Somewhat."

A man and a woman approached our table. They looked respectfully middle class and were dressed no differently than anyone else. After seeing the Grashond residents, I wasn't sure what to expect from those working toward a religiously tolerant colony.

"I'm Edwin Harrison, and this is my wife, Mary." The man looked us over, no doubt perplexed by the extreme contrast in my and Nicholas's attire. "Is there something we can help you with?"

"We'd like to buy a stake in Westhaven," said Nicholas.

Edwin instantly transformed. "Absolutely! How wonderful. We're so eager to have more people join our endeavor. Dear, would you go get one of the contracts?" He turned back to us while she went upstairs. "You must tell me more about yourselves, Mister and Mistress—"

Nicholas and I exchanged amused looks. "It's not for us," I said, though I would be affected if this worked. "It's for someone else."

A little of Edwin's enthusiasm diminished. "That's highly irregular."

"The man in question is detained," explained Nicholas. "I'll be serving as proxy."

"*Highly* irregular," Edwin repeated. Mary returned with several pieces of paper.

"I'm his attorney," Nicholas told them. "And this young lady is his—"

"Wife," I finished.

Nicholas hesitated as he took that in and then made a quick recovery. "And should Mister Harrison doubt that, you could of course show him the proof."

"It's with a magistrate in Hadisen," I said. Giving that up was a big secret, but legally, I should have a fair amount of power to act on Cedric's behalf, especially with Nicholas as legal backup. Considering the trouble we were already in, revealing our marriage couldn't really make things worse.

"Never a dull moment," Nicholas murmured with a half smile. He turned back to the Harrisons. "So, you see, there's no problem with our going forward for him."

Edwin wavered a bit more and then conceded. "Very well then. We're eager to begin our work with those passionate about our vision."

He and Nicholas began going over the paperwork. I knew a little bit about the terms from Cedric, but hearing it laid out in detail was fascinating. Most of the other colonies were founded on orders of the king, who then appointed governors and other prominent leaders. Westhaven's founding had been initiated by the crown as well, following ceding of the land by the Icori in another morally questionable truce. Unlike other colonies, the crown operated this one as a business in response to those clamoring for freedom to practice their faith. The priests of Uros might want to hunt down and persecute heretics, but the king found it easier to simply ship them off.

"Essentially, we are buying from the crown the right to lead Westhaven—though we're still a royal colony under Osfrid," Edwin explained. "Each stake helps pay off that price. We're nearly there and can begin officially drawing up charters, though we've begun some rough drafts already. Those doing the early buy-ins can take part in the planning. From that group, we'll elect who fills the important positions—eventually, all citizens will participate in such an election, but that's further down the road."

"And all faiths can worship there," I said.

Mary gave me a gentle smile. "Yes, that's our primary purpose."

Nicholas read each part in detail, suggesting a few clarifications that the Harrisons had no quarrel with. When Nicholas was satisfied, he wrote out the final affidavit on Cedric's behalf, reaffirming a commitment to Westhaven and its laws. He signed as proxy and then looked up, his pen hovering over the paper.

"I, uh, have a bit more irregularity to suggest, but we'd like to backdate this as well."

Edwin frowned. "How far?"

"About three weeks," I said.

"Some might consider that perjury," said Edwin pointedly. "Something I'm sure a man of the law would know."

"If you don't do it, Cedric will die," I blurted out. "He's on trial for Alanzan heresy, and we need to claim Westhaven's amnesty."

The troubled look in Edwin's eyes didn't reassure me, but Mary laid her hand over his. "Dear, isn't *this* what the point is? To prevent this kind of atrocity?"

Edwin took a few more moments and then exhaled. "Date it," he told Nicholas. Nicholas did, and then Edwin signed underneath as witness—also using the early date. He took my hard-earned money.

I felt like crying, but maybe that was the lack of sleep. "Thank you—thank you! You have no idea—"

The inn's door burst open, and a wide-eyed laborer peered in. "A hanging! There's going to be a hanging! They convicted that Alanzan devil!"

Nicholas groaned, but I was already on my feet. "No, no! We are *not* too late. We can't be." I grabbed the papers and sprinted for the door. Nicholas caught up quickly.

"Wait for me—the rabble loves an execution. It'll be madness out there."

He was right. We joined a flood of people heading across town, eager for blood. I wished we had horses but wasn't sure we would've gotten far in this crowd. I tried to fix my mind on the journey, not imagining what might happen to Cedric if I didn't make it. "I knew it could be soon," I called to Nicholas over the noise. "But I hoped not *this* soon."

"The governor makes the call on when the sentence is carried out," Nicholas said. "And this governor is pretty motivated to see this so-called justice done. I'm sure they'll delay enough to get a good crowd. They like an audience—scares people into behaving."

The thought of Cedric's execution was beyond comprehension. What if they did it? And I wasn't there in his last moments?

The courthouse came into sight. They'd already put up the gallows, and a few dark figures stood on it. One almost certainly was Cedric. The crowd bottlenecked when we finally reached our destination. Everyone wanted a good view, but they could only get so close. No one wanted to give up the spot they'd fought for, so pushing our way forward was difficult.

Near the back, I caught sight of Aiana. She had a hand to her eyes to shield against the sun and was scanning the crowd. She hurried over. "Adelaide! I wondered where you were. Have you seen Mira?"

"No, but I thought she'd be here. I have to get through," I said urgently. "I have to get up there."

She joined us unhesitatingly, and Nicholas asked, "Was Warren Doyle exonerated?" She scowled and nodded.

Aiana helped shove our way through the crowds. We received a lot of angry curses but pushed on anyway. It was still slow going, and we were barely halfway through when Governor Doyle moved to the front of the gallows. I could see Cedric clearly now, his good arm bound behind his back, and my heart sank. Warren stood nearby with a hooded hangman.

"Good citizens of Denham," the governor shouted. "We are here to see justice done—to help purify our colony and drive off evil forces within it."

The crowd had quieted a little, and I decided to take my chances. "Governor Doyle!" I shouted. "Governor Doyle!"

He didn't hear, but a few irritated bystanders shushed me. I attempted to move closer.

"Today, I give you a heretic—not just any heretic but one of the foul Alanzans." Hisses sounded around us. "One who practices dark arts and has unholy communion with the six wayward angels."

I'd gotten a little closer and tried again. "Governor Doyle!"

He still didn't hear, but those in front of me turned around to see what was happening. They gave way to me out of simple curiosity, and my next attempt was heard: "Governor Doyle!"

He searched for the voice and spotted me. "Lady Witmore. You missed the trial."

The crowd parted for me, and getting to the front was easy. I hurried to the gallows stairs, locking eyes with Cedric. A couple of soldiers started to block me, but Warren shook his head at them.

"Let her say goodbye." There was no kindness in his voice.

I held the papers in the air. "You can't execute him! He's a citizen of Westhaven! I have the proof. He's allowed to practice there, and you have to honor that here."

Warren's condescending look turned into a snarl. "Take your forged papers and get out of here."

"They're not forgeries," Nicholas called from below. He and Aiana had worked their way up in the crowd. "I'm an attorney, and

I completed them with Westhaven's chief representative. Everything's in order. Mister Thorn's citizenship was intact the day you found the Alanzan items."

"How convenient this just surfaced," snapped the governor. "You should've presented this 'evidence' before the verdict. This demon *will* be brought to justice, and I'll be damned if . . ."

He trailed off as his eyes lifted to something beyond me. I stood on my tiptoes and tried to see what had caught his attention. A group of riders was charging down the road, oblivious to anything in their way. The panicked crowd split up, frantic to get to safety.

"Governor!" cried one of the men when they were within hearing. "The Icori are here! A whole force of them!"

Governor Doyle regarded the man as if he was crazy. "There haven't been Icori in the city in years—or anywhere in Denham."

The man pointed. "They're right behind me! Call the soldiers!"

But as I'd noticed before, Cape Triumph didn't have a large military presence. There had been no need, now that threats from the Icori and Lorandians were nonexistent. The crown had diverted the bulk of its might to more vulnerable colonies, leaving the old fort all but abandoned. Today, crowd management was being handled by scattered militia and a handful of remaining soldiers.

I had a hard time believing the Icori claim too, but then I saw what came down the road next. A pack of nearly fifty horses approached, surrounded in a cloud of dust. As they grew closer, I saw the bright colors of plaid wool draped over the riders. Sunlight shone on heads of red and gold hair. Equally visible were swords and shields.

Chaos ensued. The crowd broke, screaming as they ran for what they hoped was safety. Governor Doyle began shouting for the militia to assemble, but it was nearly impossible to manage in this frenzy. I urgently beckoned Nicholas to come up the steps with me.

I didn't know what was happening, but I wasn't going to leave Cedric tied up when a battle was about to start. I ran over to him and sliced his ropes.

"You're okay? You're okay?" I asked, taking in the beloved features.

"Yes—yes." He touched my cheek briefly and peered around, having the same sentiment as me. "We need to get out of here. Up the north highway—take to the woods."

Nicholas nodded. "We can get help in the towns there, maybe make it to Archerwood Colony. Their militia's bigger, and they still have some army left."

We turned for the gallows stairs and found Warren blocking our path. Amazingly, only an hour after being found not guilty, he'd gotten a hold of a gun. "You're not leaving," he said. "Maybe we're all going to die here, but I'm going to be the one who finishes you."

I glanced frantically at the approaching Icori. They hadn't attacked, but there'd been no need, with everyone fleeing. The militia had finally started to assemble, but so far, there were only about two dozen.

"Stop this," I told him. "This isn't the time for a vendetta! You can get away with us. We're going north."

"Save your own skin," added Cedric. "You're good at that."

It wasn't, perhaps, the most tactful comment to use when trying to sway Warren to our side, but I doubted anything would have. A voice suddenly boomed, "Where is the governor?"

We all turned. The Icori had reached the bottom of the platform. There'd still been no sign of attack. They seemed remarkably calm, though those in the group's periphery watched the colonists warily and held their weapons tightly.

Many were painted with blue woad, just like the two Icori we'd met on the road, covered in symbols I didn't know. Women warriors rode along with the men. Copper ornaments and feathers decorated riders and horses, and their woolen tartans made a sea of color. Looking closely, I could see a pattern to it. Several riders to the side wore plaid of red and white. Another cluster wore red and blue. The group in the front wore green and black.

This was the group the speaker was in. He was in front, all tanned muscles and white-blond hair and—

He was the Icori we'd met on the road to Hadisen.

"Where is the governor?" His Osfridian was still clear.

Governor Doyle hesitantly stepped forward. "I'm the governor. You have no business here. Get out before my army beats yours to the ground." It was a bluff, seeing as the militia had thirty at most by now. I think several had fled.

"We do have business," the Icori man said. "We've come seeking justice—your help in righting a wrong done to us." His eyes flicked toward Warren. "I was told we'd need more than two people to have our demands heard. So here we are."

"You've had no wrongs done to you," said Governor Doyle. "We've all agreed to the treaties. We've all obeyed them. You have your land, we have ours."

"Soldiers are moving into our land and attacking our villages—soldiers from the place you call Lorandy." The Icori man met the governor's gaze unblinkingly. "And your own people are aiding them and letting them cross your territories."

This caused a nervous stir among our colonists, but Governor Doyle only grew angrier. "Impossible! Lorandians moving into your lands means they would flank ours. No man among us would allow such a thing."

"Your own son would."

A new speaker emerged from the Icori, bringing her horse beside the man.

And I knew her.

I hadn't picked Tamsin out right away. Her red hair had blended into theirs, and she was dressed like them too, in a knee-length green dress edged in that plaid. Her hair hung in two long, loose braids intertwined with copper pendants. I'd been stunned when I saw her with the Grashond residents. But this . . . this was enough to make me think I was imagining things.

Her entire presence was calm and composed, very different from the wildly emotional demeanor I associated with her. "Your son and other traitors are working with the Lorandians to stir up discord and draw Osfrid's army out of the central colonies—so that Hadisen and others can rebel against the crown."

Warren lowered the gun and came to life beside us. "It's a lie, Father! There's no telling what these savages have brainwashed this girl into believing. What proof does she have for this absurdity?"

"The proof of being thrown off a boat in the middle of a storm when I discovered your plans," she replied.

"Lies," said Warren. He took a few steps back, panic filling his face. "This girl is delusional!"

A man suddenly climbed up the stairs. Warren spun around to face this newcomer. It was Grant Elliott, looking particularly bedraggled today, and he didn't seem fazed by any of this. He strolled over beside me and looked as though a halted hanging, an Icori army, and potential traitors were part of an ordinary day for him.

"She's telling the truth," he said, locking his hard gaze on Governor Doyle and not Warren. The gruff Grant I remembered from the storm was back. "There are stacks of correspondence. Witnesses who'll testify."

"Elliott?" Warren gaped. "What the hell are you talking about?"

Grant's heavy gaze fell on Warren. "I think you know. About Courtemanche. About the 'heretic couriers.'"

I saw the shift in Warren's eyes, the moment when he was truly pushed over the edge by whatever those enigmatic words meant. And I knew, before he raised the gun at Grant, what was going to happen. "Look out!" I cried, throwing myself into Grant. I didn't quite knock him over but pushed him out of the way enough to just barely evade the bullet that fired from Warren's gun. That put me directly in front of him for the gun's second bullet. And I could tell from his frantic expression that it didn't really matter who he shot at this point.

Suddenly, I heard a *thwack* sound, and something moved in my periphery. The next thing I knew, Warren was lying on the ground, clutching his leg and screaming in agony. Something that looked like an arrow was sticking out of his knee. It was the same leg I'd stabbed him in. Grant knelt down to restrain Warren, but that seemed unnecessary given the wails of pain.

I, like many others, tried to figure out where the shot had come from. The Icori and the feeble militia looked equally baffled. At last, I found what I'd been searching for.

And I couldn't tell in that moment which was more incredible, that Tamsin was among the Icori warriors . . .

. . . or that Mira was standing on an overturned wagon, wielding a crossbow.

CHAPTER 31

MY SECOND WEDDING WAS BIGGER THAN MY FIRST ONE. And a lot cleaner.

I would certainly still argue that I didn't need ceremony or pomp to declare my love for Cedric. A bath and nice clothes didn't change how I felt. But there was no way I'd turn them down.

In Adoria, weddings occurred in magistrate's offices more often than they did in Osfrid, so choosing that over a church of Uros wasn't unusual. Of course, with Cedric revealed as an Alanzan, no one was really surprised. We held our after-wedding party at Wisteria Hollow, inviting everyone we knew and a lot of people we didn't. Jasper had grudgingly agreed to hosting. He still wasn't happy about his son's choices, but he'd given in and accepted the inevitable.

We spent our wedding night in the cottage of an Alanzan acquaintance of Cedric's, one who was out of town on business and had lent it to us. It held nothing of my old town house's grandeur—or even that of Blue Spring—but was charming and clean. And it was ours. All ours for the night. No fear of others discovering us. No fear of condemnation.

It felt like we hadn't really and truly seen each other in ages. Since almost no one knew we were already married, we'd spent the two weeks between the trial and official wedding living chaste and separate lives. When we'd made it back to the cottage after a long day of festivities, the jolt of finally being alone together had been so surreal that we'd hardly known what to do.

But we'd quickly figured that out.

I woke the next morning to sunlight streaming in through the bedroom's bay window. Cedric lay at my back, his arms encircling my waist. I ran my fingers over the crisp white sheets, inhaling a scent that was a mix of Cedric's vetiver, the detergent used on the sheets, and the violet perfume Mira and Tamsin had gifted me for my wedding.

"I can tell that you're thinking," Cedric said, pressing his cheek to my back. "Thinking much harder than you should be."

"I'm trying to memorize this. Every detail. The light, the smells, the feel." I rolled over so that I could look at his face. The morning sun lit up his hair, which was unquestionably disheveled. "Even you. We get to wake up together for the rest of our lives now, but it's going to be a long time before it resembles anything like this room, this bed."

He brushed my hair back and then trailed his hand along my neck. "Getting cold feet?"

"Hardly, seeing as I've married you twice now."

"Maybe we can find a reason to stay here longer."

"And miss going to Westhaven with the charter members? That wouldn't reflect well on a founder and so-called leader of the community. You'd also get arrested and possibly executed for heresy if you don't go. And all those food supplies we've got sitting downstairs would go to waste."

"Was that list in any particular order? Like, least to most serious consequence?"

"I . . . don't know." The hand that had been by my face had slipped under the covers and now ran over my bare leg—slowly, agonizingly. I was trying to keep my face and voice cool, but the rest of my body was betraying me as I curled closer to him. "You're kind of making it difficult to focus. And we have a lot to do."

"Yes." His voice was husky as he moved his mouth to my neck. "Yes, we do."

"That's not what I . . ."

He was impossible for me to resist. Or maybe I was impossible for him to resist. We melted into each other, and I forgot all about Westhaven and the hardships ahead. For the next hour, my world was a tangle of skin and hair and bedding. Afterward, I had a halfhearted urge to get up and start the day. That was soon abandoned. I collapsed into him and fell back asleep.

The sound of knocking snapped me awake and effectively shattered any remaining languor. I jerked upright. "They're here for our supplies! What time is it?"

Cedric opened one eye and fixed it on the window. "It's not time. Too early."

"Well, someone wants something," I said as the knocking continued. I climbed out of bed and searched around until I found a long, thick housecoat. I pulled it on, noting that my wedding dress was lying on the floor in the room's far corner, inside out. It was one of my diamond dresses, a fantasy of white silk and silver. "How'd that get over there?"

Cedric had been watching me dress, both eyes now open, and slid his gaze over to the corner. "You needed help getting out of it." Like that was any kind of answer.

"We'll get an earful from Jasper. I have to give that back." I finished cinching up the robe and hurried to the bedroom door.

"I think you're supposed to call him 'Dad' now," Cedric yelled after me. I paused just long enough to throw a small pillow at him.

Downstairs, the knocking had grown louder and more irritated. So, perhaps I shouldn't have been surprised to find that it was, in fact, Jasper standing out on the porch. He checked his pocket watch impatiently. "There you are."

"Sorry. We were still . . . asleep. Would you like to come in?"

"No time. I'm off to meet a man I might possibly be starting an exciting business venture with."

"And he had to schedule it during our send-off, huh?" Cedric strolled to the doorway beside me, yawning. He'd thrown on last night's wedding clothes, which were covered in wrinkles. "Or maybe *you* scheduled it during the send-off?"

Jasper didn't answer either way. "There's nothing you really need from me at this point—although I *do* need that dress back. I can get good money for that. And if this new venture works out, we might have the potential for even more. We're working out logistics for more-specific long-distance matchmaking via correspondence and classified ads."

While Jasper rambled on about the details, I went back upstairs to get the dress. It took a few minutes to assemble it all, as the various components—overdress, underdress, chemise, veil—had inexplicably ended up in wildly different parts of the room. Maybe I'd had more wine last night than I recalled. Or maybe I'd just been too preoccupied to care. Several glittering beads fell off the overdress when I smoothed it out, and I winced, hoping Jasper wouldn't notice.

When I came back downstairs, I heard Jasper saying, "—expand this business more than we ever dreamed, and you could have had a share of it. Riches beyond belief. But no. You had to marry a blue-blooded con artist and go prance off into the wilderness with some cult. I hope this new insanity works out for you."

"Father, that might be the nicest thing you've ever said to me."

Jasper scowled. "I'm serious. You've made some dangerous choices."

"But I made them myself," Cedric said. "And that's what matters."

I handed the dress over to Jasper. From the narrowing of his eyes, I think he immediately noticed the missing beads. "Is that wine on the hem?" he asked.

"Thank you for letting me borrow it," I said sweetly. "Dad."

Cedric and I stood on the porch when he left, watching until he was out of sight down the lane. When we were alone, he slipped his arm around me. "Ready for the next adventure?"

"Always."

The morning flew by as we readied ourselves and saw our wilderness supplies and few worldly possessions carted off to the Westhaven baggage train. Much like the Hadisen send-off, there was a big crowd assembling at the edge of town where the wagons and horses were lining up for departure. There'd be family and friends to say goodbye, as well as the idle and curious. When we were finally ready to go, Cedric and I cast a fond glance back at the cottage and went to join the masses.

It was as crowded as I'd expected—maybe more so. Edwin Harrison caught sight of us immediately and asked for Cedric to consult on something, leaving me alone to people-watch near the edge of the crowd.

"It must be exhausting being married." Tamsin strolled up to me. "You look like you didn't sleep at all."

I grinned and gave her a quick hug. "I slept. Some."

"Well, I'm sure you'll make up for it with all the sleep you'll get trekking through the wilderness. And whatever shack you have in Westhaven will probably be very restful too."

I thought back to the dilapidated shanty on the gold claim. It felt like a lifetime ago. "We don't even have one yet. We'll have to build it—or hire someone to, in light of Cedric's carpentry skills. Besides, you're one to talk—after living in an Icori roundhouse."

She smiled at the joke but made no comment on it. In the weeks that had passed since Warren's downfall, we'd learned a lot more about her time among both the Grashond Heirs and the Icori. She'd taken a long time to open up, and I knew there were still things she wasn't telling us. I hoped they'd come out in time when she was ready. Aiana had cornered Jasper, telling them that there was no way Tamsin could be expected to marry anytime soon after such traumatic events. Aiana had won her case, and Tamsin's contract had been extended.

She turned away and stared vacantly at the sea of people. "There's something—well, that is—there's something I need to talk to you about. Something I have to ask you."

Her sober expression was startling. Frightening even, seeing as I'd thought the worst of her troubles were over. I squeezed her hand. "Of course."

"It might be too late . . . I should have brought it up sooner . . . but I didn't want to burden you with everything else. But I know you and Cedric made a lot of money from selling the Hadisen claim, and so I thought . . . that is . . ."

"Tamsin." I'd never heard her ramble in all our time together. "You can tell me anything. Go ahead and ask whatever you need to."

So, she did.

I fell silent for a long time afterward, trying to wrap my mind around what I'd just heard. The longer I didn't speak, the more troubled she became.

"You think I'm a terrible person, don't you?"

"What? Of course not." I drew her to me again. I remembered when, long ago, she'd told me I had no idea how much she had on the line. And she'd been right. "I'm just surprised, that's all. And of course I'll help."

Her brown eyes shone with tears. "It's a lot to ask. And I understand if Cedric doesn't want you to spend the money. It's his right to—"

"Cedric wouldn't mind. And it doesn't matter. I don't need to touch the Hadisen money."

I scanned the crowd, half hoping Nicholas Adelton might have turned out. No such luck. Legally, I probably didn't need his help, but he certainly would've made things neater. After substantial evidence had condemned Warren to a ship back to Osfrid to answer for his multilayered conspiracy, a legal nightmare had ensued over the land he owned in Hadisen. In matters of treason, land like that usually reverted to the crown. But he'd had a number of leaseholders working the land, and in a generous gesture, the courts had ended up gifting those claims. Rather than deal with the excavation, Cedric had sold his for an impressive price—giving us the means to pay off my contract and build savings for Westhaven. Nicholas had been instrumental in helping us sort matters out, so I suppose he'd earned a break from us.

I spied one of the Westhaven laborers nearby, keeping track of inventory with a pen and sheaf of paper. I talked him into lending the pen and giving me a piece of paper. He was one of those who was starstruck over the truth about my past, and when I thanked him, he simply stammered, "No problem, m-m'lady."

I knelt down to make a desk out of my knees and began writing: *I, Elizabeth Thorn née Witmore . . .*

I stopped, unsure what to write next. Using my legal first name wasn't the issue. It was what came next. Or did anything come next? I'd been gone more than a year. My cousin Peter would most certainly carry the exalted Rupert's title now.

I, Elizabeth Thorn née Witmore, former Countess of Rothford, authorize the release of my surety money to Lady Alice Witmore, to be spent in the terms outlined below . . .

Tamsin watched me write each word, and I was pretty sure she didn't breathe the entire time. When I signed and finished, she read it over again, and then looked at me hopefully. "That's all it'll take?"

"It should be. That money's been isolated from any family debt for years and is legally mine, now that I'm married. It's not a lot—if it was, I would have had fewer problems. But it's enough for what you need, and Grandmama will see that everything gets followed through." I reached into my skirt pocket and produced a folded bundle of more paper. Along with a copy of my marriage certificate, it also contained a long-overdue letter. "I'll just add it to what I'm already sending her. Silas Garrett is supposed to deliver it and verify that he compared me to the portrait and saw me alive. I'm just not sure where he is."

Tamsin pointed. "He's over there, speaking with that awful Grant Elliott. He seemed so polite at first, but he's actually got quite an attitude, you know."

Sure enough, the two of them stood removed from the throng, having what looked like a friendly conversation. I still didn't know their exact connection, save that they'd both played a part in having Warren arrested. Silas was transporting Warren back to Osfrid for a treason trial while Grant remained behind in the colonies.

"He can't be that awful," I told Tamsin as we walked toward them.

"They say he was responsible for the evidence tying Warren to the Lorandians."

"Well, I'm just glad he finally seems to have shaved," she said. "He has, hasn't he? The beard looks much neater than usual."

Grizzled Silas gave me a nod of greeting when we reached them. "Mistress Thorn, I wondered when I'd see you. Congratulations."

"Thank you." I handed the bundle of papers to him. "It should be easy to find my grandmother. I'm sure she'll still be in Osfro."

Silas tucked the papers into his coat's inner pocket. "I'll find her. Anything else you need me to deliver?"

I shook my head, but Tamsin hesitantly stepped forward. "If it's not too much trouble, Mister Garrett . . . I also have some letters. The address is in Osfro. I can pay you—"

"Just get them to me before we sail in two days," Silas said.

"How is your prisoner?" I asked.

"Miserable," Grant answered. He grinned, and I couldn't tell if it was supposed to be charming or terrifying. "He's locked up in the ship's hold, and I visit him every day, just to make sure he stays miserable."

Mira joined us, overhearing that last comment. "He's probably going to be executed in Osfrid for treason. I don't think you have to worry about him feeling cheerful anytime soon."

"That conniving bastard's treachery nearly started a war that would've drawn in Osfrid, the Icori, Lorandy, the Balanquans, and Uros knows who else. It would've ravaged this land and cost countless lives. So I don't really think it's overkill to make sure he's suffering." Grant paused, almost eloquently. "I like to be thorough."

Mira rolled her eyes and turned to Tamsin and me. "Can we talk?"

We made our goodbyes to the men and wandered away. Tamsin had nearly wept after I'd written the letter, thanking me profusely, but her face was alight now, in that endearing, cunning way.

"Are you finally going to tell us, Mira?" she demanded. "Surely you won't let poor Adelaide go off into some forsaken land without telling her what you're going to do. It'd be so cruel. She'll worry the whole time."

Mira had told us recently that she'd "made a decision" about her future, but we had no idea what it was. Maybe she'd decided to marry the elderly gentleman. Maybe she'd decided to go back to Osfrid and work. Neither of those seemed likely, though, given the smile I kept seeing on her face. After her spectacular attack on Warren—which I'd learned was credited to Aiana's training—nothing Mira did surprised me anymore.

And it seemed the mystery would continue a little longer.

"Sorry," Mira said. "I can't tell you yet. But soon."

"So cruel," repeated Tamsin.

Mira caught me in a tight embrace. "Mostly, I just wanted to come tell you goodbye. It seems like we're always doing that, doesn't it?"

I pulled Tamsin into our hug. "And we always keep coming back together. I'm sure I'll be able to get back to Cape Triumph once in a while. And I hope you'll come visit me in Westhaven."

"Of course," said Mira.

"Just let us know when you have an actual house built that has enough beds—real beds, not straw on the floor—for everyone," said Tamsin. "And you can bet we'll be right there."

We laughed a little. And we cried a little. I could tell the Westhaven party was getting ready to depart, and the reality of what was about to happen hit me hard. Another journey. Another upheaval in my life.

"There you are, Adelaide. It figures I just had to look for where the most tears were around here. You two wouldn't believe all the tears in her household when we first met."

Cedric came up behind me, and I pulled back from Tamsin and Mira so that I could hug him. Then I gave him a light punch in the arm. "*He* was the one who caused most of those tears."

"And you've been smitten with me ever since."

He turned as a shout came to assemble, and his face grew serious. We had another tearful round of farewells with Tamsin and Mira, and then Cedric took hold of my hand. "My lady. Shall we?"

We walked up to where our horses were waiting—young, spry ones. Not poor Lizzie. He helped me mount, and I cast one last, fond look back at my friends. Ahead, the road stretched out of Cape Triumph and into parts unknown. Whereas the same sight on the way to Hadisen had been foreboding, I suddenly felt like all the world's possibilities were before me.

Cedric leaned toward me. "You know, I hope this new insanity works out for us."

"I think it will," I told him. "After all, the old insanity turned out pretty well."

And we rode.

ACKNOWLEDGMENTS

The conception of this series started with a few small sparks of inspiration, and once they came together, there was no stopping the blaze that swept me up as I raced to finish this book. Above all, I owe many thanks to my family during this process, especially to my husband and sons, who indulged me as I took my laptop everywhere and frequently spaced out while my mind spun ahead to the next chapter. Thank you also to my agent, Jim McCarthy, and the incomparable team at Razorbill, who all saw the potential of this story burning inside me and helped fan its flames.

Lastly, I want to thank anyone who has picked up this book and joined me in Adoria. For my longtime readers, you always take the leap of faith in following me to new worlds, and I'm grateful for that. To my new readers: welcome to the ride. There's a great adventure in store for all of us.

EVERY JEWEL HAS A SHARP EDGE . . .

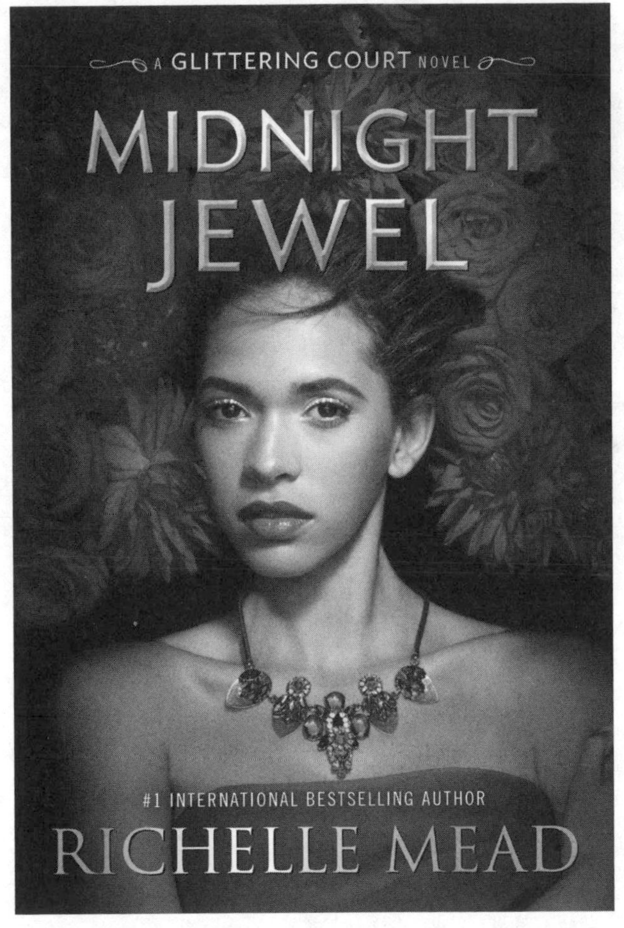

TURN THE PAGE FOR A SNEAK PEEK!

CHAPTER 1

"YOU! GIRL! DON'T TAKE ANOTHER STEP, OR I'LL RUN YOU through!"

I froze where I was, halfway up the great stone stairs that led to the cathedral of Kyriel.

The *thump-thump* of boots sounded behind me, and moments later, a young watchman rushed over to block my way. He stood almost a foot taller than me, his dark hair shaved close to the scalp as so many of the watch did. What many of the watch did not do, however, was wield a dagger with such confidence. Most kept the city's peace with heavy clubs.

I met his eyes calmly. "I beg your pardon, sir, but I'm on my way to prayer."

"Don't give me that." His face twisted into a scowl. "Everyone knows you Sims are Alanzan heathens. And I know who *you* are. I remember you and your murderous brother."

A spark of anger kindled inside me, but I kept it hidden. I had a lot of practice ignoring comments like his. "I was actually going to pray for his soul. I'm a faithful devotee of Uros. Do you think the angels would let a heretic step on this holy ground?"

I gestured up to the imposing double doors above us. A great arch, carved into the cathedral's stone, surrounded them and made the entry look even more majestic. A monk of Vaiel, hooded in deep green robes, stepped outside just then, reaffirming the sanctity of where we stood.

The watchman hesitated a moment and then grew stern again.

He kept the dagger pointed at me. "Maybe you aren't one of the Alanzans, but I know you're as much of a criminal as everyone else in your family. You just haven't been caught yet. Now tell me where your brother is."

I spread my hands out in helpless confusion, ignoring the impulse to reach for my own knife, which was hidden in a skirt pocket. "I wish I knew. I haven't seen him in over a year."

He pressed the dagger's point to my breastbone. "You're lying."

The heartbreaking part was that I'd actually spoken the truth. Lonzo had sent me one letter when he'd arrived in that land across the sea. And then there'd been silence.

"What's all this?" a new voice asked. A familiar voice.

Another watchman joined us, moving much more casually than his colleague. This man was older, portly, and red-faced. He'd left his thinning hair as it was, probably because there was too little to shave. I kept my eyes fixed serenely ahead, giving no indication that I knew him.

The younger watchman lowered the blade. "Carey, this is the Viana girl. The one whose brother killed Sir Wilhelm last year. That bastard was never brought to justice!"

Watchman Carey stifled a yawn. "Well, I don't see him here. I only see his sister. And no one ever actually proved he did it."

"But you know he did!" spat the other watchman. "We all know it. And she knows where he is! We should be tracking her every move!"

"Into a church? You think her brother is hiding here? Should I go ask that monk if we can conduct a search?"

"Sir—"

"There's nothing here." Watchman Carey managed to sound both bored and irritated. "Only a girl on her way to pray and better her soul—a girl who's done nothing wrong."

The other man's eyes narrowed at me. "She's a Sirminican. They've all done something."

Watchman Carey gestured him away. "Go make yourself useful.

Stop a real crime, not one that went cold long ago. And damn it, put that dagger away. You're embarrassing us all."

The young watchman sheathed the blade but held a finger up to my face. I didn't flinch. "Don't think I'll forget this, girl. I'll find your bloody brother, wherever he's hiding."

Once the man had stormed away, Watchman Carey's features sharpened. "Tell me he's not still in the city."

"No," I said, exhaling in relief. "But I really don't know where he is. Just that he's far away."

"You should join him."

A dull ache filled my chest. "I'm trying, sir."

"Try harder. Things like this are going to keep happening. Sir Wilhelm had a lot of friends, and they haven't forgotten." Watchman Carey suddenly looked very weary. "Look, I like you. I really do. You're smart. You know our language. But I'm not a fool. I hear about the girl who stops thieves in the Sirminican district. And that's not a bad thing—but it is something that could get out of hand one day. Just like with your brother."

"Lonzo—"

"Not another word. Sir Wilhelm was as vile as they come, gentry or not. And maybe he deserved what he got, but the less I know, the better."

Watchman Carey's forehead wrinkled up with a frown as a memory held him. He'd been the one to find Isabel, the Sirminican girl Sir Wilhelm had used for his own sick pleasures and then discarded in a river. True, Lonzo had intended to beat him to a pulp, but actually killing Sir Wilhelm? That had been accidental. Most of the watch hadn't cared about that detail—not with a Sirminican involved. Watchman Carey *had* cared and had looked away a number of times as the evidence against Lonzo mounted.

"Get out of here. You can do better." He gave me a wry smile. He was the only member of the watch who'd ever treated me as an equal. The only one who even attempted my language. "And don't take it amiss when I say I hope we never cross paths again."

He lumbered down the steps without another word, soon disappearing into the crowded street. I took a moment to collect myself and continued my journey to the cathedral. The monk remained standing near the door, having observed the whole exchange. He said nothing. The great hood hid his face, but he turned his head and tracked me as I walked inside.

My father had liked conducting clandestine business in churches. No one ever expected it. Only a handful of other people had come inside to pray during the middle of the day in this grand cathedral, one of the biggest in Osfro. They sat solemnly on the glossy wooden pews, heads bowed or eyes fixed on the sculpture of the glorious angel Kyriel that hung before us on the sanctuary wall. A priest in gold and pale green robes quietly lit candles on the altar beneath the angel, and the scent of beeswax and resin filled the air.

I scanned the nave and found the person I sought. I casually made my way over, sitting near him without making eye contact, as though my choice of pew was a coincidence. The wood creaked beneath me, and I nearly sneezed at the man's pretentious herbal cologne.

Bowing my head, I touched my brow first and then my heart. "All praise to Uros, creator of spirit and flesh," I murmured. "All praise to his six glorious angels, defenders of the faithful."

"All praise," the man beside me echoed.

I lifted my head, fixing my eyes on the glorious Kyriel. The angel held a gilded sword and shield, ready to defend mankind from the six wayward angels. My real interest was in the priest as he continued lighting candles in my periphery. When he'd finished with the last one, he retreated to a small alcove and knelt to pray.

Certain he was preoccupied, I reached into my skirt pocket and took out a small, folded piece of paper. I carefully set it on the pew between my companion and me. After several seconds, he took it and slipped it into his own coat pocket.

"Those are the names of ten Alanzans living in Cape Triumph—at least as of last spring," I said softly. "I'm sure there are more. But that's enough to get you connected. You need to memorize them and burn it right away."

He raised his head. "I know that. Give me some credit."

Around the nave, stained-glass windows depicted the other angels in rainbow colors. None of them seemed to care that a heretic was sitting beside me. Kyriel didn't leap forward with his sword. The cathedral's vaulted ceiling didn't come crashing down. Uros didn't hurl lightning from the heavens. *Maybe the Alanzans aren't the heretics*, I mused. *Maybe their way is the right way, and the orthodox who built this church are actually the heretics. Or maybe they're both wrong.*

I finally turned and met my companion's eyes. The dim lighting made them appear more gray than blue, but it couldn't hide their eager sparkle. Cedric Thorn was an extremely handsome man. Not my type—but still nice to look at. I preferred men who were a little rougher around the edges. Men who didn't so obviously deliberate on their clothing each morning.

"I give you a lot of credit. But people's lives are on the line."

His face sobered. "Believe me, I know. Thank you. And here's something for you."

My heart sped up as he reached into his coat, cast a quick glance around, and then produced a rolled sheaf of papers. He set it discreetly between us. "Your contract. Admission to the Glittering Court. A ticket to Adoria."

"Adoria," I repeated, clenching the papers. The Alanzans I knew had sworn he was a man of integrity, but until this moment, I'd had my doubts that he'd uphold his half of the bargain. Plenty of Osfridians had experimented with the Alanzan faith. Plenty had lost interest and happily turned in the real devotees.

"I made a few inquiries," he said, still serious, "but I don't think there's anything I can do to help find your brother once we're over there. They don't always record the names of bond servants. Even when they do, getting those records would require a connection to a customs officer—or enough money to bribe one. I don't have either."

"Maybe my husband will." *Husband*. The word felt strange on my tongue.

"Are you sure that's what you want? A husband?"

I could feel Cedric's gaze on me as I looked down at my hands, still gripping the papers. His polished manners and stylish clothes were deceptive. He might be pretty, but he wasn't stupid.

What did I want? I wanted Adoria. I wanted to find Lonzo. I wanted a life far away from the war and corruption that had engulfed the country of my birth. Could a rich husband and a new land guarantee all those things? No, but I'd have better odds there than I would here, where I was just another hungry refugee packed into a city that hated us.

"I want a husband," I reiterated. It was a small price to pay for all those other benefits. I would honor the contract and accept being a wife. If nothing else, I'd have some sort of choice in who I went to bed with, rather than having it dictated by my father.

As though reading my mind, Cedric remarked, "Your father was a great man. I mean, at least from what I've heard. He saved so many from persecution. He gave his life for it. You must be so proud."

"Yes," I said automatically.

"And I know you want to carry out that legacy. I know you've been protecting people here. It's noble. It's wonderful. But . . . how should I put this . . . well. You need to settle down. Not just with a husband, but in general."

"I know."

"No more sneaking around."

"I know."

"No more alley fights."

"I know."

"No more daggers to throats."

"Cedric, give *me* some credit." If we hadn't been in the cathedral, I would've shouted it. "I'll be the picture of decorum at this finishing school of yours. I'll get cultured and refined. I'll let you show me off at all those parties and wear those beautiful clothes you're always going on about." I glanced down at my worn, stained dress. "Actually, I won't mind that part. Or even the studies." The war back in Sirminica had ended my education there.

Cedric's enthusiasm returned. He really needed to work on discretion. "I know Adoria's your end goal, but try to enjoy the journey too. It won't be that bad."

"Even for a Sirminican?" I asked archly.

The bright smile faltered. I took it as a bad sign that he didn't spout off the pretty assurances and sales pitches that came so naturally to him. "Your first year's still in Osfrid. Even though you'll be at one of our country manors . . . well, you'll face the same bias you see here in the city. Adoria will be a little laxer. Sometimes. But you'll win them over. They'll see who you really are."

After almost two years in Osfrid's capital, I was skeptical, but I didn't let that show as I stood up. The priest had finished and was strolling near our side. "Thank you," I whispered. "This means everything to me."

Cedric tapped his pocket. "So does this."

"Don't come out right after me," I warned. "Wait a while."

"I know, I know. You're not giving me credit again."

I walked out of the cathedral, squinting at the bright afternoon light. The noise of midday Osfro was crushing after the sanctuary's stillness. Before me, the city whirled with life. Wagons and horses clattered down the cobblestone street, and vendors pitched their wares. Pedestrians packed the spaces in between, some headed toward a specific destination while others begged for food and work. Blocky stone buildings loomed over everything, their gloomy solidity a testament to Osfro's history.

Osfro is an old city, I thought. *A city set in its ways. There's no opportunity for me here. Lonzo knew that when he sailed to Adoria. When he left me behind.*

The cathedral doors creaked open, and I stared in surprise as Cedric emerged. "You were supposed to wait," I chastised.

"I forgot to tell you when we're leaving for the manor." He placed a jaunty brown hat atop his auburn hair and tried to block out the sun with his hand. "In four days. Wait at the border of the Sirminican and Bridge districts—by the market. My father and I'll pick you up around the first bell."

"Are you sure your father won't mind me?"

"Not his choice. He let me recruit two girls. I've picked them—sort of. I have to finish the other's paperwork." Cedric sounded unconcerned. Seeing as he'd adopted a religion that often led to death and imprisonment, a father's anger was probably minor by comparison.

"Recruit? Are you leading this girl into a sinful life?"

Cedric and I both spun around at the crotchety voice. The monk of Vaiel was still around, leaning against the arch and clutching a leather-bound copy of *A Testament of Angels*. The shadows had obscured him. Panic shot through me, and then I relaxed as I replayed our brief conversation. We'd said nothing about an outlawed heresy. Cedric and I faced no danger in discussing the Glittering Court.

"No, Brother," said Cedric politely. The monks weren't church leaders like the priests of Uros, but they were treated with the same respect, venerated for their complete immersion into study of the faith. "Quite the opposite, actually. She's joining the Glittering Court."

Even though I couldn't see the monk's face, instinct told me he was staring at me—and scowling. "The Glittering Court? Is that what you call your sordid operation? I may be removed from the world, but I know its ways. Men 'recruit' Sirminican girls all the time, taking advantage of their downtrodden situation and forcing them into despicable deeds. I saw you earlier, girl. I saw the watch interrogating you."

"We were only chatting. I haven't done anything wrong. And the Glittering Court is very respectable." I tried for calmness and humility. The last thing we needed was for him to draw the city watch's attention back to me. "I'm going to take etiquette classes and then find a husband in Adoria next year."

"And not just any husband," Cedric boasted. "She'll meet only the richest, most elite bachelors of the city. Men who've made their fortunes in the New World want equally elevated wives—and my family's business supplies them." He'd used those exact same words when we met. I wondered if the salesman in him couldn't help it.

A beat of silence followed as the monk contemplated this. Then: "Which city?"

"Cape Triumph. In Denham Colony." Cedric kept smiling, but the shift in his posture betrayed his nervousness. I didn't blame him, with that list in his pocket. Church officials wanted to make an example of native Osfridian converts. Hangings had become common.

When the monk still didn't respond, I crossed my arms and fixed my gaze on his shadowed face. I hoped I was meeting his eyes. "Good Brother, I appreciate your concern. And you're right—desperate girls with no other options *do* turn to desperate means. But I'm not one of those girls."

"Not desperate?" he asked, voice unexpectedly wry for a holy man.

"Not without options. If I don't see any, then I make my own. And no one forces me into anything." My words came out with a bit more fire than I'd intended.

"I can believe that. I'd pity anyone who tried." I could've sworn he was smiling in the depths of that hood. "Good luck to you, miss." He opened the cathedral door and disappeared inside.

Cedric exhaled. "That could have gone a lot worse. I think he must've liked you."

"They don't like anything except their studies."

"He couldn't take his eyes off you," he teased.

"You couldn't even see his eyes! Now go memorize what I gave you. Don't forget to burn it."

Cedric answered with a nod and began descending the great stone steps. "See you in four days."

I stayed where I was and looked down upon the city I'd be leaving behind. I'd come here to escape war, but I felt no loyalty. Learning to be a polished lady in some country manor was a delay in getting to Lonzo, but I was human. I wanted to sleep in a clean bed, instead of on a floor crowded with other refugees. I wanted three meals a day again. I wanted to be around books again.

"Four days." I felt my lips creep into a smile. "Four days, and my new life begins."

DON'T MISS A SINGLE HEART-POUNDING MOMENT!

EXPLORE THE WORLD OF RICHELLE MEAD

THE SAGA CONTINUES IN...

RAZORBILL

Razorbill • An Imprint of Penguin Random House VampireAcademyBooks.com • BloodlinesSeries.com

IN A VILLAGE WITHOUT SOUND,
ONE GIRL HEARS A CALL TO ACTION

"Fans of Rose Hathaway and Sydney Sage will flock to this impressive stand-alone novel."

—*Booklist*